P9-CEY-496

Hold Me
in Contempt

Also by Wendy Williams

Ask Wendy

Hold Me in Contempt

WENDY WILLIAMS

WILLIAM MORROW
An Imprint of HarperCollinsPublishers

This book is a work of fiction. The characters, incidents, and dialogue are drawn from the author's imagination and are not to be construed as real. Any resemblance to actual events or persons, living or dead, is entirely coincidental.

HOLD ME IN CONTEMPT. Copyright © 2014 by Wendy Williams. All rights reserved. Printed in the United States of America. No part of this book may be used or reproduced in any manner whatsoever without written permission except in the case of brief quotations embodied in critical articles and reviews. For information address HarperCollins Publishers, 10 East 53rd Street, New York, NY 10022.

HarperCollins books may be purchased for educational, business, or sales promotional use. For information please e-mail the Special Markets Department at SPsales@harpercollins.com.

FIRST EDITION

Designed by Diahann Sturge

Library of Congress Cataloging-in-Publication Data has been applied for.

ISBN 978-0-06-226841-9

14 15 16 17 18   DIX/RRD   10 9 8 7 6 5 4 3 2 1

I dedicate this book to single power girls everywhere.
I wrote this novel with you in mind.
I hope you enjoy it!

Hold Me in Contempt

Chapter 1

The worst thing about being a black lawyer is that everyone you know thinks you're *their* lawyer and they can call you about anything at any time. And while I'm sure that happens to all lawyers—white, yellow, brown, and beige—because I'm black it's almost a guarantee that whatever my people need me for at whatever time is likely so ghetto and/or hood, there's simply no way I can tack my signature to anything having to do with the situation. Now, that may sound uppity to some black folks and flat-out hateful to others, but I bet not one black lawyer considering my statement will disagree. And that's because it's the truth. Ugly. But true.

Case in point: My cousin Tyree got pulled over last month for speeding on the FDR Drive. Doesn't sound too bad. Add, though, that it was 4 a.m., Tyree is a convicted felon with hard-time muscles and shady gang prison tattoos from wrists to neck, he was high on crystal meth, naked, and his car was packed with frozen hot dogs he'd stolen from Gray's Papaya. (In case anyone is wondering, I can't even try to make this crap up. It was on the news.) Now, this little string of drama is totally in Tyree's range of ridiculousness, so no one should judge him. But according to the actual police report, when officers in squad cars and helicopters had their bright lights and guns pointed at his muscly black body in the dead of night on one of the busiest highways in New York City, this fool stepped out of the car and demanded that someone call his "fucking lawyer Kimberly Kind."

This was repeated more than fifty times before they wrestled his silly ass to the ground and got him into one of the police cars.

Did I mention that this was in the actual police report? And on the news?

I should've stayed my black behind in bed because I was due in court in the next morning, but you can't say no to your aunt Sissy when she calls you wailing in the middle of the night to go get her "baby boy" out of jail. No matter what I had going on, at that moment I was expected to make some kind of black lawyer magic happen—or I'd face a jury of my peers who'd find me guilty of "acting funny" or, worse, "forgetting where I came from." Luckily (or unluckily, depending on how you see it), I saved my reputation by getting Tyree off on a technicality.

Now, I knew whatever my twin brother had going on when he called this morning asking me out to brunch wouldn't be too far from Tyree's antics on the FDR Drive. As my grandmother used to say, Tyree and Kent were cut from the same cloth, and though my brother had fewer strikes behind his name, the last time he'd called at 6 a.m., it was because he'd gotten caught selling black-market Newports at Rucker Park.

Still, I agreed to meet him in Hell's Kitchen at my favorite Sunday brunch spot, 44 & X. He was paying, so it was all good.

I showed up late, but he wasn't there, so I chose a table out on the street where I could see the sun and enjoy the loud white noise of a city that had no tolerance for standing still. I ordered a mimosa, sat back, and tried to think of something lovely, but a huge black fly kept buzzing in my ear.

When Kent finally pulled up on his big black motorcycle, the engine roared so loudly that everyone seated at the sidewalk tables turned to see what was going on. He slid into a slender space right in front of the door and hopped off the motorcycle like someone was about to ask for his autograph.

Kent had been born less than two minutes after me, but thank God we looked nothing alike. My "baby brother" was always the biggest man in any room (save Tyree and his prison muscles). He'd been six foot seven, 290 pounds, and solid since we were in high school. While he was my father's only son, when he took on our father's nickname, Mook, folks in our neighborhood in Hamilton Terrace started calling Kent Big Mook and Daddy Lil Mook.

"Kiki Mimi!" Kent called out with his arms extended toward me as he padded over to my table.

He was an hour late for a brunch he'd invited me to, but I stood and grinned at him anyway. I let him pick me up and spin me around like we hadn't seen each other since emancipation. More than anyone in the world, Kent always seemed to know how to make me smile. He was my little brother and big brother at the same time.

"You're late," I said after he'd hugged me half to death and we'd settled into our seats.

"Nah. I'm right on time, love. God is always on time," he responded mystically. He'd joined the Five Percent Nation when we were in high school and still referred to himself as God.

"Well, maybe God should be an hour early next time," I said.

"Don't stress me. You been late the last few times we were supposed to meet up, so don't play," he said as our wide-eyed white waitress wearing a gold name tag spelling out *Holly* approached the table licking her lips in his direction.

"Wha chu havin' to drink, Papi?" she asked all sexy in hipster hip-hop lingo. She had a huge wooden dagger in her ear, a thin gold ring in her nose, and a tattoo of a feather on her neck. She looked like one of those Montana-bred recent NYU grads who'd been sleeping with black men since she moved out of the dorms and into an overpriced studio in the newly gentrified Bed-Stuy I hated.

"What are you drinking, Kiki?" Kent pointed at the glass in front of me.

"A mimosa." I looked at him, perplexed.

"Oh, that's what I want." Kent turned to the waitress. "Hook me up with a mimosca—"

"A mimo*sa*," I cut in, correcting him.

"Yeah, that shit, yo. Gimme that shit." He grinned like he knew the classy order sounded odd coming from a black biker in Timbs and a crisp white tee.

Hipster Holly skipped away in her Vans as I kept my skeptical eyes on Kent.

"What you looking at?" he asked.

"A mimosa? You're drinking a mimosa?"

"Yup. That's cool."

"Whatever, Kent," I said. "Look. What do you want?"

"Want?"

"Need? From me."

"I don't need anything. Why I gotta need something?"

"Negro, please. You're ordering mimosas when I've never seen you drink anything but Heineken. You asked me out to brunch in Hell's Kitchen when you never leave Harlem. And you're being all nice to me. You have to want something. Just say it." I sat back and looked at little bits of skin peeling off Kent's forehead. Then I noticed that he was a little darker than he'd been the last time I'd seen him at Aunt Sissy's second born-again baptism. The one thing we had in common was our clear sable complexion. Out here in the daylight, Kent looked a little more mahogany. "And is that a skin tan?" I added.

"Sho is a tan!" Kent grinned and sat back, taking his drink from the waitress.

"From where? Where you been? Virginia Beach?" It was late May and the city was heating up, but the sun wasn't nearly hot enough to microwave his brown skin so neatly.

Holly came to take our orders. The desire she showed toward Kent matched only by the hatred beamed my way. We gave our orders, and he answered my question with too much enthusiasm: "I was in Rio—Rio de Janeiro!"

"Brazil? What were you doing in Brazil?"

"A little vacay with the fellas. You know I gots to unwind. A god be putting in work and shit. Especially now that I'm one hundred percent legit and have a job. Workingman's money is funny, yo."

"Humph." I frowned. "Interesting. I didn't even know you had a passport."

"Well, you don't know everything about me," he said. "Just like I don't know everything about you."

"Very true. And I'm happy about that because God only knows what kind of foolishness went down in Rio. You went with Maurice and them?"

Kent nodded with a huge smile.

"I don't even want to think about it," I said, annoyed.

"Why?" He pretended to be surprised at the look on my face.

"Because everyone knows why men go to Brazil. And in a group? You guys were probably sleeping with everything that walked by in a thong. And paying for it. Horrible. Do you know most of those women are underage? And we won't even talk about the HIV rates."

"All praises to the Creator, those hoes were bad as hell, but I didn't touch not one of them," Kent protested, holding up his hands in mock innocence.

"Double negative," I pointed out.

"What?"

"The double negative you just used means you actually slept with many prostitutes in Brazil," I explained, and heard myself sounding like a complete nerd. "Look, never mind. Whatever. I'm happy you enjoyed your nasty man vacation. Cheers!" I clinked my half-empty glass against his.

"See, look at you judging a brother. Ain't even ask why I didn't sleep with none of those Mexicans."

"Brazilians. They're Brazilian," I corrected Kent, laughing. He liked to play dumb, but Kent was just as smart as I was—maybe smarter—and I was sure he knew the difference between a Mexican and a Brazilian. Racist? No. Silly? Yes. "But I'll throw you a bone. Why didn't you sleep with any of the prostitutes, Kent?"

"I fell in love." He smiled and looked off like he was starring in some Jay-Z music video on a beach with Brazilian chicks draped over both of his shoulders and a bottle of Alizé Red Passion in each hand.

"In love?" I actually laughed as Holly slid our plates onto the table. "You? With whom?"

"Her name is Lydia. Lydia Santiaga. I met her at the airport. When we walked out, she was standing there just greeting people. Shorty was mad ill, yo."

I closed my eyes and exhaled deeply before choosing my words.

"You know what, that's great," I offered lazily. "I'm happy you fell in love with Lydia, who was randomly waiting outside the airport to greet some random dudes she doesn't know. But now you're back home and everything is back to normal. Have you spoken to Keisha?"

"Keisha? I ain't fucking with her. Why you bringing my baby moms up?"

"Because she's *your* baby mama and you've been with her forever."

"I just told you I'm in love," he said. He leaned across the table and added softly, "I'm gonna marry her."

I was about to laugh before I realized that he was dead serious. Then a wave of confusion mixed with anger and maybe a little bit of caution washed over me, leaving me silent.

"That's why I invited you to brunch," Kent went on, "to tell you I'm in love and I'm getting married. I need you, yo."

"Need me? For what?"

"It's nothing really. Small fries for my big sister. See, Lydia got into some shit, so it's gonna be hard for us to get her into the country."

"Us? What? Are you kidding me? So that's why you invited me here? To get your prostitute girlfriend into the country?"

"Don't call her a prostitute," Kent said, raising his voice. "She ain't like that. She's a good girl. She just got into a little trouble. That's all."

"What kind of trouble?" I looked at him as crazily as he sounded.

"She has some family in BX, and she was here last year visiting. Five-O picked her up in Hunts Point, saying she was hoeing, but it wasn't nothing like that."

"Really?"

"Nah, yo. She was there for her cousin's bachelor party. That's all."

"So, the police just randomly found her walking the street in Hunts Point, which is known for prostitution, and arrested her?" I hoped he'd hear the insanity.

"Word!" Kent confirmed, chewing on a bite of the smoked salmon omelet he'd ordered. "And that's why we need you to pull some strings for her. They say she can't come back to the US. Not even if I marry her. And you know a nigga ain't moving to Rio to be with the meda-medas for the rest of his life, so I need you to get shorty here."

"No can do," I said flatly.

"Yes you can."

"Sure can't."

"Why not? You're the assistant district attorney for New York County. I know you can pull some strings. Call in some favors. Fuck it, call the mayor!" He laughed.

"No. I don't work in immigration, and I certainly don't call in favors for this kind of crap. I save that for things like Rucker Park . . . and what was that drama you got caught up in on the turnpike?"

"Oh, you're going to bring up that cracker trooper? A nigga was just taking a piss."

"*On* the highway," I reminded him.

"So? That's in the past." Kent sat back again, deflated. "See, I knew you'd bring that shit up. Knew you'd act funny. I thought inviting your sadiddy ass out to this spot would actually make you act right. But you ain't got no act right for your baby bro."

"That's a double neg—" I started, but stopped myself. "Act right? So, I don't have any act right because I don't want to get involved with you trying to marry some woman you just met?"

"Yup. That's how you act," Kent said in a way he knew would get to me. "Like you always forget what it's like out here for niggas like me. Just trying to find love and shit. Nah mean? Folks blow up and forget where they came from. Forget how they got where they at." His eyes cut me accusatorily.

For all of Kent's faults, his many shortcomings, he never failed to support me at whatever I was doing. Our parents became addicted to crack when we were in elementary school, and though he was ninety-eight seconds younger than me, Kent jumped into the role of caretaker. He stopped going to school and ran errands for the drug dealers so we had something in the refrigerator and coats in the winter. And even though our father eventually went to rehab and got clean, Kent stayed on the block to pay my way through Morgan State University and gave me a suitcase filled with hundreds when I was accepted to Columbia Law. It was the classic story of many families in our neighborhood at that time. Drugs took a lot away from us, but then drugs also made it possible for us to survive.

"Lydia is gonna be my wife. I love her. She's everything I've wanted in a woman—soft, beautiful, nice," he said as I ate and looked away, rolling my eyes. "She ain't nothing like these chicks here."

"I'm sure she's great, but why do you have to marry her? Why get married at all? I thought you said you didn't want any more kids. What's the point?"

"That's the thing, yo. Lydia don't want any more kids either. She already has four. She don't want no more shorties." Kent smiled like this was a plus.

"I can't listen anymore. I can't even listen anymore. This is crazy. Are you serious? You're a thirty-one-year-old man. There's no way you could think this is a good idea."

"See, you're judging Lydia. You don't even know her. Look, why don't you come through the crib tonight? We gonna be on Skype and shit. You'd like her," Kent said, trying to make it sound as if the idea had just come to mind, but it was evident that it was all a part of his plan to pull me in. "And you can see your father. I know you ain't been home in a minute." Kent still lived in his childhood bedroom in the brownstone our grandparents left our father.

"I've been drowning at work," I said. "And I can't come tonight. I'm busy."

"Too busy to meet your future sister-in-law?"

"Meet? What am I supposed to say to her?"

"Well, you ain't gonna be saying much." Kent laughed slyly. "Because she don't hardly speak no English."

"What? How do you—I don't even want to know," I said. "I'm busy tonight anyway. Tamika's son has a fencing match, and I promised I'd be there to support him."

"Fencing? What the fuck cuzzo have Miles doing that shit for? That tall-ass nigga need to be balling. He's, like, five-seven at ten. I got connects at Christ the King and St. John's, too. Get him that fat scholarship."

"She just wants him to try different things. Expand his range, so he's not stuck on the basketball thing like everyone else where we came from," I said, realizing that Kent wasn't listening to anything I was saying.

His eyes were molesting something behind me that I knew from experience likely had a big behind and huge breasts. I turned to see what he was eyeing so I could blast him for mentally groping a woman after he'd solemnly sworn his love and devotion to Latin Lydia. But when I twisted my neck, I wished I'd stayed set on Kent.

Hipster Holly was seating two people I never wanted to see again in life. Two people I'd wished dead on more than one occasion. My ex-fiancé and my former roommate/best friend. At once I wanted to disintegrate into the concrete and dribble down into the sewer—well, maybe I wanted that for them. I just wanted to disappear. *Poof.*

"Yo, honey is bad. Ass and titties on an Asian chick?" Kent was fantasizing in his own little world and probably had no idea he was speaking aloud. "She got a little black in her though. Skin kinda brown. She sexy as fuck."

"Shit." I turned back to the table and struggled so hard to swallow a gob of sad spit that had gathered at the back of my throat that I was sure everyone outside of the restaurant could hear me. I could feel my enemies turn to the table and notice me. Suddenly, I was overly aware of how my black linen slacks weren't ironed, my Hebru Brantley T-shirt looked dingy, and I was in worn-down flip-flops—not the chic stilettos I'd purchased for the sole purpose of running into them at some point. But here? Why here? 44 & X was my favorite brunch spot, and everyone knew it. They knew it. The three of us had had brunch here together. I looked like a budding lesbian who couldn't get anyone but her twin brother to take her out to brunch on Sunday afternoon.

"Real recognize real. Don't act like she ain't fine." Kent laughed like I was being petty and looked at me sinking deeper into my seat. "What? What's wrong?"

"Nothing. Look, are you ready?" I asked quickly, covering my half-eaten omelet with the napkin that had been sitting on my lap.

"Ready? What? I ain't finished eating yet." He pointed down at his smoked salmon omelet, which was covered in so much ketchup, it made me want to vomit. "I know you ain't that jealous. She's fine, but—"

"I know her."

"Oh, that's what's up. Hook a nigga up." Kent sounded relieved and probably completely missed how his suggestion undermined everything he'd invited me to the restaurant to achieve.

"That would be impossible," I said.

"Why?"

"Well, because you're allegedly in love with someone you met, like, five minutes ago and about to get married—"

"I ain't married *yet*—"

"And she's . . . on a date." Hot tears were gathering behind my eyes at that reality.

"Fuck that. Ain't no way that little nigga is hitting that shit right. I'd bag shorty in a minute." Kent laughed. "Put me in the game, Coach Kim. Hook a nig—"

"Look at the man sitting at the table, Kent," I directed, irritated. "*Look* at him."

"What I need to look at this nigga for?" Kent squinted for a minute, and then his mouth fell open like he was looking at a dead body for the first time. "Yooooo, that's Ronald *McDonald*. Your ex—" He stopped himself and looked at me. "Oh, that's the . . . Asian Kim? Wait, he's fucking Asian Kim? You ain't tell me that." He looked back at her. "I thought I recognized that ass."

"I did so tell you," I said, feeling a little tear slide from my left eye. "I told you what she did, and—"

"Oh, don't start on that shit, Kiki Mimi," Kent said, leaning toward me like a basketball coach about to pull me out of the game. "You can't let that lame nigga see you over here crying. That shit was, like, two years ago when y'all called off the wedding."

"One year, two months," I divulged.

"So. Yo, dead that. You moved on. You better than that nigga Ronald McDonald. I mean, that nigga's *real* name is Ronald Mc-Donald. Come on. You couldn't marry that clown."

He was trying to build me up, but hearing the word *marry* tore me apart, and a few more tears escaped my eyes. Then Kent placing his hand on my shoulder to comfort me opened the floodgates, so I jumped up from the table to rush inside to the bathroom before I unraveled into a mess.

I went into a stall and locked the door behind me like a monster was on my tail when really it was just my past. Ronald Mc-Donald was a funny name, but my history with him was nothing to laugh about. I loved that man intensely and without warranty. We'd met our sophomore year at Morgan State. He was skinny and too smart. He was always talking about how he was going to be a lawyer when he graduated from college and how he was going to save all the poor black people of the world. I'd always been really smart, but I had no idea what I intended to do after Morgan State. I was the first person in my family to go to college, and all I knew was that after I graduated I wanted to get a good job so I could go home, find my mother, and pay for her to go to a good rehab place in someplace like Malibu or Denver like all of the white celebrities did on television.

Needless to say, skinny Ronald McDonald and all of his big talk about plans and the future was more than attractive to me. I just craved his direction, and soon his dream became my dream. By junior year, he was my best guy friend, and we planned to go to law school together after college. But there was only one thing missing from our dynamic duo: both Ronald and I were virgins. Kent and his drug-dealing crew had scared all the neighborhood boys off when I was in high school, so I hadn't so much as made out with anyone.

All of that changed one night during homecoming weekend junior year. Ronald had pledged Kappa the semester before, and he was in his chapter's step show. I got there early with my girls and sat in the front row ready to cheer him on. We were debating who'd look the hottest onstage and who'd likely drop his cane mid-performance. I mean, some of these guys we'd known since our freshman year, and now they'd pledged and become pseudo celebrities on campus—or so they thought.

When the Kappas hit the stage, Ronald was in front of me. And he was moving his body in ways that tickled the little space behind my ears. By the middle of the show, he was shirtless and working his cane so fast, beads of sweat trickled down hard abs I'd never seen. I kept thinking, "What has he been doing all summer?" My girls were cheering and screaming his name, but I was speechless, standing there with my arms folded over my chest and feeling something new, twitching and hot, between my thighs.

Ronald didn't drop that damn cane at all, and by the time he shimmied off the stage with his frat brothers, snaking his body back and forth, I knew I was going to be waiting for him in his dorm after we finished partying that night.

I didn't say a word to my girls. In two years on the yard, I'd learned that every single one of them had a big mouth, and I was so afraid that if I did something with Ronald and told them, it would get out and people would call me a "Kappa set-out" (code for "whore"). But there was nothing wrong with doing and not telling, and I knew Ronald wasn't the type of guy to go telling his frat brothers all of his business, so once we all left the club where Ronald had been strolling with his brothers through the party before drooling freshman girls, I was waiting right outside his door.

He smiled and invited me in like it was any other night and we were about to have one of our "bestie" sleepovers and watch old reruns of *Martin* after smoking a little weed, but I told him not to turn on the television. I was already drunk enough to act out what I was feeling between my thighs, and while he was in the middle of a panicky retelling of his performance, like I hadn't been there, I jumped right on top of him on his bed. I could tell he was nervous. He hadn't ever seen me like that. His hands were sweating and I could feel his heart beating into my chest as he kissed me like the Tin Man from *The Wizard of Oz*.

That's when I felt it. I was straddling him, and at his middle something was swelling and hardening fast. I'd heard about "wood" and brothers getting "hard," and I knew what it was, so I pushed my middle to his middle and fell deeper into his chest, grinding my hips around in these kinky circles like I'd seen Patra and Lady Saw do in reggae videos on *Video Music Box*. I let my Janet

Jackson in *Poetic Justice* braids swing over my shoulders and rubbed my vagina so hard into him, something shot straight through me and I felt my whole body open up. And I mean literally—from my vagina to my heart. I rubbed harder then, and while we were both still in our jeans, Ronald's penis grew bigger again and more rigid than anything that should be connected to a human. I abandoned my brain to follow my heart, which was begging to feel the thing tapping my middle from the outside in. I am sure I didn't push my hand into Ronald's pants with any elegance. It was more of a shove and grab. I wrapped my hands around his penis and remembered that in seventh grade fast-ass Melissa Montgomery said it should feel like a banana or plantain. I decided that I needed to call Melissa and tell her that she was wrong. Because what I felt hiding below Ronald's tight abs was more like the long, thick salamis my father used to get by taking the train all the way to the Italian butcher in Bensonhurst.

My hands were on his penis, gripping it tightly and slowly fingering it all around, as if trying to confirm that it was real and moving and pulsating to the rhythm in my hips. He let out a little sigh. He placed his hands on my hips over him and next his fingers were undoing my zipper.

"You think you're ready for this?" he asked in a whisper that was more confirming than questioning. I don't think I answered. I don't remember answering. Ronald could never recall if I answered. I just started moving. Pulled off my own pants and panties and everything. Some Lil' Kim song was playing on the radio, so I was feeling all courageous.

I let him enter me while I held my breath and thought of the sounds the A train made when it pulled up at 125th Street (fast-ass Melissa Montgomery's advice). It hurt. It burned like fire. But the more I held my breath and thought of the sounds of the brakes on the subway car screeching against the tracks, the farther behind I left the pain, until I arrived at something that commanded my every sense like nothing else I'd ever experienced. I couldn't worry about anything. Think about anything. Not my mother. My father. Kent. How we were going to pay for senior year. What I wanted to be when I grew up. At that moment, when Ronald was inside of me, I had no worries, no thoughts.

I think that was when my brazen undertaking of our love began. How he stole my heart from the outside in. Because after that, I was never the same. I was sitting on top of that salami for so long and through so many days and nights, skinny Ronald McDonald became a part of me—or maybe I became a part of him, like an appendage. I got a urinary tract infection, a yeast infection, and even popped a muscle in my jaw, but nothing could keep me from that man. I stayed in position on top of him through graduation. Got accepted to Columbia Law *after* he got accepted to NYU Law and we started planning our future together. Then *we* were going to be lawyers and *we* were going to save all the poor black people of the world.

Ronald was more than clear on my plans to be with him . . . forever. He said he wanted to be with me. He said I would make a good "mate." After we graduated from law school in New York, he announced that he just needed a little more time on his own to get himself together and then he'd propose. I agreed. Hearing the word *propose* come from his lips at twenty-four was like watching a master chef cook a perfect cut of filet mignon—you'd do anything to taste the final product. Because I'd lived in adult housing through law school to avoid going home to my father and Kent, I was newly homeless and staying with my cousin, so I needed to find someplace

to live quickly. I searched everywhere, but I was broke and studying for the bar exam and I couldn't find anything I could afford that
wasn't far out in Jersey, damn near upstate, or out on Long Island.
Going home was just out of the question.

One morning my cousin Tamika, who was a booking agent
at the Wilhelmina modeling agency, said she had a client whose
roommate had disappeared in the middle of the night. She needed
a replacement fast. When I showed up at the rent-controlled two-
bedroom loft in Chelsea, this Chinese-looking girl with pecan
skin and bushy black hair answered the door in a thin tank dress.
"Please be my new roommate!" she begged like a little puppy before I could even get in the door to see the place. "Okay," I said
quickly. We laughed, sensing our equal desperation. I walked in
and she pulled me into her arms dramatically. "Wonderful! I just
knew we were meant to be when Tamika told me your name was
Kim. I'm Kim too! We're meant to be," she squealed so loudly I
knew she couldn't be any older than twenty-one. From that day on
she was "Kim 2." She pulled me to a couch that looked like it had
been in the loft since it was built and proceeded to go over a bunch
of stuff about sharing the rent and utilities. There was a neon-green
bong on the table and a pizza box on the floor near the couch, but I
was so busy looking at Kim 2's skin and wondering where she was
from, guessing about her parentage, that I hardly paid attention to
the details of my surroundings. When she asked if I'd be her roommate, I hadn't even heard how much the rent was. "Yes," I said.
"I will."

That night I was meeting Ronald for dinner in Gramercy Park
near his firm, and Kim kind of invited herself along. That was her
way. She didn't take off the nearly see-through tank dress. She slid
on some cowgirl boots only a model could get away with, and big

black shades. She wrapped her arm around mine and asked me to tell her all about Ronald—my future fiancé. I did. Told everything. Including the rap about his Bensonhurst salami. If my mother had been around, like, ever, I might have had advice to do otherwise.

There were prophetic moments over the next five years, notably an Ecstasy-fueled threesome three years in, during which I passed out after he ejaculated in her. That haunted me day and night, and might have helped me predict the psychological hell down the road when my fiancé left me in an emergency room to go comfort my roommate turned best friend.

Now, in the bathroom at 44 & X, I sat down on the toilet and cried into my hands like a stupid girl. I was done with questions about why that sad moment had happened and how it happened. I'd been numbed by the whole thing. But seeing Kim and Ronald together, knowing they were still dating and eating at my brunch spot, brought all of the pain back.

A text came through on my cell phone as I balled up a bunch of toilet paper to wipe my tears. It was from Kent.

KENT: You coming out of there?

I tried, like, three times to respond with something clear and concise that would hide the full-on breakdown I was having in the stall, something like "I'm on my way out" or "Be back in a sec," but nothing would come out right. Then Kent started writing again.

KENT: Come on. Don't let this shit go down with you hiding in the bathroom.

KENT: Hello?

KENT: Kiki Mimi, you better bring your ass out here. Yo, Harlem, stand up! I ain't fucking playing.

He was trying to make me laugh. I did chuckle a little bit at how stupid he was, but I was still hiding on the dirty toilet and probably earning a bad case of crabs for it.

KENT: Yo, you know how I am. You know I would've dropped this fool on sight behind what he did to you if I really gave a fuck about him. But I ain't do it.

The best thing about being a twin is that sometimes in such a crazy world you know exactly how someone else feels. It's like if Kent is happy or sad, I can actually feel his emotions inside of me. Like they're my own. I felt that when I read Kent's message. I felt his anger. His compassion for me. In that moment my little brother was being my big brother again. I texted him back.

ME: Why didn't you fuck him up?

He answered immediately.

KENT: Because this nigga ain't good enough for you.

And then:

KENT: He never was. I was glad when he was gone. If I put my hands on him, he would've thought I gave a fuck. I didn't. I wanted him to know that. Man to man. He wasn't good enough.

I can't say my tears went from sad to happy. That would be a full exaggeration. It's more accurate to say Kent made me smile. Made me a little tougher.

I wiped my tears one last time and flushed the tissue down the toilet. I straightened my back and walked out of the stall with the full intention of returning to the table, finishing my brunch, and moving on . . . again. *Harlem . . . stand up.*

When I was looking in the mirror cleaning streaks of mascara from my cheeks, Kent sent more texts:

> KENT: Yo, you coming out? I paid the bill, so we can leave when you walk out.

> KENT: Yo?

> ME: Yes. I'm coming out now.

The phone started vibrating again when I was stuffing it back into my purse, but I knew it was probably just Kent again, so I ignored it and headed out of the bathroom.

I took one of those deep, courage-begging breaths and pulled the bathroom door open.

And there, standing right there in front of me, was Kim 2.

I was so not prepared for that. I'm saying, if I had been, I would've said some slick Dominique Deveraux in *Dynasty* line that would cut her down at the knees and threaten her life. But a good line or practiced uppercut was so far from my mind, I just tried to walk past her. I didn't even roll my eyes.

She put her cold hand on my arm, and my first reaction was to pull away.

But she grabbed for me again.

"No, just wait," she said, trying to get a hold of me with the thin, pale hand.

"Wait? What?" I threw my arms up to escape her. "Don't touch me. Don't fucking touch me."

She reached again and I jumped back.

"Kim, stop. I just want to say—"

"I don't want to talk to you. I don't want to hear what you have to say. I've told you that so many times. Just stop," I said, repeating sentiments I'd expressed in response to the many e-mails and texts Kim had sent me after her relationship with my fiancé came to light. They had been a couple, an actual couple, for over a year before I found out. She'd met his parents. They'd gone to the Poconos together—all of this while I was with him.

"I just want you to hear me out," she said.

"Hear what? I don't need to hear anything I don't already know. You stole my fiancé. You said you were my best friend, but meanwhile you were sleeping with my man behind my back."

"We both know that's not how it went down. You guys were—"

"That's how I know the story, and that's all I care to know," I said. "I'm not one of those people who need to know why. Your motives were obvious. You wanted him from the start. You knew how much I loved him, how much he loved me, but you wanted him for yourself anyway. We were supposed to get married."

"You didn't have a ring. He never even asked you."

"So?"

"So . . . look, none of it was done on purpose," Kim 2 said. "It just happened."

"You can tell that bullshit to someone else," I shot back, "someone who wasn't nearly killed in a car your high ass was driving."

"But you . . . you . . . I never meant for any of that to happen."

"*You* what? *You* what? You, *Kim*, need to explain how when I was in surgery you were fucking calling Ronald to get *you* out of jail. Explain how when I was laid up in the hospital and the doctors thought I might be paralyzed from the neck down, you never once came to see me and you moved out of the apartment we were sharing and in with Ronald. Explain that. Did you mean for all of that to happen? Or was all of that a surprise to you, too? Because it was certainly a fucking surprise to me."

I didn't realize I was hollering at Kim 2, had my finger pointed at the little space between her eyebrows like a .22 threatening to lick a shot, until I sensed all of the eyes in the restaurant on me. I turned to see that a little crowd had gathered and right in front were Kent and Ronald.

I slowly lowered my hand and tried to rediscover my sensible mind, where the anger I'd feel over being disbarred and losing my job for beating Kim 2's ass in my favorite restaurant would outweigh the joy I'd feel after I choked her to death. And I think she was waiting for it, too, because she was quiet, and while my hands had been up before, now she was standing there with her hands raised like I was about to arrest her.

"You know what? Don't explain a damn thing," I said. "Because, as I said, I don't give a fuck."

I'd finally found my Dominique line, and it was weak at best, but I tossed my purse over my arm and walked right into the crowd, where Kent and Ronald were waiting.

I got to Ronald first, and when he opened his mouth to say God only knows what, I put my hand up to stop him.

"Don't say anything to me," I shot. "Nothing."

Kent grabbed me and pulled me out of the restaurant as I went into a list of other things I needed to say that I probably should've kept to myself.

"I sent you a text when she got up. Told you she was coming into the bathroom," Kent said after I stumbled out behind him. "You okay?"

He pulled me around the corner and pushed me up against the side of a building.

"I'm fine. I'm fine."

"I was trying to get you out of there. I kept texting you."

"I know. The phone was in my purse."

Kent's fists were balled at his sides like he was ready to fight someone.

"I was about to drop that motherfucker," he fired. "If I wasn't with you and shit, I would've stomped his ass out. But I know how you get down, so I tried to keep cool."

I don't know how I found the comedy, but I actually started laughing. And loudly.

"What? What are you laughing at?" Kent asked, looking like he was about to run back around the corner to fight Ronald.

"I don't know. I just," I started, "I guess it's funny how you said you didn't fight him before because he wasn't good enough for me, but now you're all riled up and ready to throw down."

Kent rolled his eyes and sucked his teeth like we were seven and I didn't want to play H-O-R-S-E with him on the basketball court.

"Look at you," I went on, still laughing.

"Yeah, whatever. You better be glad you're a lawyer and I knew the last thing you wanted was for some nigga shit to go down in there, because we were both about to be rumbling—sister and brother."

"Really?"

"I can't have that fool getting my Kiki Mimi all upset and hiding in a bathroom. Mess up my rep in these streets. Have niggas thinking I'm soft."

I put my arms out and pulled Kent into a hug.

"Maybe you're just soft enough. Soft enough to save me," I said, and I felt happiness wash over my twin brother.

"Ohh," Kent said. "Well, how about you save me, too?"

"What? How?" I asked. I'd already forgotten about what he'd asked me at the table.

"Lydia. My fiancée. Your sister-in-law. Pull some strings. Make some calls!" Kent backed up so I could see his begging smile.

"Ahhh, to that I still say no. Not even in a million years, Kent. No. And hell no. Nice begging smile though, baby bro."

Chapter 2

After I left Kent and the drama at the restaurant, I took a cab home to lie down for a few hours before I was supposed to be in Fort Greene for my godson's fencing match. My lower back was hurting, and I knew it would only take a little while for the consistent throbbing to spread up my spine and make it nearly impossible for me to walk or even sit up without severe discomfort. That car accident I was in with Kim 2 had left a fracture in my lower spine, and while my doctor had given me a clean bill of health, the pain never left me. Some days it was impossible for me to get out of bed. Other days I'd manage for a few hours but then I'd feel the throbbing in my spine and know the pain was back. I'd need to get home, take my pills, and lie down until they took the pain away.

I slept a little longer than I expected and missed Miles's match, but I rushed all the way to Brooklyn from downtown and got there in time to see him receive his medal and pose for pictures. I'd made it to a few of his matches, and for some reason it always surprised me that so many kids were actually fencing in Brooklyn—not hooping it up, not gangbanging, but fencing, and loving it. But it really wasn't so far-fetched. Not in the new Brooklyn with its trimmed and manicured trees and community gardens and sidewalk cafés. The newfangled Brooklyn kids lived in newly renovated brownstones and had two parents at home who went to PTA meetings and volunteered after school. While Miles clearly benefitted from it, I sometimes wondered what had happened to all those poor people and their kids who'd lived in the old chain-popping, hip-hopping Brooklyn I knew growing up.

Tamika and my other cousin Leah were giving me some serious side eye for being late. I completely expected it. Like the other parents in the room, most of whom were white and dressed liked they'd purposely gotten ready in a dark closet, they thought the most important thing anyone could do was to be somewhere supporting someone's kid. Potty poop or pottery fair, we all had to stand at attention and act like whatever they were doing was the most important thing in the world. Still, I knew my cousins' issues ran even deeper than that, so I had to accept their ridiculous criticism.

"I'm sorry I missed it," I said to them after I'd secretly slid twenty dollars into Miles's hand before he ran off to flaunt his victory medal in front of his friends. "My back was hurting and I had to lie down for a little while."

"Hum," Tamika said, cutting her eyes at me even harder. "You're his godmother. I'm just saying, it would be nice if you'd try to be here on time . . . just once." She looked at Leah for an agreeing nod that made me roll my eyes.

"Really? So, this is what we're doing? Right here? At the match?

I've been at, like, half of his matches. I know most of the parents in this room. More than both you." The same throbbing started at my spine again. I had to be careful with them. They were sisters and so catty, they'd make you feel like scratching their eyes out. When Kent and I were younger we'd call them "the wicked sisters of the East Coast."

"Whatever, Kim. He's ten. This is important stuff. He needs you to be here for him right now," Tamika said so sharply I knew nothing she was saying had anything to do with me or my tardiness.

Tamika and Leah were the children of my mother's baby sister. Like Kent and me, they grew up hard and fast while our mothers were in the street, and when most teenage girls were thinking about trying out for the cheerleading squad, they were both pushing baby strollers and collecting welfare checks. Neither one of them was stupid though. When Tamika got pregnant with Miles, she dropped out of high school, got her GED, and enrolled at LaGuardia Community College. Leah was only fifteen when she had her son, Monk, so she stayed in school, but after graduation she followed Tamika and they finished LaGuardia and City College together. Leah and Tamika were now beyond successful. They'd left Harlem for a changing Brooklyn when Aunt Donna died of AIDS in the late nineties; they were raising their sons together in a brownstone they'd purchased with the secret life insurance policy our grandfather took out on our mothers when they started using drugs. Any cliché you could apply to teenage mothers made good could be attached to their success, but my cousins remained psychologically tortured by everything that led to that actual success. The list was long, and somewhere in there was Aunt Donna's drug use, her death, and the fact that no matter how smart they were, there was nothing they could do about either of those things. But as heartbreaking as that was, that wasn't even what was at the top. There, like the final sentencing from a judge handing out twenty-five years to life, was a string of four fathers no one had seen since their children were conceived: Tamika's father, Leah's father, Monk's father, and Miles's father. It was a wound that had affected the sisters in different ways. For Tamika, it meant that she was set on making every man pay for what Miles's father had done to her by abandoning them. And since most of them had stopped coming around, I was on the list as well.

"Mika, you know I love Miles, and I'm always here for him. He knows that," I said as calmly as I could. "Please forgive me," I added sweetly before opening my arms for a hug.

Tamika rolled her eyes at me again and looked to Leah. She tried to play hard for a few more seconds, but then she softened and halfheartedly accepted my hug.

"Fine. I'll accept your apology. But don't be late again. You've been late, like, the last three times," she said dismissively, like I was one of her ex-boyfriends trying to get back in good with her. She was crazy as hell, but she was my favorite cousin. We both looked like our grandmother—had long, slender arms and dimples on either side of our lower lip.

"I won't be late anymore. I promise," I said. "Hey, Lee!" I hugged Leah and gave her twenty dollars for Monk, who was away in Washington, DC, on a fifth-grade history-class field trip. Leah had been an out lesbian since Monk was born. She never let her hair grow beyond an inch and wore jeans and Adidases everywhere she went. She was twenty-six, but she only dated women in their forties. Still, she was just as unlucky in love as Tamika, and I couldn't recall any affair she'd had that lasted past six months.

"So, how was brunch with Kent?" Tamika asked with her disposition decidedly changed. "What's his ass up to?"

"A whole lot of crazy," I said, knowing I wouldn't mention seeing Kim 2 and Ronald. Tamika felt she was responsible for the whole thing because she'd introduced me to Kim 2 and promised on the Bible that if she ever saw her again, she'd "beat her down to the white meat." Now, considering Tamika's age and success, that might sound like an idle threat, but being born and bred in Harlem, I had no reason not to believe it. If I even mentioned Kim's name, we'd be in a cab riding back to the restaurant to try to find her.

"Everything Kent does is crazy," Leah pointed out.

"Well, this is the craziest yet," I said. "He claims he's getting married."

"Married? To whom?" Leah and Tamika asked together so loudly, all of the other parents who were standing in groups turned and looked at us quickly.

"He can't be marrying Keisha. She's . . . you know," Leah said, looking at Tamika hesitantly before I could answer.

"What? Keisha's what?" I asked.

"I saw her at the club a few weeks ago," Leah answered, frowning a little. "She was with this dom I know named K.D. And I'll just say this, K.D. likes turning bitches out. I wouldn't be surprised if Keisha's next."

"Come on, Lee. We both know plenty of straight women go to the gay club for entertainment only. I've gone with you before. That doesn't mean she's turned out by some butch named K.D.," I said.

Tamika looked away like I was in denial.

"I guess the way she was grinding on K.D.'s lap was just for entertainment, too," Leah said. "I'm not saying . . . I'm *just* saying."

I stood there with my mouth agape for a minute as I added Kent's sudden desire to marry his Latin lover to the equation. He'd loved Keisha since they'd met in junior high school, and she'd gotten suspended after taking the rap for his having stolen their science teacher's wallet. They were one of those couples who lived to break up, but you always knew they'd get back together in the end.

I told Tamika and Leah all about Kent trying to get me to pull some strings to get Lydia into the US. We had a good laugh and agreed there was no way he'd ever make it down the aisle to actually marry that woman. If Keisha was that open with her underground dealings at the club, there was no way someone from somewhere didn't see what she was doing and send word to Kent. New York was a big city, but the circles people traveled in were so small. And while Leah wasn't rushing to tell her cousin anything about his baby mama being in K.D.'s arms at the gay club on account of all the drama he'd put Keisha through over the years, the cat was probably let out of the bag by someone else—someone who needed a free carton of Newports. Anyway, Kent's action was probably a reaction. We decided to put the entire case on hold until more drama ensued.

Somewhere in there, one of Tamika's archenemies walked into our little familial circle holding a glass of red punch and nodding along as if she'd been invited. One of a handful of black mothers in the room, Yolanda Johnson was a late-thirties NYC newbie whose perfect exterior and nosy nature made it easy for the other mothers to hate her. She'd had three boys but managed to keep herself a size 4, and everything from her ducktail flip to her perfectly manicured pinky toes was so on-point that it could make a drag queen envious. And that's all fine, but in the handful of times I'd seen her, those things seemed to be the only things she could talk about—

where she'd gotten her hair done, what color her nail lacquer was, her workouts with Madonna's trainer, and how wonderful her sons and husband were to her. It was enough to make anyone vomit. Or beg her to shut up. As Tamika had reminded me one night after she'd scared Yolanda off with an evil eye, Yolanda was a housewife, so staying slim and trim was technically a part of her job. And all of that stuff about her perfect sons and husband was a bunch of crap— her sweet sons wreaked havoc whenever she wasn't around, and she kept her hair and nails tight because her lawyer husband had been cheating with the single mother of another boy in the fencing class—even worse, the other mother let him go because he had a little penis, and she wasn't shy about telling people.

"Well, I think it's exciting," Yolanda said, pushing herself into the conversation at a point where there was no way she could be clear on what we were talking about. Most times she stayed away from Tamika, but Leah pointed out that whenever I came around, Yolanda would pop up. She was one of those opportunists who thought that because I was an ADA, I was a "somebody," and therefore she had to know me. "Marriage? A wedding! Nothing more exciting than that—especially when it's a brother getting married." She grinned and leaned into me, laughing. "Know what I'm saying? Who is it?"

I could see Tamika gritting her teeth to stop herself from telling Yolanda to get the hell away from us, so I jumped in.

"My brother," I said.

"Oh, that's so sweet. Are you looking for a wedding planner? Because I know the sister who planned Jay and Bey's wedding. She's wonderful. Just amazing." Yolanda's voice took on the inflection of a Valley Girl when she said "wonderful" and "amazing."

I was so stunned by Yolanda's randomness that I couldn't speak soon enough to stop whatever venom was about to come from my cousin's mouth.

"Who the hell are Jay and Bey?" Tamika spat.

Leah laughed so hard, she chortled, and Yolanda joined uncomfortably, considering that maybe Tamika was joking. Somehow, she never caught Tamika's many insults. I chalked it up to her being from Oklahoma and slow on NYC-style shade.

"You know," Yolanda said, still laughing with Lee, "Jay-Z and Beyoncé."

"Then say Jay-Z and Beyoncé. I'm not fifteen. I don't watch BET. The hell? I hate when people do that," Tamika said.

"Gotcha," Yolanda answered, looking down into her purse to retrieve her cell phone. "Well, let me give you the number, Kim. Just tell her I sent you."

"Oh, no, don't bother," I said. "I'm sure whoever she is, she's great, but she's also far from my brother's budget."

"Budget? Come on, honey. There's no budget when it comes to such things. It's his wedding—and we all know what that means: Spare no expense." Yolanda grinned at me like I was an adorable but ignorant little girl. "Oh no, I'm so sorry, dear heart. I forgot I was talking to a bunch of unmarried folks. Well, you'll all see when it's your turn to walk down the aisle." She looked around at each of us, smiling comfortingly like we were at a funeral. "And even you," she added, winking at Leah. "Thanks to Obama!"

"Yayy! Gay marriage!" Leah cheered weakly, pumping a fist in the air, but Yolanda didn't pick up on her sarcasm and pumped a fist, too.

"Well, I don't give a damn if every gay man and woman rushes to the altar to sign those papers, I'm good on marriage," Tamika said.

"What? Don't tell me you've given up on the brothers," Yolanda said.

"Oh, no, honey. I never said such a thing. Brothers come in handy, but marriage isn't for me. I've raised mine and I support myself. All I need now is a soft hand and a strong back," Tamika said.

"You are so crass," I said, laughing with Tamika and Leah as I looked over my shoulders to be sure no one could hear Tamika.

"Crass but right. To quote my mother: Men are good for two things—paying bills and giving thrills," Tamika added, with Yolanda looking at her like everything she was saying mocked her entire lifestyle.

"Stop it, Tamika. I know you can't really believe that. Marriage is a beautiful thing. When two people come together and they promise their love to one another for life, it's magical. Come on, ladies. What about you, Kim. Have you given up on men? On marriage?"

I am sure every tongue in that little brick-walled room stopped moving and every eye turned to me. Even the married men wanted to hear my answer. The boys in the back still in their fencing gear, too.

"I-I . . . I-I . . . Yeah. I . . . guess not. I mean, I do. I mean, yes. No . . . no . . . maybe not," I got out before my throat started swelling and the pain in my back wrapped over my shoulders.

"Maybe?" Yolanda repeated, her eyes disbelieving. "What do you mean, 'maybe'?"

"Well . . . I—"

"You know what, don't even answer that crap," Tamika said, cutting me off. "You'll get married when you want to get married, if you want to get married. I hate it when married women make it sound like it's the best and only thing you can do with your life, when truth be told, most of them are just fronting for the cameras. Ain't that right, Yolanda?" Now Tamika was the one serving up wide eyes to Yolanda.

"I'm not sure what you mean," Yolanda answered coolly. "Certainly some people are faking, but that's with anything. Plenty of people are happily married."

It was like a trap set for a cross-eyed bear. The moment Yolanda said that, I knew how Tamika would answer.

"Are *you* happily married? Any *small* problems lurking around?" Tamika asked suggestively.

"Why would you ask that? Of course I'm happily married," Yolanda said, laughing nervously.

"Well, that's not what I—"

Glory be to God, that Leah pulled her sister's arm and announced that they were just about to leave, because if Tamika had stood there to speak her mind one second longer, poor Yolanda would've been cursed (or blessed) with the baldfaced truth about her marriage. It was all stuff I was sure she knew, but she'd die right there on the spot if she knew that we knew. And I wouldn't blame her.

"What was that about?" Yolanda said, turning to me with a confused look. "Your cousin is so crazy."

"She's just sensitive about certain issues," I said. "No big deal."

"Well, I hope that doesn't roll over to you. Don't give up on love, Kim. I understand what it's like for you single girls."

"Oh, you do?"

"I didn't meet my husband until I'd already graduated from college, girl!" Yolanda said, as if she was, like, fifty when she graduated. "But I stayed slim and fly, and when he saw me, he knew what was up. That's what you have to do. Keep yourself up. Get in the gym!" She looked down at my hips like she'd been dying to say that to me for months. "Get your hair done." She looked up at my frizzy updo that was half natural at the roots. "Keep your nails right. Look, you're successful. You have a good résumé. Assistant district attorney in New York City! Any man would be happy to have you! I'll ask my husband if he has any friends."

I was really ready to tell Yolanda all about her little dick husband myself then. Not for anything, but if all a woman needed was a nice shape, decent hair, clean nails, and a great résumé to find love, most of my friends would be married. Someone needed to tell Yolanda to shut the hell up, but I knew her type. She would never know she was wrong, so I chose sarcasm. "Really? That's a great idea."

"Yes it is, girl. Look, don't even worry about it. And don't give up. You never know. Your blessing could be waiting right outside that door." Yolanda pointed toward the door Tamika and Leah had exited through after pulling Miles away from his buddies. She looked so sincere, I was about to burst out laughing.

"Right," I said, backing away from her slowly. "And that's a good thing, because I was about to walk out that very door. Guess I'll see you next time."

Outside, I found Leah, Tamika, and Miles awaiting my escape.

"I don't know why you continue to entertain that woman," Tamika nearly shouted at me over a siren wailing from a patrol car that had stopped to arrest some man a few feet away from the community center. Right across the street was an older park that still attracted people and daily dealings the new Brooklyn pioneers preferred not to see.

"She is crazy and delusional."

"I wasn't entertaining her," I said, watching the cop load the man into the back of his squad car. "She just came over."

"Notice she never comes to talk to me if you or Lee aren't there," Tamika said.

"That's because you're crazy," Leah pointed out.

Miles laughed, and Tamika looked at him as the cop car drove off.

"What you laughing about? You're in grown folks' business?" Tamika sounded like our grandmother. "Don't play with me. I'll knock your teeth out, boy."

We laughed because Tamika was clearly joking. As hard as she was, she could never bring herself to lay a hand on Miles.

"Yeah, you can laugh now, but we'll see later," she said, laughing at her attempt to sound threatening. "Now thank your godmother for coming all the way out here to Brooklyn to see your match." She pushed him toward me.

"Thank you, Cousin Kim," he said with his braces shining on me. He was so tall and lanky, but in his face was a baby boy our entire family raised.

"No problem, precious," I said. "I'll see you next time. And I'll be on time."

Tamika told Miles to walk ahead and turned to me again.

"Now, Attorney Kind, when do I get to see you again?"

"What do you mean? Just let me know when the next match is."

"You know what I mean. You need to get out. Why don't you come to Wind Down Wednesday with me and my girls this week?"

"You know I don't have time. And your friends are crazy. All they talk about is men and sex. Am I right or wrong, Lee?" I looked at Leah.

"I'm not in it. You know I don't hang with any of them," Leah said, excusing herself from the conversation.

"Well, what else is there to talk about?" Tamika joked.

"Anything. Politics. Social issues. Hair. Celebrity gossip," I listed. "I don't know."

Tamika closed her eyes and pretended she was asleep. After snoring a bit, she opened her eyes and looked surprised I was standing there.

"Oh, I'm sorry. I just fell asleep while you were talking."

"Look, I'll try to come, but I am not participating in some all-night dishing session about horrible dates and great sex. It's pointless."

"It's what you need," Tamika said, grinning at Leah.

"What is that for?" I asked.

Once again Leah pulled her sister's arm.

"On that note, we're out of here," Leah said, laughing, making Tamika follow her away from me.

"No, really, tell me," I said.

"I'll tell you on Wednesday," Tamika said as she waved good-bye and blew me kisses. "You better come. And you better not be late. We'll be at Damaged Goods. The old spot right around the corner from here."

Chapter 3

I got to work late the next day. My cell phone alarm went off at 6 a.m. as regularly scheduled, but I slept right through it and woke up after 10, when I rolled off the couch and hit the side of my head on one of the claw-feet on my coffee table. The alarm was blaring then, and I had, like, six urgent text messages and voice mails from my assistant, Carol.

But all of Carol's messages were urgent, so I didn't even bother with them. I'd just won a big case the week before, and I was determined to take it slow this week. I ran myself into the ground during my first years working in the DA's office, but lately I'd been feeling run-down and even considering leaving prosecution altogether. Anyway, I knew Carol had to have been texting and calling about a witness I was supposed to interview an hour before I woke up. She'd probably had to reschedule him and needed to confirm a time with me that she'd eventually pick on her own. I had to keep telling her that half of being a good assistant was thinking on her feet. And to stop calling me about every little thing every day. But she was new and young and scared by the slightest sign of trouble.

The side of my head was hurting from the bump on the table, so I had to squint my left eye to lessen the pain, and on my way to the bathroom I almost knocked the bottle of wine I'd been drinking off the coffee table.

In the mirror, I squinted to see if the claw-foot had left a mark on the side of my eye like it had before, but there was nothing I could see there yet. Still, the pain was sharp and ringing in my ear, so I could hardly get dressed and out the door as quickly as I needed to.

While I normally used the long walk from my apartment in Tribeca to the DA's office as my form of morning exercise and meditation, the thumping in my head led me to a cab, where I sat in the backseat trying to remember how I'd ended up on the couch the night before. Listening to the cabbie sing along to "Gangnam Style," I remembered lying in bed and trying to figure out why Tamika was laughing at me when Leah was pulling her away after Miles's fencing match. My back had started hurting, and I recalled looking at the clock on the side of my bed and thinking it was still early—definitely before midnight. I got out of bed and found my painkillers in the bathroom. I took two after counting out the hours since my last dose. I went back to the bedroom and lay down, praying the pain shooting up my back would go away and I'd find my sleep. But I didn't. I just lay there hearing Tamika laughing and repeating, "It's what you need . . . It's what you need . . . It's what you need . . . ," and looking down at my waist. I remembered looking at the clock beside my bed again. It was after 2 a.m. and I was wide awake. I decided to get up and walk around the apartment, thinking it would make me tired. I stopped in the kitchen and looked at the fridge. Maybe a sandwich would work. Turkey? Milk? A little tryptophan. I needed to sleep. The interview was in the morning. He was already a skittish witness. On the fence. I had to be on point. I opened the refrigerator, and there was no milk or turkey. Just the wine. A half-empty bottle of Riesling with no top. I grabbed it and went to the cabinet to get a glass, but they were all in the sink. I needed a dishwasher, I reminded myself. My next place had to have a dishwasher. That and a washer and dryer. Those were the things I hated about living in New York City—dirty dishes to wash and laundry to schlep up and down flights of stairs. I remembered placing the bottle on the table and sitting on the couch. I looked at the bottle across from me, and I saw Kim 2 swimming around inside. Thin. In a bikini. I knew I was tired then. I blinked, but there she was. Still swimming and smiling. Then I heard her: "You didn't have a ring. He never even asked you." She laughed, and then there was Tamika back at Miles's match, laughing and waving good-bye.

"That's seven dollars, mamita," the cabbie said, looking at me from the front seat of the cab. "Gangnam Style" had gone off, and we were idling outside 1 Hogan Place—a building that had consumed too many hours of my life. "You okay? You look like you dazed and confused, mami? Maybe we turn around? I take you home? Take care of you?" He grinned at me like there was any chance of that.

"Thanks, but no thanks," I said, slipping him a ten. "And for that little comment, give me my change."

I don't know if Carol had some kind of lookout person sitting outside the building waiting to announce my arrival, but when the elevator doors opened onto my floor, there she was standing with her iPad in one hand and a cell phone in the other, ready to pounce.

"Kimberly, you're here! I was just about to call you!"

"Again?" I nodded to her. "And good morning to you, Carol."

"Good morning. I'm sorry. It's just things are crazy here right now. I didn't know you were coming in late, and I . . . things are crazy." Carol was a bony Irish girl from Westchester who couldn't keep a tan—not even in the summer—to save her life. Right before my eyes, she turned beet red and looked like she was about to hyperventilate.

"Well, I'm not sure how you didn't know I wouldn't be in until later. I had a doctor's appointment this morning. Remember?" I lied, walking toward my office with her panting beside me. The floor was quiet because most of the other ADAs were probably in court or prepping for court. In New York County, we have more than five hundred assistant district attorneys in bureaus covering any kind of crime imaginable—elder abuse, human trafficking, sex crimes, public integrity. One of my classmates from Columbia Law is the ADA in animal cruelty. Last Christmas he was in the newspaper for leading the prosecution of a Russian man who'd been breeding bats in the basement of a building in Alphabet City, killing them, and selling the skin to Chinese herb shops in Chinatown.

"What? Really? I don't know how I missed that you had a doctor's appointment. It's not on the schedule," Carol said, looking down at her iPad. She clicked through a few screens. "I know I would've caught it."

"Carol," I called to get her attention once I'd made my way to my office. "Do you need anything from me?"

"Yes. I do. It's about Bernard Richard—the ex-boyfriend of that guy in the Christopher Street meth-lab case."

"Oh, I forgot all about his appointment this morning. Did you reschedule him?"

"That's the thing—I tried to. When you didn't respond to my messages, I figured that was what you wanted me to do—"

"Good. And?"

"And I tried, but he wouldn't reschedule. He's still here."

"Here?" I looked back down the hallway to the empty waiting area. "Where?"

"In the interview room. I had to put him in there."

I rushed to my computer and looked at the time. "It's after eleven. He's been here since nine?" I hung my purse and a thin sweater I'd draped over my shoulders in the cab behind my office door.

"He won't leave. Said something about people coming for him," Carol said. "Think he may be kinda . . . you know . . . crazy."

"Oh, Jesus!" I snapped, grabbing the files for the case from my desk and walking out of the office in front of Carol. "No breaks! There are no breaks for me," I added under my breath.

"Wait! One more thing!" Carol called on my heels.

"What is it? I don't want to keep this guy waiting any longer," I said.

"I know, it's just that Paul's assistant keeps coming down here, asking about your brief from the Lankin case."

"Right. He needs it. I told you to send it up last week. Is there a problem?" I asked, heading toward the interview room.

"Actually, there is," Carol started. She turned her iPad to me. "I was just looking it over before I e-mailed it, and I noticed a few things. Little errors. Nothing too big."

I read through a few corrections Carol had noted in the margin. Somehow, some of the words were misspelled, and I did see that the punctuation was incorrect in a few places.

"Must've been my computer," I said nonchalantly. "Spell-check and whatever happens when I move my files around between computers."

"I know. Your briefs are always impeccable, Kim. That's why I wanted you to see it again before I sent it. I know you would never want this out." Carol leaned into me and whispered, "Not with how much Paul seems to be coming around here now."

"Right. Good call," I said, patting Carol on the shoulder. "Look it over again and let's get it out."

"Okay."

When I started with my class of ADAs working in the district attorney's office, I vowed to work myself into the ground. I mean, I told myself I'd be the best ADA or "die trying." Although I'd never told anyone, I struggled through law school. While everything was coming easily to Ronald and he seemed to do more drinking and barhopping with his law school buddies than he used to, I basically slept in the law library and had to take writing classes every summer to keep my head above water. I think I was the most surprised person in the world when I realized that I'd actually passed the New York State bar examination. I read my name, like, a hundred times to make sure it was really me, and then I didn't tell anyone I knew I'd passed for, like, three hours. I sat on my couch and cried. I thought about my mother. None of us had heard from her in months, and the last person to see her was Tamika, who said she'd seen my mother standing in a rainstorm on Jamaica Avenue in Queens selling umbrellas but not bothering to put one over her own head. She'd had on her old favorite red hoodie. Sneakers with holes. No socks. I looked at my phone. I had no way to contact her. To let her know what was happening to me. I had no way of knowing if she'd even care. If she was alive.

Both Ronald and I applied to work in the district attorney's office in New York City. For the first time in so many years, a black man, Paul Webster, had been elected to the position, and every black law school student in the city was planning to put muscle behind him. While Manhattan wasn't exactly the impoverished district Ronald imagined himself working in to save the world, he really admired Paul. I think that was why it was so hard for him when he wasn't accepted into the ADA class that year and I got the position. He said it was cool. Reminded me of the long hours and low pay of an ADA and said he'd have more fun starting his own firm. He was too smart to be led by anyone. He'd make more money and do more good on his own.

"Bernard Richard," I started, walking into the interview room with my hand outstretched to shake his hand, "I'm Attorney Kimberly Kind. It's great to meet you."

Bernard was slumped over the table and looked like he was actually asleep, so I had to stand there holding out my hand.

When he finally stood before me, I realized he was much taller than I'd imagined based on listening to recordings of his interviews with the police officers who'd shut down a meth lab his boyfriend was operating out of the Candy Shop, a gay club on Christopher Street. On the tape his voice was soft and rather genteel for a twenty-seven-year-old male prostitute living in New York City. But in front of me, he was the same height as Kent, definitely more muscular. His hair was blond but red at the roots.

"Good morning," he said, and there was that soft voice again. Maybe he was from Alabama or Mississippi. He looked down at his watch.

"I apologize for being late. I had a doctor's appointment. My assistant and I got our wires crossed—"

"I can't leave. I have to go into witness protection," he said, cutting me off. "I won't testify unless I'm in the witness protection program. These people are after me. Going to kill me. This is big! It's—"

"Wait, let's slow down, Mr. Richard," I said, pulling him back to the table. "Have a seat and slow down. I need to make sure I'm hearing everything you're trying to share."

Carol padded in to try to refill Bernard's empty coffee mug, but I told her to bring us both a little spring water. Bernard looked anxious, and the last thing I needed was for him to be hopped up on caffeine and apparently thinking someone was trying to kill him. I called Carol to me and whispered in her ear that she should have an officer on guard just in case we realized the threats Bernard feared were real. As could be expected, he'd been reluctant to provide any information since the bust at the Candy Shop. His interviews were distant and lacked true detail. He wasn't sure about anything and never gave any names. I wanted to give him one more chance, to see if I could break through and get enough information to make my argument conclusive.

During my seven years as an ADA, I'd come to know that interviewing witnesses was by far my best skill. I was a great trial attorney too, but I had a way with witnesses that made them open up to me and that gave me an edge in the courtroom. Sometimes I could make people remember things they'd forgotten, share something they were sure they could hide, or realize something they didn't know. I always wished that could translate into my personal life.

"I can't go home. I won't," Bernard said.

"Home. Let's start there. You came here to meet me this morning. Did you leave from home?"

"Yes."

"Was there something there? Something going on that made you believe you were in danger?"

"Outside the window. My bedroom window. There was a black car."

"What time was this?" I asked, writing down Bernard's responses. While I used a recorder when I interviewed people, I always took notes as well. There was something about looking at the details on the page that turned everything into a connected web for me to follow in a way that the recordings never could.

"I don't know. Like, seven. After seven. I was getting ready to come here," Bernard responded.

"Did you recognize the car? Know the driver?"

"No, I didn't. But I know it wasn't the police because their black car is parked outside the living room window on the other side of the building."

"I understand," I said. "And please note that seeing the police car should not be reason for panic. That's just a part of protocol."

"I know. They're making sure I don't leave town. But that's not what I'm worried about. That other car, it wasn't a cop car."

"How do you know that?"

"It just wasn't."

"Well, how do you know it was there for you? Did you see the driver? Speak to the driver?"

"No. I just know," he said, annoyed.

"Mr. Richard, I'm not here to confuse you or second-guess anything you're saying," I explained. "I'm just trying to make sure we are both hearing the same thing. You're not on trial here. Okay?"

"Sure."

"Now, have you experienced anything you'd consider a threat? Anything specific that I can record and pass along to the appropriate authorities so they can help you?"

"Why can't you help me? You're the district attorney."

"I'm not the district attorney. I'm an assistant district attorney. And what you're talking about goes beyond the legal matters we deal with here. It's criminal. Now, if we find you need to be in the state's witness services program, we'll move forward with that. But I need to know there's a real threat present for that kind of action. Now, have you experienced any other threats?"

"You don't understand," Bernard whispered, looking over his shoulder at the door. "I was around the Candy Shop for a long time. I've seen things."

"Mr. Richard, Miguel Alvarez is in jail right now. And with your testimony, we'll make sure he stays there for a very long time," I said.

Behind me, toward the back of the room, there was a long wall of old law texts, wall to wall and floor to ceiling, that no one ever used. Bernard looked away from me and at the wall and seemed to leave me.

"Can I have a smoke?" he asked, reaching into his pocket without taking his eyes off the wall.

"Sorry, this is a nonsmoking building," I replied. "Everyone likes to blame Bloomberg, but it's been that way for a while."

Bernard had already pulled the red box of cigarettes from his pocket, and he started tapping it on the table.

"I'm sorry. I almost forgot I was in the 'Smoke-Free Apple.' Guess I was thinking of those cop shows where they always let the people smoke before they confess their crimes."

"Do you have anything you need to confess?" I asked carefully.

"I don't know." He paused. "Maybe. There was this girl—just a girl, a black girl—I never really knew her name. I think Miguel called her Yellow a few times, but he was always calling people colors when he was high," Bernard added slowly, still tapping the little red box on the table. "She was a dancer at one of the clubs near the pier, and she started selling a little meth for him. I knew she didn't have it—you know, she wasn't like the other girls who sold his shit in the clubs. She was just some kid. Probably a college kid. Dancing to pay her cell phone bill. She had that look. Good skin. Hair. Nails." He paused and looked at me. "She sold for a little while, but then, just like everybody else, she got hooked."

"She started using meth?"

"I was there when Miguel confronted her about it. He just asked her. Just like he did everybody else. She said no. But it was obvious. You know the look. She was skinny. Nervous. Clothes were dirty. Nails dirty. Hair dirty. It seemed like it only took a week for that to happen to her. I'd seen it all before, but there was something about her. Something different. She didn't belong there," Bernard said. "I pointed that out to Miguel, but it was like a joke to him— boxing her into a corner. He gave her more to sell. A bagful. It was wrong. He knew she was using. She'd mess up. I tried to stop him, I knew what was coming, but he ignored me. Anyway, like a week after that, here Yellow comes again. One tooth missing in the front. Holes in her cheeks. Hair in patches. Miguel and I were sitting on a couch in his living room. He made her stand in front of us. Asked about the money. Asked about the meth. She had no answers. Just shrugged and said she had nothing. Offered to sleep with him. Miguel laughed and flipped my legs from off of his lap. 'I like dick. If you don't have a dick under that dress, we're both in for a surprise if we end up in the bedroom together,' he said. 'You got a dick, darling?' he added, laughing as she shook her head. 'Sure you don't. Sure you don't.' He got up and walked into the kitchen. I was going to follow him, but I stayed in there and told the girl to leave. She just stood there—right there. She said she needed more. Just a little. She offered to have sex with me. Then Miguel came back into the room behind her and threw her to the floor. He started hitting her, punching her in the back, the arms, everywhere. I went to get him off of her, but I couldn't. He was losing it. That's when I saw the cheese grater."

"The what?" I was sure I'd heard him incorrectly.

"He had the cheese grater from the kitchen in his back pocket." Bernard dropped the cigarette box and looked at me. "I tried to grab it. I knew what he was about to do. I just knew. But I was too late."

"What happened?" I asked, gripping my fingers into my left palm really tight. Over the years, I'd learned so many horrors and knew when one was near. And each time when I had to follow along, imagining the look on some poor soul's face, I saw eyes that looked like my own. Just aged and lost someplace where I couldn't find her.

"He ran the grater up her back, so fast, so hard, and the skin tore right off like Swiss cheese piping into the little holes. The skin went from brown to white. She screamed so loud. There wasn't anything I could do. I kept trying to get that grater out of his hand, and then I was trying to get her away from him, but I couldn't." Bernard wiped a tear from his eye and tried to regain his focus on the bookshelves.

"What happened to her?"

"He beat on her some more. Yelled. Threw her out into the street without a shirt. Like trash. I went looking for her the next day. Went to the clubs. All of them. But I couldn't find her. I never saw her again."

"Did you call the police? Tell anyone?"

"You don't see someone do something like that and call the police. I was afraid. If he could do that to her, who knew what he would do to me. Some HIV-positive fag runaway from Alabama he fucks for tricks. If she was trash, what am I?"

"Mr. Richard. Look at me."

He turned from the bookshelves and looked into my eyes. "Yes?"

"He can't get to you now. He won't," I said. "No one should ever have to go through that. To see that. But if you run and hide now, if you don't share your story, what happened to that woman, the woman whose name you don't even know, will happen to someone else. That's what I'm trying to stop. That's why we're here, and that's why I need you to testify."

I reached over the table and grabbed his hand.

"It's time for you to stop being afraid. Right now," I added. "If you don't do it for you, do it for her. Tell your story."

Bernard sat quiet for a long while. And then he turned and looked at the books again.

"What do you want to know?" he asked.

"We can start with the dealings in the basement of the Candy Shop," I said. "I need you to be honest with me about what you saw there. The more information you give me about what Miguel Alvarez did and what you did and what you saw, the closer we get to stopping this thing."

"Okay," he said with new tears rolling from his eyes. "I'll do it."

While I was confident Bernard didn't need any police protection, I ordered a police escort for him. Sometimes the fear witnesses feel in cases like this one comes more from guilt than from reality. Testifying about someone else's actions was also an indictment of his inaction, and in his mind he had to create some kind of punishment for that. If the police weren't coming for him, then someone else had to. The story he'd told me, and probably even the evil in the ones he'd kept hidden, would keep him up most nights for the rest of his life looking for payback behind tinted car windows outside his apartment. Sometimes the prison sentence in the mind was worse than the real thing.

"Paul's been down here twice looking for you," Carol said, popping her head into my office after Bernard was gone and I was editing my notes from his interview.

"Twice?" I repeated. "What did he want? Did he say?"

"Said he wanted to come down here himself to congratulate you on last week," Carol said, grinning. "Said he was impressed. Good news, right? Coming all the way from the top!" She pointed up toward the district attorney's office. "That's pretty rare. Him down here just to speak to you. But then again, you were really great last week. Everyone's talking about it."

"Sure," I answered flatly before delivering a weak smile to let Carol know I wanted to be alone.

Carol took the hint and turned to walk out.

"Hey, Carol," I called. "Can you do me a favor?"

"Sure. What do you need?"

"Can you close my door," I said in a low voice, "and if Paul comes back down here, tell him I had a doctor's appointment."

"But your appointment was this morning. Right?" Carol looked confused.

"I know. I'm not really leaving. I just want you to *say* that. Okay?"

"Okay." Carol frowned at me awkwardly before pulling the door shut.

"And Carol," I added just before it closed behind her, "thanks for saying I did great."

"No problem at all. You always do."

The Tuesday before, I'd delivered the closing argument in a case that we were sure we'd lose. While I started in my ADA class focusing on what we call rackets—basic economic crimes, arson, racketeering—after my first year it was clear that my best work was in cases that involved small-business corruption with illegal drug operations, so the DA put me on Special Prosecutions. In my last case, the owner of a small vegan bakery on the Lower East Side had been growing marijuana in his apartment and transporting it to his shop, where he baked it into cakes and brownies and even croissants. It was becoming a common New York setup for the kinds of drug operations I was set to bust down: illegal pill dispensaries and marijuana factories operating out of the basements, back rooms, and kitchens of legal business fronts that allowed the dealers to function day in and out without worry. For the vegan baker, while the business itself was failing, through investigation we discovered that his drug-laced baked goods earned him upward of eighty thousand per month. He was shipping orders throughout the state and had a special baked-goods delivery service. The case seemed pretty cut-and-dry until it came out that he was only selling the baked goods to cancer patients, most of whom delivered tear-filled testimonies on his behalf during the trial. There was a teenage boy with leukemia who testified that he would've killed himself months earlier if it weren't for the weekly brownie deliveries he received from the bake shop. A broken law was a broken law, but a bleeding heart is a bleeding heart, and looking at the jury during the testimonies, I knew it was filled with bleeding hearts that might let the baker go free or settle for lesser charges. My boss hated to lose, and he despised lesser charges. I knew the verdict would come down to me. What I said during my closing could save our record and my reputation.

I'd spent days working on the argument. I'd typed it, memorized it, and practiced it, had it ready to be performed like I was Dr. King stepping up to the podium on the Mall in DC. But when it was time for me to deliver, I choked. I forgot the entire thing, and for a second I stood there looking at the jury trying to remember any word on the iPad I'd left sitting at the prosecution's desk. Then it came to me. I had to admit that the baker's actions were likely coming from a place of goodwill. I said that he could've been helping those in need, but he was also cheating the system. He was lying to his community. He was involved in vigilante justice that threatened a system that operated on the idea of change. If he wanted to change the system, he needed to work within it—not compromise it. Not take medical matters into his own hands. I went down a list of medical-marijuana champions who'd done just that. Those who'd achieved victory. I added that he detracted from their victory and lessened the power of their fight. His criminal behavior cost us more than it may have benefited the few he served. For that he needed to be prosecuted.

No matter what a counselor says, there's just no way of knowing which way a jury will go after a case is closed. So when the jury left the courtroom to deliberate, I followed my class's ritual of going out for scotch and cigars. After two days, they came back with a verdict for the wayward baker: guilty of all charges.

I stayed in my office working on the Candy Shop case a little later than I anticipated. When I got home, the bottle of wine was still sitting on the coffee table in the living room. I kicked off my shoes, picked up the bottle, and walked it into the kitchen, cursing myself for the late-night boozing that I was sure added, like, ten pounds to my body each year. I vowed to pour the little bit that was left down the drain and never ever bring a bottle of wine into the house again . . . a promise I knew instantly was a lie.

I was cursing aloud and lying some more to myself about trying to find more time to go to the gym when there was a single soft knock at the door. I never had company I wasn't expecting, so I stood in the kitchen listening for a second to be sure the knock was actually at my door and not coming from downstairs or next door. But then there was a second set of three quick knocks.

"Who is it?" I called, walking to the door.

There was no answer.

I looked through the peephole. There was someone I definitely wasn't expecting and didn't care to see.

"What do you want?" I asked.

"Open the door."

"I told you not to come here anymore," I said, looking at a bright smile in the little blurry glass hole in the door.

"I know."

"So?"

"You're going to make me stand out here forever? Come on, Kim. I just want to talk."

Against my better judgment and probably for a few reasons I couldn't admit, I undid the three locks, removed the doorstop, and let Paul in.

"Damn, you got cold on a brother fast," he said, walking in and reaching for me.

I pushed him away and walked into the living room.

"What do you want, Paul?" I asked. I folded my arms over my chest and planted my feet firmly on the floor to let him know he was not staying. "I'm sure the DA of New York County has more to do than make uninvited house calls."

"I'll start with a seat," he joked, and sat down on the couch without an invitation. "Maybe a little wine."

"Fresh out of wine," I said. "And now I wish I didn't have a couch."

"Kiki Mimi! You mad? Why you so mad?"

"Don't call me that. I told you not to call me that. That's only for family."

"I'm like family."

"No, you have a family. In Westchester. With your wife. Kids. The golden retriever. Remember?"

Paul exhaled dramatically and threw his head back to rest it against the couch. He was still in his work clothes, but his tie was missing and his shirt was unbuttoned. From four feet away, I could smell his cologne.

I never meant for anything to happen with Paul. When Ronald and I broke up after the accident, I was in the hospital for weeks and Paul came by a few times just to check on me. When I was released from the hospital, he continued to text me to send me well wishes and keep me updated on my cases. I thought it was kind, thoughtful, but when I told Tamika about it, she laughed in my face and told me we were setting a "thing" up. "He's fine as hell. You know what you're doing. Just be a big girl and admit it," she said. I denied it, but then everything became too clear. His visits and flowers, the texts way after office hours and updates I was already getting from Carol—he was coming on to me.

When I went back to work, I decided that there was no way I was going to be involved in a workplace affair—with my boss. It could ruin him. It could ruin me. He was separated but still married and had two kids . . . and that golden retriever. I couldn't get involved in all of that. Still, Tamika was right. Paul had that Blair Underwood mystique. Almond skin and sophisticated eyes that were so dark they looked black. He had perfect teeth and clean nails. His style was impeccable and his body was solid—even with his clothes on. And he always smelled so complex—rich sweet and dark spicy.

I fought off my attraction for him for a few months. Ignored his texts. I even went out on a couple of dates, and as Tamika instructed me to in hopes that I'd get over Ronald, I got my "feet wet" a few times. But nothing seemed to satisfy me. Through so many botched and just plain awkward love affairs, I was learning fast that contrary to popular belief, not all men are created equal. Some were soft, some were little, most were wack, and the others couldn't even get it up. So I'm clear: I'm talking about penises.

I don't want to make it sound like I was out there looking for nothing but a great fuck. That was far from the truth. Like anyone else, I wanted love. I wanted to find my mate. And sometimes I came close. I met some great guys, but no matter how strong the connection was, once we got into that bedroom and the private parts were released and I had to check for the motion in the ocean, if things weren't right with my body, everything went wrong with my mind. I'd go from seeing the same man every day to ignoring his calls and rolling my eyes when he spoke. It was hard to explain. I didn't understand it myself, but I thought it had something to do with intimacy. With being touched again. Moved from inside of my body. For all of her man trouble, Tamika explained it best. "It's like finding the right dance partner," she said one night when we were drinking wine on her front steps in Brooklyn. "Y'all step together. Y'all groove together."

"I came to your office twice today," Paul said, looking up at the ceiling over my couch.

"Yeah, you shouldn't have done that. Not the way everyone talks. They already think something's going on. Easter Summer keeps sniffing around, asking questions. I think she's—"

"I've missed you. I'm going crazy," he cut in.

"Paul, we had to stop."

"Why?"

"What do you mean, 'Why'? You're my boss. That's why," I said. "Don't pull me back into this. I was doing well. It's been two months. Let's just move on." I picked up my shoes and trudged to the bedroom to escape smelling him, looking at his body relaxed on my couch.

I put the shoes in place and thought about how I was going to get Paul out of my apartment.

Before, he'd broken me down without me even knowing it. I was so lonely. Soon I started responding to his texts. Then he showed up at my door with flowers one night. God, I was so stupid. But still, it felt good. Felt too good to be wanted. Sought after. Chased. He claimed the flowers were to congratulate me on some case I'd won. I pointed out that they were roses. Red roses. He laughed and kissed me on the forehead. "Maybe they're about something else, then," he'd said. Maybe that was when it all began.

"You're so fucking sexy," I heard Paul say from my bedroom door. "I never understood why you don't believe that about yourself. Make a nigga get hard just looking at you."

I turned to look at him roll his eyes up my calves and over my butt. I loved that shit about him—how he could say something vulgar and make it sound so sexy.

"Fuck," he said.

"So, that's what you miss?" I asked.

"You know it isn't about that. You know what it was," he said, stepping into the bedroom.

My heart quivered and I held my hand up fast to stop him from approaching me. If he took one more step, the sixty days I'd spent trying to erase whatever we'd been doing would die in the sheets on my bed. Paul was one of those brothers whose swagger made it hard to turn him down. Hard to say no to him. And he knew it, too. Licked his lips and grinned all day long. Said the perfect thing to make any woman melt. He used it everywhere. Even at work. When he walked by in the office, every woman stopped to take all parts of him in; even men looked to admire. I was determined to get off that train.

"I already told you, yes. Fine. We did have a connection. You're cool. We're cool, but that doesn't change the facts. You're my boss," I said.

"I'll quit."

"You're married."

"Separated. And we're talking about divorce."

"You're lying."

"You're beautiful."

I hadn't noticed it, but as I was speaking, Paul was stepping in closer to me, and then he was directly in front of me. His cleft chin was dangling over my forehead like an apple I had to bite.

"You miss me?" he asked. "Just tell me."

"Yes," I said so softly, and then I knew I was failing at mission Get Paul out of Your Apartment and likely embarking upon mission Do the Wrong Thing Again.

"Let's not miss each other anymore," Paul whispered seductively with his mouth so close to my ear, his breath sent butterfly wings down my spine and I was cured of pain. That's what he'd been to me since Ronald was gone. Something like a cure. A healer. The first time we had sex, I cried like a baby. And it wasn't because it was bad. Paul was a master performer in bed. He came at me like he wanted to take something I had. And just when I thought I was about to let him take it, he picked me up and sat me on a hard penis that made me give myself to him freely. But he didn't just sit there. He wrapped his arms around my waist and held my back up with his forearms. He wrapped his hands over my shoulders and thrust himself into me like he knew what I'd been searching for.

"I can't," I moaned, remembering how he'd come at me so many nights in the very bed that was just two feet away from us.

"Yes you can," Paul said, slipping his hand around my back to unzip my skirt. "Let me show you how much I miss you." He licked my ear and whispered, "Don't you want this dick?" before sliding my hand over his throbbing penis.

I nearly fell to the floor along with my skirt.

"Shit," I whimpered before snatching my hand away.

Paul grabbed both of my arms and began kissing my neck wildly.

I was overwhelmed. I closed my eyes but I saw everything going on in the room. Hell, I even saw into the future. How his deep dark muscles would look once he took off his shirt. Him holding my hands to the headboard from behind. His chin resting in the cup between my neck and shoulder. His pelvis jerking and his pulsating just before he climaxed. "Oh, fuck!" I sighed loudly. "Don't! Please don't! Stop!"

I took in another breath and quickly noticed that the heat that had been in front of me was gone. I opened my eyes and saw that Paul had let go of me and backed away. He looked lost, bewildered.

"What?" I asked. "What's wrong?"

"You just told me not to," he said soberly.

"What?"

"You said no and then you told me not to. You said, 'Please don't. Stop!' "

"So?"

"So, you've never said that before," he said.

"Of course I have."

"No. I would've stopped. I can't touch you after you say something like that. It's just too . . . too . . . rapey."

"Rapey?"

"Yes. Every man knows that. If a woman says no, and don't, you have to stop. You fucked up the mood." He looked down at his crotch. "I mean, my dick is soft and everything. Nothing like a woman saying those words to make a brother go soft."

"Are you freaking kidding?" I said.

"No. I'm not kidding. Nothing I can do about it now. Maybe you could . . . you know . . . get me back up."

"No. That's not what I meant," I said. "I don't care about your dick getting soft. I didn't invite you here. You just showed up. I didn't even want to have sex with you."

"Oh no, you're making it worse. Just stop talking," Paul said, laughing nervously.

"Leave!" I pointed out of the bedroom. "Since you're listening to everything I say now, follow my instructions and leave."

"Come on, Kiki—"

"Don't you dare call me that again!"

It took ten more minutes to get Paul out the front door. He pulled out every trick in the book to try to make me feel sorry for "ruining the mood," but it was all pathetic because I wasn't trying to be in any mood—especially not with him. Even if he quit his job and got a divorce tomorrow, he wasn't a better pick than Ronald. He was just a different kind of yesterday. As much as he wanted me and "missed me," he was the kind of man who wanted me to want and miss him more. That was what the whole scene in the bedroom was about. Somehow, I was supposed to be convinced that I'd ruined a perfect evening by saying no to sex I never asked for, get down on my knees and give him head to convince him to make love to me, and then thank him for giving me an orgasm . . . I never asked for.

"Can I say one more thing before you lock me out again?" Paul asked, holding his foot in the doorway so I couldn't close him out.

"What?"

"You were perfect last week. Knocked the ball right out of the park," he said, and made the cracking sound of a bat hitting a ball. "And I mean that. It's about time for you to move to the next level. You need to be thinking about that."

"I know," I said more meekly than I intended to.

"Good night, Kiki—"

"Don't call me that!"

"But it's so cute," Paul whined.

"Good night," I said, looking down at his foot in my doorway.

"Okay!" He slid his foot out, and I slammed the door on the start of another sentence I didn't want to hear. I didn't know how much longer my *nos* would last.

I looked down at my exposed stockings and panties and cursed myself for pouring the last of my wine away. It was going to be a long night.

I went to the medicine cabinet in the bathroom to get two of the painkillers I normally took before I went to sleep. There was only one left. I'd have to call the pharmacy in the morning.

Chapter 4

"It seems you're out of refills, Ms. Kind. You'll need to call your doctor."

"No. There must be an error," I said into the phone, though I could clearly see there were no remaining refills by reading the label. "I just saw Dr. Davis a few weeks ago. He's the one who gave me the prescription."

"I see that here in the computer, but it appears that you've had the prescription refilled three times in the last two months."

"So?"

"You're out of refills."

"There must be an error."

"Maybe there is. You can call Dr. Davis and have him call it in. Or we can call. Would that help?"

"No. I'll call him myself."

"Wonderful. Please give us a call back if we can do anything else to serve you."

"Thank you."

I hung up the phone and used speed dial to call Dr. Davis's office, ready to lean into whoever was unlucky enough to answer the phone at 9 a.m. I'd been to Dr. Davis's office too many times over too few months for there to be any problems with any of my prescriptions. But somehow there always seemed to be an issue, and at some point I'd be on the phone with someone, sounding like a crazy lady. Dr. Davis would want me to come in. To talk about my pain. To discuss my levels of pain—look up at the chart of scary to smiley faces on his office wall and try to pick out one to describe my pain. How consistent it was and where it was. Sometimes I'd point to ten, the harshest of pain, the crazy face with red eyes and tears streaming. "Everywhere! All of the time!" I'd say. "I feel it everywhere at every minute of the day." He'd leave the room, come back with a small square of paper with chicken scratch on it and his signature at the bottom. I'd deliver it to the pharmacy and we'd start the dance again.

As angry as I'd get, I knew he was just doing his job. Everyone was just doing their job. But my job was to manage my pain. And while it wasn't always everywhere at every moment, sometimes it felt like that. And worse, when I had to think about it, I'd have to go back to how it started, why it was there. Kim 2 and I leaving the mansion that night in the Hamptons. It was Diddy's birthday party, and Kim 2 had gotten us on the list. We were so drunk, but we had to get back to the city. I knew Kim 2 had popped some pills earlier, but I was more messed up than she was and I couldn't get caught driving drunk. She said she was okay. I gave her the keys to the rental car, and we started driving. Kim 2 turned on the radio. Taylor Swift was playing, so she turned the volume all the way up and we started singing along and laughing. The farther up the highway we went, the closer we got to the city, the fewer cars there were on the road. I tried to keep my eyes open and on the pavement. It was so late, it was early. I couldn't see the sun, but even in the night sky I saw some light shining. That was the last thing I remembered before I heard Kim scream and saw the light shining in my eyes. I thought it was "*the* light" until I came to and realized it was a doctor running along the side of my gurney as they rolled me into the emergency room for surgery. I didn't know what happened, why I was there, so I started crying and calling for Kim 2. I asked if my friend was okay. "Yes," someone said. "She's fine." Then the doctor with the light asked, "Is there anyone we can contact? Your next of kin?" That's when I realized that my entire upper body was being held in place by a brace. I couldn't move. I started screaming. Hollering. The doctors put a gas cup over my face. I went to a black place. When I woke up again, I was in a hospital bed with Ronald sitting in a chair beside me.

"Dr. Davis won't be able to see you until Thursday, Ms. Kind," the woman on the other end of the phone said when I called Dr. Davis's office about my prescription.

"I need to see him this afternoon."

"Yes. I heard you. But I'm looking at his schedule and he doesn't have any openings until Thursday morning."

"I'm out of medication and I need a refill."

"Actually, according to your schedule—"

"Schedule?"

"Yes. We have a new app where we can see how many refills the doctor has ordered for each patient and weigh that against the dosage. According to your schedule, you should have another month left."

"I don't care about any app or schedule," I said. "I'm in pain and I need a refill. I need to see Dr. Davis this afternoon."

"His next opening is on Thursday morning. I can squeeze you in at eight. First thing. How's that?" she repeated, so sugary sweet, it sounded as if she was doing me a favor.

"That's not what I asked you for, Ms.—what's your name?"

"I already told you my name, Ms. Kind. I'm Jessica Hopson," she answered. "I'm only telling you what I can do for you. There are no openings today or tomorrow."

"Look, Jessica, I am an assistant district attorney of New York County, and I am in pain. I can't go to work like this. I need for you to make something happen right now," I said, nearly growling.

"Again, I can only—"

"You know what? I don't even know why I'm dealing with you. Give me Dr. Davis's cell phone number. I'll call him myself."

There was a silence and then she said, "Fine," no doubt to cover up all of the nasty names she was calling me in her head. I didn't care. I hated to pull rank, but it had to count for something sometimes.

Immediately after she gave me the number, I hung up and dialed Dr. Davis. I don't know if she got to him first or if he'd been sitting right there while she was on the phone with me, but Dr. Davis repeated everything Jessica had said and just as smugly, just smug enough to make me and my complaining sound ridiculous.

"I could call in a prescription for ibuprofen, but you can get that yourself over the counter. Take three if you feel any pain. We'll get back to it on Thursday morning. First thing," he said firmly, and there was really nothing I could say after that but okay—or curse him out and find a new doctor. I decided to go with the former option.

For some reason, Tamika made it her mission in life to get me to come to Wind Down Wednesday. She called Carol and had her put it on my calendar, sent me text messages Wednesday morning to remind me to wear something "sexy to work that could easily translate to after-work activity," and called me three times on Wednesday afternoon.

In addition to the fact that I personally thought most of her friends were desperate, sex-crazed lunatics, my list of reasons for not being excited about a hump-day night out included that there was nothing happy about a happy hour that included an all-you-can-eat buffet of fried shrimp and French fries, divorced men with fat bellies and huge egos, and listening to sad stories fueled by watered-down well drinks. It was just a reminder that thirty was not the new twenty. In fact, being single and in my thirties was like being fifty and barren. If I went home and got into my bed, there'd be no one there to ask me if I was "seeing" anyone new, remind me that I "needed" someone to hold me at night, and force me to lament that it wasn't happening. I'd tried. I'd failed.

But I couldn't say no to Tamika's pushing, so on Wednesday night I left the office super late and took a local train to Brooklyn, to a hole-in-the-wall bar with a name that knew irony too well: Damaged Goods.

The dark bar was fairly full, with an unfair mix of many women and few men organized in circles reminiscent of high school dances. The brave sat at the bar or did a two-step on the tiny dance floor. Biggie Smalls was playing so loud, it rattled the speakers. Tamika and her friends were sitting at a high-top toward the back of the bar, the table littered with martini glasses filled with neon-green alcohol and plates of fried shrimp. Everyone looked so happy to see me that it was clear they were already drunk.

"My cousin is here, you guys!" Tamika hollered happily. "She's late, as usual, but she's here!"

I hugged everyone at the table and pulled a chair into an empty space between Heather and Tamika. Tamika had been hanging out with Heather and Monique since grade school. They met up every single week and vacationed together in Curaçao and the Bahamas. I'd never been that good at keeping track of people, so I mostly maintained my friendships on social media.

"I see you guys are way ahead of me," I said, surveying the mess on the table up close.

"Well, we've been here for over an hour," Monique pointed out. She was the pretty girl in the group. She looked like Vanessa Williams on her best day, and most men who approached her made sure to let her know. "You know who you look like, pretty eyes?" they'd ask, as if whatever they were about to say was original.

"And they have five-dollar apple martinis! I believe in taking advantage of what's available to me," Tamika said. "It's my right as an American black citizen girl lady!" She high-fived Heather over the table.

Heather was Tamika's best friend. She was a little nerdy and maybe more reserved than the other two, but just as crass. She was also the reason Leah never hung out with them. New Year's Day after Heather's divorce, they woke up together in a hotel room in Jersey City. They could've kept the rendezvous a secret if they hadn't been posting pictures of their boozy love affair on Instagram throughout the night. While the caption of the last pic of them embracing in a shower read, "This is forever," it wasn't, and the pictures were taken down after two weeks. Heather returned to men and we never spoke of it again.

I asked the waitress for a glass of white wine, but Tamika insisted that I gulp down the last of her apple martini as I waited.

"You need to catch the fuck up!" she said. "We're over here talking some grade-A classified *bit*ness, and the law requires that you are intoxicated for that."

"Oh, Lord," I said, and then of course I finished her drink.

"Good work, my dear!" Tamika said, using a comical British accent. "You have completed the mission. Now, let us continue. Monique here was sharing details of her most ratchet love affair with her new boo-thang."

"He is not my 'boo-thang,' " Monique said, looking at me. "He's technically my therapist."

"You're sleeping with your therapist?" I asked, taking my wine from the waitress. Tamika's martini tasted more like gasoline than an apple martini, and I wanted to wash it down quickly.

"He's not her therapist anymore—more like a fuck buddy," Heather joked.

"He's not a fuck buddy! He's a professional," Monique argued.

Tamika laughed and threw a cherry at Monique, adding, "A professional with his dick in your mouth."

"Well, damn," I said, feeling the mixture of cheap wine and green gasoline setting in. "What happened? I have to know."

"Well, after C.J. and I broke up, I decided I needed to see someone. A professional," Monique explained, referring to her last boyfriend, who had slept with, like, four women in her apartment building while they dated. He actually got caught one evening when he claimed he was going to take out the trash; after thirty minutes and no C.J., Monique used a GPS app she'd secretly installed on his phone to track him to a woman's apartment two doors down. "He said he was cheating because I wasn't having enough sex with him."

"How often were y'all having sex?" I asked.

"Like, three times a week," Monique said.

"Shit, I would've cheated on your weak ass, too," Heather jumped in.

"Whatever, Heather. I get tired. Between work and taking these online classes, once I get into my bed, all I want is sleep. You know?" Monique fingered the rim of her martini glass. "Plus, C.J. wasn't acting right. Who wants to have sex with someone who lies in front of the couch all night drinking Guinness and watching football?"

"I do!" Heather raised her hand jokingly.

Tamika chimed in. "See, that's the thing. Like I told you before, I don't think the issue was with you not wanting sex. I think the problem was that you two had nothing in common and that nigga was just Jim Jones grimy. Period."

"I thought we had plenty of sex. Three times a week is good," Monique said, and everyone looked at her like she was a frog with pigtails. "Please. You all are having more sex than that?" She looked at me. "What about you, Kim. How much sex are you having?"

"None right now," I said, feeling like my response was some kind of self-indictment.

"Not now. I mean, you know, when you were in a relationship," Monique said cautiously.

The mood at the table shifted to something mournful, delicate.

"I don't really remember," I said, trying to wave away the waitress's suggestion for another drink, but Tamika requested a round of apple martinis.

"Yes you do, ho," Tamika said. "Dig deeper."

I rolled my eyes at her for putting me on the spot. It wasn't because Heather and Monique were technically her friends and I didn't want them in my business. I knew how cool they were and that nothing I said to them would ever leave the table. It was that I knew the response my answer would get—and Tamika knew it, too.

"Well, maybe it was like three times . . . ," I muttered, anticipating the verbal judgment that was coming.

"See, she's like me," Monique said, nodding toward me. "Three times a week. It's enough. We're both working women, and—"

"No! Wrong," Tamika interjected. "That's not three times per week."

"What?" Heather and Monique said together.

Heather added hopefully, "Three times per day?"

"Per month," I mumbled, my voice lower than before.

The three of them went silent and looked down at their empty glasses. I wished the waitress would come back with the apple martini I didn't want.

"Ronald was very busy. It's stressful building your own practice." I hated how it sounded. "I was busy, too. Tired from work, and I also was having some . . ."

Everyone was still averting their eyes, so I just stopped talking.

"Y'all heifers can kiss my black ass," I said hotly.

And they all broke out in giggles.

"We'll kiss it," Tamika said. "Someone should've been. You know that's crazy? No grown-ass man in the world can survive a whole month only having sex three times—not if he has good pussy at home."

"No woman either," Heather said. "I mean, if she has *dick* at home—not *pussy*."

Monique and Tamika looked at Heather suspiciously. There were always new rumors that she was team switching at night.

A group of young guys walked into the bar, and Tamika nearly broke her neck to get a look at every single one of them. I tried to be more nonchalant, but the fresh crop was a sun rising in darkness. I'd done a full inspection of every man in the room, and most of them looked like somebody's uncle trying to reclaim his youth. One who'd been eyeing Monique from the bar all night looked like Jermaine Jackson—complete with the saucy waves in his hair and the slick skin.

All five of the youngsters looked like they were in their midtwenties. They were actually pretty handsome, and they were clean-shaven and dressed in business attire, which made me wonder if they were lost. Hanging toward the back was the only white boy, who looked like maybe he was Dominican or Italian. He had sharp features, a light beard that looked more like a five o'clock shadow, and skin the color of the flesh of a lemon.

Tamika turned back to the table smiling like a kid waking up on Christmas morning.

"Lookie heah nah," she said. "Seems like the Lord has blessed the church with some real material."

"Yeah, us and every other thirsty chick in this room," Heather pointed out, and we looked around to see that every table of women was turned toward the group. Two voluptuous women in skimpy minidresses and those tacky Timberland stilettos got up and took new seats at the bar, where the guys had migrated. "Just desperate. A damn shame."

"Whatever," I said. "I don't care. I didn't come here to pick up a youngun."

"You might need one. Get you past your drought. Get your numbers up," Tamika joked.

"You suck. Anyway, this isn't about me and my alleged drought. We were talking about Monique and . . . what's his name?"

"Brother to the Night," Monique said.

"What? Like in *Love Jones*? Please tell me your therapist's name wasn't Brother to the Night. Please say it ain't so," I said.

"It's his thing. His professional name," Monique explained.

"Okay. Maybe I am not hearing you correctly. He's a sex therapist? And you're seeing him because you're not having enough sex? I thought people saw sex therapists when they were having too much sex."

"He works to teach women to be more active in the bedroom," Monique said.

"Yeah, more active in *his* bedroom," Heather added.

"He specializes in opening the seven chakras and helping us raise the kundalini," Monique said, using terms I'd heard too many times at bad poetry readings.

"Hilarious," I said, laughing. "Where did you meet this guy?"

"In the Village," she said, referring to Greenwich Village.

"Sounds about right."

"No. He's very professional."

"If he's so professional, how did you end up sleeping with him?" Tamika asked.

"Well, he was trying to teach me about a tantric sex move I should try with my next partner to achieve a more spiritual orgasm, and I told him he could probably show me better than he could teach me. I'm a slow learner."

We laughed at Monique's comical confession.

She got up from her stool and started demonstrating the position, and our laughter grew raucous. She had her back to the table, pretending to be Brother to the Night as she hunched over her in what she called "the Flower Press," when one of the guys from the bar, the cutest one, with dimples I could see from across the room, walked over to our table and joined in our laughter.

When she turned around and looked completely embarrassed, he crossed his arms over his chest and smiled at her the way most men did before they pretended the rest of us weren't there and asked for her phone number.

"You know who you look like?" he asked.

"Who?" Monique replied, trying to sound coy.

"Vanessa Williams!"

"Really?" Monique sat down and leaned into the table toward him. "You think so? I've never heard that before."

The rest of us struggled so hard not to laugh.

I searched inside my glass for an escape from the ridiculous scene and discovered that I'd finished my petrol-infused martini.

"Got those pretty eyes and that golden skin," I heard our visitor add as I jumped off my stool to leave his swooning and get a more suitable drink.

After weaving around the body sandwich the women in the slutty dresses and skanky shoes were making with one of the younguns in front of the bar, I slid into a small opening between two of the older men.

"Jameson on the rocks," I hollered, trying to get the bartender's attention over the music and talking. She was all the way at the other end of the bar and she didn't bother to walk over.

"What? A Jack knife?" she called. She had a waist so tiny that it had to have been held in with one of those Body Magic girdles, and breasts that poured out over her V-neck T-shirt with Tupac's face printed on the front.

"Jameson—on ice!" I shouted, nearly hanging over the bar. "Jameson!"

"Okay. Got ya."

I backed off the bar and noticed that one of the officers had left and in his place was the white guy who'd come in with the other cuties.

Somehow I was surprised that he was standing there, since I hadn't noticed him when I walked past the other guys. He was facing away from the bar, and I kept peeking at inches of him. His watch. The tattoo of an angel on his forearm. His muscles. I guess he noticed, because he looked over at me and asked, "You aight?" sounding like Kent or one of his boys.

"Sure," I said. "I'm fine."

I looked at the table to see that Monique's admirer had taken my place on the stool.

The bartender sat my drink on the bar, and I paid her.

"You want something, King?" she asked the white guy.

"Yeah, Iesha. Let me get a Red Bull and Ciroc," he said. "Light on the Bull and heavy on the vodka."

The bartender laughed like they were very familiar and went to make the drink.

I tittered to myself about the order. It sounded like something Kent would request, thinking it was classy.

"What you laughing about, brownskin?" he asked.

"Oh, nothing."

"Come on," he pushed. "Indulge me."

"It was the drink order. It's . . ." I paused, afraid my comment would come off the wrong way.

"What?" He smiled and exposed a dimple just like mine under his lip. "Ghetto?"

"Well . . . yes," I admitted nervously.

We both laughed.

"I guess you caught me with my pants down, then," he said, and I noticed that his voice was so smooth, so easily melodic, he sounded like a late-night Quiet Storm DJ. "Ellison would say, 'I yam what I am.' "

"A *king*?"

"Oh, you're tripping on my name, too?"

"It's not every day you come across a white boy—"

"Man," he corrected me. "I'm a man. Full man."

"Yes . . . a white man named King."

"There's a lot of things about me you've never come across," he said coolly. "And don't trip on the name. It's just a little nickname I got in these streets."

"Okay."

"What about you—what's your name?"

I tried to think of a fake name quickly, but nothing would come out.

"Oh, you're trying to think of a club name?" he asked, laughing. "That's real. Word life. It's all right. I know how sisters do. We'll just call you Queen."

Monique was walking out with the guy who'd come over to our the table, and he gave King five.

"Later, yo," King said, and then he turned to me. "That's your girl?"

"Yes," I said.

"Don't worry about her. She's in good hands. I don't fuck with lames."

"That was the farthest thing from my mind," I said, picking up my drink and starting back to the table. "He should be worried about her."

"Wait, Queen," King said, holding my hand so I couldn't walk away. "You ain't going to give me your number?"

"I can't," I said. "I have a boyfriend."

"Okay. I can respect that. You be good in these streets, then," he said. "And stay fine."

When I got back to the table, Heather and Tamika were like vultures, firing off one hundred questions about the white guy at the bar and telling me that Monique was taking the young guy back to her place to try six of the tantric moves she'd studied with Brother to the Night.

"It was nothing," I said when they calmed down.

"It didn't seem like nothing. Not the way that cutie pie was looking at you," Heather said. "That's that white chocolate." She groaned and licked her lips.

"Did you give him your number?" Tamika asked.

"No, I didn't. You know I don't swirl."

"Girl, it's 2014, and that thing is fine as shit. Looking like a mix between David Beckham and Justin Timberlake," Tamika said, groaning with Heather. "Bet he got a big dick, too. I told y'all what one of the models said about Timberlake."

"Y'all are gross." I looked over my shoulder at King.

He was back talking to the bartender and laughing. He turned and looked at me like he sensed my stare, and winked.

"Oh, Lord. He's got a little swag, too! Shit. I'll take him if you don't want him," Heather said, waving at him.

Tamika grabbed Heather's hand and held it to the table. "Kimmy, I demand that you go and get his number. He's fine and he's trying to holler."

"Just because he's hollering doesn't mean he's worth my time. He's not my type."

"Well, what's your type?" Tamika asked harshly. "Must be *no* type, because you're not getting any. What are you waiting for?"

"Bring it in, cousin," Heather warned.

When Tamika got drunk she had a tendency to be even more confrontational than usual.

"No, I'm serious, Heather. She has to stop this."

"Stop what?" I asked Tamika.

"It's over with Ronald. He's gone. That's it. Move on. And to someone who's available to you." She knew about my affair with Paul.

"You make it sound like it's so easy. He was the first man I slept with. We were supposed to get married." The alcohol set in deeper. In contrast with Tamika, when I got drunk, I got weepy.

"We've all been there. Shit, I've been there," Tamika said. "So what? He left you for some fake-ass Rocawear model. I had the bitch dropped from the agency. Fuck her and fuck him. You gotta get yours."

"Gangster Mika is in the house! I know that's right," Heather chimed in. "Keeping yourself closed off ain't hurting nobody but you, mama."

Tamika pointed at me. "And quiet as kept, Ronald wasn't all that anyway. He was lame as fuck. And you know it. You only held on because of that dick. And the worst part is that you don't even know it. Shit wasn't about him. It was good fucking. Years of it. And now he's gone." She fell back in her seat and dropped her pointed index finger like she'd revealed some great secret.

I rolled my eyes at Tamika's speech and looked back over my shoulder at King. A new woman was standing in my old space, and he was smiling at her.

"So, what are you going to do?" Heather asked.

"Go home and get some fucking sleep," I said, getting up from my stool.

"Oh, don't be like that. Don't go," Heather begged. Tamika rolled her eyes at me.

"It's cool." I cut my eyes at Tamika as I hugged Heather good-bye. "I'm not mad. I have a doctor's appointment in the morning."

"Okay," Heather said.

"Whatever," Tamika jumped in, getting off of her stool, too, but I don't remember what she did after. "You just remember what I said."

"Right. I'll do that."

As I walked out of Damaged Goods, I could feel King looking at me. His eyes on my entire body so hard, I struggled to swallow. I heard his laugh, and at one point I thought I heard him call "Queen." I didn't turn around though. Something in me couldn't.

"Let me walk you out," Tamika said, grabbing my arm. "You stumbling."

"I'm fine," I said, pulling away. "I'm just getting into a cab. I'll be fine."

Chapter 5

Thursday morning I was in Dr. Davis's office describing my pain.

He sat back in his chair with his feet up on his desk, exposing some ugly orange and teal argyle socks I could tell he thought were cute, because he kept looking down at them with a little smug smile as he asked me questions.

"So, when do you start feeling pain—like, what time of day?" he asked.

"Well, I'm sure it's before I get out of bed," I answered, sitting in a chair on the other side of the desk.

He grinned at his socks poking out from under his frat-boy khakis and shook his head in a way that was neither approving nor disapproving—more a confirmation that he could hear what I was saying.

"Before you get out of bed? Every morning?" he asked.

"Yes. Early. Every day." I felt like it was the hundredth time I'd said that since he'd been treating me.

After another quick head shake, peek at his socks, and grin, Dr. Davis asked, "Are you sitting up or lying down when you feel the pain?"

"I don't know. Does it matter?" I asked. "I just feel it. That's what's important."

"Well, actually, when you feel the pain is important."

"To whom?"

"To me."

Dr. Davis turned on his polite voice to talk to me about my pain, how I should describe it, and why he was volunteering to listen. Sometimes I felt like my little descriptions were pointless, just every doctor's way of making patients pay before getting their prescriptions. And that was because really the prescription was the bottom line. It was why we were both there.

I looked around his office as he spoke. Everything was cream and red and expensive. A nautical theme with seashells and charcoal sketches of sharks Dr. Davis had done himself. He even had one of those sound spa ports that played a continuous loop of ocean waves crashing.

He said it was supposed to be relaxing.

After my accident, I wanted to find a black doctor near the office, and one of my old classmates suggested I give him a try. Hearing his name, Dr. Delroy Davis, I was sure I'd meet some gray-haired Dr. Heathcliff Huxtable wannabe the first time I visited his office. But in he walked, big and black and so in shape, I thought he was gay. And then I saw the ugly argyle socks—that day they were red and blue—and I was sure he was gay. But then, in the examination, he had me stand in front of a chair as he ran his fingers up my spine from behind. As he palpated each vertebra, telling me to relax, my spine began to loosen and I lost my balance, falling back into his chest. He tried to hold me up, but it was too late, and quickly we were on the floor, me on top of him. In my scramble to get to my feet, I noted the big bulge in his pants. Erect and new and pointed toward me. Neither of us said anything. There was just an odd look and awkward smile. Ever since, I always thought he wanted to ask me out, but he never said anything. Just smiles and grins.

"Kimberly? Kimberly? Can you hear me?" Dr. Davis called from the other side of his desk.

"What?"

"I just asked you a question," Dr. Davis said.

"What?"

"Do you feel the pain when you're asleep?"

"Asleep? What? How would I know that?" I replied.

"Well, you just said that you feel it when you wake up."

"Okay. Fine, Dr. Davis," I said, sounding dramatically defeated by his questions. "I feel it in my sleep. Okay? Is that all?"

"*All?* What do you mean 'all'?" He shifted his feet off the desk and looked at me.

"Like for the prescription. Is that all you want to hear for me to get the prescription? I feel it in my sleep. When I wake up. When I'm in the shower. Walking down the street. All day. Okay? So now can you give me the prescription?" I raised my voice with each sentence. I didn't know how else I was supposed to communicate my urgency. I had to take two shots of the Jameson I bought on the way home from Damaged Goods just to get out of bed to make it to the appointment. The ibuprofen did nothing for my pain.

"Slow down!" Dr. Davis held up his hands, and his eyes softened on me in concern.

I repositioned myself in the seat, looked off at a sketch of a hammerhead, and took a deep breath. The pain was ticking up my back again, jabbing through each muscle and bone like an ice pick.

"Are you okay?" he asked.

"I'm fine." A tear escaped my right eye.

He pushed his cream-colored tissue box toward me.

"I don't need it," I said, and then after taking another deep breath during a silence where Dr. Davis eyed me like I was nearly suicidal, I asked, "Look, can I just get the prescription? I have to get to work."

"Well, that's why I wanted you to come in today," he said, getting up from his desk and walking around to sit in the chair beside me.

"Why?"

"I'm not giving you another prescription," he said.

"What?" I laughed to let him know that if he was joking, I'd gotten it and we could move on.

"I think you're done with that part of your treatment."

"Done? What are you talking about? I'm still in pain. I need the prescription. I need to take those pills. It's so much pain. I hurt," I said, feeling a few more tears slide from my eyes. My heart was beating so fast, and my hands started to clam up.

"I don't think you do. See, I started you on placebos a few weeks ago."

"Placebos?"

"Yes," he said, and then he reminded me of a pilot program I'd agreed to take part in on my first visit. They were testing the efficacy of standard medications. They wouldn't switch my medication or try new ones on me, just play with the dosage to see how much each person needed at each point during treatment. I thought it sounded pretty interesting a year ago, but I'd forgotten all about it. "We didn't say what we were looking for in terms of dosage. The real focus of the test was patient overuse."

"Overuse?" I laughed uneasily. "Are you joking? Overuse. . . . You . . . you make it sound like I'm—"

"No. Nothing like that," Dr. Davis said, placing his hand on my arm. "We were just interested in your recovery time and the number of pills you seem to take."

"And."

"All of the pills in your last dosage were placebos—sugar pills," he said.

"I know what a placebo is—and those pills, they weren't sugar pills. They made me feel better," I explained.

"Maybe they did," Dr. Davis said.

"I know what you're doing," I said, feeling more agitated with him sitting beside me and placing his hand on my arm. "And stop. Don't patronize me. I know what I feel and I know what those pills did."

"The only way those pills could work to relieve your pain is if your pain isn't real. If it's . . . in your head."

I hadn't realized I was crying again until Dr. Davis reached over to his desk for the box of tissues and placed it in my lap.

"You weren't there. You don't know what happened. They're getting married."

"Who's getting married, Kimberly? Can you tell me? Maybe you should talk to someone about . . ."

Dr. Davis was talking about a lot of nothing. I couldn't believe he was making light of my pain. Of the kicking in my back. Every day, every night, I felt like I was cracking wide open, and he wanted to talk about some damn placebos and suggest that I needed to talk to someone?

I stood up and looked down on him. He was making it sound like there was something wrong with me and not him for shirking his duty. I mean, I was having chronic pain. My accident had caused me chronic pain, and there was only one way to deal with it. But there he was acting like Dr. Oz.

"Is this about what happened here at my first office visit?" I asked, cutting off his silly suggestion that I see one of his psychiatrist friends in Chelsea.

"What?" he asked, trying to look surprised.

"Come on," I said. "Let's just be honest. Ever since I started coming here, you've been, you know, checking me out."

He got up from his seat and looked at me in mock distress, like he didn't know what I was talking about.

"Really? So, you're going to keep on with that?" I chuckled as I stood before him. "Well, if you want to play like that, I'll say this: We both know who you are and who I am. Right?" He shook his head in agreement. "And we both know that sexual harassment is a very serious charge. One I don't take lightly. Do you understand that?"

"I wasn't . . . I-I—"

"You what?"

"I wasn't trying to do anything to you." He reached over to his desk and picked up a photo frame that had been facing away from me. He turned it to me, and there he was standing on a beach with a white girl and a little mixed toddler with a blond Afro. "I've been in a committed relationship for seven years." He tried to hand me the little cream-colored frame.

I held up my hands and backed away.

"Really?" I said, grabbing my purse. "That's your defense. You know how many men who are actually married still try to abuse their power? Whatever." I started walking out.

"Please don't leave, Kimberly," Dr. Davis said in this fake, plastic voice that sounded like he was about to do something really lame like call security.

"I'm getting another doctor. You don't want to manage my pain? Someone else will. Good day!"

He began to follow me out of the office, apologizing and begging me to contact his friend in Chelsea, but when we got into the waiting room and it was filled with people trying to get his attention, he stopped.

"I'll call you to set up a meeting," he said to my back. "You call me back. Call me back if you need anything!"

I kept walking right out into the street, where the high morning sun stung my eyes. There was no way I'd make it through the rest of the day without something. The Jameson and ibuprofen were wearing off, and already my lower back was stinging.

On the way to the office I figured I'd leave early to get into bed and come up with a plan before things got too bad, but once the elevator dinged open on my floor, Carol was in position waiting for me, arms extended, face all red.

"Oh, you're here!" she said before stepping off the elevator.

"Could you just wait until I get to my office?" I snapped. "Get in the door?"

"But it's important," she said, holding her hands out in front of me to stop me.

"Isn't it always important? Every day? Welcome to my life. Everything is important."

"We need to talk," she said, her voice thin and conciliatory. And even with my aggravation at Dr. Davis for leaving me hanging and Carol attacking me upon entry and my back pain and everything else, I knew I needed to stop and listen to her. "Bernard Richard is dead."

"Who's dead?"

"Bernard Richard. The witness. The one in the Christopher Street meth-lab case." She pulled me to the back of the elevator bank as two of my colleagues walked past looking at me with the accusatory stares.

"But he was just here. Dead?" I said, remembering him sitting across from me in the conference room. His scared eyes. The black car he described outside his window. "What happened?"

"Well, the gossip is that Alvarez put a hit out on him. Final report isn't back yet from downtown, but the word is that someone was waiting for him in the apartment when he got home last night—now that's what people are saying. But, you know—"

"Fuck. Fuck. How'd that happen? I sent an officer out there with him," I said, and then whispered. "He had protection. You know that. Right? So if that's what people are saying—that he didn't have protection—they're wrong."

Two more ADAs, one who'd started at the DA's office with me, walked by with their fake smiles and whispers. When they were gone, I looked at Carol and her still-red cheeks. "Get Chief Elliot on the phone. This won't go on un—"

"Kimberly—" Carol cut in.

"We can't have this. That man was serving the state. We can't let it get out that he died under our protect—"

"Kimberly!" Carol nearly shouted. "Listen to me."

"What?"

"He wasn't under our protection. Remember?"

"What? I sent him home with an officer."

"Yes, you did," she offered, returning to her conciliatory tone. "But . . ." She paused.

"What?"

She whispered sharply, "You didn't order full protection. He only had an escort home. That's all."

"No, I didn't." I laughed nervously at Carol's confusion. "I ordered protection for him. I listened to him in there." I pointed down the hallway toward the conference room. "I heard him. I told him—"

Carol cut me off. "You told him not to worry. You sent him home. I've been reading the transcripts."

"I—" Pieces of a blurry conversation with Bernard flashed in my mind. I remembered him looking at the bookshelves, asking for a smoke. The fear in his eyes. The story of the woman with the yellow eyes and cheese grater on her back.

I started walking toward my office again without saying anything to Carol, but she was up on my heels and still talking.

"I'll clear this up," I said over her, but it was a fool's statement. We both knew what the situation was adding up to. Where the fault would fall. And God, if the press got word.

"I think it might be too late," Carol said in a low voice, so that an assistant walking past with arms filled with folders couldn't hear her.

"What? Why do you say that?" I asked. "Is there something else? Anything else I need to know?"

"Paul."

"What? Fuck! He knows? Of course he does," I said. "Now wait. Calm down," I said to Carol. "No need to panic. I just need to sit down . . . in my office to figure this out. To get in front of it. I can do this. I can explain everything. You saw Bernard, right? You know he was high. You said it yourself. We just need to get the story straight."

"We're going to need to. And faster than you think." Carol pointed to my open office door. "Paul is in there with Chief Elliot. They're waiting for you."

"In my office? For what?"

"A meeting. They called it this morning when the word got out about Bernard."

"A meeting?" I looked down at my clothes for some reason. "What? Why didn't you tell me?"

"I called you a couple of times—even though you told me not to. I left a message," Carol said. "Kimberly, I think this is serious."

"Did you hear anything?" I asked. "What they've been saying?"

"No."

"Okay. Okay," I said, rolling through what they could want, what I had to say, what I needed to say. I handed Carol my purse, shoulder bag, and cell phone.

We stood eye to eye for a second as I adjusted my skirt and broke off to walk at top pace toward my office.

"Hold all calls," I instructed her. "And print those transcripts from the meeting."

"Yes."

When I got to my office, Easter Summer, an ADA who was always in my business with Paul, was walking toward me with her laptop in her arms. She'd started two years behind me but was fast becoming a prospective shoe-in for joining my team. And I could never figure out why. She was second-string material at best. Didn't seem to have a mind of her own and was mostly good at taking and following direction.

"Oh. I'm not too late," she said, smiling with her red lips. She was black Latin. Had skin the color of sand and black freckles on her forehead.

"Late?" I asked.

"Yeah," she said, walking into my office in front of me. "For the meeting."

Paul and Chief Elliot stood when we walked in. Elliot was a "tough on drug" hire the police commissioner put in office. One name on a short list of black police chiefs in New York's history, Elliot made sure to keep a spotless record. But he was an old-school male chauvinist whose dingy dealings with female officers and subordinates remained the talk. The *Daily News* once quoted him saying, "I'm in no way saying female officers shouldn't have guns, but I am saying that I'm sure if they did a study to compare misfires between males and female officers, the more fair sex would come out on top." Still, Paul doted on Elliot like he was the Superman of the city. He may have been a jerk, but that only gave him more credibility in a system that saw chauvinism as a part of the culture. Paul claimed he didn't like it when I pointed out the most obvious offenses to him, but then Elliot gave Paul his very own man-sized toy car in the form of a police wagon he could drive around Manhattan, running lights and acting a fool wherever he wanted, and they became thick as thieves.

Paul smiled at Easter and gestured for her to sit in one of three chairs they'd pulled in from the conference room.

"Good morning," I said, trying so hard to sound light. "I didn't know we were meeting today, so excuse my lateness."

"We didn't know we were meeting either," Paul said. "But Counselor, it seems sometimes the most essential meetings are unplanned."

"Chief Elliot," I greeted the chief, returning the nod he gave after removing his hat.

Walking to my chair behind the desk, I kept my eye on Easter as she crossed her legs and clicked on her laptop.

"So, what do we have here?" I asked eagerly, leaning toward the three of them sitting in a row before my seat. I knew it was important that I appear in control and in the know. "Now, I'm already ahead on the situation with Bernard. Very sad. A major setback, but I have other witnesses I can get to. We can still move forward. I think our real problem is with Alvarez being able to order a hit from behind bars. Anyone looking into that situation?"

"That's purely speculative and you know it. We're focusing here right now," Paul said.

Tap. Tap. Tap. Tap. Easter was typing away on her laptop like some secretary.

"Nothing to focus on. I've got it under control," I said.

"A man is dead," Chief Elliot pointed out.

"Yes. He is deceased. And—"

Tap. Tap. Tap. Tap. Easter lifted the laptop and crossed her legs, kicking a little red toenail up through the peephole in her black patent leather shoes. Both Paul and Elliot took it in.

"Look," I went on. "I know this may seem like a major bump, but I know we can—"

"Counselor, you know how serious this is," Paul said, looking back at me. "I'm sure you do. Bernard Richard was here just days ago. We have the transcripts from the meeting. He told you—"

"I know what he told me."

"I need to make sure my officers are not taking the rap for this one," Chief Elliot jumped in. "Can't get the press off my dick—now, you ladies excuse my expression. But you understand. Whenever anything happens, everyone wants to blame us."

"I assure you that won't be the case here," Paul said to him. "The blame is not being kicked around."

Tap. Tap. Tap. Tap.

"Not being kicked around?" I said, looking into Paul's eyes. "Who said there's any blame at all?"

Tap. Tap. Tap. Tap. Easter looked up at me and then quickly back down at her laptop when our eyes met.

"Counselor," Paul said, addressing me without saying my name for the third time, "perhaps I misspoke. This isn't about blame. But it is about clarity. About what we know."

Tap. Tap. Tap. Tap. Every click on the keyboard felt like a razor blade up my spine. Easter hadn't said a word, but somehow she was the beat of the conversation. Of course, I was trying to figure out why she was there. For sure, it wasn't to take notes. This was leading somewhere that I probably didn't want to be. I'd seen ADAs fired for the smallest infractions, especially ones that could blemish the DA's record or make a mockery of the department. But when I heard Elliot was in my office with Paul, I was certain this wasn't going to be my fate. They were probably just trying to kick me around, see what I knew and tell me to lie low. But Easter being included was uncommon. I knew she wanted to be on my team, so it went without saying that any loss I'd have would be a gain for her.

Tap. Tap. Tap. Tap. There was a snap in the middle of my back.

"I'm on top of it," I said, trying to breathe through the pain encircling my neck.

"He told you he was afraid. That he was being followed," Paul said.

"I sent an officer to his home with him. I thought that would be enough. Look, he was a habitual drug user. He certainly wasn't clean when he came into the office. It sounded like he was over—" Easter looked up at me.

"He was what?" Elliot pulled.

"I followed procedure," I started again. "I didn't do anything wrong." I hated the way I sounded. Like some little girl sitting in the principal's office for necking with her boyfriend in the bathroom. I was at the top of my game. Not some first-year ADA who had to explain a wrong move to a room full of uninvited onlookers who basically knew squat about the case. I was being dragged out into the wide open. Pissed on in the worst way. And Paul was leading the pack.

Tap. Tap. Tap. Tap.

I looked at Paul.

"I'm putting a new lead on the case immediately," Paul said abruptly. "Just to ward off any hits from the media."

Tap. Tap. Tap. Tap.

"No. Everything is fine. It's my case. This is just a setback, and—" I tried but Paul stopped me.

"We can't risk it," Paul went on.

Tap. Tap. Tap. Tap.

"Risk it?" I repeated. "We? We who, Paul?"

Tap. Tap. Ta—Easter stopped typing when I said Paul's name. Both she and Elliot glanced from me to him suspiciously.

"Easter just closed the Lemont case, and she's been following this one. She's a great pick." Paul smiled at Easter. "She just needs to get some information from you and Chief Elliot, and I think we can move forward. I think that's what's best. And I know we all want that."

Easter and Elliot smiled at Paul's seemingly diplomatic front.

"Of course we do," I said. "I do. But perhaps we need to talk more about this, right? Not make any rash decisions just because of the media. And we don't even know what's going to happen. If it's even a story."

"We had to move fast either way. Be proactive. We can't afford to be behind," Chief Elliot said. "We have to protect ourselves from this error."

"It was an innocent mistake. How was I supposed to know that he was going to—"

"You were supposed to know because it's your job," Paul snapped.

Tap. Tap. Tap. Tap.

"I am not some psychic. I am—"

Tap. Tap. Tap. Tap.

"And what are you typing?" I shot my eyes at Easter.

"Counselor, don't do this," Paul said, and again eyes in the room rolled from him to me.

"Do what? I asked a simple question."

"I'm . . . I'm—" Easter tried.

"No. Don't say anything, Easter," Paul commanded, pointing at her.

"Oh, she's Easter, but I'm Counselor?" I said.

Tap. Tap. Tap. Tap.

"And don't you type another thing I say," I shot at Easter.

Chief Elliot's eyes darted back and forth again, and he stood up with the hat he was holding on his lap in his hands.

"Don't do this now, Kimberly. Not here," Paul said.

"Do what? What am I doing?" I asked. "Better yet, what are *you* doing?"

Chief Elliot quietly put his hat on and looked at Paul, who was still sitting beside Easter and her crossed legs and red toenail polish.

"I believe I have a meeting elsewhere," he announced, sounding as if he'd just said the first thing he could think of to get away from the tension in the room. He caught Paul's eye and grimaced knowingly.

After Easter and I stood to shake the chief's hand, Paul walked him out of the office and left us standing there looking at each other.

Silent, we could hear Paul whispering to Elliot about rivalry and getting everything straightened out.

"I'm sor—" Easter started.

"Don't," I stopped her. "Don't you dare say you're sorry. Not for this. Because we both know you're lying, and with the kind of morning I'm having, I can't stand here and pretend I give two shits about your fake sorry. You're not sorry. Not one bit. So save it."

"Kimberly, I admire you—how you've—"

"Oh, stop it, Easter. I can see right through your type. A glorified fucking secretary." I pointed at her laptop. "You don't have the brains to get to the top, so you take the notes for the boys, study hard, and maybe sleep with a couple of people to get to the top. Is that the plan?"

Easter stepped toward my desk, and her eyes went so cold, she looked like she was possessed. "Was that the plan for you?" she asked.

There are times in every Harlem girl's life when who she wants to be is called into question and who she was proves too strong for restraint. When in her diamonds and pearls and Chanel and Gucci, she is pushed to a place where she regresses to those old Timbs in the back of her closet and the wad of Vaseline she knows to rub into her cheeks so not one scratch from the fight that's about to start will ruin her complexion. That's where I was taken so quickly when Easter came out of her mouth at me like she wasn't standing in my office and didn't have a clue about who I was or what I was capable of.

Hurt back, neck, and all, I was no one's punk and I was getting tired of everyone, everywhere I went, treating me otherwise.

I didn't even say anything.

Easter's eyes widened as I got two inches shorter because I'd stepped out of my shoes and then reached to my earlobes to remove my earrings.

"Look, we have to—" Paul stepped over the threshold of my office and surveyed the scene. "Wait! What's going on?"

"I was just about to make an impression on Counselor Summer that it was time for her to leave my office," I said sternly.

"And I was just about to make an impression on Counselor Kind that I'll leave when the meeting is over," Easter said, looking like she was in no way going to stand down.

Paul stepped between us just before I was going to come over the desk after Easter or she was coming for me from the other side.

"No one is asking anyone to leave." His body was facing me, but he looked back and forth between us.

"Really?" I said, testing him.

"Easter," Paul started, his eyes stuck on me, "please return to your office. I'll be in there in a minute to give you further direction."

"Yeah, that's what I thought," I said.

"But I still need the—" Easter's voice had tumbled to a whine.

"Easter, please!" Paul glanced at her but kept his head facing me.

"But—"

"Please!"

Locked in with Paul, I watched Easter stuff her laptop under her arm and roll her eyes at us. "Guess I got my answer," she murmured before walking out.

"What is this?" Paul asked when she was gone.

"You tell me. I came to work and I was basically ambushed in my own office," I replied as he turned to close my door. "A heads-up would've been nice."

"There's no heads-up in this. A man died, Kim. Do you understand that?"

"Oh, now I'm Kim?"

"What's gotten into you?" Paul walked around the desk and looked at my bare feet.

"I'm having a really fucked-up morning," I said. "There's a lot going on with me. And the last thing I need is to get here and have the fucking chief of police and some glorified secretary with some law degree in my office talking about they're taking over my case. My case! And you didn't even tell me what was about to go down. Our shit aside, I thought you had my back."

"Don't you dare question my goddamn loyalty!" he hollered so loudly I knew everyone outside the office could hear him. I looked at his chest and realized he was wearing the red and purple Vitaliano Pancaldi tie I'd bought him last Christmas. "You made your decision. Now you live with it. No different from anybody else around here."

"No different from Easter?" I asked suggestively.

"Easter? Are you fucking serious?"

"I saw how you were looking at her. The same way you looked at me before I was dumb enough to take the bait." I laughed coolly.

He whispered angrily into my face, "This is not about us. You know what we have. This is about you."

"Me?"

Paul leaned against my desk and crossed his arms before resting his head in his hands.

"Me?" I repeated, feeling the weight and worry in his stance. "What about me?"

"I wanted to wait. I thought maybe things would change, but after how you just reacted in here, I see it's impossible," he announced gravely.

"Wait for what?" Those ticks were coming up my back again.

"You haven't been the same lately, Kim." He finally looked at me. "Your work, it's weak at best. I got that Lankin case brief from Carol, and—"

"She wasn't supposed to send that to you yet," I said before calling out for Carol. "Carol! Carol! Ca—"

"Stop it, Kimberly. I sent her to lunch."

"Lunch? What?" The ticks in my back reached my neck again, and I had to sit down. "Why did you do that? What's going on here?" I reached down to my purse for the painkillers I'd forgotten weren't in there.

Paul grabbed the bag. "I need you to listen to me."

"I can't. My back hurts right now. It hurts and I need my painkillers." I tried to pull the bag back, but he snatched it and threw it to the other side of the desk.

"You're a fine attorney. The best here," Paul said.

"Oh my God, you're firing me." I was shaking. I saw my mother. Kim 2 and Ronald at the altar. Me pushing Kim 2 out of the car, getting behind the wheel, and pressing the gas pedal really hard. Screaming. Screaming.

"No. I'm not firing you. I just—I'm suggesting that you take a vacation."

"No. No. No." I tried to get up, but Paul held my hands in place on the arms of the chair. "I'm fine. I don't need a vacation."

"You're burning out. Missing things. Late to work most days. Not communicating with people. Your reports. Now this thing with Bernard Richard. I've seen it happen before. You need some time. You can't burn the candle on both ends."

"No. This isn't about burning any fucking candles, Paul. This is about your dick," I countered. "You're pissed off because I'm not falling for your shit anymore. I mean, just yesterday you were down here talking about how great a job I am doing."

"I was trying to encourage you."

"No, you were trying to get back into my bed," I charged. "And I'll tell that sexual—"

"Don't do that. We both know everything between us was consensual," Paul said.

"That's not how it will look," I said, and the knife in my voice surprised me.

"You wouldn't."

"I don't need a vacation. I need you off my back. Off my case."

Paul lifted his hands and backed away. "Take a week. Take two weeks. Take a month. Just step away. For you and the press," he said. "Hand your stuff over to Easter and take some time for yourself. Get yourself together. Please, Kimberly. I'm asking you now. Next I'll have to tell you."

Paul had a car with a driver waiting for me downstairs. I still don't remember how I got downstairs or what I said to the driver. Just the web of pain over my whole back, spinning over my shoulders, making me sob.

The car started moving. The driver, an old black man with gray dreadlocks and silver studs up his earlobes, hummed along to some gospel song on the radio.

I wanted to say something to him. To ask if he knew what I should I do. Where I was going. How to make the pain stop. But he kept humming and the car kept rolling through the busy late-spring New York City afternoon and I couldn't think of what to say, what to ask, how to begin.

I looked down at my purse in my lap and thought about who I could call. Whose number I could dial who would say, "Tell that man to drive you here. I'll take care of you. I'll comfort you."

I unpinned the bag and started searching, rummaging past my wallet, lip gloss, lotion, writing pad, and then at the bottom I saw my phone and the half-full bottle of ibuprofen I'd purchased at the pharmacy.

I reached for it.

The driver's humming got louder. I snatched the top of the bottle off and poured half of what was left into a shaking hand.

Now the driver sang along with the music coming from the speaker behind my head. *"His word said he won't. I believe it. I receive it. I claim it."*

My hand was shaking so badly, some of the pills fell to my lap and then the floor.

"No, he'll never put more on me—"

"Stop singing! Turn off the music!" I shouted as more pills fell to the floor.

The car went silent.

I rolled down my window and took in as big a breath as I could.

"Whatever it is, you don't need those pills for it," the driver said.

I could feel him looking at me through the rearview mirror, but I kept my eyes on the buildings and people and bikes and cars rolling past outside the window. I took two more breaths and dropped the rest of the pills.

"I'm fine," I said, my voice cracking and unexpected tears rolling down my cheeks.

"I'm glad to hear that. Now, is there somewhere I can take you? Someplace where you have someone who can handle—"

"There's no one. Home. Just take me home."

I told him my address and he rolled the rest of the windows down, saying he thought I needed more air. He started talking about his grandson who was in business school at Columbia. How hard it was; how he kept telling "the boy" he had to be strong because the devil is out there working in the streets.

I nodded, out of respect, and kept watching the world move along as if mine hadn't just stopped. It was the only thing I could do to stop my tears. Then I went back to gathering the pills off of the dirty car floor. I had a feeling I was looking for something. Waiting. Beside us in the downtown traffic, a couple with California-blond hair canoodled in a Saleen S7.

"But you be strong, girl," my driver said, "and focus on who and whose you are, because your maker is stronger than your enemy. And that's what I tell him."

The S7 sped off when the light finally changed, and behind three more taxis in a hurry was a silver Bentley that shined so brightly in the sunlight that it forced two last tears out of my eyes.

"I say to him, 'You focus on God, boy. Because that's how you make it through,' " the sermon went on over the steady hip-hop beats rattling from the Bentley. "You put your faith in the Lord and his son, Jesus Christ, and you can't go wrong. You know that? Salvation is through the King of Kings! Glory!"

Nodding, I watched the silver car and the sun bouncing off its every surface. We were stopped at a light again, and I peered into the darkened back windows to try to see inside. I wasn't looking for anything. Just maybe something. A rapper. A face I knew that I could tell someone else about later. Tamika and I always shared our celebrity sightings in the city.

I am sure I was almost leaning out my window when all of a sudden the back window of the Bentley came down a little and smoke rolled out in sweet marijuana-laced waves. There was someone laughing inside, a white face with a thin beard. I thought I knew the face but couldn't recall how and when I'd seen it. That's when the man started laughing and the tilt of the head took me back to the bar that night with Tamika. Back to Damaged Goods.

"King?" I recalled aloud. "King!" I felt a happy flutter in my stomach—as if I was seeing an old friend. Or had known him beyond our two-minute meeting in a dank bar in Brooklyn.

"That's right! The King of Kings!" the driver repeated my words when the light changed and we started moving again.

"No, King! King!" I pointed to the car like he had any idea who I was talking about. "Stop!"

King must've heard me, because he looked around outside the window.

I waved and said his name again, but his car was speeding up and mine, of course, was slowing down.

"The King?" the driver repeated again, tapping his brakes. "That's right! We stop for the Lord! Brake for the Lord!"

"Never mind. He's gone." I watched as the shiny silver car rolled away.

I stopped at the store in the lobby of my building. Watched as the clerk slid a cold bottle of Jameson into a paper bag. He'd asked why I was home from work so early. Mentioned that he didn't think he'd ever seen me during the day before. I smiled politely and tucked the bottle into my work bag before heading toward the elevator. Besides the doorman, no one was around. And it was so quiet, I could hear the elevators sliding up and down the cords between floors.

As I waited I tried to free my mind of Paul in my office. Take a week off? Two weeks? What was he saying about me? I had no way of knowing anything was going to happen to Bernard Richard. If Paul had seen him sitting in the conference room staring off like a meth zombie, he would've made the same decision. This wasn't about me or my work. I wasn't burnt out. I was moving on with my life and not falling for his lies anymore, and he couldn't handle that. God, what men will do when they feel threatened. But to bring it to my job? To humiliate me in front of simple-ass Easter Summer and Chief Elliot, who probably wanted to see me go down because I'm a woman? I couldn't let Paul get away with that. He was right that I wouldn't escalate the situation and accuse him of sexual harassment. I actually had just as much to lose in that kind of battle as he did. Anita Hill and Clarence Thomas proved to all working women that there was no predetermined victor when women stepped up with information about sexual advances, no matter how crass or vile, against men in power. In spite of his nasty-ass Coke-bottle pubic-hair comments, Thomas went on to the Supreme Court, and

Hill and her tired, worried face were hardly seen beyond a short list of random television interviews and late-night news panels. I'm sure that wasn't the life she'd imagined as a rising star when she took the job beneath Thomas at the Department of Education.

And as much as I hated to agree with anything Paul said, he wasn't lying about my part in our affair. I'm a grown woman, and I know there were two people in our tango, and as many accusations as I could chuck at him, he could lob double in my direction. Still, however we handled whatever happened between us needed to happen where it started. I wasn't about to put my career on the line for that.

Like the lobby, my apartment was quiet with noontime nothingness. In the kitchen, I opened the Jameson and took three shots to calm myself before pouring a glass with three ice cubes. I took the glass and bottle to the couch, where I looked at the blank television screen and thought to turn it on but decided against it. Instead, I looked at my reflection, alone and frozen like a Zoloft commercial for single women who'd failed at everything. I remembered King calling me a queen. Me not answering and walking out of the bar like I didn't know he was talking to me. Maybe I knew he was joking or thought he couldn't be right. Some queen I would be. I couldn't hold anything in its place. All this spectacle in my life, and there I was with no power to do anything about it.

I poured another glass and lay back on the pillow I sometimes used to ease the pain in my lower back. I needed a plan. I could get everything back in place if I could just focus. I thought about King and how he moved with so much confidence around Damaged Goods. The woman behind the bar laughing at his jokes. His eyes direct but relaxed in a place where most men who looked like him would be either unwelcome or placed under constant speculation that could end in a horrible fight to prove his masculinity.

I finished my drink, but the ice cubes were still there, so I poured a little more Jameson and lay back again.

Men and their masculinity. Dr. Davis and Paul acting like I was the reason for their problems. Like I had the issue. I'd fought to get where I was. Every single step of the way I'd fought. Through college. Law school. I'd handled those cases all by myself, and now I was out of line? Me? I needed a break? To go sit in the fucking corner with a dunce cap on? Fuck them!

I drained the glass and slid it onto the coffee table. I didn't need a break. I needed everyone off my back, so I could move on. I placed the pillow in the small of my back. My eyes closed and everything went spinning into a disorienting tornado of images that led to someplace in my memory, in my past.

It was Ronald's apartment.

Kim 2 was sitting on the side of the bed in one of those thin bras from American Apparel that only girls with A-cups could wear. I was still in my green sundress, standing at the door with my hands behind my back, looking at her. The creamy little breasts that led to ruddy nipples, brown and red at the same time.

Ronald had insisted we leave the lights on. In a group text message between the three of us, he'd said he wanted to remember this. To see everything and record it in his memory in case it never happened again. Kim 2 responded with a smiley face and "SURE" in all caps.

Bassnectar was playing on the radio beside the bed. The music Ronald usually worked out to. He was in the bathroom off the other side of the room, and I could hear him taking deep breaths, like he was doing pull-ups on the bar he'd installed in the doorway.

Kim 2 stood and ambled to me. Through her thin panties peeked a freshly shaved vagina. I felt myself back up a little, like she was a nude stranger, because that was how it felt.

"Calm down," she said, taking my hand and slipping something into my palm. "Take that. Lie down and just relax. I'll handle this."

"What is it?" I looked into my palm and found a round yellow pill with a happy face etched into it.

"A little Ex for your nerves. You'll need it." She laughed. Took the pill from my hand and held it up to my mouth until I opened wide and made a bed of my tongue. "It won't take long." Her words slurred into a cadence that matched the music. "Just relax."

She pulled me to the bed and told me to lie down.

"It's nothing. Just remember you're doing it for him. Right?" she whispered into my ear, looking at the bathroom door. I nodded. "It'll be great. Legendary."

My head was pulled back onto the pillow by something strong and fluid inside of me. There was a rush from my toes to my brain and then needles dancing from my palms up my arms.

Kim 2's laughing turned into the music, and where she was positioned at the foot of the bed, I couldn't tell if she was dancing or standing. There were just her red nipples and nude, pubescent vagina first under and then outside of her bra and panties.

"You're naked," I said, trying to lift my hands to point at her, but I couldn't move.

"You are, too!" She cackled like a witch into the music and pointed at me.

I looked down at my breasts parted on my chest, so cold I was covered in goosebumps. "I'm cold," I said, wondering where my green dress had gone, and hearing in my voice a slurring whine that made me sound more like Kim 2 than Kim 1.

"Bitch, you're fucked up already," Kim 2 said. "You'll be fine. It'll pass in a few minutes. Then you'll be ready to play."

She started dancing, and I tried to focus on her body, to keep pace with something so I didn't pass out from the pressure in my head. My eyelids were so fucking heavy, and my brain was dragging my mind into the pillow with it.

Ronald walked out of the bathroom naked with his dick fully erect and tapping at the nappy black hairs over his protruding belly button.

"What? Hold up!" I tried to get up to tell him he was naked and I wasn't ready for that, but I hardly made it to my elbows before I fell back again.

"Oh, you're already ready for us?" Kim 2 said, sauntering over to my first lover with a grin. "And here I was thinking about how we were going to get your dick." She laughed.

Ronald looked at me and sort of smirked before Kim 2 was in his face and turning his chin to her with her index finger.

With his attention, she got up on her tippy-toes and started sucking on his neck and stroking his dick.

"You're so hard," she purred between nips at his neck, running her fist up and down the shaft of his dick with a visibly tight grasp, making him moan.

The weights at the back of my head were dissipating, and I managed to sit up.

"You okay, baby?" Ronald walked over to the side of the bed and stood just close enough to reach over and touch my hair.

"She's feeling it now. Aren't you, Kiki?" Kim 2 walked over to me too and pushed the finger she'd been holding over the tip of Ronald's dick into my mouth. "Suck it," she demanded naughtily.

I looked at Ronald and he nodded.

And then my lips were squeezing her finger as she teased it in and out of my mouth and the salty taste of Ronald's pre-cum mixed with my saliva.

Ronald bent down to kiss me, but Kim 2 pulled her finger from my mouth and slipped it into his. Then she came back to me and started dipping it in and out of each of our mouths, teasing us toward each other until finally our tongues met and we were kissing intensely and deeply. I started sucking Ronald's tongue, feeling like all I wanted was something in my mouth to ease the vibrations coursing through my body from the tip of my clitoris to my tonsils.

Kim 2 had climbed on top of me and was straddling my waist with her knees, popping her pussy to Bassnectar's "Wildstyle Method."

"Suck his dick," she said rather wistfully as she swayed her hands offbeat in the air like a drunken belly dancer. "I want to see it."

Ronald stopped kissing me and stood erect with his hard dick. I stared and tried to remember what I was doing. Why I was there.

"Do it," Kim 2 instructed then. "I know you're not scared. Don't act like you haven't sucked that dick before. I always hear Ronald moaning through the wall at our place. Let me see. Come on."

Ronald wrapped his hand around the back of my neck and pulled my face toward his head. I looked up into his eyes, and he smiled, leaning back on one foot. It was his birthday. This was his birthday wish. I remembered. A threesome with my roommate. The last thing he wanted to do to sow his wild oats before getting engaged. Just the thought of that opened my mouth wide, and I took all of that dick into my cheeks until the back of my tonsils burned and I felt like I might cough up the strawberries and red wine I'd had earlier.

"Fuck yeah," Kim 2 coached like an accomplished porn star as I rolled my lips back and forth and up and down his venous shaft as it pounded into me so many times that tears trickled into the creases of my eyes.

Ronald had been the only man I'd ever had sex with, the only penis ever in my mouth, but I'd practiced this art to completion too many times to fail—and I certainly was not about to fail in front of Kim 2 and her ruddy nipples and buff pussy.

Ronald's penis became more rigid in my mouth, and I held my breath to stop the fluttering in my tonsils. I thought of that train coming into the station at 1:25 and began to disappear into the sensations detonating in my pussy.

"Fucking, bitch," Ronald said, holding my neck in place. We caught our usual rhythm, and first my lips and then my tongue and then my tonsils and then my throat went to work. I pulled his dick past the bump at the back of my throat by tilting my head up and took him down my neck.

"Oh shit, you're turning me on," Kim 2 said as she played with her vagina over mine.

Ronald looked at her desirously as I gave my throat a rest by jerking him hard with my hand. His pupils rolled around in melting swirls.

"I want to see you eat her pussy," he said, dribbling, trying to focus in on Kim 2's mouth.

She laughed demurely, tilted her head to the side like a Catholic schoolgirl, and stuck her index finger into her mouth.

Since Ronald had started talking about a possible threesome with my roommate, I'd imagined what it might be like: I'd dreamed up awkwardness and shy playful touching that ended with Kim 2 running out of the room. We'd laugh and go back to our usual one-on-one knowing we'd been there and done that and could move on with our lives into forever. I'd agreed to it because I knew Ronald had a little crush on Kim 2. Why wouldn't he? She was exotic and wild and experienced. But still, not what he'd want in a wife. Far from it. She had no accolades behind her name. Hadn't suffered with him through law school. Won the ADA position he'd failed to win. She had bad credit and little more in the world than good looks. He wanted to fuck her and that was it. I could give him that and we could be done.

I tried to keep reminding myself of that. Kim 2 was no threat to my ascension. This was now, but later would be more. I tried so hard, but in every second of that Ecstasy-laced night there was proof that I was lying to myself. This show was on the road, and I wasn't making it to the next stop.

Kim 2 climbed off me and jerked my legs open like she'd done it many times before. Sitting in the middle of the V my legs made on the bed, she tickled her hands up the insides of my calves as Ronald and I looked on at the show. She was in her space. Eyes on her. Live on the runway.

She lifted my knees and pushed my ankles back, making little pyramids of my legs. Then, like a stretching Siamese, she rolled her breasts down to the empty space on the sheet in front of my pussy. As her lips neared my lips she was blowing and whispering at my vagina, words that turned to senseless purrs in my Ecstasy-sheltered ears. She lapped at my clitoris hungrily.

"Your clit is hard," she said, face-to-face with my pussy. "Let's see if she's wet." She looked up at Ronald before pulling her right index finger from beneath my legs and slipping it into my vagina, where she danced her pad from a hook to an arrow like she was beckoning something within me.

My legs and my lips opened wider.

"Yeah, she's wet," she confirmed to Ronald, and then she disappeared beneath my curly mound and became only sensations I couldn't see, and then I was riven, wide and flowing. Cake on a plate.

I'd lost focus, falling back into the bed and closing my eyes, going to a black space with explosions of red and violet beneath my eyelids. Kim 2's mouth was steady, sucking me hard, but I still heard her whispering into me. I heard more utterances of pleasure and recognized the voice as my own.

When I opened my eyes, Ronald was standing in front of me at the foot of the bed. His head was hanging back and his chin pointed at the ceiling. His chest was rocking to me and away in short, rhythmic taps. His arms were stretched forward and hanging low to where I couldn't see his hands because of how flat my head was on the bed.

Then I felt rocking between my thighs, and the whispering I'd heard inside of me became heavy panting and moaning in desirous agony.

I pushed back up on my elbows to find Ronald's fingers and discover what had become of Kim 2 between my thighs.

Gradually, as I came up, I saw my boyfriend's lower arms, wrists, and then hands spread apart on either side of Kim 2's ass as he bucked into her so hard she screamed.

In and out my boyfriend went, and Kim 2's screams got louder and more thunderous, like something great was swelling inside of her and this was the preamble of what was to come.

She wrapped her hands up around my legs to hold herself in place and leverage her weight, and I felt her push back into his dick.

"Fuck this pussy. Fuck it hard!" she directed him with such force, it was nearly demonic.

Ronald looked down at me with no expression and bucked hard and hard and hard and hard at her ass, and she stayed right in position.

"Yes, give me that good dick. You know how I like it," she let out in breathy syllables.

Clouds parted in my mind and opened, and the significance of those words would forever haunt me.

But Ronald kept bucking and my roommate held tighter to my legs, and soon her nails were digging into my flesh like razor blades.

"Kim! Kim!" Ronald cried, flushing deeply. He was calling my name. Twice each time. Two times. Two. "Kim! Kim!"

I looked at Kim 2 and she was looking at me too. Her Asian eyes pierced through me.

"Ronald," she called, staring at me. "Cum inside of me right now. I want to feel it again. Let me feel it."

He bucked and shook the entire bed again and again, and soon the red left his body.

Chapter 6

I woke up on the couch in my apartment unsure if I'd dreamed of Ronald's birthday wish with Kim 2 that night at his place or had actually relived it. I had to recall my entire day beginning with Dr. Davis's office and then continuing with Paul and Easter and Chief Elliot in my office, the black cabbie, and King in platinum rolling beside me to remember where I really was. And it wasn't actually an upgrade when I did remember. Nearly fired? Everything but accused of overusing my pain medication by a doctor who really wanted to get into my pants? A mess. I wanted to go back to sleep for a really long time, even if it meant seeing Kim 2 and Ronald fuck raw right in front of me. Maybe I could try to change some things the second time around.

My cell phone started rattling on the coffee table, so I rolled over, taking my eyes from the ceiling, and saw from the direction of the light coming in the window that a lot of time had passed since I'd knocked out.

I reached for the phone and looked hard at the empty bottle of Jameson beside it. On the floor, the glass I'd been drinking out of had been shattered to diamond pebbles.

I wondered if maybe the guy downstairs had been playing his loud music again while I was sleeping and it had caused the glass to fall off the table. Maybe the bottle had fallen too and that was why it was empty. I'd only had two glasses. No way I drank that much. But how did the bottle get back onto the table? I looked at the floor. Where was the liquor? Maybe I'd gotten up in the middle of my nap and cleaned it up and placed the bottle back on the table. I tried to remember these events, but they were fuzzy. I'd call the apartment manager in the morning to complain about the guy downstairs. He'd led to the demise of so many of my glasses, I needed to send him an invoice.

The phone rattled again before I could open it to see that there were three text messages from Tamika:

MIKMIK (1:32 p.m.): Hey, KK. Miles will be a little late getting out of practice today, so no rush. Like 4:00pm will work. I know that time sucks for you, but thanks for agreeing to help me out . . . and spend time with your godson!

MIKMIK (3:37 p.m.): I tried to call you twice. I called your office and your secretary said you were out for the day. Guess you're on the subway headed to Brooklyn now. I'm about to go into the fashion show. They're taking our phones. I'll call you when I get out. Make sure Miles doesn't eat too much. And no fried rice from that greasy-ass Chinese spot on the corner. Thanks again.

MIKMIK (3:40 p.m.): OK. Last message . . . I promise. I know you hate it when I send these long-ass texts. But don't let Miles go to that park across the street from the community center today. There was a shooting out there last night and you know how things have been going with those gangs on the basketball courts. I know there will be retaliation. Don't want my little prince caught up in their bullshit. OK . . . that's all. Walking into the show now. BABUY!

I looked at the texts and tried to recall what she was talking about. Pick up Miles? I hadn't agreed to that. The last time I saw her we'd been at Damaged Goods and I walked out because she'd pissed me off. Maybe she thought she was texting Leah. I read through the messages again and saw that she was addressing KK, so that wasn't it. And I knew she wasn't asking Kent to pick Miles up from fencing. Pick Miles up from fencing? We'd talked at the bar about me spending more time with Miles. I remembered something about a fashion show. Tamika's walking out of Damaged Goods with me, insisting she help me into a cab. But I told her I was fine. She'd walked me out? I agreed to pick up Miles? Was it Thursday already? Had I agreed to Thursday? I read the messages again and remembered the conversation outside of Damaged Goods.

"Shit!" I jumped up ready to act, but my foot landed in the pile of broken glass and I screamed "Shit!" again. I hopped away from the table and balanced on my left foot, so I could pull the other one up and inspect the damage. Luckily, there was just pain, but no glass or cuts.

By the time I slid on my shoes and hopped to the elevator and down into a cab, it was already four o'clock. It would be at least thirty minutes before I was even in Brooklyn fighting against traffic and red lights. Miles would probably know to wait for me that long, so I sat back and looked at the clock on the dashboard, counting down seconds and saying to myself that he would know what to do. He had to.

At four fifteen the cab was being held up at a red light three blocks from the bridge and I was thinking that taking the train would've been a better idea. I started counting minutes again to relax, and I swear, like, ten passed at that one light. We were at the mouth of the bridge into Brooklyn at four thirty, and I was trying to give the cabbie directions to get there sooner. Times like that I wished Tamika wasn't so strict and had let Miles get a cell phone. But each year since he was seven, when I'd tried to get him one for Christmas, she'd say, "I didn't have a phone and I survived Harlem. He doesn't need a phone to survive Brooklyn." Good point then. But terribly inconvenient now.

At 4:45 I tried calling Leah to see if she could get Miles, but she didn't answer, and then I remembered that she'd gone to Atlantic City with her girlfriend.

"Come on, you can go faster," I said to the driver when we were three blocks away and it was five o'clock.

"It's rush hour," he said in his thick African accent. "We get there fast, mizz."

I opened the window and poked my head out of the moving car like that would somehow send telepathic signals to Miles letting him know I was almost there and to wait for me before he decided to walk home on his own or do whatever kids did when someone was over an hour late to pick them up—it was 5:05. I could never forgive myself if anything happened . . . not to mention Tamika would kill me.

I looked up at the sky. Clouds were swirling, and even though it was late May, a kind of winter darkness was settling in overhead. Maybe a storm was coming.

I started shaking and counted the blocks again and realized we hadn't moved.

"I have to get there!" I said to the cabbie, but he didn't even nod. It was like he couldn't hear me. "I am in a rush! Drive!" My back started aching and I had a sick feeling in my gut, and that's when I heard that familiar, unmistakable sound that echoes in the heart of anyone who's ever lived in a place where violence is expected: a gunshot.

"Miles!" I'd screamed this three times before I realized I was out of that cab and running toward the community center. "Miles!"

There was an eerie silence everywhere. The clouds were thickening, and I knew instinctively that in minutes a mother would be crying, kneeling down over her son's body on the sidewalk or street corner, begging anyone to explain what happened.

"Miles!" The bottom of my foot was stinging from what I would later realize was a needle-sized shard of glass I hadn't seen during my quick inspection at the apartment, but I kept running. The cabbie was on foot behind me, but I kept running and screaming like I knew that bullet had Miles's name on it.

"Miles!" I ran to the steps of the community center where he always waited after his practices, and it was empty. No one was there. Not a soul. Just a balled-up Bon Ton potato chip bag.

The shaking got worse. My back was fresh beef being pounded by a mallet.

I looked at each step twice. Maybe I was missing something. He had to be there.

Then I heard the sirens and the screaming. I turned to see a crowd huddled in the middle of the basketball court in the park across the street.

"Miles!" I was about to run over to the park when the cabbie jumped in front of me.

"You pay!" he screamed, holding an empty hand out to me. "You pay now or I call the police!"

"I can't! Miles! He's across the street in the park!" I pointed and tried to get around him, but even though he was shorter and slimmer than me, he stopped me.

"You pay now!" he demanded. "You drunk! You drunk! I smell!"

"You don't understand! He's over there!" I pointed, trying to break loose.

"Hurry and pay. I leave cab!"

Realizing there was no way he was letting me go, I opened my purse to hand him my entire wallet so I could run across the street, and that's when I saw Tamika's name on the screen of my phone.

"Mika!" I screamed, answering the call. "Mika!"

"Kim?" Tamika said too calmly.

"It's Miles! He's—" As if she could see me through the phone, I pointed to the scene in the park, where it looked like the crowd was dispersing.

"What is it?" Tamika asked.

"I was late," I said. "Late and—"

"I know you're late. I just spoke to Miles."

"What?" I looked over the cabbie at the crowd.

"He went home with crazy Yolanda and her sons. She was kind enough to take him when you were late," Tamika said, her voice as cold as the cabbie's accusing eyes.

"But I was . . . I didn't know I was supposed to get him," I tried to explain.

Tamika laughed but not happily. "You know, Kim, I am getting tired of this. I ask you to do one thing, and you can't even do it."

"I had a bad day. There is so much going on," I said.

"Well, I'm having a bad day, too," Tamika replied. "You know why?"

"Why?"

"Because someone left my son waiting outside on a street where I specifically told her I didn't want him hanging out."

"But Dr. Davis and then Paul—there's been so much today," I said. "I just forgot, I guess."

"You forgot about my son?" There was that angry laugh again. "Look, Kim, I don't know what the fuck is up with you, but you need to get right because you're fucking up. And I don't want to be a part of it."

Tamika hung up and I was left listening to a dial tone.

"Hurry and pay. I leave cab!" the cabbie demanded again.

I pulled two twenties from my purse and handed them to him. "Take it," I said.

When he walked away, looking back a few times to give me dirty looks, I saw two women who had been in the crowd in the park walking out.

"What was going on there?" I asked them.

"Some dumb motherfucker playing with a gun. Nearly shot himself," one said.

"Fucking shame. Can't a day go by in the hood without this shit," the other added. "At least ain't nobody get hurt."

My whole spirit was about dead. I was unprotected. Like a storm had come and gone and left me wet in the rain. Something in me sank down really low and hurt me so bad I actually felt the pain in my heart. Thank God nothing had happened to Miles. But standing there outside the fencing club, I was forced to really stare at what was happening to me. How could I forget that I was supposed to pick him up? Why was Tamika angry at me? Why was everyone so against anything that I wanted to do?

I was done with riding in cabs and talking to cabbies and talking to just about anyone at that moment, and so I just started walking. I put my one sad foot out in front of my other, aching foot and took little steps, like a baby who was just learning to walk and trying to figure out how not to fall down. I was so numb, I couldn't even feel my back. To press my toes hard and deliberately into the ground was about the only way I could know I was still standing and maybe headed somewhere. But where?

One foot. One aching foot. Three steps and then four. Soon I was on the corner looking up at the sky witnessing the twilight. Even in my sadness there was something beautiful and familiar about it. Everything in the world above me was in its place. Controlled by some silent organization that hadn't ever failed. Hadn't ever gotten sidetracked or derailed. Focused. Resilient. Even in Brooklyn the sun, moon, and stars were at work.

"Get your shit together," I said to myself, turning the corner and looking out at the world before me. The sidewalk went straight forward in a path that was cracked and crumbling in places.

A sound, something that echoed like bass booming from speakers, caught my ears, and I looked up from my path on the sidewalk.

There, hanging right in front of me, was a black sign with honey-colored neon letters flashing DAMAGED GOODS. The name flashed slowly like the signs on those old-timers' jazz lounges on Lenox Avenue where Kent and I used to find our father passed out.

"Jameson. Double," I requested, finding myself on a bar stool with my wallet in my hand.

The same bartender who'd been on duty the night before was behind the bar. She smiled at me with some familiarity and went to pour the drink but then turned back, confused.

"What you want with it, Queen?" she asked in a cliché Brooklyn Puerto Rican accent that was more Rosie Perez than . . . Rosie Perez.

I heard that she'd called me Queen, but didn't think anything of it until after I said I wanted it straight up and she responded, "Any ice, Queen?" She said it more like a name than the common way brothers in New York addressed women they respected.

"Yes. Sure," I answered. As she poured my Jameson, I looked around the grungy bar for signs of life. The music was bumping, and it was dark and ready for the coming night crowd, but save three or four old men who were obviously locals playing pool toward the back, it was empty.

"Here you go," the bartender said, setting my drink down.

"Thank you." I placed my credit card on the bar.

"Tab?" She picked up the card.

"No," I answered, then changed my mind: "I mean, yes. Yes. Bad day. Horrible day for me."

"Right place then, Queen." She nodded and turned to the register right behind her.

"Hey, Iesha, right? Why do you keep calling me Queen?" I asked her back as two long-haired Puerto Rican women in tight black pants and pastel thick-bottomed stripper-style stilettos walked past me from the back of the club and waved at her.

"I'm sorry. I thought that was your name," she said, turning back to me. "Wasn't that what King called you last night?"

"King?" I repeated, trying to sound like I hardly knew who she was talking about, but when it was apparent she was on to my attempt at minimizing, I said, "Oh, yeah. That white guy I spoke to last night."

"Yeah, him," she said, and giggled with a little *you know damn well you remember him* in her voice.

Trying to seem nonchalant, I added, "Oh, I think he just meant it like the way all the brothers call women queen. You know?"

"No. I've never heard him say that to anyone before," she said confidently.

"Really?" I tried not to sound interested in the information, but the Jameson in my hand had me feeling unfastened or excited and I'd hardly had a sip.

A beautiful woman walked from the back of the club, and I saw that she had come from the kitchen.

"So, have you seen him? King?" I kicked the nonchalance up to ten, for my own benefit as well as Iesha's; I could rationalize that I was trying to shake off my blues by focusing on something other than my bad day. "Not that I care—just asking."

"Sure. I've seen him," she said curtly, and turned to walk from behind the bar without another word. She went to the back where the woman had walked out of the kitchen.

"Okay. Guess I shouldn't have asked," I said to myself before looking for solace in my glass of liquor and melting ice cubes. I hadn't started drinking or even smoking until I went to college, and for years the closest I got to hard liquor was Alizé and Hypnotiq. I liked the sweet stuff that went down easy. It made drinking seem fun. Feminine and silly. Not dark and piss-infested like the drunks I'd known growing up. I'd sip a little something and laugh with my girls or Ronald. Get a little nasty. Maybe even pass out, but still it felt innocent. When I got to law school, though, that soft, feminine liquor didn't do anything for me. There were too many headaches in the morning. Too many vomit fests over the toilet. I had to stop it, but I still wanted to drink something. Have a little sip to take the edge off after a late night studying. Or after dealing with my mother being found somewhere down and out and there was nothing I could do about it. That's when the liquor with men's names came into my life and I learned to love the purity of straight alcohol with no sweet lies. Jameson became my best friend. It had bite and nerve. Let you lose control but made you feel like you were in control.

"Hey, young blood," I heard one of the men near the pool tables say, and I looked over at the men crowding around.

In the middle of their circle of wrinkly brown skin, thick glasses, and old-school Kangols was one white face with a thin beard. It was King. It was like he appeared out of nowhere. I couldn't tell if he'd walked in when I wasn't looking or come out of the kitchen.

As the men chatted, laughing and slapping five, Iesha walked out of the kitchen and returned to the bar, where she went on working like we hadn't spoken.

I watched the scene at the pool table for a second and then started coaching myself about not appearing thirsty or too excited to see King, or like I'd come to the bar to see him, so I turned around. I told myself I wasn't interested in him. It was purely a product of circumstance. Desperation. I was in Brooklyn to pick up Miles, and after that went awry I needed a drink and I didn't want to wait until I got back to my place, so I stopped at the bar. Right? Then I wondered why I was explaining myself to myself. I took the last swig of my Jameson and sat the glass down hard on the bar to signal for another.

"Somebody said you were looking for a King." This was heard over my shoulders. The smooth baritone voice fell on the rear of my left ear with a tickle that swam down my back and made me squirm and jump a little.

"Oh, I'm sorry," he said, sliding onto the stool beside me. "I didn't mean to scare you."

"I'm not scared," I said with more determination than needed.

He noted it, too. "Well, I ain't never scared either," he responded in equal register.

After a few chuckles we let an expectant silence sit between us.

"I—" I started, but he opened with the same word and we laughed again at the butting of heads. That time it was more familiar. Not like we'd known each other for years, but like we'd been checking each other out. I knew my embarrassment showed in my eyes, so I looked away. But I could still feel him beside me, and that made me more excited. His presence felt overwhelming. Like a man in charge. I blamed it on the new double, which I'd nearly finished.

"You go first," he said.

I was about to tell him about seeing him in the Bentley in Manhattan, but I opted against it. I didn't want to seem too pressed, like I was looking for him, and lead him into anything.

"I was going to say that I didn't know you worked here," I said, looking back at him smoothing his beard slowly.

"I don't work here," he said.

"But you were in the kitchen, right?"

"Oh. That." He looked away. "I just help out sometimes."

"Oh. Well, what do you do?" I asked, and felt a foot in my mouth. While asking those kinds of questions was acceptable in most circles I moved in, I knew there, in Damaged Goods, it probably seemed more like sizing someone up or being nosy. And what did it matter anyway?

"I do many different things," he said so coolly that if my eyes were closed I might've thought he was a brother. He wrapped his arm around the back of his head to tend to an itch, and there, on the inside of his biceps, was the Black Power fist tattooed in red ink.

"I'm sorry. I didn't mean to be all up in your business. I was just making small talk, I guess."

"No hesitation," he responded. "I get it." He grinned.

"What? You get what?" I smiled back and felt my eyes flirting, and I didn't look away this time.

"You're sizing me up," he said, and we laughed again.

"No! I'm not!"

"It's cool. That's how women like you do." His eyes were flirting then.

"Women like me?"

"Sisters. Black women."

"Ohhh! Now I see. You're claiming you know something about black women? About sisters?" I took a full sip of my drink, leaving the ice cubes lonely in the glass again. Without even asking, Iesha came over quickly to pour another glass.

"I know a lot about black women. Probably more than you." He nodded at Iesha, and she winked back.

"Humm," I let out. "How is that?"

"How do you think?"

"So, you're one of those white men who dates black women?"

"Exclusively."

I rolled my eyes the way black women do when white men make declarations like that. It brought up cellular memories of rape on plantations, images of white men prodding the wide hips and bouncy buttocks of Sara Baartman, "the Hottentot Venus," on display in London, of white men sleeping with black women to "see what it's like," anger at a widely held belief that black women were more sexually driven and promiscuous than any other women on the planet, dirty, dick-sucking bitches . . . and a bunch of stuff our fathers whispered in our ears about why we "bet not eva bring no white boy home!"

"Guess you're one of those 'once you go black, you never go back' folks," I said cynically.

"Not exactly. More like, I ain't go no other way. I've only dated black women. It's what I like." He leaned toward me, and the tickling that was still playing at my ear shot down my back and split my ass cheeks. "And I like what I like."

Somehow that new double got back into my hands and I downed it like it was water. I wanted something stiff inside of me. My ass cheeks spread out on the stool, and I felt King look before placing his hand on the small, innocent, but suggestive space between my back and my buttocks.

"Let's get Queen some water," he said to Iesha.

"Water?" I looked at him. "What, you think I'm drunk?"

"No. Not at all, Queen. I just want to keep you sober."

"Why?"

"Because I'm about to beat your ass back there on one of those pool tables," he said, pointing to the table the old-timers had abandoned.

"Now, that might be a little hard for you to do. I'm not bragging, but my brother and I were the reigning champions of the Harlem Kids Pool Tournament for five years in a row. You don't want none of this!" the Jameson in me said.

The cute guy Monique had hooked up with the night before walked into the bar and up to us with his hands in his pockets and a slight look of worry on his face.

"Yo, let me holler at you," he said stiffly, showing his deep dimples though he wasn't smiling at all.

King didn't turn around. He rolled his lower lip into his mouth and held it with his teeth.

There was a palpable tension between the two men and I tried to cut it with a smile at the guy, but he kept his eyes on King's back.

"I got that," he added vaguely. "Holler at me."

"Holler at Truth," King answered tersely. "I ain't on."

"Come on, my nigga. Ain't shit. I got it." He reached out to put his hand on King's shoulder but stopped himself. "Come on, yo. Don't be like—"

King turned swiftly. "D-Black, I just told you to holler at Truth. You don't want this."

An hour and two more doubles later, I was at the pool table, losing and laughing. Martini glasses filled with green potion and red cherries and platters of fried shrimp were floating around a bar that was nearly packed. Women in Timberland boots and men with gold grills and fresh Caesar cuts lined the bar. Most people who walked in looked over at King and me, and some waved or nodded at King, but no one really came over except the waitress, who kept our drinks filled and whispered in King's ear for responses he gave with a pointed finger and serious tone.

"You're a pretty popular guy for someone who doesn't work here," I said as King set up a shot.

"You're a pretty horrible pool player for someone who was champion of the pool association," he retorted, leaning against the table for a masterful play that made it clear he was no stranger to backroom pool.

"I bluffed," I admitted, smiling.

"I figured."

We hadn't really shared much in the way of revealing conversation in the hours we'd been chatting. It was more small talk and stares along body parts. I didn't mind the surface chitchat though. It was nice not to be known. He never asked my name again or what I did. And that cut me away from my life for a little while. It also stopped me from thinking much of anything about him beyond what I saw.

I paced the table to see if I had a shot, but the only angle I could find would require that I jump up on the green felt.

"Let me help you," King advised, seeing my trouble. He took my hand and pulled me to the far left corner of the table. "You see that?" He stood behind me so close and whispered in my ear. "Right up the middle. Set up just for you."

"Yeah," I said, all dreamy.

"Bend over," he commanded, and immediately my brain went to Monique's Flower Press practice with Brother to the Night. Just then I wanted to know what the move was and imagined King in it. I exhaled before I realized that I'd already assumed the appointed position and King was standing behind me with his hands gripping my waist. "Arch your back."

"What?" I asked, pulling myself out of my daze. "Why do I need to do that? This is—"

"Just do it," King ordered, his tone sharp. "You'll see."

"Okay," I said, dipping into the green with the stick in my hand.

"Now hold that thing close to you."

Somehow King was standing straight now, but it sounded like his lips were on my ear and his baritone caressed me from lobe to nipple. The cotton crotch in my panties was damp against my skin. I blamed the Jameson and decided I'd need to leave in a bit.

When the stick hit the ball, it rolled into the hole like water down a drain. I almost jumped up to give King five but tried to keep my cool.

"Good job," he said, smacking my ass.

I jumped to turn and ask him what he thought he was doing touching me in that way, but the way he stepped back with his feet apart and his chest forward, I felt like maybe it was okay.

"So, what are we playing for?" he asked.

"I don't gamble."

"That's too bad. I have the grand prize if you want it," he said.

"You're a great flirt, but I'm not here for all of that. I just needed to unwind. Been having the worst week ever. Work. Family. Drama—"

King cut me off: "I'm not your man, Queen. I'm not here to hear about your bad times. I want to make good times with you."

"Why?" I asked, implying a clear distinction between me and the women who were clearly waiting on standby at the bar, watching us play.

"I like your style. Your attitude. Ain't no other bitch in here got shit on you, Queen," he said, nodding toward the gawking lineup. "Bad thing is, you don't know it. Good thing is, I'm going to show you."

I laughed nervously before saying, "I don't need you to show me anything. I know I'm beautiful."

"Do you? Do you really?" he asked, and I couldn't say anything. He walked around the table for his shot. " 'Cause I'm looking at you and I know some nigga got you fucked up. And I'm not having that. You know, the best thing about me and you—about the difference in your black skin and my white skin? I can see your beauty more than you ever will. I can tell you everything about it. Because I watch it. Because I don't have it."

I was rendered speechless. I watched him move, his white skin glowing softly under the pool-table lights.

"So you want to help me see my beauty?" I asked, as if it was impossible.

"If you let me."

Two guys I hadn't seen before walked into the bar, and all eyes except King's transferred to them. One of the women at the bar whispered to the woman beside her, who turned to get a look before peeking back at King and returning a whisper.

The men, one as big as Kent and the other a little shorter but just as wide, said something to Iesha and then headed toward King.

King put his stick down and told me to wait for a second.

He stopped them just feet from the table, where I could hear dribbles of words and see that their conversation was less than friendly.

I tried to play cool but stepped a little and closer to them so I could get some words.

"Tell that nigga what I said," King directed. "Ain't shit matter but that. Truth know."

"Man, fuck. Nigga D-Black ain't about to let that shit ride," one of the guys said.

"Trim that fat, then," King said, and their voices went so low as I struggled to hear.

I was practically in the huddle with them when King turned to me.

"Sweetheart, can you wait here for me for a minute?" he asked. "I got some folks outside I need to holler at."

"Oh, that's fine," I said. "I'll practice my new shot."

"Aigght."

When King and the two guys walked out I was left standing before the stares of the women at the bar. If my Harlem upbringing hadn't made me bulletproof against eye shoots, I might've taken some serious hits, but I shrugged and reminded myself that I was on their turf down in Brooklyn. ADA or not, Brooklyn girls didn't play, and I didn't want them to think I was there for a fight.

I broke the standoff by pretending to look for something in my purse. I pulled out my cell phone to see that I'd missed three back-to-back calls from Kent and a text asking me to call him back ASAP. I knew he was calling about his alleged fiancée and I didn't feel like lumping his drama onto my own, so I responded with a short text telling him I was stressed and I'd call him back later.

As soon as my response went through, the phone rang again with Kent's name on the screen. I sent him to voice mail, but he called right back.

"What do you want?" I answered harshly, pressing my ear to

the receiver. "I told you I'm busy. I don't have time to hear about your Latin prostitute, Kent."

"It's about Mommy," he said gravely. "I need you to get home. To come home right now."

"What? What is it?" I asked, my heart jumping into speed with scenarios of my mother being found dead or near dead. Because that was always a thought. Always the possibility. Just waiting for a conclusion. "I'm out, you know, so if it's not anything really bad, just tell me."

"Kim, we need you to come home."

"I'm having a fucked-up day. I can't do this here," I blurted out, feeling my heart swell in the mystery of worry. Right then, I wished I wasn't in the strange bar with the strange man, doing whatever I was doing. "If she's dead—if that's it, then—"

"She ain't dead," Kent said. "But she been here. Daddy has proof."

"She's been there? Mommy's been there?"

"Yes. Come home."

When I exited Damaged Goods, I nearly walked right past the silver Bentley. My gut in knots as it usually was where my mother was concerned, I saw the car but also didn't see it, or maybe I didn't care that I was seeing it. I just needed to get home. To my real home. I was relieved to know my mother wasn't dead, but the paradox was that she still wasn't alive. She was the shadow she'd always been. Always would be. What I chased. What I ignored. What I couldn't hold.

Lost in my thoughts, I found myself standing in the street right in front of the Bentley. I reached out to hail one of the dollar taxis waiting at the corner.

"Queen! Where you going?"

I turned as if it was a shock to find anyone else outside in the world as I was rushing to another disappointment.

When I answered him, King was opening the back door of the Bentley to get out. Just before he closed the door, I got a glimpse of the guy with the dimples sitting in the car. In the few seconds it took for King to get on his feet and close the door, I read the panic on the guy's face.

"I have to go," I explained to King.

"But I thought we were finishing our game," he said.

"I'm sorry, it's an emergency."

He stepped closer to me and searched my face.

"You need anything?" he asked, the way Kent or Tyree would, and I knew instantly that by "anything" he meant a wide range of things.

"No. It's nothing like that. It's just my mother," I let out. "It's family. That kind of thing."

"I understand. You need a ride? I can get you anywhere you—"

"No. It's fine. I can get home."

"You know I got you," King said, wiping a tear I couldn't keep in my eyes.

"It's fine. Really. Nothing new."

He pulled me out into the street, and I swear he hardly lifted his hand before a dingy dollar cab stopped right where we were standing.

He opened the back door to let me in and requested my cell phone so he could add his number.

"You call me if you need anything," he said firmly in a way that somehow made me feel protected. "Doesn't matter what it is. How late it is. You understand me, Queen?"

"Yes. I do," I said, getting into the cab.

He shared words with the driver about making sure I got to where I was going safely and closed the door. As we pulled away, I watched him out the window.

Behind him, the doors of the Bentley opened, and the two men who'd walked into the bar got out.

Chapter 7

It was late by the time I made it up to Harlem. I found Kent and my father in the backyard in the dark. My father was sitting on the ground beside the rusty metal doors closed over the cellar. He had a drill in his hand. Kent was standing over him holding a flashlight, complaining that my father should let him work the drill and take the flashlight.

"What are you guys doing back here?" I asked.

"Hey, babygirl," my father said, looking up at me. "Your brother tell you your ma been here?" Both of my parents were first-generation New Yorkers whose parents left the Deep South looking for whatever work would take them off plantations that still meant a death sentence for blacks years after slavery ended. My father's parents were from Mississippi, and while they made a home in Harlem, they moved onto a street that primarily housed people from their hometown, so they still lived and spoke in old ways and passed that down to my father. Kent and I used to joke that in one sentence my father could switch from New York City slick to country-boy genteel.

"Yes, Daddy. That's why I'm here," I answered him, getting down on my knees to kiss him on the cheek as I'd been trained to do.

"Guess I shouldn't have asked that. You don't come uptown and see about your pa no way. Too busy I know," he complained, looking at me through blue eyes that had once been brown, pushed into early cataracts due to his drinking. His sobriety plan had never included his drinking. His standard nightly routine since he'd returned home to us without our mother was stopping at the liquor store on the corner to buy a fifth of whatever was cheapest and fall asleep in bed in his work clothes with his bottle wrapped in a brown paper bag on the nightstand. Some nights he'd sob aloud and call my mother's name. That was when Kent would sneak out and come back with Baggies and vials and cash and candy stashed in his pockets.

"Daddy, don't start with that, please," I begged. "I can't today. I really can't."

He shrugged and went back to drilling.

"So, what happened?" I asked. "How do y'all know she's been here?"

"Daddy set a trap," Kent answered, gliding the light over a sand walkway leading from the gate on the side of the brownstone to the cellar doors.

"Duke and Mrs. Amelia on the corner said they saw her over here a month ago. Then Lil Richard, the one work over in the auto body, said he saw her walking up the driveway a week ago," my father explained, pulling a screw out of the door.

"A week ago? But no one told me," I said. "Why didn't anyone tell me?"

"I wanted to tell you," Kent said, "but Dad said to wait."

"I didn't want you to get worked up. Get your hopes up about your ma," my father replied. "You know how you get. Got that job. Need to focus."

"How I get?"

Kent and my father looked at each other.

"I just figured it'd be better if we knew something before we went and broadcast it, getting folks upset," he went on. "So I set these traps. Let me know if she's really been around here."

"The sand was my idea," Kent divulged, widening his eyes at my father.

"But these could be anyone's footprints." I pointed to the trail that had two sets of prints—mine and a much smaller pair.

"Ain't nobody coming back here," my father said. "And, plus, I got me some proof." He pulled another screw from the door and stood to let Kent pull the door off the hinges. He pointed down the steps.

"What?" I looked into the darkness of the cellar, where seven chipped concrete steps that I'd fallen down too many times as a child led to a storm door that had a trick lock only Kent, our parents, and I knew how to open. "She's been down there?"

My father and Kent looked toward the darkness.

I didn't wait for another word. I descended as if I didn't know the harm that could come with one misstep. Something like an anvil was sitting on top of my heart. And although both Kent and Daddy said my mother wasn't in that basement, there was no stopping my brain from constructing the image of her sitting in the middle of the closet of our stored memories, holding her hands out to me, smiling, asking me all about my bad day.

I undid the lock with three shakes and a turn to the left, and a turn to the right, then I gave the door a kick. I could feel Kent right behind me just as he'd always been when we were younger in these situations involving our mother. Quickly, we were ten again. I looked at him when I put my hand on the light switch.

"It's okay," he said. "It's fine."

The light illuminated a space that hadn't changed ever. Old cribs and decorations. Cash registers and boxes of hangers from the store my grandparents once owned on St. Nicholas. A box of Kent's old basketball trophies. The dusty Barbie Dreamhouse that had made its way from my bedroom floor to the backyard to the basement. Little islands of stories from everyone's past.

"It's in the corner over there by that old mannequin from your granpap's store," my father said, coming into the basement behind Kent. "My proof."

I looked over to the withering white woman with the Kewpie-doll blue eyes and a permanent smile. There was an unraveled blanket and scraps of paper on the floor at her arched feet.

"Been unusually cold these last few weeks," my father said as I went over to the mess of out-of-place things. "I think she been down here resting."

I bent down and picked up the blanket. It was a ripple pattern crocheted in an ugly purple and black I always complained about. The anvil sank down.

"That's your old blanket," Kent said.

I nodded.

"The one from your bed."

"It's been down here in a box since you left for college. Thing got mildew and whatever else on it," my father said. "Think I'll wash it. Put it back down here with some canned food. Leave it by the steps where I put her old red sweatshirt she took from down here last spring."

"The one Mika saw her in on Jamaica Ave.," I reminded him, knowing he liked it when he could confirm that he'd had some kind of contact with my mother.

He went on, pretending he was unaffected. "Maybe I could put a refrigerator down here for her. Not one of those big ones. A little one," he said.

"That's a great idea. Because then you could put a note on it telling her to knock on the front door?" Kent joked in a way that I'm sure our father found inappropriate, but it was what any other family who hadn't been through what we'd been through together would ask. Why wouldn't my mother just knock on the front door and come inside for a warm bed and a hot meal?

"She don't want us to see her. You know that, boy," my father said. "Not the way she is. Not until she's ready."

I looked down at what I'd thought were scraps of paper but that I could now see were little cut out squares from pictures. I handed the smelly blanket to my father.

"What's this?" I asked.

Kent rushed over to help me pick up the squares.

One by one, I looked at the faces on the squares. Me. Me. Me. All of the faces in the little squares were of me. Me at seven with pigtails. Me at three still holding a bottle. Me at six crying because I didn't want to go to church on Easter Sunday.

"Where'd these come from?" I asked. "How'd they get down here?"

My father walked over and looked at the pictures in my hand. "I thought you'd remember," he said.

"What?"

"Your ma was supposed to throw those out. You don't remember?"

"No. What happened?"

"You took those pictures out of her photo album and cut them up. Said you had some project for school and needed pictures of yourself from every age," my father said, laughing. "Think it was right before you went to high school." His voice dropped. "Right before we left. You really don't remember?"

I shook my head no, and tears rolling down my cheeks sprinkled my face in the pictures.

"Your ma called up to that school to see what the project was supposed to be about, and they told her you was supposed to have pictures of both you and your ma—some Mother's Day art show. And y'all had a big fight about these pictures. She said she didn't have copies, no film. Nothing. No way of replacing them. You got all mad and tried to stomp off with the little cutouts of your face. Said they was pictures of you and you could do what you wanted with them. Your ma ain't like that. She jumped right on you. I guess she was about to give you some licks. But you about fought her back. Pushed her off of you and you called her a—" He paused. "Said you was embarrassed she was your mother. It was the first time you said it to her face, and it really hurt her. I know it. Next day y'all wasn't speaking. You'd dropped out of the art show and your ma was set on throwing those little squares of your face away to teach you a lesson. Guess she kept them." My father took the square of me crying before Easter Mass and laughed. "I remember this day. Lord, you showed your behind so bad, saying you didn't want to go to church. I made you put on this here dress, and we was about to go out the door. Then your ma stopped and said maybe we shouldn't go if you didn't want to go. And we didn't."

"We didn't?" I looked at him. "What do you mean? I remember that. We went to church that day. It was Easter. I had on that dress." I pointed at the picture.

"No. It was Easter and your ma asked you what you wanted to do since you didn't want to go to church," my father said. "Ice cream. You wanted to go to get some ice cream and sit in Riverside Park. And that's what we did. Pretty day. We ain't take no pictures of that though. You remember that, Kent?"

Kent nodded and handed me the pictures he'd collected.

Though there were only ten or twelve squares, the images in my hands felt like hundreds of memories. And I wondered what my mother thought when she saw them. Why she'd looked at them and if she ever thought of what I looked like now. If she cared. My heart started crumbling under the weight of the anvil, and I reached out for Kent to catch me, to keep me from falling to pieces with it.

"It's okay, Kiki Mimi," he said when I fell into his arms. "It's going to be okay. You know that. Right?"

I sucked in my tears and laid my head on my baby brother's shoulder. I agreed that everything would soon be all right, but none of us really knew that it would be and none of us really knew what "right" meant. The idea was just comfort. Just a word that signified an end coming someday.

In the house, my father explained that he was removing the storm doors because he thought they were probably too heavy for my mother to hold up when she was coming in and out of the basement and he didn't want one to fall on her and knock her down the stairs. He said it so passively, like he was simply making sure to shovel a sidewalk after a snowstorm to ensure his wife didn't fall on her way into the house with groceries or laundry and not to create shelter for a drug-addicted wife he'd maybe seen a handful of times in fifteen years.

Sometimes I wanted to just scream in his ear that she was gone and never coming back to him, not the way she was, but it wouldn't be any use for a man like him. Loving my mother was all he knew. They got together at a time when men married the first girl they loved, made a home for her, gave her babies, came home every night—no matter what they did in the street—and prayed to die first to leave everything he had—even in death—to her. I knew my father felt he'd failed at most of that. And for men like him, even ones who got fucked up using drugs, it made him feel like less of a man. His only chance at redemption was that she was still out there. It would break his heart more to give up on the idea that she'd come back to him.

Daddy picked up his fifth in the brown paper bag and kissed me on the cheek good night.

"Work in the morning," he said, heading to the staircase.

"Good night, Daddy," Kent and I said.

"You know, Kiki," my father said, turning to look at me from the third step, and it was rare because he never said a thing else to us after he'd said good night and mentioned that there was "work in the morning" and also because I'd maybe heard him call me Kiki three times in my life, "I've always been sorry you had to grow up without your ma. You done a good job making yourself what you are, but I just know . . . I know you always been missing and needing her. I'm sorry to you for that."

Daddy finished his thoughts and started climbing the steps

again. Kent and I didn't say anything. He almost never opened up to us like that, and when he did we both knew not to say too much afterward. A thank-you would just embarrass him. He needed the moment to come and go.

"Thought you were going out," I said to Kent when we heard Daddy's bedroom door close.

Kent had gone into the kitchen and come out with two Heinekens.

"Why you say that?" he asked.

"Because you always do . . . you know, when something happens with Mommy."

"Can't. Got too much on my mind." Kent sat down at the table and placed both beers in front of himself.

"Oh, no beer for me?" I asked.

"I don't think you need any beer," he said. "I've been smelling liquor on you since we were in the backyard. Where were you when I called you?"

"Some bar in Brooklyn," I confessed. "A place Tamika and her girls took me to."

"You know you can't be fucking with those hood rats in BK, right? Where'd you go?" He clipped the top off one of the Heinekens.

"Damaged Goods."

"DG? The fuck you doing in there?" Kent looked at me strangely.

"It's a cool spot."

"Come on, Kim. You know better. I don't even fuck with Brooklyn niggas, and I know about that spot. What the fuck were y'all there for?"

"Five-dollar apple martinis and fried shrimp. And it wasn't so bad. I went there today to relax a little bit. Take my mind off of some stuff happening at work," I explained, and there was no way I was going to tell Kent about Paul sending me home. We'd be sitting up debating it for the rest of the night.

"Stay outta there," Kent said after taking a long, mannish gulp of his beer. "Ain't shit for you in there."

"Jesus, Kent. You make it sound like I'm still sixteen and you can forbid me from dating that guy on the football team again."

"Nigga was a thug."

"He's a congressman now," I said.

"Exactly. And he's still a thug." Kent finished his beer and moved on to the next.

"A married thug. With two kids," I quipped, laughing. "And I'm still freaking single. Listening to you."

"So, you don't need that nigga. You don't need no niggas. Just one nigga . . . your bro. And I need you."

"Here we go again," I said. "You can stop your speech right now, because I'm not trying to meet your Brazilian girlfriend, and I damn sure am not helping you bring her into the country. So let it go."

"I already have," Kent replied unexpectedly.

"Like days ago you were madly in love. Lydia was everything. What happened?"

"Man, fucking Keisha and shit." Kent sat back heatedly like he was back in high school and arguing with Keisha about smoking his weed.

I had to stop myself from laughing. I could tell by the quick anger in his eyes and his furrowed brow that he knew about the butch-lover gossip.

"I thought you two were done. Why do you care about Keisha?"

"Man, she out in them streets, Sis. Fucking up," he said. "I ain't want to say nothing, but I'll tell you, I think she playing for the other team. Got turned out and shit."

"No," I said, trying to sound surprised. "Not Keisha."

"Yeah, man. Shit's like a virus right about now. Mad bitches fucking bitches. Fuck niggas. Nobody want a nigga no more. Just get a nigga bitch."

"Right," I said, trying to make sense of Kent's puzzle of logic. I decided to point something out that was pretty clear, something most women had been wanting to ask men for a minute: "Why do you think that's happening?"

"Motherfucking gay indoctrination. Shit on television. Obama. Everywhere."

I let out my laugh then. I had to. "So what about before all of that? Why were women gay then?"

"Maybe they was bored. I don't know. And we ain't talking about all women. We talking about Keisha. My baby mama. Your niece's mother." He looked at me, and I promise a little tear was floating on the rim of his eye.

I pulled my laughter back in by biting the tip of my tongue. "Deep and contemplative Kent" was even more comical than "in-love Kent."

"I know what you're thinking," Kent went on. "It's me. That's why she riding plastic dicks. I fucked her up. Ain't never treat her right. Go on and say it." Kent looked at me.

"Okay. Yeah. You aren't the best choice of mate," I said with all of the attitude I could just for Keisha.

"I know! I know! I ain't shit. I need to get my shit together. I done fucked too many hoes on Keisha. And I lied about Brazil. I did fuck mad hoes in Brazil."

"Not a surprise."

"That's why I have to call this thing off with Lydia. Got to let her know I can't marry her," Kent said soberly. "I love Keisha and I want to get myself right for her."

I couldn't hold my laugh in anymore again. "Make-a-change Kent" was more funny than any other version. Like that time he decided to join me at Morgan State and tried to move into the dorm. Within a week he was selling weed out of his dorm room window and fucking half the senior class—that was his freshman year.

"What? Come on! Don't laugh at me," Kent said. "I'm being serious."

"Serious about what?" I asked. "I've heard this before. You get all upset about something Keisha did to get back at you for something you did, which usually involves a girl, and you promise to do right, and that works . . . right up until you meet the next girl. Then you sleep with her and it starts again."

"That's what I'm saying. I have a problem. A sex problem," Kent said. "I have an addiction. I'm a sex addict."

"I'm done," I announced, standing up and looking for my purse. "You've lost your mind."

"No, don't go." Kent stood too. "Don't. I'm serious. I have a problem. And I'm getting help."

"So, now you're Tiger Woods and that's why you can't keep your dick to yourself?"

"No," Kent said, stepping to me. "I'm the son of two addicts, and so I recognize that there's a strong chance I might have a problem, too."

"Where's my purse?" I tried to leave Kent in the kitchen to go into the living room, but he grabbed me and held me tight. "Let me go," I said, feeling tears welling up from nowhere. I didn't know what they were for.

"Stop it, Kim!" Kent ordered. "Listen to me."

"No! I'm going home."

"I'm getting help. And I want you to support me."

"Let me go!" I hollered.

"No." Kent kept his tight grip. "I need you."

"No. You need an excuse," I argued. "Mommy and Daddy have nothing to do with your fucking up. That's bullshit. And I'm tired of you saying that every time something is wrong in your life. So what they were addicts. That has nothing to do with us. I'm fine. I went to school. I'm successful. You chose what you are. You choose what you do every day."

"It ain't that simple and you know it," Kent barked back. "No I ain't about to put no pipe in my mouth or no needle in my arm, but I still chose my drug of choice. We both have."

"Fuck off, Kent," I said, peeling him off my arm by scratching the top of his hand with my nails.

"Fuck!" He flinched when I drew blood. "What the fuck is wrong with you?"

"I'm out!" I ran out of the kitchen and found my purse on the couch in the living room.

"Kiki!" Kent came out after me. "I need to talk to you."

"No! Don't touch me again!" I grabbed the purse and ran out of the house, down the steps and onto the street. Kent was screaming my name from the front porch, but I kept running. I had to get away from him and his excuses. I couldn't be party to the lies he told himself to make up for all of his "am nots." He always tried to do that to me. To pull me into his feelings and make them mine. There was nothing wrong with him or us or me. We were fine. We were what we wanted to be.

"Miss! Miss! You need a ride?"

In the street beside me were the bright lights from the dollar cab that had dropped me off.

"What?" I looked at the driver. "Why are you still here?" I hadn't told him to wait for me. He even refused to take my money when I got out.

"I take you home. Right? Make sure you safe," he said in an Arab accent.

I got into the car after looking behind me to discover that Kent had gone back into the house.

"Where you live?" the cabbie asked. "Where you go?"

"I don't know," I said, remembering King's orders when I got into the back of that cab in Brooklyn.

"Hello?" King answered the phone on the first ring.

I tried to answer but I was crying too hard. All I got out was "I need . . ." and then my voice went weak.

"It's you, Queen?" he asked.

"Yes."

"You all right?"

"No."

"You don't have to say anything else. Tell Baboo to bring you to the spot. Everything's going to be okay. I got you."

I cried most of the way from Harlem to Brooklyn. Laid my head against my purse on the back window and cried at the day, the long, long day. All of the losses. The pain coming back at me and how powerless I felt under it all.

I looked out into the street and imagined every shadow was my mother: hunched over, black, and alone with no home.

My worry ushered me into a deep sleep that wasn't broken until I felt the driver pulling me out of the car.

"Come on, lady. You wake up. We here. See? We here?"

I muttered something I was saying to Kent in my dream because the driver's words had become Kent's. But then he pushed me to open my eyes.

"You look. You see. See? Open your eyes. See! Please see!"

"Wha? What?" Though I could feel that I was standing then, I knew I was leaning over too. I could smell the cabbie's curry dinner. I opened my eyes one at a time and saw a concrete block and above it the familiar behemoth of a clock, aqua-colored, with Roman numerals.

"The Clocktower?" I slurred sleepily, lifting my head off the cabbie's shoulder. "Why am I here?"

"It's where he lives. His home."

"Who? Who lives here?"

Just then King came rushing out the front door with the two guys from the bar.

The guys took me from the driver and I nearly fell over into someone's arms.

"Thanks, Baboo," I heard someone say.

King came in close to look at me. He was wearing black slacks and a wifebeater that lay transparent over a maze of black tattoos on his chest.

King turned and the men holding me up under each arm followed him into the Clocktower Building.

"Everything okay, Mr. McDonnell?" the doorman asked, rushing to meet us at the elevator.

"Just fine, Frantz," King said. "In fact, I'll take it from here." He reached out to take me from the two guys, and I was scared I'd fall over on top of him, but when his arm went under my arm and around my back I felt more support than I had with two men. His muscles seemed to expand. His body was steady and planted. I let my whole weight fall to test him and closed my eyes again.

King helped me into the small glass elevator where the ding of the doors closing startled me, so I pressed my head into his chest.

"You okay?" he asked, looking down into my eyes with worry.

"I'm tired," I said. "Very tired."

The elevator doors opened, and King led me into a space that looked like an art gallery. There were some couches and chairs, a television, and tables scattered in different settings around a huge, open space, and on every wall there was a work of art that was big, colorful, and, no doubt, very, very expensive. But that wasn't what was stealing my vision, what had me wondering if I was still in the dollar cab and dreaming. It was the clocks. Four fourteen-foot clocks, one in the center of each wall, drawing my eyes to windows that let in a breathtaking 360-degree view of Brooklyn, the East River, Manhattan, and the Manhattan Bridge. I was in the Clock-tower, in DUMBO's most expensive apartment, the one that real estate tycoons had been bidding on for years until some private buyer outbid the likes of Jay-Z and Ralph Lauren. It had been a front-page real estate story in the *New York Times* for months.

"You live here?" I asked King.

"Most of the time," he said, leading me to the nearest couch. He made sure I was standing up on my own and quickly cleared the pillows from the couch by pitching them to the floor. On his back there was a huge black and gold jester's hat I could see through his wifebeater.

"Who are you?" I asked.

He stood and looked at me. "I'm your king," he proclaimed. "Any more questions?"

"No." I fell into King on purpose that time. I wanted to feel his lips against mine and taste his tongue in my mouth. To smell him.

My nose brushed against his as I slid his top lip into my mouth. He slid my bottom lip into his mouth, and we tasted each other's newness through bated breath, and everything in my past dissipated. And we weren't even touching.

King's mouth on mine set a hungry pace that promised my body so many things.

I sighed and let him take control.

I opened my eyes to watch him kiss. To see us kiss each other. The bright lights from the big city peeked in at us. We were shadows. Not black and white. Just hungry shadows.

My pussy quivered, and I reached for King's hand to put it there and let him feel its begging.

All time stopped when he pulled away from me. Withdrew his hand from my hold. His lips from mine.

"What is it?" I asked.

"You sure you want me there, Queen?" he asked, and I discovered just then looking into his eyes that they were glittering azure blue and looked like captured birthstones. He looked down at my pussy.

"I just want to feel better. Can you make me feel better?"

King answered with a soft kiss on my lips.

"No," I said. "Not like that. Not soft. I want to feel something. I want to feel it."

King took my desire as a command and moved fast.

This time his hand found my vagina on its own. His full palm cradled the heat emanating from inside of me. He caressed my right shoulder with a voracious mouth, teasing sighs out of me.

I was about to reach to pull my skirt up and my panties down, but he snatched his touch away again.

"Wha—" I started, thinking he was done with me, but I couldn't finish my one syllable before this near stranger had me up in his arms, wrapping my legs around his torso, my brain wondering how he'd moved so quickly to get me into that position.

When he started walking, I thought he was carrying me to the bedroom, so I was surprised when I felt my ass being set on a cold, hard surface. King left me to turn on a light, revealing a bathroom shining in bright white tile and metal trimming everywhere.

"Why are we in here?" I asked as he came back over to me, pulling off his undershirt. "You want to see?"

"No," he said, picking me up from the counter beside the sink and spinning me around to a colossal floor-to-ceiling mirror. "I want *you* to see *you*."

He started kissing my shoulders again as he removed my skirt and then my shirt and underwear with near-perfect precision, hardly requiring me to take a step.

I watched him in the mirror. He watched me watch him. But never once did those blue eyes look at their own reflection.

"You see you?" King said. "I'm going to make sure you see you, Queen."

He moved my feet apart and grabbed me by the back of my neck, pushing his fingers into my hair.

"You're fucking beautiful," he said to my image.

I looked down at my breasts in the mirror. His free hand played with one of my nipples, and in between his white fingers my chocolate skin was brilliant.

"You see?" he asked again, sliding a condom from the counter beside us.

"Yes!" I answered through moans, taking everything in.

King slid his dick into me like I was the only woman he'd ever enter again. His eyes were on me in the mirror with the most sincere intention of pleasure.

We didn't have to say another thing about what we were doing, because seeing him looking at me on the outside as he pulsated on the inside, I knew this was something to him. He was making love to fucking me.

Once it was clear that I knew that, King left me alone with my image in the mirror. He moved his eyes off the mirror and started beating into me, giving me exactly what I'd asked for: a feeling.

"King!" I cried.

"Queen!" he answered, thrusting me so close to the mirror I could see my panting in a cloud. "Queen! Queen!"

Chapter 8

At 8:15 a.m. I was usually headed into the district attorney's office, but after my night with King in the Clocktower Building, I found myself standing on Park Avenue outside Wilhelmina New York cloaked in yesterday's clothes with wrinkles of last night's gossip.

I knew Tamika would still be mad at me for leaving her hanging the day before, but I just could not hold my news in until she decided to calm down. On one hand, I could count the number of times I'd had sex with a man that quickly—and that included King. I felt a euphoria that sent butterfly wings fluttering in my gut every time I thought of King's fingers grabbing the roots of my hair as he held my head in place over the bathroom sink. At every second, my thoughts took me back to his long stroke, pulling his penis all the way out of me and then pressing forward until my ass stopped him;

he'd called out "Queen" so many times, I looked in the mirror and considered that maybe it was my name.

Tamika walked into the building with one of her male co-workers who usually rode the train into Manhattan with her from Brooklyn. She was wearing low black Chuck Taylors but had heels tucked into a small reusable grocery bag on her arm.

I was sitting on a bench beside security sipping a latte I'd purchased from a food truck.

"Oh hell no, Stan," Tamika started with the security guard after noticing me sitting beside his desk, "you know we have tight security here. Can't let strays in Wilhelmina." She rolled her eyes at me and took a sip of her coffee.

Stan knew me from my many visits to the office, so he laughed at Tamika's show, but she, predictably, kept up her matinee performance.

"I get so tired of the fakes. The wannabes. The liars and duplicitous individuals. Lock them all up, I say. Throw away the key," Tamika declared so dramatically, her coworker laughed and excused himself to go upstairs. "No need to leave me. There is nothing down here for me."

I stood and walked over to Tamika, who was standing in the middle of the lobby like she was Cleopatra or Queen Nefertiti and I was about to bow to her.

"Humpf," she murmured to my face. "Looks like the chicken-heads have come home to roast."

"Malcolm X quotes at eight a.m.?" I joked. "And that's *chickens* have come home to *roost*."

"Actually that was *Tamika*—because I'm about to *roast* a *chick-enhead*," she added, but even though she was extending the humor, she had a sour face and I knew she was cool on me. Other workers, hardly awake and looking more like the extras from *The Walking Dead* than a healthy workforce, trickled in through the sliding doors, and we had to step to the side with our standoff.

"I'm sorry," I said.

"For what?" she asked.

"For letting you down by not picking Miles up from fencing."

"No. You let your *godson* down," she said.

"Okay. I did that."

"And you let *yourself* down."

"Okay. I did that, too," I said.

"And you let *Malcolm X* down!"

"Him too."

"And *Spike Lee and Denzel*."

To that, I rolled my eyes. "Fine. Them too."

"Now, say it," Tamika demanded, looking off.

"I am not saying all of that," I said.

"Humpf." Tamika looked at me. "Guess we're done here." She stalked off in her sneakers and headed for the elevator.

"Mika, wait!" I followed her. "I have hot gossip."

"Tell someone who cares," she snapped.

"No, really. It's good." As she was about to join a crowd of sluggish coworkers on the elevator, I got close up on her ear and added in a low voice, "I slept with the white cutie from the bar."

She froze and then her entire disposition changed. "I'll see y'all upstairs," she said to the person holding the door open for her. "Go on. Get! Skedaddle!" she ordered the elevator door as it slowly closed on the widening eyes inside.

She turned and looked at me with electrified eyes, and we

screeched liked groupies, pulling each other out the front door to gossip in private.

"Oh, my God! I can't breathe," Tamika said. "This is crazy. I can't believe you fucked him! Damn, he was fine! Damn! Whoa. You're such a slut!" She hugged me like I'd just won a trophy, then backed up and looked into my eyes. "I'm proud of you though," she said in pretend sincerity. "Sometimes being a slut wins. And I can tell by looking at you that you won last night. Yes, Gawd! Yes!" She laughed and looked me up and down. "Was it good?"

"It was, girl! It was," I confirmed.

"Okay! I need all of the details. Every little bit." She bit her lip like she was about to tear into a bag of Funyuns. "And wait, just know this does not excuse your behavior yesterday. I am still not your friend. But we both know that juicy gossip overrides anything any day! Now, spill the pork and beans!"

Telling the story of my night with King was like reliving it, like leaving that morning outside Wilhelmina and returning to the Clocktower. Back to me heaving over the sink and thinking King had cum, but then feeling him pick me up and carry me into the bedroom with a hard dick pressed into my back. Him whispering, "I'm not done yet." Him making me feel like everything sexual was new in his bed. I was lost, disoriented, found, and perfectly in place all at the same time.

"I must meet this man who did you right," Tamika said in her fake noble English accent, and we laughed. "So, after all of that, what the hell are you doing here . . . like, with me?" she added, fanning herself.

"I did the old 'I'm cool and I have to go' routine. You know, didn't want to seem too thirsty," I informed her. I'd hardly slept in King's bed. I lay there watching the moonlight dancing on the ceiling and thinking about how crazy I was for being there with King, but still not regretting it.

"Well, there's also the fact that you had to go to work," Tamika blurted out. "Wait, why aren't you at work?" She looked confused.

"Just a few days off. Vacation," I explained. I hadn't even considered what I'd say once people realized I wasn't going to work each day. "You know I won that big case last week. Figured I'd take some time myself. Relax."

"You ain't never relax before," Tamika said. "Shit, you've had a straight pole up your ass since forever. Got to get some drinks in you to calm your tight ass down half the time."

"Well, all of that is behind me now. I'm turning over a new leaf. Good times ahead!"

"Really?" She stepped back and looked at me with a grin. "I guess Mr. King is the new boo-thang?"

"Girl, are you kidding? No way. There's no possibility of us getting together. He's all Brooklyn, and you know I'm Harlem world," I joked.

"Just get your feet wet for once. Enjoy yourself. You deserve it. Plus, I hear Monique's been hanging out with that guy she met there—I think his name is Vonn or something. Isn't that your guy's dude? Y'all can, like, go on a ghetto double date. Go see a movie at Kings Plaza. Make them buy y'all some high-top Reeboks and shit like we used to do back in the old days."

"Yeah, they know each other," I said, laughing, "but I don't think King's the make-out-at-Canarsie Pier type. He seems a little classier than that."

"Classy?" Tamika chuckled. "And hanging out at Damaged Goods? *No comprende!*"

"I know, but there was over one million dollars in art in his condo," I said. "His sheets—they were Frette! Fucking Frette!"

"Well, then something doesn't add up," she whispered, looking devious and crossing her arms.

"Well, I think he owns the club. I mean, he didn't say it, but it was evident by how people were treating him."

"Humph." Tamika pursed her lips shadily. "I'm sure there's gold in the club, but that's not Clocktower money, honey. He'd have to own, like, half the clubs in Brooklyn to be up in there. And Manhattan, too. You know that. We both read the *Times* Real Estate."

"Look, Mik, King is cool. But, like I said, that was a one-time thing. Who cares about how he got up in the Clocktower? I was in, now I'm out." I jumped over an imaginary line on the ground. "I'll never see him again."

"Right. Right. Famous last words."

After Tamika and I said good-bye, she walked into the building, leaving me on the sidewalk. Two svelte women who were obviously models walked past me in oversized clothing that exaggerated their frail frames. Still, there was something so sexy or mesmerizing about them. Even on a gray New York City street corner with hundreds of blank-faced people whizzing by in the morning rush, they were special. Something to look at and admire and seek out. People seemed happy at the chance to lay eyes on these images of perfection, of what women should want to be, but in a cruel twist of irony, never could. I remembered how I'd felt walking the streets with Kim 2. How men would stop walking and rush over to talk to her. They could hardly say anything substantial. They'd babble like idiots and beg for her telephone number like circus monkeys begging for bananas or peanuts. It didn't matter what she was wearing or how she behaved. She could look homeless and gaunt, like, near death, and act like a raving bitch, and still these men would grovel to get her to smile at them. Handsome men. Rich men. Famous men. They'd call the apartment all through the night. Just to have her say she'd go out with them, they'd send Luxor roses from Banchet and NōKA chocolates and boxes of La Petite Coquette lingerie and airline tickets to wherever.

One of the models must've seen my stare. She rolled her eyes and nudged the other woman before they walked into the building.

Kim 2's time at Wilhelmina took a turn when she gained three pounds. It was nothing—that's what I'd told her as she lay on the living room floor crying about what I felt ridiculous for calling a "fluctuation." She said I didn't understand—those three pounds, and her inability to lose them, were a demarcation in her existence, an indication of the beginning of the end. I wanted to laugh. But I didn't. I actually felt bad for her. That she thought three pounds could mean anything. In the end, she was right though. The agency stopped booking her for shows. The reason: She looked "different" in the clothes; they couldn't send her out if she couldn't exactly fit the items designers provided on the rack; and one designer asked that the agency stop sending him "Puerto Ricans," saying the last one they'd sent (Kim 2—who isn't Puerto Rican) had a big ass and he couldn't send that down the runway. This made Kim 2 cry and made me feel horrible for her. I decided to try to cheer her up by having Ronald hook her up with one of his decent friends. While she always had men trying to get at her, most of them were trifling or crazy. I thought maybe a romantic distraction could get her on track again.

The day Ronald was supposed to hook up Kim 2 on a double

date with his coworker Alonzo, a Cuban attorney who not only looked like a model but had a brilliant mind, I was held up at the office and Alonzo was stuck at an airport in Miami. Kim 2 and Ronald ended up at the restaurant alone.

She texted me a picture of them waving from the bar at Ginny's Supper Club in the basement of the Red Rooster. She captioned it, "borrowing your boo for the evening." Hope you don't mind. Thanks for looking out for me, bestie.

It took me a long time to look back at that moment without quick tears. Other times, I wondered if her joking or their play with each other, sneaking into each other's lives in front of my face, was just suspicion on my part. But for some reason, when I read that text, I just knew something was starting. That was the beginning. I sat at my desk in my office surrounded by papers I needed to organize by sunup, thinking about my perfect-model best friend cozying up to my boyfriend in the snuggly, twenties-inspired décor at Ginny's. Men walking by and seeing Ronald with Kim 2 and thinking how lucky he was to have her. Ronald feeling that and leaning in . . . definitely leaning in. Loving it.

I tried to call him, but there was no answer. I texted that I was on my way, and he said there was no need. Everything was fine.

Standing outside Wilhelmina with my memories, my back started to hurt and I reached into my purse for my pill bottle. Then I realized there was nothing there. I backed up against the side of the building to try to take some of the pressure away and let something cool touch the pain that had suddenly shot through me like an arrow.

I hadn't felt a single pain all evening or morning, and then suddenly, seemingly out of nowhere, there it was, so sharp and clear.

I tried to take deep breaths. My heart began to quicken. Nervous sweat gathered at my hairline.

My rushed breathing slowed to something so shallow, it scared me. I could hear my heart beat. Literally feel my pulse in my hands. My back felt like someone had stapled my skin to a pole and was ripping me away. I would've screamed but I couldn't find my voice, and it wasn't until a bent-over, wrinkled woman in a crowd of five or six spoke to me that I remembered I was standing on a street corner in New York City at 9 a.m.

"Dear, are you all right?" she asked, pointing at me with an index finger supporting the weight of an enormous fake-diamond ring.

The woman and the crowd flipped in and out of focus.

I could see that people were talking, but I couldn't tell if they were speaking to me or one another, and then I thought maybe I was imagining everything—even the people standing right there.

"Maybe she needs a doctor!" I heard. "Someone call 9-1-1!"

Inside my body and beneath my pain, some voice of my own begged me to get myself together. The voice pleaded and begged, and then I heard myself say to someone, "No! I'm fine. I'm fine. Just need to get home. Stomach virus. Just a little sick." The voice told me to smile. To push off the wall and through the crowd. Smile the entire way. "I'm fine. Thank you."

"You sure, dear?" The old woman walked beside me. "Someone get her a cab!" she instructed before asking, "You need a cab?"

"Yes," I said, feeling new sweat in my palms. My skin vibrating like I was in a steam room. My knees feeling like balls of gelatin connecting toothpicks.

Three more people confirmed that I didn't believe I needed a doctor before continuing on their way. Soon, it was just me, the old woman, and a bicycle deliveryman with a huge bag slung over his back standing there as a cab slowed to pick me up.

I thanked them both for their help, secretly hating them for being witnesses.

"Hello. My name is Kenton Kind. And I'm a sex addict." That's how I expected my twin brother's speech at the sex addicts' meeting to begin.

Three of Kent's voice mails, each more sad than the one before, had invited me to the meeting. After lying on my couch for two days, surviving frequent bouts of back pain on a calculated mixture of ibuprofen, sleeping pills, and Jameson, I decided to show my face and do what Kenton claimed he needed on the second message: have his "back this one time." He'd said he wanted someone who knew him to be there when he told his "truth," and he couldn't think of anyone else but me. It sounded kind of gross to me—the idea of listening to why my own brother thought he was a sex addict in a tale that would no doubt follow his every filthy encounter blow by blow—but the more I thought about it, the more I really knew that I was the only person my brother could call on to be there. He'd always had a lot of friends—although many of them were now dead or locked up at Rikers—but I'd always been the only person he confided in about personal things. I was probably the only person he'd told about the meeting. Plus, I still thought the whole thing was a sham. A bunch of bullshit Kent maybe believed about himself to explain why he was such an asshole when it came to women and why he'd made an irreversible mess of the only woman who'd ever really loved him. I didn't think he had a sex addiction. He was just a womanizer experiencing a tragic dilemma caused by his whorish ways. I figured that maybe if he sat through the meeting with me there, he'd realize that and stop focusing on the wrong thing. Get his shit together.

Kent sat up front, planning to speak, and I sat in the back of the room, looking around at the seemingly healthy people chatting, eating brownies, and sipping cheap coffee and wondered who they all were. I wore a fitted Yankees cap and a high-collared sweater with my jean skirt to be sure no one saw me walking in, and I planned to hide beneath Kent's arm on the way out. The meeting was in the basement of an old church turned community center, at the back of a hallway of rooms with signs on the doors indicating other evening gatherings in progress—group meetings for everything from drug and alcohol abuse to anger management.

The meeting began when Jake, who introduced himself only by his first name and as the team leader, went over the rules and read through a pamphlet on addiction.

"Addicts are defensive," he said. He peeked out over his expensive-looking wire-rimmed glasses at us. "We all know what this means. You're constantly faced with the truth about your addiction, either from recognizing the addictive behavior yourself or through others, and you fend off the confrontation by being defensive. You wonder or you're asked if maybe you've done too much, have had too much or just overindulged, and you fight yourself or someone else about all the reasons the confronted idea is wrong." Jake's demeanor was so dignified, his language so articulate, that I wondered if he was a college professor or a doctor. He'd said he was a recovering sex addict, but looking at his pale white skin and thin, girlish arms and legs, I wondered who would actually have sex with him. "You try to ignore it. Tell everyone to focus on something else. You become violent. You hate everyone for thinking they know better than you. Then you start convincing yourself that *you* know better than *you*." Everyone laughed, including Kent, who sat sandwiched between two women I thought he'd be trying to hit on in any other scenario.

"Right, we laugh," Jake went on, laughing himself. "But we all know that moment when your addiction makes you start thinking about yourself in the third person. Makes you schizophrenic. Why? Because that same you who became defensive then tries to prove to yourself and everyone else that you don't have a problem by attempting to regulate your own addiction. You say you won't do this or that for this amount of time. Maybe forever. But then it comes back. And hard." A woman in the front stood up like Jake was delivering the gospel at church. Then the woman beside her stood up and they hugged. "It comes back to help you realize that you're not in control at all. But you remain in denial. And then you get defensive again. And thus begins a whole new cycle of your addiction. Leading back to the beginning. And then back again."

Jake went on, but I stayed on that one for a little while. I thought of the sharp pain in my back a few days earlier outside Tamika's office. The ride to my apartment in the taxi and how it was only a little after ten in morning when I made it upstairs and thought that if I could just have my painkillers and maybe a drink, I'd feel better. Now, I knew I didn't have an addiction to pills, but looking for the Jameson in the kitchen and feeling my heart sink when I realized I'd just finished the last bottle, I thought maybe something was really going on with me. Then I felt the sharp pain again and I rushed to take ibuprofen, but I knew it wouldn't be enough to get through. I went downstairs to buy more Jameson and drank only enough to get me right. Just enough to sleep. When I woke up from the nap, I still felt the pain and I needed more, but I made myself wait. Just three more hours. I just needed to wait.

When Kent got up to speak, I lowered my body in my seat and pulled my cap down on my head. He introduced himself like a thug about to do an Easter speech. Jake had to remind him not to use his last name and to turn off his vibrating cell phone—probably some woman calling him, I thought, laughing to myself.

"How has my addiction shown itself?" Kent nervously read off of a piece of crumpled paper he was holding. He gave a sad chuckle and looked toward the back of the room where a clock was hanging over my head. "Okay. I promised myself I'd tell the truth, so I'm going to come right out with it, yo. No more hiding. No fucking fear."

"That's right, brother! No fear," the black man who was dressed like a Fruit of Islam security officer broke in.

"I can't remember the last day when I didn't have sex, yo," Kent revealed. "And that includes yesterday and even today."

I felt myself gawking and closed my mouth. That was just like Kent—talking about having an addiction and then still doing it anyway. I looked at my watch and cursed myself for coming. If he wanted to do this ridiculous routine to feel better about being an asshole, he could do it on his own.

"I ain't perfect, but I guess that's why I'm here," he went on. "I fuck—I mean, I sleep with a lot of women I don't know. Shorties I be meeting at the club. No names. No numbers. Wedding rings. Bathrooms. Just sweating. And those ain't the worst ones. The worst ones be the ones I see more than once. Shorty I met online, this white girl in Staten Island, I was going to the crib two times a week. Fucking—sexing her. Her baby was there. I think she was married. It didn't matter. I'd get it in the kitchen when I walked in. She ain't even want me to take my motorcycle helmet off. I didn't care. We both knew what I was there for. The baby would be crying. Husband calling. I'd hit it and bounce. It's whatever."

He looked down at the paper again and read another question. "My low? That's easy. It's how I realized there was a problem. My baby moms, I fucked—had sex with her lover—some chick— you know—that gay shit. The shit was crazy, yo. And I knew it was crazy—kept telling myself that while it was happening, but I wouldn't stop. I went to her spot to confront her about sleeping with Keish, and I was looking at her—she's one of those girls that be dressing like boys—and I was like, 'Yo, what the fuck?' " I slid even lower in my seat and covered my face with my hand. "She was talking about how she ain't never been with no man before and dick ain't shit. I was like, fuck that. I was so mad. And I kept thinking, I need to get even—even with Keish for fucking this ho and this ho nigga for fucking my girl. You know?" Kent was off in his thoughts and started pacing the front of the room like an actor delivering a soliloquy in a Shakespearean tragedy.

"Right there, yo, I decided I was going to get shorty to give me head and I was gonna fuck her. I knew everything I needed to say, everything I needed to do to get at her. She was saying she ain't never want no dick. Ain't never fuck no nigga. That just made me more excited to do it. And I did. You know, a woman is woman. Even dressed as a nigga, she still a woman. I sat down on her couch and told her what to do and she did. Got down on her knees and did it. And then I tapped that. Made her call out my name—told her, 'Call this Keish's dick'—made her scream it. And she did. And I felt like I was high. Not, like, sexually, but in my head. Like I won something. When it was over, she was talking about how we wasn't gonna tell Keish and let it ride. All this bullshit. Like she ain't even know at some point it's gonna get back to Keish—it always do. When I walked out that door, the high left me. I was mad. First I was mad at Keish for fucking that ho, then I was mad at the ho for fucking me. Then I started thinking about me. See, I was mad at the girl for getting ready to lie to my baby moms, but I was doing the same thing. Lying to this girl I know love me. Lying like it's a fucking sport. Like it's a joke. And I know it's gonna hurt her. Bad enough. Real bad. She gonna find out. I'm gonna tell. And I'm gonna have to deal with it. Worse part is, I think I knew all this when I did it."

After the speech, I waited in my seat with my cap still down low waiting for Kent to say good-bye to all of the people who'd rushed to his side with well wishes, hugs, and matching stories. A few people tried to talk me up, but I said little enough to make it clear that I wasn't looking to make new friends.

When the room had emptied of everyone but Kent and a woman who seemed hell-bent on stuffing into her purse what was left of the Entenmann's chocolate chip cookies, I stood to head out with Kent.

We coupled up shoulder to shoulder like we'd been attached that way at some point in the womb and walked out of the building without saying a word.

My thoughts had taken so many turns during his speech. I was angry and then I was ashamed. Then intrigued. Then embarrassed. Then sad. When it was over, this man who was bigger than any man I knew in my life was seriously holding back tears. He was nervous about something. And I knew it wasn't the crowd. Kent was a showman. No crowd could make him afraid. It was then, just as he started talking about our parents' addiction, that I finally decided that maybe he was right about his situation. Maybe his sex addiction was real.

"Go on and laugh," Kent said, breaking our silence when we'd made it outside.

"Laugh about what?" I asked.

"What I said in there. I know I sounded crazy."

"No. Not crazy. You're not crazy."

"Really?"

"I think what you did in there was brave. Now, what you did with that woman—that might have been crazy," I said. "But you being open about how it made you feel, that wasn't crazy."

"So, you don't think I'm just doing this because of what's happening with Keisha, like you said at the house?" he asked.

I thought in silence as we stepped down the concrete stairs to the sidewalk. It was getting pretty dark outside, and clumps of people looking to enjoy the warm evening strolled past.

"I honestly don't know," I admitted. "You've done some fucked-up shit. Does that make you an addict? It might just make you a fucked-up person."

Kent shrugged in agreement as other people from other meetings that had let out rushed past us on the sidewalk.

"But what I saw in there was that you believe you have a problem, so I have to support you," I said. "Guess that's why I came. I didn't want you to be out here by yourself—not if you didn't want to be. You wouldn't let me go through this by myself."

Kent gave me one of his bear hugs. As he held my head on his chest, I could tell maybe one or two tears had fallen from his eyes, and I also knew they'd be gone by the time he let me go.

He whispered, "I don't know what the fuck I'm doing. But I

think if I figure this shit out, I can understand a bunch of other things. That's all. I've gotta start somewhere. We both gotta."

And then against everything I thought I knew about Kent, he let me go in time to see one of his tears. One innocent and strange-looking droplet decorated the outside of his left eye. If it had been black, it would have looked like a gang murderer's tattoo.

Before I could figure out why he wanted me to see his tears, I asked, "Do you think I drink too much? Is that why you invited me here?"

"No. This was about me."

"Kenton, please! You weren't really even supposed to have a guest here tonight. I saw the sign on the door saying no guests allowed. And who in their right mind would want me there to hear all that crazy shit? Just stop it. Did you invite me here to see all of this stuff because you secretly think I drink too much and you want me to get on the self-help bandwagon, too?"

"Do you think you drink too much?" he shot back, sounding rehearsed.

"Don't answer my question with a question," I said. "Because there's a reason I asked. The other night at the house, you said 'we' have our drugs of choice. You didn't say 'people.' You said, 'we.' You included me."

"Fine, Kim. I'm not around you enough to say. But sometimes, when I am around you, the way you drink and the way you act, it reminds me of Dad. Would you say he has a problem with alcohol? That he's a drunk?"

I took a few steps away from Kent. Rubbed my palms together.

"I'm not like him," I said. "I just asked if you thought *I* had a problem."

"Yes." Kent's response was swift. Planned. We weren't touching, but I felt him exhale.

I took the hit to the chin and stood firm. "That's all you had to say," I said, and then I popped out a smile. "I'm fine. See? I heard you and I'm fine."

"You plan to do anything about it?"

"Well, I'll push back. I'm a big girl. I can take your criticism," I said playfully. "I don't think you mean any harm, so I'll back up. And you know, to prove to you that I don't have an addiction to alcohol, I won't be defensive, as Jake pointed out in there. I'll just listen and back up." I grinned.

"Shit! You got it. That's some kind of change from how you came at me at the crib. Right?"

I perked up again and served another smile, this one with teeth and gums. I wanted to look like the perfect pupil or someone who was a believer. I was ready for the conversation to end. I didn't want to go deeper. Be pushed deeper by Kent and his suggestions. When I agreed to come, I knew that was as far as I'd go. On the other side of me agreeing to stop drinking for a little while, hearing myself agree in front of Kent, was the empty bottle of Jameson falling out of my trash bag at the incinerator the night before. The old judge from up the hallway with his gray toupee and arthritic limp bending over to pick it up even after I told him to leave it alone. Him doing it anyway and looking at me oddly. Judging me with his old-fart ass. Like there was something odd about a woman finishing a bottle of Jameson. I wanted to give him a piece of my mind. But I settled on an exaggerated eye roll that stopped at my nude navel. That was when I felt the wind whipping through the hallway, hardening my nipples. And they were bare too. Somehow, I'd forgotten to put on my shirt when I'd taken out the bag of glass. I cursed the old judge out for looking at my nipples. And inside the apartment there was no relief. After I got myself calm from the incident in the hallway, I rocked myself to sleep and met in my dreams what was becoming a recurring theme—Kim 2 and me in that car headed into New York at sunrise. Only in the dreams everything was furry. I was in the driver's seat instead of sleeping. Kim 2 was awake. I was screaming. She was covering her ears. Trying to grab the steering wheel.

"I understand if that's all you want to share right now. Maybe you'll share more with me later?" Kent said distantly before adjusting his motorcycle helmet under his arm to let me know he was ready to go too. He looked into my eyes. "I love you, Sis." He turned away.

Chapter 9

$\mathcal{I}$ was sitting in the backseat of the dollar cab for ten minutes before I realized it was the same Indian driver who had taken me to King's house. When Kent pulled off on his motorcycle, the cab showed up seemingly from nowhere. I told him my address after he'd started driving.

"I know you," I said just a few blocks from my house.

"Yes, miss. I am Baboo."

I sat back perplexed for a minute, deciphering the pattern in his colorful, gold-tubed turban that made him look too regal to be sitting in the front seat of a squalid New York City dollar cab. There was no permit posted on the dashboard. Just little bottles of dried-out air freshener and pictures of a little boy and woman with long black hair taped to the glove compartment. What sounded like Indian pop music played a little too loudly on the radio.

"You know him?" I asked vaguely, looking out the window.

"Yes."

"Really?" I sniggered, uncomfortable but sort of charmed at the thought that maybe King had sent Baboo to come get me. Then I asked, "Did he send you there tonight? To get me?"

Baboo nodded.

"Okay. So he knows where I was tonight? Where I am?" Suddenly, every image I saw outside the window in the night looked like a spy, someone watching my movements. I didn't know if I should feel stalked, but mostly I was intrigued. Who was this man of such mystery and power? I felt myself blush, my chest heat up. It was the unmistakable feeling of being made special.

Baboo didn't answer my other questions.

"Okay, you can't say anything, I guess. Makes sense." I watched spies outside watching me. Wondered where King was in the crowd crossing the street. The car beside us? I turned to look for the silver Bentley. "Well, you can tell him that I don't need any cab rides from him. And I don't need you following me around. That's actually kind of creepy. You got that?"

He nodded again but I could tell he was smiling.

"Yes. You tell him all of that. And make sure you add that I'm very sorry but I'm not interested in him." I poked my nose into the air like a woman who was offended. King had called and texted me a few times. I didn't respond. I'd meant what I'd said to Tamika. Our night together was all that, but it was just a night. Just a one-night swirl. I mean, what else could it be? I deleted his number, erased my call log and his messages.

"Yes. Will do," Baboo said.

The car stopped outside my apartment.

Pier, the doorman, approached the car to open my door. I looked up at the building, so many flights up to my floor, to my dark apartment, curtains drawn and no one inside. I remembered King's kisses up my spine.

"No!" I said impulsively, holding the car door closed before Pier got his gloved hand on the handle. "Wait one minute!"

Baboo turned to me.

"Can you contact him?" I asked quickly. "Can you—do you know where he is?"

"Whatever you like, miss. We go. Baboo can do it."

Pier watched me, waiting in his white shirt and black vest from the other side of the window, like I was a fish in an aquarium.

"You getting out?" he mouthed.

I shook my head no and waved good-bye as my tattered chariot started rolling away before making a wide and illegal U-turn to head to Brooklyn.

Sitting in the backseat, I felt exhilarated, like I was sneaking out of the house with fast-ass Melissa Montgomery, doing exactly the opposite of what I'd just promised myself. I covered my mouth and chuckled in a way that I hadn't in so long. What was I doing messing with that white boy again?

As Baboo talked on the phone, I heard him call out "Queen," and I wondered how many times he'd done this same thing for another woman King found interesting or had invited to his home after meeting her at Damaged Goods. I told myself this was nothing. Just some fun. Something to do to get myself off the couch and away from thoughts about Paul and work, Ronald with Kim 2, Kent and my parents.

"Sooo . . . remember those famous last words?" I whispered into the phone to Tamika after Baboo informed me of King's instructions to bring me back to the Clocktower.

"Biiiiittttccch!" Tamika shot back theatrically. "Shut the front fucking door!"

"No, I can't close the door because I'm about to walk into it!" I cracked.

"I knew it! I told you your ass would be back swirlin'," Tamika teased. "Pink diznic got you sprung!"

"I ain't sprung. Just bored. Need a little excitement, like you said."

"Tell me about it, girl. I'm over here looking for some new-new online. Blackfolksmeet.com is like a prison hookup site right about now. I could use a little David Beckham of my own."

"You're an ass."

"Yes, but I'm also honest," she said. "But be safe and savor every detail, so I can get a full report in the morning. Okay? And don't forget to wrap it up. Last thing we need is some curly-head baby fucking up our Afro family pictures."

I laughed so hard, it turned to a deep chortle that made Baboo look at me over his shoulder.

"Oh, yeah," Tamika started again. "And ask Jungle Fever about Vonn—that dude Monique was fucking with. I've been calling you. She asked me to have you ask your friend if he's heard from Vonn."

"Why?"

"She said he disappeared. He was supposed to show up at her house that night before you came to my job I think," she explained. "He never showed up. Ain't answer his phone. Typical nigga shit. But then when she checked, like, two days later, the phone was disconnected."

"That just sounds mad random. I'm sure it's nothing for her to worry about." I remembered the guy with the baby face walking into the bar when I was talking to King. How he looked at me. Him sitting in the backseat of the Bentley.

"Oh, I know that. Shit, I told Monique that Vonn ain't want no more of that old wrinkled pussy. Fool had to change his number to escape."

I chatted with Tamika the rest of the way to Brooklyn to calm my nerves and stop myself from thinking.

When we got to King's place, both Baboo and the doorman at the Clocktower rushed to help me out of the cab. Each took one of my hands and smiled meekly without looking into my eyes, nearly bowing his head to me as he pulled me from the car like a royal thing. I felt like the moon was shining down from the sky on me alone.

I forced Baboo to accept the cash in my wallet before the doorman, who'd introduced himself as Frantz, insisted I take his elbow to be led into the building.

"Will you be needing any help upstairs?" Frantz asked with high spirits, as if we'd taken part in this routine for a very long time.

"I think I'm fine," I said. "Wait, isn't King here?"

"No, miss. Mr. McDonnell sent word that he will be here shortly. He has advised me to allow you into his home."

Frantz pressed the button to call the elevator for me and asked again if I needed his assistance.

I refused and headed to the far corner of the elevator, where I watched the door slowly close out Frantz and the lobby.

As the elevator ascended, I tried to think of every reason I had to turn around and go back to my place. Every reason why what I was doing was wrong and maybe even reckless. Random sex with a random man was just wrong for me—no matter how bored I was, no matter how pissed off I was, no matter how hurt and lonely I was. What was the point?

My cell phone buzzed. There was a text message from a number with no name that I'd later lock in for good.

> 917-555-1212: I see you made it home, Queen. I'm finishing up some work. Try not to have too much fun without me. See you in a few. Relax. I'm rushing home to be with you.

The elevator opened with me feeling like King was reading my mind. I even looked up to make sure there wasn't a camera spying down on me.

I stepped out and stood there for a minute, looking at my cavernous surroundings. From floor to ceiling and wall to wall, the space felt more magnificent than a home. More like a museum.

I tried to look casual, walking around touching things with open, anxious palms. I felt like Little Orphan Annie entering Daddy Warbucks's estate.

For a few days I'd been trying to remember why the last name Frantz had used to refer to King in the lobby that first night I'd visited sounded so familiar and stayed in my brain even though I was halfway out of it. I'd heard it so many times, but I couldn't place it until Frantz had said it again downstairs. Then it all came back to be. There was this documentary I'd watched on the History Channel in March when I was home sick in bed with a cold the day of the St. Patrick's Day parade. I remembered that day because Paul called me early in the morning all worked up about Chief Elliot arresting some Irish gang members who'd actually tried to buy enough dye to dump into the Hudson River to turn it green for the day. After getting off the phone with him, I couldn't sleep, so I turned on the History Channel to see that they were featuring a documentary on Irish families of New York. It sounded like great sleeping material, but I got caught up in it because the narrator kept saying one of the family's names the way Robin Leach would have on that old television show *Lifestyles of the Rich and Famous*—"the McDonnells of New York."

The narrator documented a history of New York that many people both outside and inside the Big Apple didn't know. Apparently, for a long time, the Irish ran the city. They were the mob, the gang leaders, the businessmen and moguls. There were still dribs and drabs of that old Irish glory in New York, in finance and law enforcement and even in the Catholic Church, but most of the treasure that remained of the Golden Clans was seen in wealthy real estate deals where descendants locked up chunks of upper Manhattan soil along what came to be known as "the Irish Gold Coast." The McDonnells were the wealthiest, most public clan of New York's old Irish.

While I knew plenty of people in New York had that name and there was little chance some guy I'd met at a bar in Brooklyn was the descendant of rich white folks the narrator claimed moved out to Rye, New York, and changed their names, King was fully a mystery to me. Not that we'd spent so much time together that I should know a lot about him, but Tamika was right—some things didn't add up. So when I heard his name and remembered about the New York McDonnells, my mind couldn't help but make fanciful conjectures.

My eyes darted about in search of anything holding a clue to who King was; then I gave in and decided a full-on snoop wouldn't hurt anybody. I was just being safe.

I tiptoed around the place, turning over this and that, going through the garbage cans in the kitchen and bathroom (Tamika taught me that), while listening for the elevator, talk, shoes scraping the floor . . . any sign I was busted.

My little investigation led me in so many directions in the sprawling triplex, I felt like I was lost and that King would pop up at any moment. Then I imagined him watching me like a CIA agent on one of those hidden spy cameras and started looking for those, too.

My quick search resulted in no information and no cameras—nothing. Not even a photo album or piece of mail. The place was clean.

My heart racing, I sat on the couch to catch my breath and consider what one of the detectives from downtown would do. Just as I leaned into the cream-colored leather, the cables hanging over the elevator started turning and twisting.

"Be cool," I told myself, switching positions two or three times to try to appear as natural as possible. I tried to slow my breathing to stop my heart from pounding, but once the cables had pulled the cab into position in the all-glass elevator bay, I lost my total cool again.

There stood King, strong, legs apart, shoulders relaxed, and hands folded in the center of his pelvis. He wore a black suit and gray shirt that fit him so well, I knew quickly that no matter how cool I was, this night would be a repeat of the last time we were together.

He stood erect like a model used to the spotlight as the doors rolled open in enthralling slow motion.

He stepped out like he was going to say something subtle but memorable. And he did: "Welcome back, Queen."

To that, I answered with a grin: "Not like I had a choice."

"Not like *I* had a choice," he remarked, climbing two steps to the platform where I was sitting on the couch and kissing me on the forehead like he was blessing me in a ritual. Even with inches between us, I could smell the hints of pepper in his cologne, strong and bold. It made me want to hike up my skirt and remind him of what had happened the last time I'd been here. But the shy girl in me made me do otherwise. As he walked to the kitchen, I crossed my legs and led us into conversation more natural to friendly strangers—the weather and recent changes in Brooklyn.

It was interesting to hear him talk about simple things like cloudy days and those annoying bike lanes taking over the streets in Brooklyn. As he took off his cuff links and excused himself to get out of his suit, walking in and out of his bedroom, I did my normal basic-knowledge test to size him up—see how informed he was, throwing in ideas and facts from a few articles I'd recently read in the *New York Times* or features I'd listened to on NPR. I could hear King chuckle like he knew exactly what I was doing, then he'd mention the journalist and give a little bit of information that wasn't included in the story. And of course he'd do it in his gruff King, Brooklyn accent, sounding like an educated mafioso.

"Wine?" King asked on his final exit from the bedroom, wearing jeans and a polo. He headed toward the kitchen. "I'd offer to make you a drink, but I don't know shit about mixing drinks and I think Terra's been getting me for all the good liquor anyway."

"Terra?" I repeated, sure he'd slipped his lady's name by mistake.

"Yes. That's my cleaning lady." He grinned. "I hate to call her that. Makes me sound like a bitch. Right? Maid and shit?"

We laughed, and King went on about how easily some men he knew carried on about their "maids" like they were old white women.

"So, what do you want?" he asked, standing beside the bar separating the kitchen from the living area, where I was still on the couch. Looking at those jeans sitting on his waist just right and the tattoos peeking out from beneath the polo, I thought of so many ways to answer that question. "Queen?" he called with a slight smirk. "What do you want . . . to drink?"

"Nothing," I said, shaking off the images from the bathroom in my head.

"Nothing to drink?"

"Yes. I'm kind of pulling back on the alcohol," I pointed out nonchalantly. "Maybe just a little water."

"Got it." He headed toward the refrigerator and pulled out two bottles of water. "Think I'll have a little agua myself. Got to keep hydrated." He brought the water over to me and sat down beside me on the couch.

We smiled at each other for a second like we were impressed and maybe surprised to be sitting so close again.

"Any reason for getting on the wagon?" he asked.

"Just getting a little chubby in the stomach area," I lied.

"Chubby?" King looked at me like I was delusional. "Not to be too blunt, but I was holding on to your stomach for a long time the other night and I didn't feel anything out of place. Now, a sister has to have a little thickness on her, that's what I like, but ain't nothing chubby about you."

King's declaration turned the water I was sipping on into wine.

It went right to my head, where it exploded like eight shots of Golden Grain alcohol. I licked my lips really hard and gulped down some water.

"Good to see you feeling better," King said, watching me drink.

"Feeling better?"

"Last time I saw you—every time I see you—you seem stressed. No?"

"It's nothing really—just family stuff. Work. Bullshit."

"I feel you. We all get fed up with the bullshit sometimes," he said.

"What bullshit do you get fed up with? Like, at your job?" I asked.

"At my job?" He looked surprised.

"Yes. Where you work . . . Where *do* you work?"

"You said it before."

"Damaged Goods? So you *do* work there?"

"From time to time."

I laughed and looked right into his eyes. "Come on," I said, switching to my Harlem accent. "Stop playing me like I'm from someplace in Arkansas. I know ain't no way someone who just works at a bar in Brooklyn can afford a place like this."

"I feel you," King offered aloofly.

"What?" I pushed after an elongated pause where he was supposed to explain himself but just kept sipping his water.

"What?"

"You can't stop there. You have to answer."

"Look, my family owns some clinics, and I worked in the business for a while, but I'm getting out." He rushed through this casually.

"Clinics? Your family owns *some* clinics?" I laughed, remembering that documentary. "Come on, you can't just throw that in there on me. How many?"

"It's not something I like talking about. My family—there's a lot of shit. You know how it is. A lot of good shit and a lot of bullshit. Like I said, right now I'm putting myself into position to start my own thing."

"So that's why you're working at Damaged Goods?" I asked.

"Something like that . . . ," he said, his tone detached. "Something like that."

I sat back knowing I'd pushed King as far as I could in that moment. I didn't know much about him, but the bit I knew about dealing with dudes like him was that pushing him for information for too long would shut him down. Then there was another side of me that listened to his story and hoped he wouldn't turn the tables on me. I wasn't exactly feeling like talking about what I did. It just seemed so regular, almost common and boring, sitting there with King. And that was interesting and even relieving. I'd gotten used to getting set up with guys who looked at me like I was some kind of unicorn because I was so successful in my career. They acted like I was Michelle Obama just because I had an assistant, benefits, and vacation days with pay. Sometimes it seemed like I was constantly paying for my success with the men I dated. One night Ronald had the nerve to suggest I quit my job at the DA's office and work as his legal secretary. I'd gotten in late and drunk after losing a case that had been kicking my ass for months, and he started complaining about what the job had been "doing" to me. He said something about not wanting to be married to a zombie and he didn't want to think about having that kind of example around his children. He went into a "leave your job or else" speech, where he claimed being his secretary could help launch me into something else at his firm.

"Bull and shit!" I'd screamed when Kim 2 came over to let us know our hollering had the police at the door.

"So, what made you come see me tonight?" King asked, pulling my hand into his and turning it over to look at the web of lines in my palm. "I was surprised when Baboo called me."

"Surprised? Really?" I laughed doubtfully as he traced the lines to my wrist and planted an abrupt kiss there. "I doubt that. I'm sure your little stalker sent you a full report of my every move."

"Stalker?" King smirked. "I can't control where that man chooses to drive his car."

"So you're claiming you didn't send him to find me?"

"Nope." King smiled.

"Well, I know how to spot a liar when I see one. I only ask that if you send someone to stalk me, you send someone with a better cab. Like a Mercedes or something. Come on, son!"

King laughed and nodded in agreement.

"All right. I got it," he said. "I wasn't trying to scare you. I just really, really wanted to see you again, and with you not answering my calls, I got a little desperate. I didn't mean anything by it. Please don't call Queen Latifah on me or anything. Again, I just wanted to see you."

"You wanted to see me?" I asked as he started moving his fingers up my arm so softly it felt like light tickles, sending playful pulses to my spine.

King pulled me to him, and facing me nose to nose, he looked into my eyes.

"Yes," he said before kissing me so intensely, I regretted every day I'd been away and couldn't even remember why I had.

I still tried to push him away though, playing coy as we kept up the game of chatting about nothing I'd remember. I'd only take away from the moment his serious sea-colored eyes on me, working more dexterously than his hands. I could resist a touch, but there was no defense from those eyes; they tugged at me and soon had me lying on my back on the couch, missing my shirt. Caught in his gaze, I couldn't even say who removed the shirt or suggested the position. I was just looking into the sea and riding a wave that rolled with the sound of King whispering something about tasting me.

Then I realized he was on top of me, spreading my knees apart with his hands.

His eyes left me and I felt his tongue circling my nipple.

"You okay with that?" he asked between tender licks.

"What?"

"Me tasting you?"

I didn't respond. I loosened my legs and pushed my pelvis up to him like he was a doctor.

King slid down and raised my jean skirt up to bunch at my hips.

He didn't bother to remove my panties. He set his mouth on my vagina and plucked my erect clitoris with his tongue, making me wince and sigh in rotation until my panties were so loose with my wetness that he could move the crotch to the side with his tongue.

"Fuck!" I shouted as he slid his tongue into me. My legs were splayed so wide, I had to arch my back to keep from falling off the couch. "Fuck! Fuck!"

King put his hands on the small of my back to prop me up as I danced on his tongue and he flicked my clitoris up and down.

My body was melting into something weightless as I shuddered again and again, sending his tongue a torrent of evidence of my pleasure.

And then, right where King's hands anchored me in place,

there was a snap that turned my "Ohhh-ooohhh" to "Ouch! Ouuuucccch!"

Something in my back had popped, and my body tensed up fast, leaving me petrified.

"What happened?" King jumped up from my crotch and looked at my face.

I could only reply through more pain: "Ouch! Ouuuucccch! Ouuuccchhh!"

I pushed him away and adjusted myself on the couch to relieve the pressure kicking at my lower spine.

"What's wrong?" King asked.

"My back! It's my back!" I said, trying to breathe through the sharp pangs.

"Where does it hurt?"

"Down here," I replied, pointing to my lower back.

"Well, calm down and keep breathing," King ordered confidently. "We need to get you to the bedroom."

"For what?" I looked at him sideways.

"No—not for that." He chuckled, trying to pull me off the couch. "If the pain is in your lower back, you may just have too much pressure on your lower discs. We should lessen the weight. Lying on your stomach helps."

King helped me to his bedroom and laid me on the bed with a neck roll under my stomach to lift my lower torso.

"I'll be right back," he said, walking out of the room.

The pain didn't go away, but I immediately felt some relief in the position.

He returned with a cool cloth he placed on my neck before sitting in the chair beside the bed with a new bottle of water in his right hand.

"Here. Take these," he said, his left hand displaying two little white pills with *V*'s etched into them.

"Vicodin? What are you doing with these?"

"What are you, the police?" He laughed, handing me the pills.

"No. I'm just saying, I'm not supposed to take strange pills from strange men," I said. "And most people don't just have these things hanging around."

"Well, Ms. Detective," he opened. "First, it's not strange—you just said it was Vicodin, and I'm not a strange man—you're in my home. And I told you my family owns clinics. Mostly pain-management clinics. I keep the pills in the house in case something happens. Basketball injury. Whatever. You never know. Hope you don't turn me in."

"I won't," I answered, laughing and swallowing the pills down with the water. "Well, tell me," I went on. "Since you seem to know so much, what's up with this cloth on my neck? How does that help my pain, doctor?"

"Oh, that's something my *maimeó*—my grandma—taught me," he said. "It's just to keep your mind off the pain. That's all. See, you're not even thinking about the pain right now. Are you?"

I thought about it and confirmed, "You know, your grandmother is right. I'm not thinking about the pain. I'm really not. Smart lady."

We laughed, and King got up to get a blanket to put over my bare back. He spread it out over me and kissed me on the cheek like he was saying good night.

He sat back in the chair, where I could see him looking at me.

I told him a little bit about the car accident, leaving out the parts about Kim 2 and Ronald at the hospital. The new dreams that were beginning to feel truer than my actual memories. He asked about my doctor and what kinds of painkillers I'd been taking. I shared parts of the story about Dr. Davis and his crush stopping my prescription and that I needed to find a new doctor.

As the Vicodin set in and every one of my muscles sagged into a relaxation that made me slur my words, I kept insisting that I get up and head home, but King wouldn't hear any of it.

"You're stuck here with me," he said. "Face it. You're not going anywhere. Not tonight."

I remember trying to disagree and roll off the bed to get to my feet, but my eyelids were so heavy. I just wanted to close them for a little while. The last thing I said was that I'd take a nap and wake up in a minute to be on my way.

My minute-long nap turned into ten hours of deep sleep that only ended due to the unmistakable sound and scent of bacon frying in the kitchen.

I opened my eyes on the chair next to the bed, empty except for a folded white T-shirt. The room was made bright by the morning sun.

"Good morning," I said, walking into the kitchen.

King was standing at the stove in basketball shorts and no top. He turned around and smiled. "Good morning." He walked over to me holding a greasy spatula, the bacon sputtering in the frying pan behind him. "I see you found the shirt I left out for you," he added. He looked so different in the sunlight coming in from the east. Maybe more striking than handsome. His cheekbones were tight. His eyes digging. I considered that this was maybe the first time I was seeing him so clearly and up close. I wondered what I looked like to him and thought that maybe I should've stopped in the bathroom to fix my hair before I came out to the kitchen.

I stood on my tiptoes and kissed him on the lips anyway. "Perfect fit," I said. "You made breakfast?" I nodded toward the stove.

King ran back over to the stove, grimacing. "Just some bacon," he said, making it in time to interrupt a growing cloud of black smoke. He removed the frying pan from the stove and sat it right on the granite countertop before turning back to me. "It's all I know how to make. I'm not much of a cook, but I figured you'd be hungry."

"Thoughtful." I couldn't help but grin at his gesture. I climbed up on a stool at the island in the middle of the kitchen.

"No." King laid the spatula down and came over to me again. "Not at all. Thoughtful would've been getting up early enough to have this ready to surprise you in bed. But I didn't want to move. You looked so beautiful when you were sleeping." He cupped the side of my face with a big, solid hand. "I didn't want to wake you. You were so peaceful."

"Yeah. That's funny. I've been having a lot of nightmares lately," I said, noting that I'd slept at King's place for the second time and those were among the few times lately when I hadn't dreamt of the car accident. In fact, I couldn't remember dreaming of anything. I was floating.

"You were knocked out."

"I'm happy I got any sleep after my back went out on your couch." I frowned, remembering how crazy I must've looked contorting my body to get rid of my pain and then lying stomach down on King's bed in nothing but a jean skirt and a blanket thrown over my body. "I'm so embarrassed that happened. Like I'm some kind of old lady. I'm sorry for ruining the night."

King went and picked up the frying pan and brought it over to the island, setting it down on the counter in front of me.

"You really did ruin the night," he said sarcastically. "I had to work hard to help you into bed and keep watch over you all night.

Do you know you snore? I normally charge top dollar for my nursing services. I don't come cheap, sister."

I laughed. "Really? Well, I'm pretty broke, but I can make it up to you in other ways. You have any ideas?"

"Hum . . ." He leaned into me and I couldn't help but slide my hand up his chest. "I do have some ideas," he said.

"Like what?" I felt his hardening nipple.

King fell back, laughing. "Whoa, girl. Get your mind out the gutter. See how y'all harass us male nurses? I was actually thinking of something a little less steamy." He paused. "I want you to spend the day with me. Here. Let's play hooky."

"Hooky?" I giggled, thinking he had to be joking.

"Yes. I already canceled all of my meetings and told Terra not to come today. I'm all yours. I don't know. I just was thinking, I want to just do some plain shit. You know? Sit in the house and watch daytime television. I don't even know what comes on anymore. *Maury*? What the fuck. We can order in and keep on our nightclothes. And"—he took my hand and placed it back on my chest— "see what happens after that."

"You're actually serious?" I asked.

"Okay. Maybe it is a dumb idea. Forget—" He was about to step back from my hand but I grabbed him.

"No—I was just confirming that you weren't playing with me," I said, remembering my lonely couch at home. My peaceful resting at his place. "I think it sounds pretty cool. I'm yours too."

I moved my hand from King's chest to his cheek and pulled him to me for a long, wet, and hot kiss that might've led to us skipping some of the steps in his plan for hooky day had there not been a skillet of pig meat on the counter between us.

"So, where are our plates?" I asked King after letting his lips go.

"No plates," he said, plucking a piece of oily bacon directly from the skillet. "I eat my pork right out the frying pan. Tastes better that way."

"What? You're supposed to drain it on a paper towel or something. You can't eat that right out of the pan. You'll die of heart disease. Hypertension," I protested.

"Oh, I'm not a brother," he joked, before picking out another piece and teasing me with it. "I'm good. I may burn in the sun, but it takes a lot more than some pig fat to knock an Irishman down. Remember that."

So, people still go on Maury Povich's show to let all of America know that they have no idea who their baby daddy is, and apparently it's pretty easy for your best friend to sleep with your girl-friend. King and I snuggled under the covers in his bed and tried to act like we were above watching this silliness unfold between trailer-park drama queens and project papas, but it was too good to turn away. We lay there enjoying the TV antics and eating bacon out of the frying pan like it was popcorn—and I admit, it did taste better right out of the grease. For a long time our conversation never went deeper than disgust at a wrongfully accused father or tears at a toothless dad reunited with his daughter after twenty-five years—all in front of Maury Povich. Still, I felt like something was going on between us. Yes, I could tell he was trying to keep up this hard persona, but his laugh was becoming the most honest thing about him. Even if I didn't find something funny, if he laughed, I laughed at him laughing. And he laughed a lot.

My cell phone was on the nightstand set to silent, and I looked over at it a few times to see that Paul had called me twice since sunup and left one message. I was about to listen to it, but when I reached for the phone, King reached for my ass cheek and I kind of got tied up with him for an hour. By the time I looked at the phone again, my battery was dead and I just really didn't feel like plugging it up. Why? Paul was the one who'd put me on vacation. Anything he had to say could wait until I was ready to return—wasn't that his advice?

We ordered Thai and pizza. Chicken wings. Closed the blinds. Watched too many gangster movies. Reenacted the scenes. He was an Irish Tony Montana and I was a young Michelle Pfeiffer turned Foxy Brown with a mean walk. We washed each other's backs in the shower. We talked a lot.

King opened up a little more. He wasn't one of *the* McDonnells from the History Channel. But he was *a* McDonnell. His great-grandfather Rig actually was on the second ship to arrive at Ellis Island. He'd come to America a thief who'd originally been denied entry, but he used blood money to get a spot on the ship. When he got to New York, he vowed to leave his past in Ireland behind, but he had little choice and too many opportunities to do the wrong thing. But then he met King's great-grandmother, whom he fell madly in love with and married in secret to stop her parents from sending her to a convent to avoid them hooking up.

King seemed so proud of his long-ago ancestry, but the closer he got to his present, the more vague and tight-lipped he became. He'd look away. Make sudden transitions. He did let on about where he thought his love of black women came from though. His great-grandmother's parents had good reason to try to stop their "true blood" Irish daughter from marrying a white man. They were keeping a big secret. King's great-great-grandmother wasn't Irish at all. She was half black and half white. Had come up to New York from Georgia in the 1870s and used her ivory skin, green eyes, and hair blond from the roots to change her history. She told her husband all of this when she met him at a soup kitchen near Castle Garden days after he'd arrived at New York's original immigration station from Ireland. He didn't care. He was in love and vowed to keep her secret. But nearly twenty years later when their daughter, who they were lucky to have come out with skin and hair just like her mother's, announced that she was in love with an Irishman, they worried about what her children would come out looking like, and then came the threat of the convent.

"So, you have a little black in you?" I laughed, looking at King. I could see it then. I imagined that was what made his skin so beautiful.

"I come from a long line of men who love black women," he said. "It's funny because they claimed they were passing, but I look at pictures and they both looked black to me. My grandmother had an Afro—she used to iron it on the ironing board though. Never went out in the sun."

The second morning I awoke in King's bed, I got up and went around the room trying to put together pieces of the outfit I'd been wearing when I got there.

King sleepily called out, "Stay. What do I have to do to make you stay?"

I returned to bed and went back to sleep. We played hooky a second day. Kept the blinds closed so tight it was easy to forget the world outside was still in motion. I forgot to plug in my phone. Maybe I didn't want to plug in my phone.

Morning three, I got up again. King called out again.

"I can't," I answered before he finished.

"Why not?"

"Because . . . I can't. I have to go. I just have to."

King got out of bed and met me in the living room, where I was looking for my shoe. "Why?" he asked. "Why can't you just stay here? With me?"

I stopped my search and smiled at him. "You're not tired of me yet?"

He approached me slowly, trying to con me back to bed with his eyes. "I'm definitely tired . . . but not of you. I'm tired because of you."

He almost pulled me in with his stare, but I walked away. "I have to go."

Inside, I felt the same way he did. I wanted to stay there in the darkness with him and forget about anything outside. But every once in a while the sunlight would shine through the blinds and I knew I couldn't pretend my world didn't exist. Being with King, I felt like I was safe in a cocoon or a cradle. But even caterpillars and babies have to leave their confines sometime. And though King seemed perfectly content in the high-rise Brooklyn Eden we'd been creating out of Chinese delivery and On Demand movies, I knew his outside world was catching up with him too. His phone was rattling all night. A few times he'd left the room to make a call and returned out of his fun mood. Sometimes I felt like he was running away from something just like I was running away from something. I didn't know what he was running away from. But I didn't know what I was running away from either.

Downstairs, Baboo was waiting in his car, but I demanded that King have Frantz get me a random cab off the street.

"No more tabs on me," I said.

"No more ignoring my calls," King answered.

"No more."

He kissed me on the cheek so sweetly and helped me into a cab Frantz had led into the circular drive in front of the building.

"Here," King said, handing me a little Baggie filled with pills he'd pulled from his pocket.

"What's this?" I said, taking it. There were maybe fifty pills inside.

"A little extra in case your back starts hurting again."

"I don't need it." I frowned, trying to return the Baggie, but King lifted his hands and stepped back.

"Throw it away if you don't need it. I just want to make sure you're okay."

I stashed the Baggie in my purse, vowing to throw it away once I got home, and waved at King standing in the drive as the taxi drove off.

The city looked so strange to me after coming out of the darkness King and I created in the Clocktower. Summer had come while we were in our cocoon, so though it was late morning and rush-hour traffic was just slowing, the sun was already pounding down on the concrete, making me wish I had worn the dark summer shades I usually saved for midsummer walks.

The ride back to my place was slow and silent. The driver was white with a head of gray hair. The name on his permit was George Thomas. He wasn't wearing a colorful turban, and his cab wasn't dingy.

When we got to my place, he happily accepted my money and pulled off like he'd never see me again. And he probably wouldn't.

Standing in front of my building, I looked up at my dark living room window.

"Welcome home, Queen," I said to myself in a low voice before stepping toward the front door.

I was about to walk inside, but something told me to look back over my shoulder.

Taking the empty spot where the taxi had been was a familiar police wagon with the front window down and familiar eyes ogling me.

"You getting in pretty early," Paul said, hanging out the driver's side window. He'd often drive the wagon around the city when he was on "official" business or just creeping. "Your daddy know you keeping company with folks this time of morning?"

"My father knows I'm a grown woman and doesn't keep tabs on me," I answered from the door.

Paul laughed. "Oh, I wasn't talking about your *father*. I meant your *daddy*—big daddy." He pointed to his face.

I was supposed to laugh. I didn't.

"So, you're just going to stand over there? So far from me?"

"You're the one showing up at my place randomly . . . once again," I said. "I thought we had an agreement about this."

Paul chuckled at my resistance as the old judge from my floor and his wife walked out of the building pretending not to see me.

I stood waiting for Paul to get out of the wagon.

"You always want things your way," he complained, coming to me and attempting to open the door.

"My way? What are you . . . look, what do you want? Why are you here? Again?" I pulled his hand off the door handle to make it clear he wasn't even walking into the building with me.

"Calm down. Shit. I was just making sure you were okay. I've been calling you for days. No answer," Paul complained. "I'm saying, I'm not just your lover. I'm also your boss. It's my job to make sure you're all right."

"Paul, news flash: You're not my lover. And your position as my boss is under question as we speak."

Paul grinned. "So, you got a new job? Is that where you're coming from?" he probed, looking at my attire. "I'm not sure what kind of firm allows attorneys to wear jean skirts, but okay."

I crossed my arms over my breasts and poked out a hip, making sure my pose conveyed my disinterest.

"So, you're not going to tell me where you were?" Paul asked.

"Not at all. Want anything else before I go upstairs . . . alone?"

"Fine. You want to play hard. We'll play hard," Paul said. "I'm actually here on official business. I need to talk to you about something."

"What?"

"I can't tell you about it down here . . . on the street. Why can't we go upstairs?" He reached for the door again, but I swung my hip to the other side to stop him from walking past me.

"Kim?" he pushed.

"Paul?" I answered, mimicking him. "Just tell me what's up. You said it's official business; let's be real official."

He pouted and gathered himself again. "We have a new case starting up. You're the only person who can work it."

"Well, the 'only person' is on vacation, so that's settled. Why don't you try passing it on to Easter?"

"I'm serious, Kim. This is gonna be really big." Something in Paul's eyes changed out of playing mode and shook us back to our work. I compromised and agreed to sit and talk to him in the wagon.

He told me about a case he'd been following with Elliot. Jim Reddy, the DA in Kings County, had contacted them months ago about a growing drug ring in Brooklyn that had been gaining attention in headlines for years. They were selling prescription pills to students at Brooklyn College, Pratt, and LIU, in dorms and at parties. Reddy had known about the operation for years. It was common for dealers to sell to students. But the ring was growing more powerful, elusive, and unpredictable. They seemed to have an endless supply of money and pills they pumped onto the campuses by way of strippers and call girls sent to provide comfort to the bored and dejected. He'd been working with his chief and the Brooklyn PD to just get a face, a name behind the operation, but they kept following weak leads and the small charges they did get through on the dancers and prostitutes seldom led to indictment, and none of them snagged the leader. Reddy contacted Paul because the streets were talking and the ring was open for business in New York County—our county. They finally had a face and a name.

"I wouldn't trust the case with any other prosecutor. I want you to be cocounsel with me," Paul said. "Now, Elliot is working on the arrest, but we already have some of the report, stuff sent in from Brooklyn and even the Bronx, and I want to have those charges ready to go before the grand jury once Elliot moves, so we can get an indictment. You know the faster we move with things like this, the better. Don't want their lawyers to see it coming."

"When do you need me back?" I asked, reverting into my old role so anxiously I actually felt a thirst in my throat and twitching in my fingers. As he'd laid out the details, I'd thought of the charges. Knew the words to write. The calls to make.

"Meeting is tomorrow," Paul said, and I heard the thirst in his voice, too. This was what we loved. What we chased. "I think this is it, Kim. If I nail this—if we nail this, then the writing is on the wall. I can't lose. It's my ticket—"

"Mayor?" I said, recalling something he'd whispered to me in bed one night.

He nodded.

"You think people will be looking at this case like that?" I asked, considering what that could mean for me, too.

"These guys are moving on to NYU and Columbia."

"White kids."

"Jewish kids." He looked at me. "I'd get the godfather behind me," he added, and he wasn't talking about a fictitious Italian Don Vito Corleone. Sanford I. "Sandy" Weill was rumored to be the most powerful man in New York City, maybe the world. The former CEO and chairman of Citigroup, he'd bought every New York mayor since the 1980s. No one brokered a deal in the city without his backing. When the president came to town, he met with Sandy.

"I'll be there in the morning," I said, getting out of the police wagon.

Paul watched me walk around the front of the car. I felt his eyes all over my body.

"Kim," he called when I was back up on the sidewalk and steps away from the driver's side door. "I don't care where you were all these nights. Just know that wherever you were, whatever it was, I won't let it come between us."

"It's none of your business," I said, feeling like he knew more than he was saying—that was always a possibility with Paul. He never ever made a move or a statement like that unless he was sure of the terms. He wasn't the type of person who lived in ignorance. He faked it.

"You're right. It's not my business right now," he responded distantly. "So don't make it my business."

The same four bare walls I'd fled days ago for Brooklyn were waiting for me upstairs. There was no million-dollar art. No marble anything. No bacon in a skillet. No King. No nothing. And if it had felt quiet and lonely before, upon return it was dead. I turned on the radio and the television. Powered up my laptop. Plugged in my cell phone. Tried to remember what in the hell I'd ever done with myself in that apartment before.

I sat on the couch and noticed a water ring on the table where I normally sat my glass each night. Beside it was the faint ring from the bottle of Jameson.

I looked at the clock. It was just a little after noon.

I got up and checked messages on my voice mail once my phone powered up. There were messages from Kent and Tamika. Another one from Dr. Davis begging me to call him to set up a meeting. Texts from Carol about the meeting with Paul tomorrow. She'd copied the police reports and put them on my drive so I could look at them from home.

After thanking her by text, I decided to take a nap.

I went into the bedroom and lay on my back. I closed my eyes and waited but I couldn't find rest through the commotion I'd created between the television and radio. Still, it all seemed so quiet. I wondered what King was doing and turned over to the phone I'd placed on the bed beside me.

I picked it up and was about to call him but decided against it. I didn't want to seem too thirsty. I'd just insisted on leaving his place.

I decided to call Tamika instead. She'd be an earful. And never one to disappoint, she picked up before the first ring was finished.

"Girl, it's about time you called me back!" she spat out in her most suspicious voice.

"Hey, Mika!"

"Hey yourself! You listen to my message? You hear about Vonn?" she blurted out.

"What? What is it?" I asked.

"It's on the news. You see it on the news?"

"I've been busy. What is it?"

"Oh, no. Girl, you sitting down somewhere?"

"Yes," I said, suddenly sensing the urgency in Tamika's voice and sitting up in the bed. "What's going on?"

"He's dead, girl. Vonn is fucking dead."

I felt like she was telling me news about someone I actually knew. I asked, "How did he die?"

"Was murdered! Shot in the back of the head. They found him on the bank of the East River last night. Wrapped in plastic. Fucked up!"

"Who killed him?"

"Fuck I know? Fuck I want to know? They're saying it may be drug-related on the news. Dude has a long-ass rap sheet. And you know you don't get shot in the back of the head and dumped in the East River by no stick-up kids," Tamika went on speculating. "This had drug shit written all over it. Monique's all fucked up about it, too." She lowered her voice. "Don't tell nobody I told you, but she might be pregnant by that motherfucker. She swore me to secrecy, but this shit is too crazy for me to keep my mouth closed."

"This is horrible," I said. "Does she know anything? What happened? Nothing?"

"No. She didn't speak to him since I last spoke to you when he was missing. The po-po were knocking at her door last night asking when the last time was that she saw him. Said they found her number in his phone—" She paused. "That's why I was calling you."

"What?" I felt a lump pushing through my throat.

"Rig McDonnell—that's the other person he spoke to before . . . ," she said. "They asked her if she knew him. She said she'd never heard the name. But then they showed her a picture. It was the white boy."

"King?"

"Yes," she said in a low voice.

"Is she sure? This is crazy," I said, remembering that King had told me his grandfather's name was Rig, which meant "king" in Gaelic. "I need to call him. I was just with him, and he was fine. I guess he didn't know."

"Do you think he—"

"He what?" I cut Tamika off, knowing where she was going. "He killed him?" I laughed. "Are you kidding? That's not like him. Plus, you asked where I've been all these nights—I was with him. Okay? So, there. He's fine. King is fine."

"Well, that's good news. I was worried. You know? With the cops having his picture and shit. They made it seem like he was . . . involved."

"No way. And I can confirm that. The man didn't leave my sight for two days," I said. "We were locked up at his place."

"Did he say anything about Vonn? Did you ask him like I told you to?"

"I forgot," I said. "I wasn't exactly thinking about Vonn then. Slipped my mind. Guess I'll call him now. I'm sure he must know by now."

When I got off the phone with Tamika, I called King immediately, but it kept going to voice mail. I didn't leave a message though. I didn't want to mention his friend dying if he didn't know about it, and I didn't want to seem like I was all up in his business either. I sent King a text asking him to call me back, and he responded with one word: *OK*. Then I lay in bed with the phone in my hand for hours, waiting.

Chapter 10

In *Poor Richard's Almanack*, Benjamin Franklin wrote, "A countryman between two lawyers is like a fish between two cats." One of my law school professors who said he "left the profession to hide in the academy" made my class write a five-page essay about the quote. I admit that I completely misunderstood the statement and spent my five pages writing about how insulting the quote was. Franklin was writing in absolutes. Generalizing. Pushing ideas that contributed to those horrible lawyer jokes that commonly opened with two lawyers drowning in the ocean and no one wanting to save them. I wrote about how Franklin's statement didn't take into account those of us who wanted to see true justice in the world. To make things better and have an impact. To change and protect. My professor put a smiley face on the top of the paper and a fancy "F" beneath it. On the last page, he wrote, "Come back and see me in two years."

It didn't take two years for me to experience what Franklin was really talking about. After six months in the DA's office, I rewrote the paper, sent it to the professor, and got a sad face with an A underneath it, and on the last page, he wrote, "Welcome to the practice."

My new paper was about the fish's blood and what I saw it doing to me and every single lawyer I knew. At the end of the day, no matter what preconceived notions or ideals a new attorney has about her profession, her training in law is about winning. Not compromising. Certainly not losing. Winning. To win, you use your knowledge and understanding of the law, which you later realize is simply human-written conceptions of what justice is and isn't based on the needs of the percentage of people who have the power to enact the laws. Training makes you so thirsty for this win, you'll go to battle with anyone to get it. Use your laws like armor and weapons to offend and defend and win. After a while, your opposition is always the other lawyer, whatever laws they're using to win. Your battlefield is the courtroom. Your audience is the jury. Your trophy is the ruling. Nowhere in there is mention of the countryman who led the two lawyers to the gathering. He became just a fish. A nobody who met his demise in the full stomach of the lawyer who prevailed in the end.

Walking into the conference room in the DA's office the next morning, I smelled blood everywhere. It was like I was a cat in a seafood restaurant and all around me were my back-alley hunting buddies, who were coming up with a plan to crack open a tank filled with plump pink salmon.

Paul sat at the head of the table in his favorite blue suit. Two other ADAs, one from Rackets and one from Narcotics, and I sat to his left. Chief Elliot was on his right followed by Reddy, the DA from Kings County; his chief; and a police detective from their precinct in Downtown Brooklyn.

I'd been away from the office for nearly a week, but when I walked into the conference room with my coffee cup in one hand and my laptop in the other, I smelled the blood, and sitting down in my chair to Paul's right was like sinking my teeth into a rare piece of fish steak—the first bite. I let the feeling rush through me and looked around to see that we were all enjoying the same invisible meal. These men, all men, were determined to fill their bellies.

I found Carol at her desk. I was unusually happy to see her. We'd actually hugged, and then she'd launched right into her notes for the day, asking if I'd had a chance to open the files she'd placed on the drive about the case. I lied and said I had. Really, it was only a half lie. I did open one of the files, but I couldn't focus on anything after I got the news about Vonn and was waiting to hear back from King. I was so on edge I wanted to go downstairs to the store and get a bottle of Jameson. But I remembered my promise to Kent, so I took two of the pills King gave me instead and got into bed with my iPad and the case notes opened.

As soon as I started reading the first paragraph, my cell phone started buzzing with a new message. I rushed to pick it up from the nightstand, sure it was King. It wasn't. Just a mass text from my gym letting me know about the "summer sizzler sale."

I decided to take a short nap. Just a few minutes to calm myself down and then I'd get back at it. While it was an honest plan, that nap tumbled into a restless slumber that led to another car-accident nightmare, where I was yet again behind the wheel.

When I awoke in the morning, I found my hand clutching my cell phone.

"LeTiffany Tedget, known on the street as 'Yellow,' was arrested at Brooklyn College two months ago for prostitution and intent to sell prescription drugs." Reddy had gotten up and started giving the background information on the drug ring with reach into both boroughs. He'd opened with the basics Paul shared with me the day before. "While Major Narcotics Investigation tried to hold her and get some information about her supplier, we didn't have a whole lot on her, so we had to let her go." As Reddy spoke, on the conference room projector he flashed arrest photos of a frail, light-skinned black woman who looked noticeably strung out. While the craters in her cheeks and pale peeling lips suggested that she was a meth addict, it was easy to tell she'd been beautiful in another life. "A week later, Yellow's body was found on the bank of the East River." He flashed crime-scene photos of her nude body spread on the riverbank. Her eyes were open and white with film. "She'd been shot in the back of the head." The images switched from her muddy breasts to black bloody clumps of hair at the base of her skull, right above long keloids that looked like garden snakes beneath her skin slinking up her spine.

"What's that on her back?" Paul asked, pointing.

"Lesions from some kind of incident. The coroner's report says they're fairly new," Reddy said, looking down at the report in his hands. "Likely from trauma caused by some kind of instrument."

"A cheese grater," I said, looking at the large image on the screen and remembering how Bernard had described the dancer Miguel Alvarez brutally attacked in front of him, the skin tearing off her back like Swiss cheese.

"Yes," Reddy said, looking up at me. He was an old prosecutor whose remarkable instinct made him very popular throughout the state. Like Paul, he liked working closely with detectives and police officers. He liked to keep his ear to the street, connecting law with order. "That's what the coroner suggested."

"You know this woman?" Paul asked me.

"Bernard Richard mentioned her attack during an interview about Miguel Alvarez and the Candy Shop indictment," I said. "She was a stripper. Started selling for Alvarez. He turned her out. Beat her up pretty bad. Guess she moved on to Brooklyn."

"That's how Special Victims Bureau got the lead on her supplier. They started passing her picture around, showed it to a Dominican stripper they busted in a car in back of Pumps," Reddy said, referring to a strip club in East Williamsburg that was known for prostitutes. "If they took her in, it would've been her first trip to Rikers, so she started talking really fast. Said Yellow was her roommate. She'd stopped working in the club when her old pimp scarred up her back. And since then, she'd been on the street selling for this man—"

I was taking notes on my laptop, so it took a minute before I looked up at the new image on the screen.

"Rig McDonnell," Reddy started, and the two words stung me harder than King's face in a mug shot behind Paul's head, "is the co-owner of Damaged Goods, a hole-in-the-wall bar in downtown Brooklyn."

I felt like King's blue eyes were staring right at me—his eyes and everyone else's at the table. Like the next picture on the screen would be of me. The next question aimed at me.

Reddy added, "For a long time, Narc has known about Rig's dealings in organized crime. His father, Dr. Rig Conor 'R.C.' McDonnell, started opening pain clinics in Bedford-Stuyvesant in the early nineties." Reddy switched to a map of New York with, like, twenty stars dotting neighborhoods throughout the boroughs. "Soon that ballooned into operations in middle-income communities in the Bronx, Brooklyn, and even Westchester."

"They were nothing more than pill mills pumping oxycodone," one of the Brooklyn detectives, Kern Strickland, said, jumping in. "Narc shut most of them down in 2000." I knew Strickland from a few cases I'd taken on that led me to Brooklyn. He was a brother. Had a bald head and a distinct distaste for lawyers. I always noticed it in how he spoke to me or over me. At first I thought he was just like the other boys who thought girls shouldn't be playing on their ball court and resented me for whatever power I had, but then I saw that he treated all lawyers with the same judgment—man or woman, black or white, he held us all in contempt.

"But before that happened, the clinics made him a very rich man. And even when Narc shut down the clinics and took his license to practice in New York, McDonnell opened legal pain clinics and had his old doctors writing prescriptions for him like bus passes. Dr. Stan Xuhui Li, one of the doctors on McDonnell's payroll, wrote more than seventeen thousand prescriptions in thirty months," Reddy said, flashing pictures of Li and King's father on the screen. "We took Li down last year. Tried to get to McDonnell, but he used his muscle and his money and went underground. But he's still out there. We think he's in somewhere in Central America—Belize maybe."

"That brings us back to his son—Rig. He goes by 'King' on the street," Strickland said when King's photo was on the screen again. Strickland fit the typical profile of a black Brooklyn detective—tall and muscly with a walk that carried the weight of the heavy-ass chip on his shoulder. He was no lawyer, but he wanted blood, too.

"You okay?" Paul whispered to me. "You look sick."

"I'm fine," I replied. "I'm just a little thirsty." I kept my eyes low and off the screen, so Paul couldn't read anything into my reaction to King's image—if he hadn't already.

He reached past me and picked up the carafe to pour water into the empty glass beside my laptop.

Reddy went on, "As I said earlier, Rig has been using his daddy's money to make moves through this nightclub." He showed a picture of Damaged Goods. "Working with a couple of local thugs—small-time dealers—for a while. We've kept our eyes on them. Kept our eyes on Rig."

Reddy explained that King had the perfect plan to move drugs out of Damaged Goods. The girls at the club, and at that point I was assuming it was the beauties I'd seen lined up at the bar at Damaged Goods, had prescriptions from actual doctors throughout the city. He registered a pain clinic to the club's address, legally dispensed pills to the women using their prescriptions, and even acquired medical insurance payouts for the drugs. They then went out and sold the pills. Gave King 90 percent of the profit. The women played it safe though. They were all strippers who used their beauty to work the college scene and sell to an audience that couldn't get enough until it was all too late. They sold everything from codeine to Ritalin. They hosted "welcome back" parties at the beginning of the semester. Had payment plans to collect student loan funds and even took credit cards. They were working the stripping parties legally and just added the cost of the Baggie to the cost of the dance. It all appeared legit until the kids started dropping off like flies toward the end of the semester, showing up at addiction clinics shaking and begging their suburban parents for more pills.

It was hard for me to hold the Cronut I'd eaten for breakfast in my stomach as I ingested the information about King. As Reddy and the detective carried on, I pretended to take notes to keep my eyes off of the images, but all I could feel was King all over me. Hear him in my ear. Feel him inside of me. There was buzzing in my ear. The croissant/doughnut tossing around in my stomach. I was asking myself every question that began with "What the fuck?" and ended with "How didn't I know?"

The last week was in instant replay in my mind. Every minute since I walked into Damaged Goods. Since King walked into Damaged Goods.

I heard Reddy say, "We had reason to believe McDonnell was behind LeTiffany's murder." Through the corner of my eye, I saw King's mug shot beside the photo of Yellow's body beside the river. I took air fast into my nose to calm an uneasy feeling growing in my stomach. "We have statements from her roommate that Yellow was afraid because King's crew heard about her arrest. They thought she was talking to us, and that was how she got dead."

"Real dead," Strickland chimed in.

"I don't get it. If you had the statement from the roommate, how didn't you get an arrest?" Paul asked.

"We brought all the guys in," Reddy explained, moving his slides along to a collage of pictures of every one of King's friends I'd seen with him at the club—including Vonn. "We were ready to go. But then the roommate lawyered up. She suddenly had a whole bunch of money. Recanted her statement, saying the officers set her up. Turns out one of them was her old john. We can't touch her."

"But we did have one ace in the hole—LaVonnte Russell—a member of the crew the feds nabbed a long time ago on the Jersey

Turnpike with a shitload of cocaine," Strickland said. "He was moving his own stuff but said he'd give intel on a boss behind a bigger operation that was growing and about to take over the city—move into Manhattan."

Vonn's picture grew larger.

"He'd been wearing a wire for us for weeks," the detective added before Vonn's mug shot changed to the crime-scene image of his body washed up along the shore. "We found him yesterday morning."

"You think McDonnell did this?" Paul asked.

"Number-one suspect," Strickland answered. "Vonn betrayed McDonnell. Vonn's dead. That's what we got. Motive, but it's all speculation right now. We can't seem to get anything to stick to McDonnell. He operates like the old mobsters did back in the day. Never gets his hands dirty. Just orders and orders through so many ears, he comes out clean every time."

"So no charges?" Paul added.

"No. We're just bringing him in for questioning. Try to shake things up. But these guys always have alibis," Reddy jumped in, switching the picture back to a close-up of King's mug shot that spread so wide on the screen, his blues eyes became huge pixelated cubes that nearly looked demonic. "We'll ask where he was the night Vonn was murdered. And there will be something. A girlfriend. Probably one of the strippers. You know the drill."

The men at the table traded knowing stares.

The Cronut pieces shot up my throat, and I jumped out of my seat to stop myself from vomiting.

"Bathroom," I said, rushing out with my hand over my mouth.

I locked myself in the bathroom before staggering into a stall and vomiting Cronut bits into the latrine.

"Oh my God," I said, bending down over the yellowing water, my knees on the dirty floor and hands embracing the bowl. "Fuck! Fuck!"

Hunched over and heaving, I kicked the wall and cursed some more. Vonn's waterlogged body washed up on the shore and Reddy's comments about King's alibi sent the last bits of Cronut and bile up my throat, and my body contorted to stop myself from vomiting.

"Get it together, Kim!" I cried with the bile in my throat burning so much it forced tears to my eyes. "Please! Please! What the fuck is going on?"

I felt in my pocket for my phone and pulled it out.

"No! Don't call! Don't call!"

There was knocking at the door.

"Kim? You okay?" It was Carol.

"I'm fine, Carol!" I answered. "Tell them I'll be right back. Just a little nausea. I'm fine."

Still heaving, I looked up at the ceiling and asked myself what was happening.

"Just get it together!" I cried as a tear rolled down my cheek. "Please!"

When I left the stall and stood in the mirror to wipe my tears, I looked at myself and thought of how my father always said he could see my mother in my eyes. I never saw it. Sometimes I thought maybe I couldn't remember what her eyes looked like. Still, I looked at my eyes and pretended they were hers. Thought of what she might say if she was standing there looking at me. How she might say it. But I heard nothing. Maybe I couldn't remember her voice either.

"I got this! Yes! I do. I can do this," I snapped, and suddenly wiped my tears and sucked up the snot in my nose. "We're good. We can do this," I said to myself before washing my hands with methodic coolness to redirect my tension. "This is your career, Kim. You will not let anyone fuck it up." I stared into my eyes. "No one."

"Kim! Come open the door. It's Paul."

Paul started knocking in a way that made it clear he wasn't going to stop until I unlocked the bathroom door.

"Oh, I'm sorry. I didn't realize I'd been gone so long," I called from the sink.

"Open the door," he said again, as if he hadn't heard me, and continued his annoying slow knocks.

I left the mirror and opened the door. "Yes," I said, stepping out into the hallway with him.

He looked at me suspiciously from head to toe to head.

"You sick?" he asked. "You look like you've been crying. What happened in there?" He nodded toward the bathroom.

"Nothing. I was just feeling sick," I said defensively as I tried to lead him back to the conference room. "I didn't think I'd been in there that long. Why did you leave the meeting?"

Paul grabbed my arm.

"Sick like what? Did you vomit in there?" he asked, sounding rather nervous.

"Now you care if I'm sick? Really?" I laughed at his clear desperation. "Wait. This isn't about you caring. You're"—I pointed at the bathroom—"Wait. You think I'm"—I pointed at my stomach. "And by you?" I laughed again. "Not a chance."

"You have been acting funny lately. And not talking to me." He stepped closer to me and whispered, "Maybe that's what all of this not-wanting-to-see-me bullshit is about."

"Get over yourself, dickhead. I'm not pregnant with your child," I said. "And if I was, I wouldn't be here. I'd be at a clinic. Look, let's just go back into the meeting. We can *not* talk about this later." I started walking toward the conference room again.

"Too late. Everyone's gone," Paul said, stopping me.

"Gone?"

Paul said, "The detective squad from the Eighty-Fourth Precinct picked McDonnell up an hour ago. Reddy said we can sit in on the interview. See what kind of animal we're dealing with."

"We? I don't want to sit in on the interview. I'm not—"

"Now you're joking right? Come on. If we're going to take this guy down, we have to be in the loop with the cops. You know that." Paul chuckled, pulling the keys to the police wagon from his pocket. "Ride with me. We'll use the sirens. Be in Brooklyn in ten minutes."

The Eighty-Fourth was the big bad bully of the Kings County precincts. Its choke hold on a grid of the moneymaking businesses in downtown Brooklyn, signature-signing aristocrats in Borough Hall, and the major courts in Brooklyn that called the precinct home made it a lion with a silent growl and an invisible reach that few could ignore. That probably sounds strange when speaking about an entity that was essentially created to shuffle criminals in and out as law enforcement sought to make Brooklyn a pleasant place to call home, but there was so much more the officers in any precinct controlled. As the old saying goes, "If you want to do business in Brooklyn, it'd better be a blue business." That meant you needed the cops on your side to survive. Sometimes those cops were good guys. Sometimes those cops were bad guys.

The Eighty-Fourth's close proximity to the Brooklyn and Manhattan Bridges meant that officers, officials, and attorneys on either side of the East River often worked together or bumped heads over crimes and casualties.

When Paul and I walked into the Eighty-Fourth, it felt the same way it always had—like walking into a room filled with sorority sisters who may have slept with your husband. Everyone was all hugs and "Hey, it's been a while," but careful with what they said and what they didn't say because too much of either one wouldn't be good for anyone.

Greeting everyone as we walked in, I kept my smile wide and casual as I had in the police wagon with Paul on the way over. Under the blare of the siren, he'd told me about what I'd missed at the meeting with Reddy after I left. With so much pressure on his operation, Vonn had let on that King was slowly moving his business into Manhattan and had set up a new operation just a few blocks from the DA's office. His goal was simple. He wanted to move on from the college crowd in Brooklyn and into the deeper pockets of the upper class in Manhattan—entertainers, executives, socialites, and tech geeks, an entire population of addicts who preferred drugs that came with prescriptions. In the wagon, I kept up the conversation with Paul, trying so hard to seem concerned, but King's next move wasn't at the top of my list. While no one aside from Tamika and her friends knew about King, just the thought of me being attached to him in any way was heartbreaking and even embarrassing. I was worrying about where he'd been and whether everyone else was going to find out that I'd been with him. I didn't want King to see me—I couldn't let him see me. But I couldn't exactly refuse to go into the interrogation. I didn't know why, but I could feel Paul watching me. I could tell he was trying to figure something out.

One of the detectives who'd just been at the meeting chatted with Paul as they led us into the observation room, where we could watch King's interrogation through the one-way mirror. The room was dark and as small as a walk-in closet. Four chairs were lined up in front of the glass.

I kept my eyes on my feet to avoid looking at King, whose presence I immediately sensed. Even in my nervousness, I could smell and feel him. Memories of our every second together made the scene surreal and what I knew I should be thinking about and feeling at that moment. The stranger on the other side of the glass was my enemy. The lover on the other side of the glass was no stranger.

Paul and I sat beside each other, leaving two seats for Reddy and Norman Delli, the Eighty-Fourth's Egyptian psychologist who used to sit in on interrogations in Manhattan before he transferred to Brooklyn. He'd once told me that people always thought the traditional one-way mirror was a joke—cops spying on suspects, as other cops played "good cop, bad cop," taking turns trying to push a confession. But the one-way mirror was no failure. Its success, he'd said, was about the psychology of what happens when someone knows he's being watched. Most guilty people looked away from the mirror when they felt anxious or trapped in the small interrogation room. Sometimes they'd lash out or curse at whoever was spying from the other side. The innocent always looked right into the glass, as if they were looking for allies or some support system, someone to witness what they were going through.

"Motherfucker ain't look over here yet," Paul said, elbowing me to get my attention when Reddy and Delli came and sat beside Paul, signaling that they were about to start the interview. Paul leaned over to me. "Always a bad sign when they don't look up at the mirror," he whispered.

I quickly rolled my eyes over to Paul to avoid the spotlights on King. "Yes. It is."

Paul turned from me and started talking to Reddy.

The door in the interrogation room opened and slammed close. I raised my eyelids just enough to see Strickland's shoes walking toward the table where I knew King was sitting.

He pulled out his chair and sat down. I kept my eyes on his feet the entire time.

"Some weather out there. Looks like it's going to be a hot summer." He used his feet to drag the chair closer to King, and it scraped loudly against the concrete floor. "I don't care if it's hot. I prefer the heat. I hate those rainy summers. I was raised in Seattle. Moved to New York to escape all that rain." He paused. "You ever been to Seattle?"

"I'm not in Seattle right now?"

I heard King's voice, and without any internal agreement on the matter, my eyes went to find him. He was smiling at the detective. Had pulled his chair to the table and was sitting back, holding a coffee cup in his hand like he was meeting a friend at a café.

"Do you think you're in Seattle?" Strickland said. He was holding a folder in his hands. He slid it onto the table slowly.

"Come on, Strickland. You know we've been on this date before. What you want from me?" King asked in the deep voice that rang with more authority than the detective's bassless tone.

"Can you believe this motherfucker?" Paul said, crossing his arms.

"What do you think I want?" Strickland asked.

"Fuck I know? Dick?" King put his cup down and leaned toward him. "You know I don't get down like that."

They laughed. King tilted his head back and looked at the detective smugly.

"Y'all brought me in here. Got me in this room for two hours by myself. You come in here to talk about Seattle?" King said.

"He's annoyed," Delli whispered.

"I know you're from Seattle, Strickland. You already told me that story about your wife and moving to New York to escape the rain. Fine. We're friends. What the fuck do you want from me?" King asked.

Strickland sat back in his seat too, leaving more space between himself and King.

Delli stood and walked to the mirror. "Strickland's messing up."

"LaVonnte Russell," Strickland started, but then he paused.

"La—who?" King looked confused.

"LaVonnte Russell," Strickland repeated.

"I don't know who that is. Is that what this is about? Why you have me down here?"

"You know who he is. We both know you know who he is. Vonn—one of your boys. He hangs with you at the club, Damaged Goods. You have him doing your dirty work. Right?"

"I don't know what you're talking about, Strickland. I really don't. I know Vonn, but I didn't know his name was LaVonnte Russell. We're just cool. That's it. Why? What did he do? He got locked up? Baby mama tripping again?"

"No, McDonnell. He's dead. Vonn is dead." Strickland plucked the folder from the table and handed it to King.

King took the folder and leafed through it. From the look on King's face it was clear that he'd found pictures of Vonn's dead body inside.

"Nigga fucked up. Shit. Who did it?" he asked coolly, looking at the pictures with a detachment I knew Delli was looking for. People who are guilty usually focus on one part of the picture, the victim's eyes or some piece of the crime scene they remember or wish to recall. The innocent look at the entire puzzle with clear detachment. Their eyes bounce around at everything they don't know or haven't seen as they try to understand what they're looking at.

King's eyes were bouncing.

"He wasn't there," Delli confirmed, looking at us over his shoulder.

Strickland exhaled and stretched his arms and neck as if he'd heard Delli or knew the same thing. "We're trying to find out who did it. You know anything about it?"

"I didn't even know Vonn was dead," King said, sliding the folder and picture back onto the table like an old newspaper he'd read.

"Seems unlikely. A member of your crew goes missing. Body washes up in the East River and you don't know anything. Give me something."

"Nothing to give. I'm a businessman. I keep telling y'all that. I don't have a crew. Whatever Vonn was doing to get himself killed and thrown in the East River was on him," King said. "I actually heard he had a pretty long rap sheet. Y'all look into that? Shit, all the tips I'm giving y'all, maybe I should be the detective." King looked at the mirror. "Who back there watching? Reddy? Fucking Delli? LaPaze? Williams? All y'all sitting around watching me like I got the answers. I don't have any answers. I'm a businessman. I told y'all that." He smiled at us, and when his stare came closer to where I was sitting, he peered more directly into the glass.

"McDonnell, where were you the night before last? The night Vonn was murdered?" Strickland asked.

"No—ain't no old heads watching me right now," King said, seemingly in a trance at what he saw in the mirror. He wasn't listening to Strickland. I knew he couldn't see me, but that wasn't how it felt. "New people. Who's watching me? Hunh?" He smiled slyly and winked.

Paul and Reddy looked at me like they thought King could see me too.

"Stop fucking around!" Strickland shot. "Where were you that night? You let me know and we can be done with this. You say you had nothing to do with Vonn's murder? Prove it. Where were you?" Strickland leaned in toward King again.

"Busy," King answered, looking back at him.

"Busy doing what?"

"Busy out. Doing shit I always do," King said.

"Where?"

"I was at home."

"Were you with anyone?" Strickland asked, and the blood circulating in my body turned to ice. I couldn't move. The only thing of use inside of me was my heart, which pounded with so much fear.

King paused and looked at the mirror again.

"What night were you asking about?" he asked, looking perturbed. "Oh yeah. Two nights ago? I wasn't home. I was out." King looked down and to his right.

"Were you with anyone? Can someone confirm that?"

"He's lying," Delli said. "Covering something up." He looked back at Reddy. "He doesn't want us to know something— something about his home."

"No one can confirm where I was. I was out alone." King kept his eyes down. "Riding on my Hayabosa—the Queen. It was a nice night. Wanted to take her out. Open her up."

"The night your boy was killed you were out on a motorcycle alone? No alibi anyone can confirm?"

"Nope. Just me and the wind." King looked at Strickland and sighed dramatically before straightening his shirt like he was getting ready to stand up and walk out the door. "We done here?"

"Done?"

"Yeah. You're not charging me with anything, right? Just a chat." King chuckled. "If I was going to be arrested, you boys would've charged me with something by now. I think I've said enough without a lawyer or some reason I need to be here. Anything more and I might incriminate myself. Wouldn't that be a shame?"

Strickland looked at the mirror. He had no choice but to let King go. He stood, picked up the folder, and signaled for King to follow him out.

When he opened the door and King exited, I felt like my body of frozen veins had been thrown into a pot of boiling water. Everything I'd witnessed flashed before me in a fury of accusations and questions about where I'd been and how I knew King and how long we'd been sleeping together. I heard all of these things and imagined it like I'd been sitting in the room beside King and Paul was the one asking the questions. My back started hurting immediately, and the pain was so bad I was afraid to stand.

Strickland walked into the room with his head lower than mine had been when we'd arrived.

"He's hiding something," he said. "I know it. I've interviewed this guy, like, three times, and as cool as he seemed, this was the most nervous I've ever seen him."

"What do you think it is?" Paul asked.

"Something about where he was," Delli tried. "Who he was with. Maybe that's who killed Vonn. Maybe that's why he doesn't want to say anything." He looked at me. "What do you think, Kind? McDonnell looked right at you—seemed to anyway. What did you see in his eyes?"

All of the men with their arms crossed over their chests looked at me for a response.

I struggled not to look down or to the right, signs they'd be looking for if they thought I might have any reason to lie. I kept my eyes glued on the person asking the questions.

"Didn't seem like he knew anything," I said to Norman's eyes. "I think we might be overthinking this."

Outside the Eighty-Fourth, I had to refuse three of Paul's offers of rides back to the office by saying my back was hurting.

"No, I'm fine. I'm just going to hop in a cab and go home to get into bed. I'll get up in a few and start working on the case," I said.

"Great idea! I'll come with you. We're cocounsel, right?"

"Paul, you know we can't do that," I said, looking behind him to be sure King wasn't anywhere around. "Let's not even start that way. I'll go and read over the rest of the files and meet you at the office tomorrow."

"Why do you keep doing this, Kim?" he asked.

"Doing what?"

"Putting this barrier between us like you don't know what's happening."

"What's happening?" I looked at a silver car behind Paul that turned out to be a Chrysler 300.

"I'm doing this for you. For us. If I become mayor, you know what that means. I'm done with my old life. We can be together."

I looked Paul in the eye. "Be together? Don't make me say it again, Paul. You know the deal. You're mar—"

"She signed the papers this morning," Paul revealed, cutting me off. "I didn't want to tell you we'd decided to move forward with the divorce until it was final. Didn't want you to think I was lying or trying to get you into bed again. This is it. I'm signing the papers tomorrow."

"A divorce?" The new panic sprang up in me. "You're getting a divorce?"

"Yes!" Paul chuckled gleefully. "God, yes! I'm divorced—well, when I sign the papers."

"I don't get it. What about the kids? The house? How did you come to an agreement on all of that? You two had a life together, and you—"

"I gave her everything, Kim. She's keeping the house. The cars. We're sharing custody. I get a new life though." He smiled at me and cupped my chin in his hands in a way he never would have in public before—and definitely not in front of a precinct where officers we knew were walking in and out and waving at us. "A new life with you."

I stepped back to remove my chin from his hold.

"What is it? What's wrong?" he asked.

"I need to think about this," I said.

"Think about what?" he spat out. "This is what we wanted, right?"

"Before . . . but now you . . . and I . . ." I couldn't complete one thought without my mind going back to King with a confusion that actually led to clarity about my feelings. "I can't do this right now. There's too much going on."

"With that other nigger?" Paul asked, pulling me to the side of the door. "With the motherfucker you were with the other night?"

"I wasn't with anyone. There is no one," I said.

"You say that, but that's not how you act. You cut me off and I was okay with that. I thought it was because you wanted something definitive, and now I'm giving you that and you don't want to talk about it? What the fuck, Kim? How is it not another motherfucker?"

"Just stop," I said to Paul as Reddy walked out with Strickland and nodded to us. "We can't do this here. Not here! I'm going home and I'll talk to you about it later. I just need to think. That's it. There's no one else. I just need to think."

Chapter 11

"I need you to meet me at that cheap rental-car place on Adams by Borough Hall. Can you be there in an hour?" That's all I said to Tamika when she answered her phone. All I had to say. Her response was just as direct: "I got you. I'll tell Leah to get Miles from fencing. Walking out of the job in ten minutes. See you there." She hung up without saying good-bye. It was the always satisfying result of the emergency response system we'd been taught as children growing up in the ghetto in New York. When someone called you and uses a certain voice, no matter what you were doing, you asked where they were, slid on a hoodie and Timberland boots, and set out in less than five minutes. If you had a car, the gun would be under the front seat, the music would be down, the windows would be up, and you'd be on your way to scoop whomever from wherever they were, ready to do whatever was next. And that re-

ally meant whatever—stalking, tire slashing, breaking and entering, breaking up, or moving on.

Tamika wouldn't let me down. Though we were a few feet out
of the ghetto and it was only a little after 5 p.m. and the new summer heat would make showing up in a hoodie and Timbs look ridiculous and suspicious, she rolled up in front of the car-rental place
in less than an hour.

I'd already gotten one of those dated compact cars with roll-
down windows, powerless-locks, and an actual CD player. I'd requested a low-key color, something black or gray, but the thing was
white with absolutely no tint on the windows. I don't know why I
thought the tint would be of use or that the car needed to be a dull
color. I wasn't even sure of why I was renting the car yet. Or whether
that was a bad move or could be seen as one by someone later on
at some point. What was I about to do? After I'd gotten away from
Paul, I'd thought back to the nights I'd spent at King's place. Who
knew I was there. Who'd seen me and could confirm that I'd been
with King. There was Baboo and Frantz. They didn't know who I
was, and if it came down to it, neither could say how long I'd been
at King's place. Then I remembered the video cameras all over the
Clocktower. On the corner, in the lobby. They'd been watching and
recording everything since I'd walked in the door the first time.
Delli and his suspicion about where King was the night of the murder, and why he'd switched so quickly from talking about being at
home during his interrogation—it was only a matter of time before
he passed his speculations on to the detectives, and that would lead
them back to the Clocktower and those video cameras.

I was parked outside the car-rental place going over the plan
when Tamika got out of her cab. I beeped so she could find me.

"What's up?" she said, getting into the car wearing a silk navy Lauren dress and the Louboutin flats I'd bought her for her birthday. It wasn't the emergency-response attire for what I had in mind, but it would do.

"It's bad, Mika. It's really, *really*, really bad," I said, keeping my hands on the steering wheel though we weren't moving. I looked at her. "It's King. He's a . . ." I searched for the words to describe what I'd just learned about the white man I'd been sleeping with. "He's a drug dealer—a kingpin."

Without interruption, I sped through the details of the slide show in the conference room, King looking through the one-way mirror, the fact that I was on the other side of his stare and that I was the one he'd been with the night Vonn was killed. No one could ever know that. No one.

"Why didn't he say anything? Why wouldn't he say he was with you?" Tamika asked. "Do you think he knows who you are?"

"I never told him. I never let on about anything. He doesn't even know my last name."

"Does he know where you live?"

"No—well . . . yes. He's never been to my place. But yes, he does," I said, remembering Baboo dropping me off. "He knows people who do, but I'm not worried about that. I don't think he would do anything to me. He's not like—"

"Are you joking, Kim?" Tamika widened her eyes on me. "You just said it yourself. He's a fucking drug dealer, which, I might add, isn't all that surprising."

"Don't do that. I've already beat myself up about it. How didn't I know—whatever. This isn't about that. This is about right now," I shot back. "I get it. I fucked up. And that's it, but I can't change that right now. And besides, you were the one who told me to sleep with him. Remember? *'Try something new'? 'Get a little dick'?"*

"Yes. I said to fuck that white boy *one* time. Not make him your fucking boyfriend!" Tamika scolded me like I was a wayward teenager.

"He's not my boyfriend."

"You have feelings for him. Don't lie to me, Kiki. I've known you forever. You've been feeling dude since day one." Tamika waited, and we let my lack of response confirm her pronouncement. "I'm not going to cuss you out about it right now. We ride with each other and that's it. What's the plan?"

"I need to get that tape. I have to figure out how to get the videotape of me at the Clocktower before the detectives from the Eighty-Fourth figure out what King is hiding."

"How are we going to do that?" Tamika asked, looking out the front windshield in the direction of the Clocktower, which poked up just a little over the other buildings downtown.

"I guess we're about to find out."

"No doubt! I got you, cuz. You know that!" Tamika squinted at me and puckered her lips mischievously in a way that told me trouble was on the way for both of us.

Now, if this was *NCIS*, there would be a freeze-frame shot of me pulling out of the space in front of the car-rental agency. The director would want to give viewers a chance to really think about what was about to happen. At that moment, I could've stopped everything: dropped my crazy cousin off at home, driven straight to the office, told Paul that I'd slept with Rig McDonnell and needed to be removed from the case, and vowed to never ever hear anything about King again. If only life were that easy and people always made those right decisions. In that moment, nothing in that line of thinking sounded rational to me. In fact, it seemed irrational. It would've meant career suicide, because if I opened up to Paul about anything concerning King, he'd want to know everything about our short fling. Legally speaking, by telling the truth, I'd then be obligated to tell the "whole truth and nothing but the truth." And that would mean me being dragged into the case, too. I could already see the headline on the cover of the *Daily News*: ADA BLOWS DEALER. They'd be all over me. Stuff would come out about my family, my mother, maybe even my involvement with Paul. I'd seen it done too many times not to know how a headline assassination could annihilate a career in a New York minute. I'd end up with no career, no future, and no place to go but back home with my father and Kent.

I pulled out of that space in the rental car. My crazy cousin riding shotgun was the perfect costar, and we were busy plotting and planning like it was 1990 and we were setting up to break into the water-gun balloon-game booth at Coney Island to steal a three-foot-tall pink and purple teddy bear Tamika felt she'd been cheated out of by the cheap manager. We'd actually gotten away with that. Certainly, we could handle this.

So, an hour later, Tamika was running and screaming into the front door of the Clocktower Building with her hands over her head and no Louboutins on her feet. "Oh my God! He took my shoes! My shoes! My purse! He took my purse and my shoes!" she screamed a little more dramatically than we'd discussed when outlining our half-baked scheme to get Frantz away from his desk in the lobby, so I could find out where the videos were from the cameras around the building.

"Miss, is everything okay?" I heard him say. Tamika had

punched in my number, set her cell phone to speaker, and stashed it between her breasts so I could hear everything they were saying.

"No! Some crackhead just stole my purse and my shoes! I need help!" Tamika answered. "Help me!"

"I can call the police?"

"The police? Are you kidding me? He took my Vuitton and my Louboutins! I need help right now! Come with me! We have to catch him!"

"What am I supposed to do?" Frantz said, and I felt we were losing already. It was a stupid plan anyway. The cat chase only worked in the movies. Not in real life. There was no way Tamika was actually going to get Frantz to chase after someone who'd just mugged her.

"Please, mister. I'm helpless and I need you!" Tamika's voice was softer and sweeter now, and it sounded almost as if she was curtsying to Frantz or maybe even bending over so he could see her breasts.

"Come on, Mika!" I complained to her voice in the speaker, though I knew she couldn't hear me with the volume off on her phone. "This isn't a freaking date. Oh, God, this is ridiculous. What am I doing?"

I banged my head into the steering wheel, sure Tamika would come hopping out to the car shrugging at Frantz's lack of response to her "chase my crackhead mugger with me" request. But when I looked up again, there were Frantz and Tamika running at top speed down the middle of the street. I ducked so Frantz wouldn't see me and quickly got out of the car when I saw that Tamika had led him around the corner.

"This is crazy! This is crazy! This is crazy!" I repeated as I padded quickly toward the Clocktower trying not to look suspicious.

I wanted to turn around and get in the car and go home and forget everything that was happening, but it was too late. *It* was happening.

In the lobby, I slid behind Frantz's desk and looked around at the compilation of live feeds from cameras throughout the building. The cords at the backs of the flat-screen monitors led to a hole on the desktop. I looked under the desk thinking I'd see a VCR and a collection of VHS tapes, and right then I realized the error of the plot—it was no longer 1990.

"What the fuck?" I cursed, bending down over a computer hard drive. "What am I supposed to do with this?" I peeked up over the control desk to see if anyone had walked into the lobby. Before Tamika had gotten out of the car to run into the building, we waited to see if King would walk out. He was the only person in the building other than Frantz who knew my face, and we couldn't risk me running into him. By some stroke of dumb luck, he'd left in his Bentley just minutes after we got there.

"Okay. I'll just take the entire computer," I said to myself, sizing up the nineties hard drive. I started pulling the wires from the base, rushing because I knew Frantz and Tamika would be back at any minute. I couldn't hear anything but garbled noises on the phone and figured it was glued to Tamika's breasts.

"Who are you?" I heard from above when I was disconnecting the wires.

"What?" I popped my head up, sure I was caught.

Standing at the desk in front of me was an awkward-looking white girl who couldn't have been older than ten or eleven with a mix of freckles and preteen acne decorating her cheeks and forehead.

"Me?" I said.

"Yes. You. Where is Frantz? Are you trying to steal his computer?" Her tone was privileged, accusatory. She sounded like she was going to scream for the police.

"Me? I'm-I'm . . . ," I stuttered, keeping my eye on the doors behind her. "I work at"—I looked at the computer monitor—"Hewlett-Packard, and I came here to pick up the computer so I can take it to our lab to get fixed." I casually picked up the heavy hard drive and smiled at her. "I guess I'll just leave now." I started walking out from behind the desk when I heard more garbles on the phone in my pocket.

I could feel the nosy little girl watching me limp along holding the hard drive, but I kept walking and smiling, praying I'd make it to the front door and out into the street before she decided to scream bloody murder, the cops arrived, and my fake-thug ass was loaded onto a bus to Sing Sing—in my mind it would all happen that quickly.

But she didn't say a word and I made it outside with the clunky computer in tow. And for a second I was able to feel the ecstasy of escape criminals must experience when they've gotten away with something. It was like that first sip of Jameson. The first toke of a joint. Everything outside seemed wonderful. I just needed to make it to the car.

As I said, the feeling was fleeting. As soon as I turned the corner to where the car was parked, Frantz barreled into me with Tamika right behind him screaming, "Mayday! Mayday! Abort! Abort!"

The hefty hard drive fell to the sidewalk, where it cracked and flattened.

Tamika and I winced at the damage and looked at each other,

ready to give it a Harlem run, but Frantz must have been from Harlem too, because he caught both of us by the wrists in some kind of ninja hand lock before we could get away.

"I know you," he said to me. "You're King's girlfriend."

"Girlfriend?" Tamika and I said together.

"What are you doing here? Why are you taking my computer?" He looked at Tamika. "And why are you with this crazy woman?"

"I am not crazy! Ain't my fault your slow ass couldn't keep up!" Tamika snapped before I cut her off.

"Listen," I started. "I can explain everything. Just don't call the police. Please! I beg you. I'll explain everything."

In the back office of the Clocktower, Frantz was sitting on top of a desk, leering down at Tamika and me. He'd called in some other guard to stand post out front.

I'd just finished telling him my entire story—well, not the true story (I wasn't that stupid), but the version I concocted that I thought could at least get Tamika and me out of the Clocktower without handcuffs and a one-way ticket to Sing Sing.

"So, you mean to tell me that you two came here to steal my computer because you're married to a government official who might be in the running to be the second black president of the United States and you don't want there to be any evidence of the affair you've been having with a white man?" Frantz repeated the case I'd pleaded back to me, somehow managing to make the elaborate story I told sound pretty crazy.

"I know that's hard to believe, but you have to trust me. My husband is well connected, and I can't let this ruin him!" I said. "I like King. But I just won't risk everything I've built and throw it away!"

Frantz stared at me for a minute, and then he just started cracking up, laughing so hard it was obvious there was no way he believed me.

I tried to get Tamika's attention so we could prepare to run again.

"Look, forget all that, mister. Let's have a real talk," Tamika said, getting up from her seat slowly and slinking toward Frantz as if he were the teacher and she a bad student.

I could only rest my face in the palm of my hand in disbelief. I imagined the police sirens closing in on the Clocktower. The DTs from the Eighty-Fourth laughing as the cops brought me in for booking. This was it. I was going down. Kim 2 and Ronald would have the last laugh, after all. Not only would I be alone forever, but I'd be alone in prison.

"Talk about what?" Frantz looked puzzled.

Tamika stood in front of him and played with his cheap uniform tie as she spoke. "We can forget everything that's happened here today. All walk out of here with nothing but good memories."

"Oh, I was going to walk out of here with good memories anyway," Frantz said, seeming like he was on to Tamika's game.

"Well, I can make those memories even better," she said, pushing the tie between her breasts.

"And how will you do that?" Frantz asked.

"I'll make love to you real good," Tamika purred. "If you make that little ol' recording disappear and let us walk out of here. You won't regret it."

"Oh God," I complained into my palm.

Frantz sucked his teeth and flicked Tamika's hand from his tie.

"Sit down!" he commanded so harshly that I felt it in my back and Tamika straightened up and actually took her seat next to me. "You . . . are a horrible actress," he said to her after getting up from the desk. "And you have daddy issues I suggest you work out with a therapist." Then he turned to me. "And you, what the hell are you doing? I don't even know you, and I know you're better than this. Running around here stealing computers like you ain't got no damn sense. And bringing *this one* with you?" He pointed at Tamika, and I shrank in my seat from the scolding. "Don't you have any other friends who would've maybe given you better advice?" Tamika and I glanced at each other, discomfited.

"I was just—" I tried, but Frantz stopped me.

"No. Don't. Please don't say anything else about your husband or anyone wanting to sleep with me. That insults my intelligence. I'm the doorman at the most expensive residence in Brooklyn. I have a goddamn master's degree. I probably make more money than both of you." Frantz exhaled and stood in front of me. "Listen, sweetheart. I know you're hiding something. And I know you really, really want that surveillance footage. That's the only thing that would make someone like you do something stupid like this—" He stopped and looked at Tamika.

"What? It was her idea!" she said.

"Sure," he went on. "And because of that I'm going to let you off this one time. Let you go think about what you're doing and maybe stop yourself while you're ahead." He looked into my eyes. "There's a lot of trouble to be found around here. And I wouldn't want you to be caught up in it. You understand me?"

"Yes," I answered humbly. "And does that also mean you're giving me the footage?"

Frantz went back to his seat at the desk. "Nothing to give," he said frankly.

"What?" Tamika said.

"You know how much it costs to live here?" Frantz asked. "I'll just say this—all of the residents at the Clocktower aren't exactly operating on the up-and-up, so to speak. Half of my residents are the side-pieces of Manhattan gangster and Wall Street rainmakers."

"So?" Tamika pushed.

"So, we don't keep the footage. No way. No how. Not from the lobby anyway. What you see are the cameras and videos we use to make the good, white people, celebrities, and old farts feel nice and safe here at One Main Street. The feed goes into the computer, where it's stored for twenty-four hours. And if nothing happens—like two crazy people coming in and trying to steal the computer"—he pointed to the busted-up hard drive on the floor beside the desk—"it's erased."

"Erased?" I repeated.

"That's right. Those images of you here that night when you came to—you know—they're gone." Frantz folded his arms and smiled at me. "Been gone. So, you came all the way over here to start trouble with your little Bonnie and Clyde routine for nothing. Besides, even if you'd gotten away with the computer, it wouldn't have been worth anything. The feed uploads to an online server. That old hard drive has nothing on it. These are all things real criminals would've checked out."

When Tamika and I left the Clocktower and fell into the front seat of the sad little white rental car, we looked at each other like strangers who'd met in the bathroom at Webster Hall in the nineties and had sex with no condom in a coked-out haze. Disgusted by our partner. Embarrassed by our behavior. There was nothing to say. We should just go our separate ways forever and forget anything had ever happened. But we weren't strangers. We were cousins with mothers who were sisters, so any shame we could feel because of a ridiculous act like trying to break in to the Clocktower and steal security footage would not go unnoticed by two humans going separate ways. Not at all. It would be confronted and beat out by . . . laughter.

"Oh my fucking God!" Tamika howled hysterically, laughing, chortling, and screaming all at the same time. "Can you believe that? Can you believe what fucking just happened?"

"No! I can't! I fucking can't!" I was trying not to laugh, but there was nothing else I could do with the nervous energy ballooning inside my stomach. My heart was still racing in disbelief. Like I'd just walked out of the biggest surprise party ever.

"You were so good, Kim!" Tamika turned to me to recap the events. "The way you spoke to Frantz. Those tears! I believed you, girl. You deserved an Oscar for that shit!"

"I was not crying!" I protested, already laughing at recent memories of me sitting before Frantz like he was a judge.

Tamika mocked me. " *'I like King. But I just won't risk everything I've built and throw it away!'* "

"How do I sound like a broke-down Marilyn Monroe begging for change on a street corner?" I joked. "I was much better than that!"

"Not better than me! I deserve an Oscar-Tony-Emmy for my portrayal of Mrs. Halle Berry on a New York City street corner in the epic Negro classic *Jungle Fever*," Tamika said reverently before repeating Halle's classic line, " *'Yo, Daddy. I'll suck your dick good for* . . . those Clocktower videos!' "

"You were ridiculous! Oh my God. I can't believe you said you were going to sleep with that man," I charged, finally starting up the car to escape. It was dusk, and the rush-hour traffic was just beginning to slow. Though we were still in the middle of something that could get both of us into a lot of trouble, our childish joking worked to lighten the pressure from the longest day I'd had in a while. The day wasn't even over, and already I'd only returned to work after being sent home by my boss/former lover, sat in on a meeting where the white man I'd been sleeping with was implicated in two murders and deemed a mastermind drug dealer, witnessed his interrogation about said activity, been confronted by my boss/former lover about his divorce and what I owed him once it was finalized, and gotten caught trying to steal the computer from the most prestigious address in Brooklyn. The joking was more than necessary. It had been earned.

"I was awesome," Tamika said. "Don't knock my shine, because you couldn't pull off a Halle impersonation. And Frantz was cute too."

I looked at Tamika and we burst out laughing again.

"You're a mess. Let me get your ass home to your child before we get into more trouble," I said, pulling out of the parking space having looked only to my right to be sure no cars were coming down the street.

Once the car was in motion, though, I had to brake fast because I'd missed two people coming off the curb on the left.

"Wait!" Tamika ordered, just in time for me to tap the brake to avoid hitting the pedestrians.

I looked up, and there, walking right in front of the car, were Strickland and the other detective from the Eighty-Fourth.

Strickland held his hand out to stop the car, barely looking at me behind the wheel before trotting across the street toward the Clocktower.

"That's the heat, isn't it?" Tamika asked, observing their blue suits and dorky detective sunglasses.

"Let's get out of here," I said, pressing the gas hard and not letting up until I was down the street.

Once we got to Tamika's house, after her hassling me, I parked the car to go inside and say good night to Miles. I hugged him and kissed him, commented on how tall and lanky he was getting, and went to his small, blue-painted room with the glow-in-the-dark sticker constellation stuck to the ceiling to look over his prized collection of fencing trophies. It was interesting how that little moment with my big godson slowed my thoughts and brought me back to my world. His braces and chin acne, the little anxious wild hairs sprouting around his upper lip were just so unaware of any of my mania. For just a second, I couldn't think about myself. "I love you, Miles," I said to him. "You be safe." He smiled and replied, "I love you. You be safe, too."

Tamika wanted me to stay on her couch for the night so she could know I was safe, but I told her I really didn't feel like King would try to do anything to me. Why would he? He hadn't even replied to my text from the night before when I tried to contact him about Vonn, and I was sure he hadn't seen me at the precinct. I had no reason to believe he even knew who I was. Or cared. Maybe he'd moved on and I could just forget about my whole walk on the wild side. Wake up in the morning to my old life.

My old life?

I walked outside in the darkness thinking of that past. What was it? Before King and this? Was that my old life? Paul? Was that it? The accident? What was it? Where was it? Where was the old life I wanted to wake up to?

The streetlights along the block were half out, and the one over the white rental car was blinking and buzzing, threatening sudden death.

Halfway up the block to the car, I looked back at Tamika's house and then out to the dark street that was so quiet for Brooklyn at night. There was not one cat running in the gutter, not one dollar cab twisting through the street, not even a teenage couple snuggling on the front stoop. It seemed like it was just me, the moon, the rental car, and the banged-out streetlights.

While I felt a little spooked by the solitude, I was determined to keep a level head and rushed quickly to the safety of the car. I made it into the car just in time for the streetlight to shine its last glow.

Shaking, my nerves wrecked, I shoved the key into the ignition to flee some ghost that I'd thought was on my tail. I sighed in relief at my escape. "Calm down, girl!" I ordered myself. I turned the ignition and went to pull my seat belt on when I saw something black in the backseat over my left shoulder and felt something cold under my right arm at my breast.

My first instinct was to scream, and I started to, but a hand covered my mouth, muffling the sound.

"Don't scream!" a male voice said.

The hold over my mouth tightened and the cold object in my side warned me to stay in place. I held my hands up and tried to get a look at who was behind me, but I couldn't see in the rearview mirror.

"Do not scream!" he said again, jabbing the cold steel into my stomach.

I shook my head to confirm that I wasn't going to scream.

"No screaming. All right?" he said.

I shook my head again.

He let go of my mouth slowly, keeping what I assumed was a gun in my side and moving his arm to my chest, where he held me against the seat.

"Who are you? What do you want?" I cried, trying to look down at the gun. "I don't have any money. You can have my purse. It's just Marc Jacobs though. Not worth a lot. Please don't kill me!" I looked down again, and although the gun was hidden beneath my shirt, I could see the hand holding it. It was white. And a few inches from the wrist there began a tattoo sleeve I'd studied one night in bed when someone's arm was wrapped around me. "King?"

"Shhh!" he whispered in my ear. "No need to let the entire street know it's me."

"Oh my God! Don't kill me! Please don't! I didn't say—"

"Just drive, Queen," he ordered.

"Drive? Why do you want me to drive? Where are we going?" I blurted out.

"Your place. Drive me to your place."

"Why are you going to shoot me there?" I cried, looking down at the gun again.

"Shoot you?" He laughed and then his eyes followed mine to the gun. "What? You think this is a gun?" He pulled the barrel from my stomach and held it up. "My iPhone. Not exactly the most efficient killing device."

"Oh my God! You scared the shit out of me!" I said. "What the hell was that about? You didn't have to play like you were going to kill me in order to talk to me. Jesus Christ! I thought you were some crackhead trying to rob me."

King let me go and fell back in the seat. "No. I'm not a crack-head." He looked at me in the rearview mirror. "Can we go to your place now?"

"For what? Why do you want to go to my place?" I asked. "Look, I know everything. I know you lied to me—about who you are, what you do! You lied!"

"I ain't never lied to you, Queen. Not once," King said. "Look, the cops are all over my spot. I just need somewhere to lie low for a little while, and I think we need to talk. You say you know about—well, I know about you, too."

"How do you—" I tried, but he cut me off. "How I know doesn't matter. We just need to talk."

"There's nothing else to say."

"Queen," King called to me in the mirror. "Listen to me. You can scream and kick me out of this car right now and never ever see me again. I'll never bother you, and you won't have to worry about our little secret. Or you can do what you really want to do and take me back to your place, so we can talk and I can tell you everything you want to know, everything I want to say. It's your choice, but you need to make it now and you need to make it fast."

My eyes still on King's, my hand moved the gear selector to drive and my decision was made. Just like that. I didn't know it, but right there I'd let go of the possibility of waking up in the morning to my old life. Whatever I thought it was. I shifted my stare back to the street and put my foot on the gas. Two turns and that car was set in the direction of Manhattan.

I went upstairs before King. He instructed me to get out of the car and walk straight toward my building. He'd get out alone and walk around the block the long way. Although he didn't think the cops had tailed him to Tamika's house, he didn't want to risk them finding him at my place.

Those few minutes I was upstairs alone felt like I was awaiting a verdict from an unpredictable jury. I paced the floor and looked at my phone and then out the window. The blizzard of feelings I had to confront in the car driving over the Brooklyn Bridge with King in the backseat beat me into honesty about what he'd made me feel. The reason I couldn't think of my good life before him was that most of it was so gray or just uninspired. It was always me fighting against something or for something, and I was growing weary of the defeat everywhere.

There was a tap at the door. I looked over from the window where I'd been searching for King. For the first time I considered that maybe someone had been following us. Who was at the door? The police? Strickland? Paul on one of his late-night visits? Maybe it was him and Strickland and the cops had King in a car downstairs. That was it! Frantz had lied about the video and they were all downstairs. Coming for me.

I crept to the door lightly, my heart pounding, and looked through the peephole.

"Oh my God!" I said, opening the door to let King inside, then locking every one of my six locks. "I nearly . . . I thought . . . I thought . . ." I placed my hand over my beating heart.

"You thought what?"

I was thinking of what I was going to say, but then out of nowhere I jumped on King and started pounding him with angry, passionate punches. "Liar! Liar! Fucking liar!" I punched and pushed him until he got a hold of my waist and pulled me so close I could only rest my arms at my side and try to wriggle out of his grip.

"Calm down. Just stop," he said, without raising his voice. "Just stop it. I'm here. I'm right here. Just stop it."

He started kissing my forehead and then my cheeks.

"No!" I pleaded. "I don't want you to kiss me. Stop it! Let me go."

"I didn't lie to you," King said, loosening his hold.

"You're a drug dealer. A fucking drug dealer!" I pushed away from him. "I can't believe this. I can't believe any of this. I should've fucking known something. Everything you said—everything—just all lies. And you never gave a fuck about me!" I shouted. "You were just using me. You knew who I was the whole time! You knew!" I pointed at him. "You were setting me up."

"I didn't know when we met. I swear to you. I didn't know anything until after that night we spent together. I didn't."

I walked over to the window and looked out at the cars, the traffic. "You just wanted me to be your alibi. That's why you held me in your place those nights. Not because you liked me. Because you"—I looked at him—"you had Vonn killed. Vonn and Yellow. Didn't you? That's what everyone's saying. You did it."

"No. I had nothing to do with that. There's more to it. I promise you."

"You know how many times I've heard that from people like you? That's what I do. I put liars like you in jail, and it's always someone else's fault. Even the court's fault. Always more to it," I said. "That's what men like you say. Always an excuse. The point is that those people are dead and your name is the only name connecting theirs."

"It's not what you think," King said, sounding tired. He walked over to sit on the couch. "I'll offer myself a seat," he said, sitting down and looking around the living room like he was taking it in.

I looked out the window and said very calmly, "You're a drug dealer, King." I looked at him. "I'm an assistant district attorney in New York County. I put men like you in prison." I laughed lightly to mark the moment in irony. "I don't sleep with them."

"*Men* like *me*." King returned my laugh. "A man. A man." He looked at his lap.

"What?"

"I ain't no man," he said, looking back at me. "I'm *traill*," he added in a Gaelic accent I'd only heard when he'd mentioned his grandmother. I knew a few Gaelic words from some Irish officers I'd worked with. I'd heard *"traill"* many times as we'd prosecuted business owners who were a part of the Irish mob. A *traill* was an Irish slave. "Remember what I told you about my great-grandfather coming through Ellis Island? Well, I didn't lie—old Rig was on that second ship. He'd been denied a place on the first ship leaving Ireland, so he bought his way onto the next one—like many other men did at the time. Back then there wasn't anything in Ireland for men like my great-grandfather. He had no choice. He sold himself. He sold all of us."

"What? What are you talking about? That's crazy," I said. "The Irish mob is dead—dying at least. There's no way you could still—"

"The debt is for five generations." He looked down again. "We're White Hand. The brothers make you rich. The richer you are, the richer they are. You pay them back. It keeps going. You only leave when you die."

"King. The White Hand hasn't been in operation since the thirties. I mean, even the Westies are done. We ended that organization three years ago, and they were only half functioning. Thugs who wanted the fame and the name of the Irish mob," I said.

He looked back up at me, and somehow he seemed so much softer and broken than I'd ever seen him. "The finest trick of the devil is to persuade you that he does not exist," he said, quoting Baudelaire.

"Maybe you're the one who doesn't want to exist and the mob is long gone and you're just saying all of this to persuade me otherwise," I said.

"I wish I was lying, Queen—"

"Don't call me that," I said. "And if all of this is true and the only way out is death, then where is your father? Is he dead? Because the detectives said he's—"

"My father was a favorite. The bosses took a liking to him. He was so smart, and they figured if they sent him to medical school, he'd somehow magically make all their dirty asses Ivory soft and clean. Then they could enjoy their wealth and shit on the up-and-up—move to Fifth Avenue. Eat at the Russian Tea Room. They put so many men like my father through school. Only to bring them out and set them up and steal from them for the rest of their lives. All their clinics—all of it—that was their enterprise. My father had no choice."

"Your great-grandfather? Your father? What about you? You have a choice?"

"They called me everything from Chalky to Leprechaun—I was never anything more to them than an Irish nigger," he said. "My skin is too dark for them." He laughed. "Isn't that funny? Most people see me as white—call me white boy—but to them, the obvious traces of my past were too much to just call me Irish. I wasn't going to be anything but a street dealer for them."

I knew better than to call King a liar about that. If he was telling the truth about the mob and his family's connection to it, he would be set out to do whatever the heads told him to do. Most mob families operated like a caste system. Your vocation, relationships, and connections were dictated by rules and orders that you hardly knew about. That was true in any crime family. If King's lineage went as far back in the mob as he said, they would have some rank, some solid ties, but that meant nothing in the history of an operation that had its roots in the early 1800s in New York City, when many Irish immigrants were indentured servants and some were just street beggars. Soon, the poorest of the poor in the city united and got organized. They made profit by bullying business owners. Soon they became the business owners. And some bought their way out of the mob.

"When the cops came down on my father, we lost everything. They took everything from us. And then the brothers took what was left," King said. "And what they couldn't take, they moved onto me. My father's debt became mine. That's how it works. A father's debt becomes his son's debt."

"That doesn't make any sense. You're rich, King. I've seen it myself. You live in the Clocktower penthouse; you drive a Bentley. You don't exactly look like someone who's struggling under the oppression of the Irish mob. Come on."

"You don't understand—the richer I am, the richer they are. They only care that I'm not broke. You make money, they make money—that's the rule. Anything that might interrupt that is cut." He leveled his hand to signal cutting something off.

"Vonn?" I said delicately. "Yellow?"

He nodded.

I looked back out to the street. A police car zoomed past with its siren screaming. The black pavement was slick and shining from a fast night shower. I thought of Monique.

"Vonn was my boy. My friend. I grew up with him," King said, getting up from the couch. "I kept telling him not to fucking talk to the cops. They were just testing him. Trying to see if he'd snitch. Half of those cops are dirty. They're in the organization."

He came over to me and looked into my eyes intensely. "I can't do this shit anymore. I got to get out. That's why I'm moving to Manhattan. Get more money. Get the fuck out of here."

"And go where?" I asked. "The DA's already on to you. Building a case against you as we speak," I said. "He smells blood. He wants you. To put you away."

"You want to put me away?" he asked.

"It's not my choice," I said. "It's my job." I backed away from him.

"You always have a choice."

"A choice about what? All of this stuff you said aside, you're still a drug dealer—you sell drugs to people. It ruins their lives. I've seen it. I know. It ruined mine," I said. "I choose not to support anything that can do that. Not to anyone."

King tried to reach for me, but I pushed him back.

"Kim . . . I can't . . . I . . . ," he tried, then just stopped and looked at me, with everything he couldn't say in his eyes.

"No!" I shouted. "You can't!"

"I—"

"Don't say it," I begged, knowing what the thing he was about to say would require from me and what that would mean to everything I was.

"Tell me you don't feel it, too," King dared me.

"I can't do that. I can't. You're a—"

"A drug dealer," he said. "And I love you."

"No! No!" I started walking toward the door, but King followed and grabbed my hand. "Stop it! Let me go!"

"I love you, Queen. You don't have to say it back, but I want you to know that. I love you."

He wrapped his arms around my waist, but I kept my back to him.

"I just met you. I don't even know you," I said, afraid to look at him.

"That doesn't change how I feel. What happened. I've never been like that with anyone," he said. "I was myself. Just me. It was like I was alone but really with someone for the first time when I was with you. I never wanted you to leave me."

He wrapped his arms tighter around my waist and kissed my shoulder.

"It was just sex," I whispered, but I felt the heat from his lips spread down my side and weaken my knees. "That was all. It didn't mean anything."

He kept kissing me and I was growing weaker. Soon tears were in my eyes and my breathing became labored.

"No, King!" I begged. "I can't. I don't want to do this."

He stopped kissing me and whispered softly in my ear, "Do what?"

I looked up toward the door and answered, "I don't want to love you. I don't want to get hurt. Not again."

I pulled myself free and walked to the door, wiping my tears. "You have to go! That's it. I have to stop this now. This isn't who I am. I am an attorney and I can't do this." I undid two locks and held my hand over the third. I could feel King breathing behind me. "You understand?" I said, undoing the third and fourth and fifth locks just as quickly as the first two. "You just have to leave," I added, putting my hands on the sixth lock. "Okay?"

"I'll understand if you can undo that last lock," King said. "If you can, then I'll know you don't feel the same for me and I'll leave. But I want to say one last thing to you."

"What?"

"I need you to look at me."

I kept my right hand on the lock and turned around to look at King. "What?"

"I did have someone get some information on you. I did know who you were. But, like I said, it wasn't until after that first night we spent together. I told myself exactly what you just said—there's no way we could be together—but then, the more I thought about it, the more I knew that there's no way we can't be together. I'm not afraid of anything. I wasn't built that way. But in this short time I've known you, I know I'm afraid to lose you. I can walk away from all of this, but I can't walk away from you. I'm not going to."

I didn't know I'd let go of the sixth lock until my arms were around King's neck. My lips were going toward his. He was holding me up against the door, the door that wouldn't open that night. That lock would stay locked.

Chapter 12

The next morning, I rolled out of bed on the same side as always. I took the same morning shower. Brushed my teeth with the same pink toothbrush and whitening toothpaste. Put on my same work clothes and walked out into what I was expecting to be the same world. But when I set foot on the sidewalk, the cracking city concrete I'd been walking on all my life, I knew nothing was the same. I was different. My New York was different. And it was all because of the terrible secret I had inside of me.

As I drove the rental car into Brooklyn early in the morning, the world looked so fake. People and stoplights, buildings and cars were orbiting me like those rolling images in the old Fisher-Price Music Box TVs. Everything was moving along exactly as it should, without question or confusion. Like fire ants building a new colony. And there I was in the middle of it all, not knowing what direction I was supposed to go in, what I was supposed to be doing, filled with questions and confusion. I was off course. And it was frightening because I didn't want to be in the music box pretending anymore. I didn't want to be a fire ant. Doing all the same stuff and walking along like things were going to just somehow get better if I worked a little harder and pushed through. How many years had I done that? What had that gotten me?

Lying on King's chest in my bed the night before, I kept thinking that nothing was better before him. I'd escaped Harlem. I'd become an attorney—a top prosecutor—but I was still struggling. Hurting. And doing it alone. And here was this man, the most unlikely candidate, whom I felt drawn to like my tongue to the sweet slush on the bottom of a twenty-five-cent Italian ice on a hot July afternoon, saying he loved me and didn't want to be without me, and for every wit inside of me I knew he was telling the truth. That was just without question. Without confusion.

I rolled over and looked at King. I whispered in his ear as he slept, "I love you, King."

He didn't move, but seconds later he whispered, "I love you, Queen."

I started kissing his chest, and then I sat up and made love to him.

When I awoke, he was gone.

After I returned the rental car, I took the train back into Manhattan and got off a few blocks from work. I was headed toward the office from a different direction than usual, but somehow I fell right in line with the same people I always saw walking to work. The interesting thing about morning commutes in New York is that even in a city so packed with humans, if you left your doorstep at the same time each day, you wandered into your day with the same people—the dog walker with the three poodles and one overly sophisticated Afghan, the man talking on his cell phone while padding through moving traffic and always looking like he was about to get hit, the blonde whose long hair was wet even in the winter, the black nanny with the white twins in the stroller. You never waved though, or acknowledged one another. In New York, that would be rude and crazy. You raise your nose into the wind and mind your damn business.

We were a moving mass of colors too muted for the spring around us—office-friendly grays and browns, navy blues and black. There was an occasional yellow blouse or pink sweater, but mostly we were so uniform, it was hard to know where I started and the next person began.

I wanted to stop walking, to turn around and go in a different direction. Or just stand there and scream. Tell them all to just try something different. Or let me.

And then I saw it. Something different in the crowd. Right in the middle of everything, a glimpse of red. At first it was just a sliver moving between two shades of gray, but then it got bigger and seemed brighter, and there was something about the way it moved, something so familiar, that I started skipping around people to catch more of it.

Soon, the slivers in front of me turned into a red hoodie pulled up over a head that I could tell from the gait belonged to a woman. She was a little taller than me, much thinner, but she walked like me, with her shoulders back and her head tilted to the left like she was thinking about something.

I kept pulling myself through the crowd to see more of her. I excused myself as I passed between couples and reached past people's shoulders, trying to get a hold of the red sweatshirt, but it was always just beyond my reach.

"Wait!" I called out to her back. "Please wait!"

People around me looked sideways, not wanting to commit too much attention to my outburst—New Yorkers not wanting to get involved.

I called out once more before lunging forward over the shoulder of a woman holding a cup of steaming coffee.

"Shit!" the woman cried after the hot coffee sprayed over her arm and chest.

"I'm sorry! Oh no!" I said, stopping to help the woman, while looking over my shoulder to see the red drift away from me.

"Sorry? Watch where you're going! Shit! I just got this shit out of the dry cleaner!" She used a napkin she'd been holding in her other hand to try to wipe up the spill. "Now I'm going to be late!"

"I'm sorry. I thought I saw someone I knew. Someone I haven't seen in a long time."

She gave me a customary New York eye roll. "Whatever," she said, walking away. "Just watch where you're going."

When she was gone, I looked up ahead and took a few steps to see if I could find the hoodie again but there were just too many people rushing by. I tried to convince myself to stop and head to the office. I told myself it couldn't have been her anyway. There was no way. Not in Manhattan. Why would my mother be there?

I decided to turn around and go to the office but as soon as I took a step in the opposite direction, I bumped into someone else.

Embarrassed as we knocked heads, I said quickly, "I'm so sorry!" before I even looked at the person I'd collided with. I stepped back as a woman's voice accepted my apology.

"It's okay—" she started but stopped when she looked at me.

"Kim!" we said together.

"Oh, hell no!" Kim 2 tried to push past me like the other woman had.

"No wait! Wait!" I said, remembering my dream. "I need to talk to you." I tried to grab her arm, but she was already out of reach.

"There's nothing for us to talk about. You're crazy and I don't want to have anything to do with you!" she shouted so loudly that people around us started slowing down to get an earful. "You stay away from me and stay away from Ronald, too!"

She started to walk away again, but that time I caught her sleeve. "What do you mean, stay away? I haven't been around you or Ronald."

"You call phone calls at all hours of the night staying away? Talking about killing us? That's staying away?" she asked.

"Wh-wha-what are you talking about?" I stuttered, considering what she was saying. "I never called you. I haven't spoken to you since I saw you that morning at breakfast."

"No. You're lying!"

"No I'm not. You're lying!"

Kim 2 reached into her pocket, pulled out her cell phone, then handed it to me with her call log on the screen.

"See!" she said.

I looked through three calls with "Kiki" listed. All were from between three o'clock and five that morning.

"How do I know this is really me?" I said in a low voice but feeling somewhere that it had been me. Some kind of choppy and slow-moving memory floated into my mind.

"Well, you probably wouldn't remember calling me because

you were so fucking drunk. Blabbering on about me selling my pussy to the highest bidder and being a dick digger and that I was really a fat ass and that's how I lost my modeling contract," she said softly with pain in her eyes. She snatched the phone back and stashed it in her hoodie pocket. "I don't need your shit. Things are hard enough for me."

"I didn't say those things," I said, but I remembered it. I could hear myself saying them. Sitting up in my bed and saying those things into the phone. Kim 2 screaming back, *"I'm calling the police if you keep calling me!"*

I started feeling sick to my stomach, light on my feet, and like my head was floating up and up. I felt myself stagger toward Kim 2.

"I don't feel so well," I said breathily, trying to stay on my feet. "I think I need to sit down."

Kim 2 held me up.

I placed my arm over her shoulder, and she propped me up.

She walked me to a little coffee shop a few feet away and sat me in one of the chairs out front.

"Wait out here," she said. "I'll be right back."

She returned with a cup of water and handed it to me.

"Sip some of that," she said, sitting across from me at the table.

One of the waiters from inside the shop came to the door and looked at me.

"She's fine," Kim 2 said to him. "Just a little dizzy."

"I don't remember calling you. I really don't."

"You didn't call last night. And there was nothing for, like, two nights a few days ago. But you do most nights," Kim 2 explained, her anger now dissolved and her voice sympathetic, while motioning for me to finish the water.

"I don't understand. Why would I do that?"

"I don't know. I know you're angry with—I guess you should be, but I just wanted you to know that"—she looked away—"we were doing the best we could. We tried to stop it, but you kept doing—"

"Doing what?" I asked.

She bit her lip before speaking. "The drinking. It started with the drinking. You were so fucked up. And Ron just wanted to help you. That's how it started—us talking to each other. We were just trying to help you."

I put the water down and stared at her. "I didn't need any help. Yes, I was drinking, but we all were. You were doing drugs. We were all partying. It wasn't just me. You're trying to make it sound like it was just me."

"Do you remember the first time the police came to the loft? When you came in drunk?"

"I'd had a few with coworkers. We lost that case. So what?"

She looked at me and took in a deep breath, released it. "I kept telling Ronald you'd get better and that it was just the work. We could help you. He came over that night before you got home—"

"I don't want to hear this shit!" I said.

"No, you need to, Kim. I've been trying to tell you this, and you need to hear it," Kim 2 replied. "He came over because we were talking about trying to get you some help. Getting you into rehab."

"Rehab? Fuck you!" I was about to get up, but Kim 2 placed her hand over mine.

"You were so drunk that night. He took you into your room and tried to talk to you."

"Yes. He did. I lost a case and that dickhead proceeds to tell me it was time to leave my fucking job. Really? That's helping me? That's rehab? Saying I could be his fucking secretary?"

"That job was killing you," Kim 2 said. "I saw it every day. You couldn't get through the day without drinking. Ron just wanted you to see that. He was scared, Kiki. We both were."

"No, you both were jealous of me," I shot back. "I was more successful than both of you, and you were jealous, because I'm stronger than you. So you wanted to make me look weak!"

"I never said you were weak. I know you're strong. Trust me, I know that, but how can you keep being so strong, Kim? Always? With all the shit in your past? How can you keep it all up?"

"Right. I'm so strong but I can't keep it together, so you two decided to fuck each other? That's was going to save us all? Give me a break."

"You hit him! What was he supposed to do? It was bad enough he had to lie to the cops and pretend he'd fallen down. His eye was swollen for days. He had to take off work so no one would see it."

"He told me to be his secretary! I'm not a secretary. Do you know what I've been through?" I said. "All of it? I didn't do all of that to be put in my place because he can't handle my success."

"So, what about me? I can't handle your success either?" she asked. "Is that why you tried to kill me? To kill both of us?"

Those questions tore open a scab that bled out a past I was reliving in dreams. The memories that were just echoes and shadows came back at me like a boomerang upside my skull.

"You shouldn't have let me drive," I said in a voice that I didn't recognize as my own. "Not the way things were. You knew I knew. And I was fucked up. Why would you let me drive?"

Kim 2 told her version of events. That we'd left Diddy's party. We were drunk. And tired and it was so dark. I was more messed up than she was, and she begged to drive. I agreed. Gave her the keys and then she started driving. There was the Taylor Swift song.

We were laughing. Traffic started to thin. The highway got darker. Kim 2 needed to go to the bathroom, so she pulled over at a gas station.

"When I got back to the car, you were behind the wheel," she recalled. "I kept saying you were too drunk to drive, but you said you were fine and just wanted to get home. I tried to pull you out of the seat, but you insisted. We stood in front of that gas station for ten minutes and you wouldn't get out of the car, so I got into the passenger's seat."

She said once she was in the car, I got really quiet. I turned off the music, rolled up the windows, and held both hands on the wheel so tightly, she could see the tips of my nude thumbnails turning red. Something was wrong. She saw tears rolling down my cheeks.

"You started driving so fast. I told you to slow down, but you wouldn't. You said you knew everything. That I was sleeping with Ron and that we were planning to leave you all alone," she said. "I told you that wasn't it. That we were just friends and I could explain. But it was too late. You pressed your foot on the gas and said you were going to kill both of us, so he'd be the one alone. I tried to stop you. I reached over you for the wheel, but it was too late. The car started rolling."

I felt the pain ticking up my back.

"We went right off the side of the highway, over the fence, and into some field." Kim 2 looked like she was remembering something so bad it probably gave her the same nightmares I'd been having. "I was awake the entire time, spinning and spinning, but when the car stopped and I was getting out, afraid it was going to blow up, I saw that you weren't moving. You were knocked out. Then I heard the sirens. I wanted them to help us, but I started panicking."

She looked at me. "Kim, you were behind the wheel and so drunk. I knew what that would mean for your career. You'd be disbarred. I couldn't let that happen. I pulled you out of the car and laid you out on the grass. When the cops and ambulance got there, I told them I was driving."

"I was driving," I said.

"I don't know what happened. Why you were so pissed. What would make you snap like that," she said. "I'd never seen you so angry, so split in half."

My mind continued to gather the echoes, and I could see Kim 2 walking toward the gas station building. She was laughing. Waving at me from the bumper and doing some stupid drunken dance. "Hurry up," I yelled. "I need to get home." She giggled a little more and staggered into the building. I sang along with Taylor Swift. Then Kim 2's phone clattered in the console between the rental car seats. I looked at it and "Ronald" was on the screen. My heart started pounding. My mind bounced to every single time I'd suspected something was happening between them. I looked up at the gas station to see if Kim 2 had come out of the bathroom. I picked up the phone and put in Kim's pass code: 1908.

RONALD: We have to tell her about our plan really soon. I can't live this lie anymore. I just want it to be over, so we can move on. Let's do it in the morning when you get back from the Hamptons.

"He was talking about the intervention," Kim 2 said when I told her about the text message I'd read and erased before she'd gotten back into the car.

"No he wasn't. You're lying to me!" I cried. "If it was all about me, why would he leave me at the hospital? Hunh? Leave me in a hospital bed all by myself to go and be with you?"

"I was in jail. He had to bail me out," Kim 2 whispered sharply. "There was no one else. I didn't have any money. Who else was I supposed to call? I'd just saved your ass, and I was sitting in a jail cell because of it."

"No one ever told me that."

"You wouldn't talk to us. You never answered the phone. You'd never hear me out. I know you don't believe me," Kim 2 said with tears coming to her eyes and her nose turning red, "but that was all really hard for me. I know I was some bullshit. I fucking know that. The shit I did back then, sleeping with you two. I know it was bad, but I saw you like my sister and I only did that because in my fucked-up way I thought it was what you wanted because you asked me to do it. Ron was the only person there for me when you cut me off. That's when it happened. Okay? That's when we got together. But only then—after."

I started crying too. I knew she was telling the truth, but I wasn't ready yet to admit it.

She got up and stood over me. "I want you to forgive me some-day. I know it might not be right now. But maybe someday. Because I really miss you, Kim," she said, tears streaming. "You remember all the bad times, but I remember the good." She wiped her face dry with her sleeve and smiled thinly. "Call me when you have some-thing nicer to say. I'll pick up every time."

"You're late!" Paul said, standing at the elevator.

I walked around him and kept on my path to my office.

I felt him following me, but at some point he stopped.

I found Carol in my office, sitting at my desk when I walked in.

"What are you doing at my desk?" I asked as she got up.

"Uploading some audio files Paul just gave me." She looked into my eyes as we passed each other, trading places at the desk. "Your eyes are swollen. You've been crying?"

I ignored her and moved the computer mouse with my index figure to clear the screen saver and see what was on the desktop. There was an icon showing that audio files were uploading.

"What? You didn't believe me?" she said, laughing nervously.

"No. I do. I'm just having a horrible morning."

"I understand. We all have those days. Right?" She smiled encouragingly before walking toward the door. "Don't you fret. All is well. You'll be fine in no time. How about I order one of those macchiatos you like from Bluebird? I'll have a messenger bring it over."

"I don't want that. I'm okay," I said.

"Suit yourself." She frowned.

Carol walked out, but I called her back when the audio files had finished loading.

"What is this?" I asked.

"Not sure. Didn't listen. Paul gave the memory stick to me earlier. Oh yeah"—she gritted her teeth in embarrassment—"good thing you stopped me. He wanted me to tell you to make sure you didn't lose the memory stick. I think it's the only copy or something. That's why I loaded it onto your computer for safekeeping." She grinned and slapped her head. "Jesus, I must be getting old. I also almost forget to tell you about lunch. He told me to put him down for two p.m."

"No," I said.

"What? No, I'm not getting old?"

"E-mail Paul and tell him I can't make it."

"But there's nothing on your calendar."

"Well, make something up. Okay?" I glared at Carol. "And close the door, please." I smiled and sat in the chair. I waited for the door to click closed and pressed Play on the file on my desktop.

There was just static at first. Then there was one of those long recording beeps. Next was King's voice:

"Quinn, why aren't you answering my calls? Come on, man. Things can't be that sweet in Belize. Look, I need to make sure you transfer that stash. Closing up here and it's about to go down. Do me that solid."

There was another break and then a beep.

"Got your message. Put the stash in RC's name. There's no nine-digit that will connect it here. We'll do the rest on our side."

The messages continued, and on each one King was moving money around between offshore accounts. He kept speaking in pounds and sometimes used lingo detectives associated with the Russian mafia, money laundering, and transfers between Britain and HSBC. He never used numbers, but he couldn't be talking about less than a million each time.

When the last recording played, I looked down at the memory stick. In pillow talk after King and I made love the night before he promised he was going to leave everything. He just had to find a way to separate his money from the business and leave a little behind to satisfy the brotherhood, so when he disappeared no one came looking for him. He'd asked me to come with him.

I snatched the memory stick out of the computer and dropped it into my purse. My heart drumming, I moved the pointer on the mouse to hover over the audio file. I right clicked and scrolled up to delete. I right clicked and scrolled up to delete.

I right clicked and scrolled up to delete.
I right clicked and scrolled up to delete.
I right clicked and scrolled up to delete.
I right clicked and scrolled up to delete.
I right clicked and scrolled up to delete.

"We got him!" I heard, and immediately dropped my hand from the mouse. I looked up. Paul's head was in my doorway.

"What?" I snapped.

"You listen to the tapes?" He laughed like he'd just eaten a full fish dinner. "Classic. Somehow these guys are so good at hiding their drug activities but always go down for something else. What's on there will get him at least twenty-five years RICO. Can't outfox the law. Right? You listen?"

I could feel my hands shaking under the desk. RICO was the racketeering act we used to put away mob bosses operating in New York County. It was simple but efficient. All we needed was for two major state charges to stick to someone to show a pattern— money laundering or transporting—and then all of the charges based on suspicion of the drug enterprise, charges we couldn't previously pin on the boss because he'd been giving the orders and not participating—murder, street sales, whatever—could legally be pinned to him as the head. We called it "pin the tail on the donkey" because once the DA posted the indictment with the list of charges, even before the trial, he could seize the boss's belongings and completely stop the enterprise. This usually led to them pleading guilty, getting locked up quickly, and serving a minimum of twenty years. It was how the Gambinos, the Luccheses, even the Latin Kings went down. Simple. Efficient. They seldom saw it coming.

"You sure it's him?" I asked.

"Yes. The guy on the tape—Quinn—feds have been taping his

phones for years. He was connected to that HSBC scandal in 2011. Got off and, just like they always do, went right back in. Feds are closing in on him. That leaves McDonnell to us," Paul said confidently. "You know, at first I thought this was just about the mayor thing, but now it's so sweet. Brooklyn couldn't stop him, but all those calls were about his start-up in my borough. My city! I've got him, Kiki. He's mine—well, ours." He grinned. "So, what's for lunch? I was thinking Siggy's. Been craving that wild salmon burger for some reason."

"I can't do lunch. I need to catch up on the case," I said.

"Thought you were doing that last night. You were home, right? Working on the case in your apartment?" Paul sounded like one of the detectives grilling a criminal. Like he knew something. I imagined him sitting outside my place in the police wagon watching shadows of King and me from the street.

"Well, you can never know too much," I said. "I'm caught up, but with this new information, I need to add—"

Paul cut me off. "No, you *need* to decide what you're going to do, Kim."

"What does that mean?"

Paul had stepped into my office, and now he walked closer to the desk and said with a smile, "I called you back to work. I didn't mention anything that happened before you left. I just let that shit go. Right? Took the heat. Figured out how to keep all the details out of the media." He smiled wider. "Now I need you to play with me. Either you're here or you're not here." He sucked his teeth dubiously. "I, for one, want you here. But the final decision is yours. I'll see you at Siggy's at two," he said with a smile.

He left me in my office with the flash drive in my purse. He didn't mention that it was our only copy.

Carol came in to apologize for missing Paul heading into my office. I told her it was okay and that I'd actually meet him for lunch. She slid a macchiato onto my desk and said she'd figured I'd need it and that she'd be at her desk if I needed anything.

I sat back in my seat and stared at the coffee cup with steam hovering over it for a few seconds or minutes, every one of which felt impossible. I wanted to knock the cup to the floor, lie down on the desk, cry and rock myself to sleep. I felt like I'd climbed to the top of a hill with a weight strapped to my back and lost my step, and the weight took over, and now I was free-falling to the ground. I hadn't even gotten over the reality of the car crash—had time to think about it, or King and what we'd whispered entangled the night before, or anything. There was no time for me to try to catch hold. I was just falling. Any clarity or energy I thought I'd found when I rolled out of bed that morning was exhausted. I wanted to go back to sleep. I wanted to quit everything.

I turned to the computer and it looked so strange. Anything I ever did on it felt forgotten and foreign. What were my cases? What work had I done? I looked around my office—the room I'd danced in on my first day. Whose name was that on the door outside? Who was she? Really? At one time this job and this place had meant everything to me. Now it felt like a hard-to-remember dream.

Kim 2 had said I was strong. She didn't blink one time. Didn't look to the right. Said she knew I was strong. But if that was true, then how could I have needed her to save me?

I looked up at the calendar and counted off the days since I'd told Kent I wouldn't drink again—just for him—to please him. And I realized it wasn't the first time I'd looked at the date. The whole time I'd been counting the hours. Every little circumstance left a lingering thirst on my tongue. I could taste Jameson at the back of my throat. I'd ignored it. Left it without acknowledgment. Re-placed it with . . .

I picked up my purse and searched through everything to find the Baggie of pills King had given me. I fished it out and looked at it. "Overuse," I heard Dr. Davis saying.

I threw the Baggie of pills into the trash can.

"No more," I said, pointing at it like it was a bad-ass kid. "No more!" If I could let the alcohol go, then I could stop taking the pills. I would be fine. Kim 2 and Ronald, Kent, they all thought I had a problem, but I'd be fine.

There was laughter out in the hallway. I looked up and saw Eas-ter walking by with another ADA I hardly spoke to. They looked back at me and surrendered fake-ass waves. When they passed my threshold I heard Easter say, "Oh, she's back? Guess membership *really does* have privileges." They laughed some more and trailed off.

I looked down at the Baggie in the trash and reminded myself that anyone would be able to find it there. I picked it up and placed it back into my purse.

Paul was sitting outside Siggy's in one of the wooden chairs be-side the ALIENS EAT FREE chalkboard sign where people commonly crossed out *aliens* and replaced it with *rappers* or *strippers* or *whores;* Paul and I once put in *attorneys.*

"There's my pretty girl," Paul said, standing up and stepping forward to kiss me right in front of the packed late-lunch crowd of workers and tourists and I'm sure a few lawyers who knew him.

I moved back, stunned. "What are you doing?" I asked.

"It's okay, baby. It's fine." He came at me for another kiss, and held my arm so I couldn't move. He kissed me on the lips and loos-ened his grip to rub my arm.

Months earlier, I might have died for that kind of public display, but now I only said, "Why are you sitting out here?" I usually found him down the long hallway at the last table in the back of the restaurant. He'd rush through lunch and promise to come to my place later for his kiss.

"Damn, girl! Come on! You're gonna have to stop this mean shit! A handsome man like myself kisses you, and all you can do is complain about the table?" He started laughing but stopped when he noticed my distance. "What? I was joking about the handsome part. God! Let's get you a seat and some food in your belly."

He pulled me to the table and I sat down.

"I've taken the liberty of ordering the very tasty salmon burger for my sweetheart," he said, fingering his phone on the table. "Don't have long. Supposed to meet Terrance and Brocket at the courthouse," he added, referring to two other ADAs who also worked Special Prosecutions as he responded to text messages. "Getting ready to go before the grand jury on that Crips murder case from last summer." He put the phone down and looked at me.

"That's fine," I said.

"I remember the first time we came here. That was just a few weeks after you came into the department. I wanted to get to know you. I admit it, my mind was so fucking blown the first time I saw you. I was like, 'This sister is bad!'" He smirked at me seductively. "You are so beautiful. I knew we'd be together."

"Really?"

Paul jerked backward like he was surprised. "There it is again," he said.

"What?"

"You rolled your eyes again. Like you're still mad at me about something. What did I do? I mean, correct me if I'm wrong here, but I thought we were making progress."

"Paul, I've been thinking about things, and I'm happy you're getting a divorce, but I hope you're not doing it for me, because—"

"I'm not *getting* a divorce, baby. I *am* divorced. See. You can stop being angry. Okay. I'm done. I'm ready." He smiled and held out his arm. "I'm all yours."

"You didn't let me finish—"

"I had important news. I wanted to get it out."

"And you did it again," I pointed out.

"Okay then. Go ahead, honey. I'll wait. You get it all out." He rested his elbow on the table and held up his chin to show he was listening. His cell phone was clattering with incoming text messages.

"I don't even need to keep going, because you're doing exactly what I have a problem with. What I didn't have a problem with before because I was so fucking happy that you were just paying any attention to me. And who wouldn't be? Look at you! God!" I looked at the women sitting behind Paul who kept looking over at his back, his shoulders, seeing what all women saw in him. "And then I thought the sneaking around, the excitement of it, the good— really great sex, that all went to my head and I was thinking I was feeling things I probably wouldn't have otherwise."

"*Wouldn't have otherwise?*" Paul shook his head. "I don't get it. What are you saying?"

"I don't think this is going to work," I said.

The waitress came out and put the sandwiches on the table. "Can I get you two anything else?" she asked.

"No!" we both said, still staring at each other.

When she left, Paul laughed uneasily. "You're making a mistake. This guy you're seeing got into your head and he's got you confused."

"What guy? I keep telling you there's no guy."

"Let him go. Just stop now. Before it gets out of hand." He picked up the burger and started eating it like he was hardly attached to the conversation. He waved at people walking into Siggy's like he was already running for mayor.

I waited and waited. Watched him eat and smile at people until I couldn't stand his smirk anymore.

"Eat your food. It's Siggy's. You like it," Paul said, pointing to my burger with his mouth filled with food. The phone on the table started clattering again, but he silenced the call.

"I'm not hungry." I pushed the plate away.

"Why?"

"Because of the things you said. Where do you get off threatening me?"

"Threatening you? I didn't threaten you."

"You said, 'Just stop now. Before it gets out of hand.' I take that as a threat."

Paul laughed. He looked down at his food and laughed like Chris Rock and Dave Chappelle were standing at the table telling jokes.

"I love you, Kim. That's it. And I'm not letting anything come between us. Not even you. Now, you may think you know what you want right now, but I know what's best." He gazed at me. "I can't wait to see how this all works out for us." He reached under the table with his left hand and patted my knee while continuing to eat until he'd stuffed the last bite into his mouth. I sat silently watching him. "Now, I certainly hate to eat and run, especially with such beautiful company, but I have to get to the courthouse," he said, wiping rogue bread crumbs from his lips and chin. "You stay here. Eat your food and get some sunlight. Getting a little thin and pale. Turning into a white girl on me." He laughed and stood up, straddling the chair and leaning over me, blocking the sunlight. "See you at the office, baby?"

"Sure. I'll see you there," I agreed, though I wanted to question him about what he'd said concerning how things would work out for us—there was no "us." But it seemed like no matter how I said it, no matter how I acted, Paul could only see what he wanted to see. Not that any of that was a surprise, but his pushing was making it clear that he wasn't about to walk away from me easily. I guess that should've made me feel good—to have my boss, the DA of the greatest city in the world, sweating me. It didn't. It made me afraid.

Paul bent down and kissed me softly on the lips with his eyes closed. I didn't close mine. I watched him to see if he believed what he was saying. If he'd open his eyes and stare at me like a fish. He didn't. His mouth closed, he twisted his lips on top of mine dramatically like we were soap opera stars. He kept his eyes closed tight like he was dreaming.

Then he stepped back from the table and said good-bye and the sunlight returned.

The women at the table behind us watched him walk away and get into his illegally parked police wagon right at the curb. By how he moved, I could tell he was aware of their gawking.

"Didn't like the sandwich?" the waitress asked, appearing at the table.

I looked at the table where my untouched salmon and Paul's empty plate sat in contrast.

"Just not hungry," I replied.

"Oh. That's too bad. After he already paid." She smiled before digging, "Us girls got to eat free sometimes. Want me to wrap it up for you?"

I waited for her to return with the bagged salmon and left a tip on the table before walking to the curb to catch a cab back to work.

I felt like the sun followed me from the chair to the cab, beating down on me so hard, it felt like the middle of July. Opening the back door of the cab, I looked up at the sun and said, "Damn!"

I slid my left leg into the backseat and had started telling the driver where to take me when I felt the door handle tug back from me. I looked over my right shoulder.

Pulling back on the door was a black woman with a slender frame in a bright yellow Tory Burch brunch dress that screamed "housewife in the city."

"Sorry, this cab is taken," I said to her huge sunglasses and tight frown. I tried to pull the handle again, but she wouldn't let go, and moved in between the car and door. "Umm . . . , I said, this is taken," I said sarcastically. "No worries. It's New York City. Another cab will be along in a minute."

"I know it's New York, bitch!" she said sharply, snatching off her sunglasses.

"Lawanna? Oh . . ." I shrank recognizing the face I'd studied so many times in pictures in Paul's office and at events where she was glued to his arm.

"I knew if I followed that nigga around long enough, he'd lead me right to his new pussy. Fucking liar," she said, looking like she was about to spit on me.

I stuttered out, "I-I know what it looks like, but he's my boss— that's all," while the driver, who should've been telling Lawanna to get the hell away from the car, was peering nosily over his shoulder, enthralled by the exchange.

"Bitch, please! There's nothing stupid about me. You don't stay married to a nigga like Paul for that long being stupid. I know his moves like clockwork. And I know for sure that you're the bitch he's fucking," she said. "Just own your shit. You know, I was born and raised in 40 Projects. And where I'm from, a bitch fucking your man is grounds for a fast beat-down. And it's even worse when she denies the shit."

"I didn't mean for it to happen. I was going through a lot," I whispered, seeing in her eyes the same rage I felt when I discovered Kim 2 and Ronald were together. "It didn't start the way it ended up. I was having a hard time." And then I heard myself sounding like Kim 2.

"Well, I hope you don't mind having a hard time, because that's all you're gonna get with Paul. He don't make shit easy, and he made my life a fucking hell. All these clothes and cars, and the houses— and we ain't nothing but two hood rats playing dress-up." She came in closer to me and looked into my eyes. "Oh, you didn't know that. You think Paul is some fucking Alpha-Kappa-Omega-bitch boy?" She laughed. "Oh, no. He's a nigga in a suit. Don't be confused. Think I let him get off so easy in this divorce for nothing? Please. I just wanted my house and my kids and for him to go away. Now he's your problem."

Lawanna stood at the car door without moving for too many seconds. She didn't say anything. She just watched my face like she was trying to remember it or share something else with me.

At first it was awkward and I heard the cabbie cough to signal that it was time for her to go. But then it was chilling, scary. Almost made me want her to curse at me some more or haul off and slap me like angry wives did in the movies.

"It's over between us," I said, deciding that was why she was still standing there studying me—she wanted to hear that, but it was the God's honest truth.

Her response turned her voice so dark and macabre, the sun seemed to black out, as if Paul was standing over the entire city watching us. "It's never over with Paul," she uttered. "Not until he says. Thanks."

Lawanna stepped back from the door like a zombie, put her shades back on, and waved good-bye with a cryptic smile when the cab took off.

"*Ay, Dios mío!* What the fuck was that?" the driver said in a thick Spanish accent while making the sign of the cross.

My heart was beating too quickly for me to respond. I just pointed straight ahead and ordered, "Drive!"

"That *puta* was crazy as hell, eh?" he added, looking back at me. "You sleep with her husband? Shit! That's nothing to play with, *mami*. Bad blood. You know. As we say in DR, 'Karma is a bitch'!"

"Thanks for your solid advice, cabdriver man," I said, still pointing ahead. "Just drive."

"Whatever you say, *mami*. Just don't put that woman on me," he said. "Hey, if you need some help, maybe you can go see my cousin Demaris in the Bronx. She crazy as hell, but she got the Santería. Sell you a candle or something. Right?" He looked back at me again.

"I don't need any candles. I just need to get back to my job," I answered, though candles and Santería did sound pretty comforting after Lawanna's hard black-girl stare.

When I got back to the office, I was still worked up and scared and I headed straight to Carol's desk, where she was playing Spider Solitaire.

"Carol," I said, startling her from behind.

"Oh, shit!" She jumped and turned around to face me. "I know what this looks like"—she nervously pointed to the computer screen behind her—"but I'm really just on a break."

"I don't even care," I said. "Look—"

"*You* don't care?" She looked at me like I'd gone crazy.

"Carol, listen, I don't want to see Paul at all for the rest of the day. Okay? If he comes around, you say I'm not here," I said. "I need you to do that. And I'm leaving early." I looked around at the other ADAs who were walking in the common cubicle area, looking at me but pretending to be doing something else. I wanted to scream out that I knew that they knew what was going on. I wondered if Lawanna had come to the office in her yellow dress before I'd gotten there. Maybe plastered up a poster in the bathroom with the word "*Ho*" beneath my picture.

Carol sighed and said in a low voice, "Is something going on with you two? People are talking. And I know things have been strange around here, but I need my damn job. You know I just bought that condo in Jersey."

"You're not going to lose your job," I assured her, but really, with the day I was having, I couldn't guarantee anything to anyone. "And what are people saying?"

Carol stood and whispered to me, "That Paul got a divorce and that you"—she looked warily over at the assistant in the cubicle beside hers and lowered her voice more—"you might be the reason." She then quickly snapped back and smoothed out her shirt like she was detaching herself from the guilt of office gossip. "Now, I'm not the one to judge. The baby Jesus knows for sure I've done my share of dirt with the married kind, hoping it would all turn out in my favor, but"—she looked at me the same way Lawanna had—"all us grown women know that it never works out the way we hoped and prayed it would. Seems our grandmothers were right—*the beast you free from the swamp is that beast you have to take home.*"

"I've never heard that before," I said.

"Oh, well, my grandmother was Geechie with one good gray eye, so who knows what she was talking about. Point is, I don't care what decisions you make. I just need to make sure I'm okay. You know?"

"You're fine, Carol. We're both fine."

"Whew! That gives me relief. And hand to God"—she kissed her right palm and held it up to the ceiling—"I'll never play Spider Solitaire at work. Don't want people to think our little team isn't doing any work."

"Well, that's good to hear."

Carol's focus moved from my face and bounced over my shoulder and up above my head like there was an ugly gray cloud hovering there about to storm down acid rain that would burn me alive. And I felt it too. In seconds, I felt what was written on her face and I knew it was the last straw for me. I didn't want to turn around and face whatever monster storm was brewing behind me. Was it Paul? Lawanna back to give me more of the evil eye? I didn't care and I didn't want to know. I wanted to knock Carol down, jump over her desk, and run right out of the office without ever looking back to see what was lurking.

"Detective Strickland? From Brooklyn, right?" Carol said with a crinkle between her brows.

"Yes. It is I."

Carol smiled. "I remember you from that albino drug murderer case you solved years back. Totally weird. Was all over the news. Folks were talking about it all around here. I'm Carol Southland, Counselor Kind's assistant. Pleased to meet you." She extended her hand to shake Strickland's, and I saw his brown hand slither past my waist to meet hers.

"Great to meet you, too," Strickland said. "And to run into

Counselor Kind on this beautiful day. I thought for sure you'd be out and about in the city," he added into my ear. "Shopping or getting your nails done. You know how you womenfolk get during the spring—taking care of all your little beauty secrets."

I turned to face Strickland as he and Carol laughed. "I don't have any secrets," I said.

"Really?" He grinned at me in his maroon suit. "I never took you for the type who didn't have secrets."

After reminding Carol of my explicit instructions, I led Strickland to my office and offered him a seat.

Sliding behind my desk to sit opposite him, I asked, "How can I help you, Detective?"

"Let's not be so formal," he said. "You don't want this to be a formal visit." He peered into me and I knew what I'd feared was true. "In fact, before you take that seat, you may want to go and close your door. Wouldn't want any prying ears." He nodded at the door.

"Okay." I walked and closed the door and stood behind him looking at the flatness of his bald head, the little ant-shaped shaving bumps at the base of his skull. "So, what's going on?" I asked, walking back behind the desk and finally sitting. I struggled to sound calm, but I already heard my voice shaking.

Strickland gave a short and wicked laugh before talking about Delli's suspicions about King's alibi the night of Vonn's murder. How at first he wasn't going to make a move on the psychologist's suspicions, but soon he found himself asking the same questions, and those questions led him to the Clocktower.

"You've been very busy, Counselor," Strickland said, looking at my degrees on the wall.

My hands on my lap behind the desk, I fought trembling that

shook me from my ankles. "I didn't do anything," I said, hearing in my voice the panic I would've read as fresh blood on the lips of any guilty person I was interviewing. I told myself to shut up and be calm and look forward without moving.

"Maybe you didn't. But this isn't about what you did. I already know that. It's about where you were and why." He paused to clear his throat. "See, my sources put you right at the Clocktower on the day of Vonn's murder. Seems, in fact, that you were there for a few days. Been keeping company with the suspect—the suspect in a major investigation that's currently on my desk."

"What's your point?" I asked, determined not to admit to or deny anything Strickland was implying. We both knew the game.

"Look, I don't care who you fuck, Kind. With all of the single and desperate black women in this city, you're bound to fuck a white guy . . . or a criminal . . . or a white criminal, in your case, at some point. But when you fuck with my case, you fuck with me. And you being at the Clocktower the night of the murder and not telling anyone and that white bastard protecting you, that's fucking with my case."

"You have no proof of any of this," I said.

Strickland's laugh was long and wicked. "Oh, sister, I've got plenty. You know the doorman? The one your little hood-rat cousin volunteered to suck off? He's blue."

"Frantz?" I let slip out, and I felt those razor blades scraping up my spine again.

"He's talking. Told me all about your little visit. Even you and McDonnell cuddling in the elevator. How sweet." Strickland batted his eyes mockingly.

"That doesn't mean King did anything," I said.

"Oh, now you motherfuckers are on a first-name basis?" he asked. "And none of that interests me anyway. As I said, I'm on to the why. Why would a woman like you fuck a man like that? Why were you with him the night of the murder? And why wouldn't you tell authorities when you realized we were on to him?"

Strickland leaned forward and tapped his nails on the wooden desktop. I knew this was to mash at my nerves. I tried to breathe to ease the pain in my back, but it was only tightening with each tap. "See, I'm a detective and I'm naturally curious. Want to know things. Understand. And what I came up with is that you didn't tell my team about your involvement with McDonnell when you were in Brooklyn because you and that snake you call a district attorney were trying to ruin our investigation so you can have McDonnell for yourself. Or, you had no clue who McDonnell was and you were too afraid to tell us anything because you wanted to protect your little career. I hear you have your eyes on being the next DA?"

"You don't know anything about me," I said, trying not to leave any traces of alliance with Strickland's words. I knew what he was looking for in me, a lean-in to admit to his theories.

He sat and stared, waiting for a move.

"Yeah," he said after a while. "I guessed those were both wrong. Then I came to my next hypothesis. Want to know what it is?"

"What is it, Strickland? Humor me."

"Well, maybe you know everything and you're playing the game for McDonnell. That's where your interest is. Isn't it? Protecting him? Hiding his secrets? You're just playing us. Been siding with McDonnell the whole time."

I looked down at my purse on the desk where the memory stick with King's audio file was.

Strickland caught the glance and looked there too.

He said, "Who knows where your filthy hands have been. What evidence you've hidden. Information you've stalled. I know your kind."

"I haven't been hiding anything for anyone," I stated adamantly.

"Oh . . . not you . . . right?" he said. "Please. Drop the good-girl routine. I looked into your past. I know about your parents, that alcoholic father of yours, who stumbles down your old street every day crying about his lost wife." Strickland smirked. "And that mother? A straight crackhead. A rock-smoking homeless prostitute."

"My mother is not a prostitute!" I said, getting up with tears in my eyes.

"Oh, did I pluck a nerve!"

"Get out of my office!" I said.

"You don't want to hear the truth about your mother? How I found her sucking dick on the side of the road for five dollars?"

"No! That's not my mother!" I screamed. "You don't know anything about my mother. Now get the fuck out of my office!"

Strickland stood, but his face was unaffected by my orders.

"Oh, I do know the truth about you, Counselor Kind. And soon everyone else will, too. That you can take the girl out of the projects but you can't take the projects out the girl. You'll be subpoenaed. That face will be on all the newspapers. You'll be ruined. The only place you'll be able to work is on that show *Mob Wives*," he said. "Now, you do have a choice."

"What do you want from me?" I asked, fighting to keep back my tears. I refused to let him see me breaking down.

"You tell me all about McDonnell's operation. What he's doing. And I'll keep your little Clocktower dick ride a secret."

"I can't do that. I don't know anything," I pleaded.

"Kind, you don't expect me to believe that. I know about pillow talk. I know he's told you his story about the Irish mob. About his father living in Belize."

"I told you I don't know anything," I said. "Now, would you just leave!"

"Fine, Kind," Strickland said, walking toward the door. "I'll go now, but I'll be waiting for you," he added, opening the door. He nodded and tipped an invisible hat before walking out.

I let out my breath like I'd been underwater. And the pain in my back was ornery. I was standing, but I had to look at my hands to make sure I hadn't fainted. The tears I'd held back now dripped to my palms, and I screamed so loudly I saw red streaks in my eyes. "Shit!" I walked back to my seat and tried to think of what to do. If there was anything I could do. I thought to call King, but if Strickland was on to me, he'd probably had my phone tapped.

"What is it?" Carol said, rushing into my office. She quickly closed the door on the prying eyes of people who'd heard my scream.

"I can't do this!" I said to myself, standing in the middle of the floor afraid to move.

Carol came to my side. "What did he say? I knew that Strickland was bad news. Was it about Paul?"

I heard her but I wasn't listening. I was being pulled right back down that mountain with the weight around my waist.

"You need me to call someone? An ambulance?" Carol asked. "I don't think you're well. I think you need an ambulance."

"I'm fine," I said. "I need to get out of here. To get home."

"But you're not well," Carol said. And then she looked at the little slip of paper on my desk with Dr. Davis's name and number on it. "Maybe we should call your doctor—Dr. Davis," she said, handing me the paper.

"No! I don't need him!" I snapped at Carol. "I'm just going home."

"Yes! That's fine," she agreed.

I picked up my purse, and through tears, I looked around the office as if I'd never be back there again. I remembered King asking me to run away with him. To go away and leave this place.

I walked out of my office past assistants and other ADAs lined up along the walls with closed mouths and perked ears.

"I'll call you later," Carol said, walking out behind me and trying to make it sound like everything was okay. "Feel better. Just a migraine. You'll be fine."

I walked along the line keeping my eyes ahead.

I could hardly see Easter, but I knew she was the last person I was passing before I got to the elevator.

"Feel better," she said, touching my shoulder. "I really mean that."

I pulled away, rushed into the elevator crying. I felt like everyone was chasing me, following me like a mob with pitchforks, threatening to burn me alive. I started sweating and feeling clammy. The elevator was vibrating in and out with the beats of my heart. On the loudspeaker there was Strickland repeating what he'd seen my mother doing. I fell to the back corner and covered my ears. "No!" I said. "She wouldn't do that!"

Once the elevator doors opened again, I ran out of my corner, through the lobby, and into the street, where I stopped a cab with my body and an outstretched arm like I knew where I was rushing to. But when I got into the back of a cab, I couldn't remember where I was going. I couldn't hear the cabdriver. I just watched his lips moving so fast. He kept saying the same thing again and again, but I couldn't hear him. I couldn't answer him either. He reached back to me. I was handing him a slip of paper. The world around him started closing in, black all around. And then he was gone. Everything was gone.

Chapter 13

I was swimming in the ocean. It was so big and blue and deep all around me. Water as far as I could see. Up above there was more blue in the sky. No sun. Just clouds that looked like the waves. There was no sound. No people. Just me feeling the salt water carry my body in its expanse.

Up near my breasts, the water was chilly and choppy, but at my feet the undercurrent was warm and so calm. I stopped kicking and pushing myself through the waves and sank down deep to feel more of the warmth. I wanted to stay there. To never leave or find land again.

Underwater, I looked up at the sky. That was it. I was going away. I closed my eyes, drew the salt water into my lungs, and let myself slip down, down, down.

"Kim!" I heard through the water. "Kim!"

I felt an arm belted around my waist.

"Kim! Don't give up! You can't! Wake up, baby! I need you to wake up!"

I opened my eyes again and the blue water was gone. I was lying on a couch with a sketch of a shark on the wall behind it, flanked by seashells in frames. I could hear the recorded sounds of the ocean through the sound spa port.

I looked over and saw Dr. Davis standing beside a man with his back to me.

I couldn't speak, but I reached out to them.

"She's awake!" Dr. Davis said, looking at me and then rushing toward me.

"Kim!" The man turned around.

"Kent!" was my first word.

My brother ran to my side.

"You okay, Kim?" Kent said, getting on his knees beside me. I could see so much worry in his eyes.

"I'm fine," I answered. "I was just dreaming." I looked at Dr. Davis. "Why am I here? How did I get here?"

"You gave a cabdriver my number. Told him to bring you here," Dr. Davis explained.

"Do you remember anything? What happened to you?" Kent asked.

"I don't know. I was at work. I just wanted to get away. I was having a bad day. A really bad day," I said. "I must've fainted."

"I think you just had a little panic attack," Dr. Davis declared, stepping in front of Kent and checking my heartbeat with a cold stethoscope. "You were barely awake when you got here. You were saying something about your mother. And then you passed out. That's when I called your brother. You had him listed as your emergency contact."

"Oh my God, I'm sorry. I'm so sorry!"

"There's nothing to be sorry about." Dr. Davis placed his fingers on the glands on my neck and then gave me a thumbs-up to let me know I was okay. "I'm glad you thought to call me." He grinned. "You weren't answering any of my calls. I was starting to feel a little hurt." He stood up straight and looked at Kent. "She'll be fine. I'll leave the two of you alone. Let me know if you need anything."

My brother sat down on the floor at my side and stroked my hair like I was his child. "What happened to you, Kiki Mimi?" he asked.

"I was at work, and there was . . . ." Though my thoughts were still blurry, I could hear Strickland in my ear like he was standing beside me.

"There was what? What happened?"

"Just this guy. We're working on this case together, and he said some things to me. I was just—it was a bad day."

"What's his name?" Kent asked with his jaw tightening.

"Name? I'm not telling you that. I'm not crazy." Even with my head spinning in the waves from Dr. Davis's ocean soundscape, I still managed to chuckle at Kent's request. "You'll go over there and act a fool—and don't show up at my job. He doesn't even work at that office."

"You know I'll fuck him up, right?"

"It was just work stuff. The boys play rough," I said. Strickland's language was vile and his approach was just out of line, but it was nothing compared with what I'd seen and heard from men there. On any other day I could've taken his insults, fought back, and probably would have won, but in the bottom of the bag of everything else it was like the perfect right hook on the cheek to just knock me out—literally. "I've been having a hard time," I admitted softly to my brother. "A really hard time. And I don't know what to do. I feel like I need to get away to just leave everything. Start over."

"Why don't you just do it, then?"

"Leave? You think I should leave?"

"Why not?"

"What about you? Daddy?" I asked. "Mommy?"

"We'll be fine. Ain't none of us going nowhere. You know that," Kent answered. "Kiki, I know I'm supposed to tell you to stand up—right? Give you that 'Harlem stand up!' pep talk. But the truth is, you've been standing up strong all along. All this time. Standing stronger than all of us. And if you want to sit down for a little while and let us pick up the slack, go on and do it. Maybe you keep thinking that you want to get away because you need a break. Take it. Stay away as long as you like. Like I said, the fam ain't going nowhere. And you know I always got your back."

When I am asked to provide an emergency contact, I usually give the first name that comes to mind—Kenton Kind—and scribble down his cell phone number in a rush as if the question is a nuisance, an unnecessary aspect of whatever form I'm filling out. That's because I'd never been in a situation where an emergency contact was needed and I couldn't imagine one.

With Kenton Kind sitting there stroking my hair with his big heavy hands that could've used a little shea butter at the knuckles, I was so grateful for him being my twin, the other side of me, and for being the one whose name I'd put down without even thinking. He was right: He always had my back.

Dr. Davis wouldn't let us leave without me signing up for physical therapy for my back and agreeing to make an appointment to be evaluated by a drug abuse counselor for possible dependency on prescription pills. While I initially fought him about his idea that

I was abusing painkillers, when I pulled out the Baggie King had given me as evidence of my lack of desire to take the pills, I realized that I was nearly through the stash. I didn't even remember taking the pills.

"The best thing we can do right now is ask questions," he said, walking Kent and me to the door. "If we get the answers we were expecting, we can move on. If we don't, we can get some help."

"Thank you, Dr. Davis," I said. "Thank you for not giving up on me. And for harassing me."

He laughed and smiled at me. "I knew you'd come around. You're too smart not to."

Kent and I took a cab to my place, and he came upstairs to make sure I got in okay.

"I'm really fine now. You can go," I said, walking into my apartment in front of him. "I'm just going to lie down. Probably call the office. I know my assistant is going crazy. She's probably called every hospital in the city."

"Need me to do anything before I go?" Kent sat on the couch as I went into the bedroom to slip out of my shoes. "Maybe I could make you soup."

"Soup? It's spring. What do I need with soup?" I laughed, walking back into the living room with bare feet.

"I don't know. Ain't that what people eat when they sick? Chicken noodle soup?"

"That's for a cold, crazy." I sat beside Kent and leaned my head on his shoulder. "You know, you have your flaws, but you're really the best brother in the entire universe."

"The universe? Really?" Kent leaned his head on top of mine. "That's mad competition. I beat the fucking aliens, too?"

"Yup. Yup."

He pointed at the table. "Where's your Jameson?" he asked. "That's where you normally keep it."

"No more Jameson," I answered, shaking my head. "I told you I was stopping. You didn't believe me?"

"Saying you're stopping and actually stopping—" he trailed off, ". . . you know."

"Yeah. How's your thing going?"

"Great. I lead the meeting next week. Want to come—"

"I'm good," I answered, giggling. "I think I had an earful last time."

"All right. Don't say I didn't invite you though."

We sat there a little longer. I felt so safe leaning on him that I fell asleep listening to him breathing.

When I woke up, the sun was down. Kent was sitting there looking straight ahead into the dim living room.

"I fell asleep," I said. "I think I was really tired."

Kent wasn't saying anything. He was just looking ahead.

"You okay?" I asked him.

"She probably ain't gonna get better, Kim," he said firmly.

I didn't have to ask who he was talking about.

"I been sitting here thinking about what I could say to make you feel better. Something about what I think is really bothering you," he said. "I think you worrying about Mommy. You always been. And I think I need to tell you she gonna be all right. But I don't think she will."

"Me neither," I agreed with tears in my eyes.

"I ain't never want to say this to you, but we might need to prepare for the worst." Kent put his hand on my knee. "Our mother might die out there in those streets. She might not ever come home. You understand that?"

"Yes." I closed my eyes and let the tears fall. I watched my mother's red hoodie disappear into the darkness beneath my eyelids.

I had a long cry on Kent's shoulder. One of those good cries that builds into sniffling and bated breath. I didn't say anything though. I just sobbed over everything I couldn't forget about my mother, everything I couldn't remember, everything I'd probably never know.

Kent comforted me through my wailing. He draped his arm around my shoulder and nodded along with what I was thinking but not saying. It was as if once again my thoughts were ours. He knew what each sob was for.

"So, where am I going to be visiting you? Bali? Dubai? Australia?" Kent said, trailing me to the door after my swollen eyes couldn't produce another tear and I convinced him that it was safe to leave me alone to go to sleep. I wasn't tired at all after my nap, and it was still pretty early, but my brain was exhausted and I really wanted some alone time to dig through the day and prepare myself for tomorrow. Dr. Davis advised me to get a mental health evaluation as soon as possible. He wanted me to talk with a professional about why I'd had a panic attack that led to me passing out.

"Atch-scray on Australia-ay," I said, speaking the pig Latin Kent and I'd used to pass messages to each other in front of our parents as teens.

"Oh, you just went old school!" Kent said, chuckling, as I started unlocking the locks on the door. "But why scratch Australia? You know all y'all bougie black females going to Australia right about now."

"I'm saying, you're trying to ship your sister off already? Let's wait and see how things go before you start planning stamps in your passport."

"You know what I figured out when I was in Brazil?"

"What?"

"You only here once. Maybe there's a heaven. We don't know. But you only here once. And you should probably do some shit while you here," Kent said introspectively.

I unlocked the last lock and turned to take in his depth. And for a few seconds every word of what he'd said sounded like it had come from the lips of Nietzsche himself. But then, after looking my brother over, his Timbs and fitted cap, his slang and swag, I burst out laughing.

"What? Why you laughing at me?" he asked, laughing too. "Niggas can't get deep?"

"So, is that how you ended up proposing to Latin Lydia— because we're *'only here once'*?" I asked.

"Shorty was bad, yo! For real!" Kent explained, regressing from Nietzsche to Tupac. "Could've been wifey—"

"Right! If she wasn't a prostitute!"

"True! True!" Kent said as I pulled the door open. He started walking out but stopped to hug me and ask if I was sure I'd be okay.

"I'm fine," I repeated. "And thanks for coming to my rescue."

"Anytime, Kiki Mimi. You know that."

I pulled the door all the way open to let my oversized twin out and stepped into the threshold behind him.

Our laughter turned to gasps as we saw King standing there outside the door.

I let out an involuntary "King!" but Kent's fast reaction to the unexpected person beside my front door led him to draw back his fist to swing. I quickly jumped between Kent and King, ready to try to stop my brother's blows.

"Wait! No!" I cried to Kent. "Don't!"

"Fuck is you?" Kent asked King.

"Fuck is *you*?" King spat back, stepping in toward him.

"I'm the nigga that's about to split that wig," Kent said.

King just laughed at this as I fought to keep them apart.

"Oh, you want to see? You want to know what's up?" Kent started patting his lower pelvis where he kept his gun.

"No!" I cried. "No! He's my friend." I looked at King over my shoulder. "This is my brother!"

"You know this fool?" Kent asked me.

"Yes. He's here to see me."

Kent kept his hand on his jeans but backed up from me. "Fuck is he standing out here by the door like a stalker if he's your friend?"

"I invited him," I said, though I hadn't. "I told him to come here."

I pulled Kent reluctantly down the hallway toward the elevator, tussling with his pushing and cussing the entire way. I was nervous but not surprised. If I'd thought about the two of them meeting, I'd realize it would have to go something like that.

"It's fine! Everything is fine! He's my friend!" I repeated to soothe Kent when we were at the elevator and actually couldn't see King anymore, but Kent was still bucking up like he was ready to fight.

"I don't like that shit! You know that!"

"Just calm down!" I insisted the way my mother would when Kent would get on some boy who'd shown up on our doorstep just to talk to me.

"That's the cracker from your job? The one who was up in your face today? He ain't look like no fucking lawyer. He look like a dope dealer."

"No he isn't and no he doesn't," I argued. "Look, just go home. I'll call you later."

"I don't like that ofay—tell him I said that shit, too. I ain't feeling it. You saw how he was about to come at me?" Kent asked.

"You threatened to shoot him in the head, and you grabbed for your gun. What did you expect him to do?"

He ignored my logic, of course, backing into the elevator. "Tell him we ain't finished yet. I'll catch that ass on the flip side. He better be glad you was here. For real."

"Sure. I will." I blew Kent a kiss as the door closed on the rest of his rant.

I rushed back to my apartment. The door was closed, but I knew he was inside. I turned the knob and let it swing open.

King was standing by the window. He was wearing the same blue jeans from his place and a thin white polo.

He turned from the glowing city outside and looked at me. His blue eyes were like lasers through my skin. They could see any emotion I was even thinking of trying to hide to keep my distance from him. There was something like a buzzing or alarm in my ear. It wrecked all of my defenses and swept away the dirt of the day.

We ran to each other like there was a football field between us. Embraced and kissed and felt each other's faces like it had been forever.

I hugged him again, and my desperate hold proved that support can come in different ways from different people. With my brother, my sorrows came out by leaning on his shoulder. With King, I collapsed into his arms, resting my heart against his, and the tears all poured out. He held on to me.

"I'm here, Queen," he said, and I realized for the first time that unlike Ronald and Paul, he'd never once called me "baby." I was always Queen. He held me closer and kept repeating in my ear, "I'm here. I'm here."

I suddenly pushed away, remembering Strickland's threats, Paul's work with the feds. "You have to go! You have to leave now!" I shouted fearfully.

"Why? What's going on?"

"Strickland—he was at my office today. He knows about us. Frantz told him—he's undercover."

"I know about Frantz," he said pensively.

"Strickland is moving fast. He doesn't want Paul to get the charges on you. He wants Brooklyn to claim your arrest."

"Figures. He's had it in for me for months. It's okay though." He reached for me and laced his arms around my waist. "He won't find anything to stick to me. I shut down operations in BK. Just like I promised. I told you, I'm getting out. I meant that."

"No—there's more, King. You don't get it. Your case has been moved to New York County now . . . We're—"

"Shhhh," he said, trying to quiet me. "I got it. I've been working the law since I was a kid. I know what's up. I ain't worried about the DA. You don't have to worry either."

"You don't know him. He's got a target on you, and he won't back down. It means too much to him. He's working with the feds. They've got tapes."

King stepped back, clearly stunned as I told him about Quinn on the tapes. He sat on the couch and rested his head in his hands.

"Those offshore accounts—even if they can't get you for the drugs, they'll take you down for that if one dime came back into

New York. They'll slowly pin each charge to you. Twenty-five years."

"RICO," King uttered.

"Yes," I said, remembering the memory stick in my purse. It wasn't even worth mentioning. I might stall Paul for a few hours, but he could easily get another one from his contact—if the files weren't already online. Later, after everything had gone down, I'd find the memory stick in my purse and look at it strangely. Part of me would wonder how it got there. How I'd turned into someone who'd even think to take it out of my office. I was the law. I represented that. I'd upheld that. It used to be what moved me. What made me important. When did I lose it? "See," I said to King, falling to my knees in front of him on the couch, "you have to go."

He looked up from the ground and at me. "You're coming with me?"

"I can't. I . . . I'm—" I stopped.

"Then I'll stay."

"Don't be a fool!" I protested. "You stay here and they'll lock you up for the rest of your life. Paul will see to it. I know it."

"You said you'd come with me, Queen," he said simply.

"That was just a fantasy. Night talk. You know? Not real," I said, trying to convince myself and my heart as images of King and I walking along so happy somewhere on the list of places Kent had named—Dubai, Brazil, Australia—looped in my mind. I felt so happy and free, but those were just images. This was my life. "I can't just leave to be with you!" I cried. "Everything I have is here."

He grabbed my shoulders and pulled me to him. "Everything you need is here," he said, pointing to himself. "I'm not leaving you. I refuse to."

There was a knock at the door. Just one rap at first, then three quick ones.

"Who's that?" King asked.

"Shhh," I warned. I knew the knock.

"I know you're in there. I saw Kent downstairs. Open up!" we heard from the door. And then there were three more fast knocks.

"Who is—" King tried, jumping up, but I got up too and stopped him from charging the door.

"Shhh!" I repeated, hoping the knocking would just stop, but it didn't.

"I'm not going away. I need to talk to you. Stop being like this, Kiki!"

King looked at me.

More knocking. I began to panic. I tried to pull King back toward the bedroom.

"What are you doing?" he asked as Paul called from the door.

"I need you to wait in my room," I said quickly, knowing there were only two places to hide in my tiny one-bedroom—the bedroom or bathroom. "I have to handle this. You can't be here," I pleaded.

"I'm not waiting in the room," he said.

Paul was still knocking and repeating, "Open up!"

"Please! I'm begging you! I just need one minute! It'll be bad if you're here. Please just do it." I kept pulling King, but he wasn't budging. I whispered in his ear, "I haven't asked you for anything, but I need you to do this. Please! Please! For me."

"Kiki!" Paul hollered. "Open the door! I'm not leaving!"

The knocks had turned to loud bangs by the time I'd pulled a half-willing King into the bedroom and run back out to the living room to start undoing the locks.

"Stop being so loud," I ordered Paul as I finished. "My neighbors will call the cops."

"Let them come. We can have a fucking reunion up in here."

I let Paul in, and immediately I could smell alcohol on him.

"I've been looking for you," he said, stumbling toward me. "You left work early today. What happened?"

"Ask your wife," I said. "Lawanna was stalking you today, and she showed up at Siggy's when you left."

"Crazy bitch. I told her to stay away from us," Paul slurred, trying to hug me, but I wouldn't let him get his arms around me.

"You're drunk!" I pushed him away.

"Probably!" He laughed demonically. "Been out celebrating." He backed away from me and started padding around the living room with his eyes fondling every surface.

I stepped in front of him to get his attention on me. "Celebrate what?"

"Victory!" He pumped his fist into the air. "Or as Charlie Sheen would say, 'Winning!' " He laughed.

I forced a laugh too. "Winning what, Paul?" I struggled to free my voice of worry.

"Well, I'll be filing the order early next week," he said.

"Filing the restraint order against McDonnell? Isn't that kind of soon?" I asked, trying to mask my immediate alarm. The restraining order would be Paul's first step in seizing King's belongings and stopping him from leaving the country—if he could leave at all. He'd be arrested, a high bail would be set, and if he couldn't afford it, he'd sit in jail until pretrial.

"Too soon? Are you serious?" Paul quickly stepped past my body barrier and took his eye snooping toward the kitchen. "He's a fucking criminal. How much longer are we going to tolerate having him on the fine streets of New York?" His tone oozed mock reverence for the "fine streets of New York."

"I know we're not dealing with a Boy Scout here. I'm just saying, there's more research to do."

"We have plenty between Brooklyn and the laundering. Enough to get him the max. And with the murder connections, we may be able to go for the death penalty." Paul stopped his spying to stare at me.

"Death?" I felt my worry. I knew he could see it in my eyes. Ever since RICO was enacted, DAs had been toying with the notion of using it in the more serious cases, especially those with gang violence. "It's extreme, Paul, and you know it. Don't you think you should've come to me with this? I'm cocounsel."

He smiled at me like I was broken. "Cocounsel?"

I was standing beside the kitchen table, and he started moving toward me with menacing steps. If it was a movie and I didn't know him, this would be the part when I'd reach behind my back to grab the shiny knife from the butcher block.

"Yes. We're working on this together."

"No we're not," he said plainly.

"We're not?"

He pointed at my chest. The tip of his index finger tapped at my heart as he said, "You've been very busy doing other things. Very. Very. Very. Busy. Right?" He produced one of his newspaper-photo smiles. "I heard about Strickland coming by the office."

"He's just trying to shake things up. He thinks we tried to sabotage the McDonnell case in Brooklyn, so you can prosecute him in New York County and claim the charges yourself."

"Where would he get an idea like that?" Paul's words were like matches striking my skin.

"I don't know," I said, trying to look away from his scorching eyes. "He was making things up about me."

"Was he really?" Through the corner of my eye, I could see Paul's smile. "So he was just making things up?"

"He doesn't know anything," I said. "He thinks he does, but he doesn't."

"I told you there'd be trouble. Didn't I? Said there would be trouble if you didn't stop. So many times I told you."

I looked back at him. "Didn't stop what?" I asked, although I realized right then that Paul had known about King for a while. Maybe all along.

"Late night at the Clocktower. Hanging out at the club." He looked disgusted. "Sleeping with him."

"I didn't—"

"Please don't insult me. Do you really think anything can move in my city without me knowing?" He looked toward the bedroom. "I told you, I'm not going to let you fuck this up. It's bad enough you slept with him. I figured you were just acting out some fantasy. I never thought you would've taken it this far. But when you took that memory stick, I knew—"

"That was a test? You gave that to me as a test?"

"I'm just trying to protect you. That's all I've been trying to do. Trying to help you see what's going on. Who this guy really is."

"I don't need you to do anything for me."

"Yes you do. You don't know who this man is. What he's capable of." He started stepping toward me, forcing me to back up to the wall that separated the kitchen from the bedroom.

"He's not a bad person—he's just—" I stopped. I felt tears on my cheeks.

"He's a fucking criminal. And he's gotten into your head, Kim. He's probably just using you. Trying to get to me. To stall the case somehow. Make no mistakes about it—you're disposable. These types of men, they only think about themselves." He wiped my cheek. "But don't worry. I won't let him use you anymore. We'll come clean about the relationship—say he threatened you, took some pictures of you and bribed you. Make you the victim here."

"But I'm not a victim," I uttered.

"Yes you are." Paul stood tall over me again, this time blocking out the light in the kitchen and caging me against the wall. I felt myself getting smaller. Feeling defenseless.

"Get out of my way," I said, trying to get away from Paul, but he grabbed my arms and held me in place. "Let me go and get out of my house!"

"No, Kim!" Paul shouted, shaking me. "I'm not letting you go. Not until you snap out of it and realize what this motherfucker is doing to you."

"Get off of me!" I screamed.

Paul shook and shook; his hold tightened. My head hit the wall with a crack.

"Get away from her." I heard a steady and bold growl.

Paul looked over his shoulder and very quickly let go of my arms before backing away from me.

King was standing behind him with his hands at his sides.

He didn't look at me. For a minute, it was like I'd disappeared as he and Paul sized each other up.

"Romeo finally shows his face," Paul cracked, laughing. "I thought you'd stay in that room all night like a little bitch."

"Are you okay?" King asked me, ignoring Paul's taunting.

"She's fine," Paul said before I could answer.

"I'm fine," I said.

"Okay." King looked at Paul. "I believe she asked you to leave," he said confidently. "And I'm going to give you a chance to leave on your own right now."

Paul listened intently, then started laughing. "Can you believe this motherfucker?" he said to me before looking back at King. "So what happens if I don't leave on my own? What you gonna do?"

"Guess you'll have to wait to find out."

Paul kept laughing. "Do you even know who I am? What I could do to you?"

"Everybody just stop!" I said, feeling the tension between them growing. Paul's shoulders were higher than I'd ever seen them. He was trying to look bigger and stronger. While King was still cool in his stance, his lack of expression was scarier than anything. "Let's just stop this now before it gets out of control."

"I'm not the one around here threatening people," Paul said sarcastically. "Personally, I'm feeling a little concerned for my safety. It might be time for your company to leave." Paul looked at me expectantly. "Tell him to leave," he said.

I didn't know what to say. Who should leave or stay. There was no telling what Paul had waiting outside for King. And there was no way of knowing what Paul would do if I made him leave my place. Any option was a gamble. And the stakes were too high.

"Tell him to leave!" Paul repeated with the laughter gone from his voice.

"King," I started, "I'm—"

"Just tell his ass to leave!"

"King, I—" I tried.

"I'm not leaving you here with him," King said.

"Oh, please. Enough of this undying-love shit," Paul said. "Just go."

"Fuck you!" King said, charging toward Paul.

Paul jumped back and reached behind him. He pulled a silver, long-barreled gun from his pants and so quickly had it pointed right at King's heart.

Standing beside Paul, I felt the image of him with that gun pointed at King burn into my vision to remain forever. It would be the fastest second I'd never forget.

"Oh my God! What are you doing?" I screamed. I wanted to reach for the gun, but I knew instinctively that could lead to more dangerous results. While I wouldn't have thought Paul was capable of using the gun and shooting King, before this I'd never have thought he'd show up at my place with a gun in the first place, so there was no way to predict what he'd do.

"You won't leave? I'll make you leave!" Paul said to King, whose facial expression had hardly changed. He only backed away from where Paul and I were standing beside the wall and stood at the threshold between the tiled floor in the kitchen and the hardwood in the living room.

He put his hands up and spoke calmly to Paul. "Come on, man. You're not going to use that," he said.

Paul answered, "I won't have to if you get the fuck out of here."

"Just put that thing away and we can talk like men."

"Men? Not likely. See, men like me don't talk to men like you," Paul said.

"Paul, what the hell is wrong with you?" I asked, careful not to move. "He didn't even do anything. You can't shoot him."

"He didn't? He didn't do anything?" Paul said distantly, and

I saw something wild in his eyes, something angry and so cold. "That's not how I remember it—"

"What are you talking about?" I asked.

"See, how I remember it, I was stopping by to check on a colleague after she left work early sick. And when I get upstairs, I hear screaming and banging on the wall. The door is open, I rush in, and who do I see holding my colleague up against the wall, beating her viciously? One of the state's top drug kingpins we were just moving in on."

"You planned this?" I said, remembering everything Paul had done and said since he'd been in my apartment.

Paul went on with his eyes glued to King, "I try to get him off of her, and we fight, wrestle. He pulls out a gun and tries to shoot me, but I gain control, and luckily, just in time, I fire once to save my life—POP!—he's dead."

"He doesn't have a gun!" I said.

"That's not what detectives will say when they run it. The numbers on this sweet piece of silver will lead them right to bullets from the head of a detective found dead in the East River just hours ago—I'm sure Strickland's comrades will be happy to solve that crime. Too bad you'll already be dead."

"Strickland's dead?" I asked.

"Couldn't let him rat you out, baby," Paul said. "He was threatening to go to the chief. I took care of it. That doorman too."

"Oh my God, Paul! You're crazy!"

"Just put the gun down," King said, but Paul just ranted on, about protecting me and making the cover of the newspaper. I noticed King take tiny and steady steps toward him. He kept repeating, "Put the gun down."

"You think you can take her away from me? You think you're a better man than me?" Paul shouted with his arm still pointed at King but wavering now under the weight of the gun. Sweat beads bubbled at his brow. He transferred the gun from his right hand to his left and spread his legs square to shoot. "Don't take another step toward me," he ordered with his hand on the trigger.

King jumped back and I saw Paul's finger tightening to pull the trigger.

"No!" I hollered, dreading the future, and then something in me pushed me toward the gun. I don't know if I was going to jump in front of it or try to wrestle it away from Paul or just buy some time, but I lunged at Paul with my hands ready to grab the gun.

There was a shot—POP!—just as I got my hand around Paul's on the gun and lifted the barrel toward the ceiling. The sound made Paul and I freeze like two people who had no business handling a weapon.

King rammed Paul's chest, knocking me out of the way with his arm before reaching for the gun.

They stumbled and scuffled and cursed. I stepped back to try to keep my eyes on the gun so I could jump in and get it away from them, but it disappeared as they fought on my kitchen floor, buried in the scuffle.

In those seconds, I thought to try to get the gun or try and go get help or jump between them, but no action could be the correct one.

Just then, Paul rolled on top of King and I saw the gun in his hand as he drew it up to aim at King's temple.

I jumped on his back and grabbed the gun again, pulling Paul back toward the tile with me to let King up.

Paul fell on top of me, but he still had the gun, and I couldn't get to it.

King jumped on him again, swinging at his face and chest as I eased back to the wall to escape the weight of their bodies. I tried to keep everything in view, but I missed something and then there was another pop.

Everything went slow.

King was still on top, but his body slumped down toward Paul's. There was a lifeless curve in his shoulders.

"No!" I howled. "No!"

Forgetting or not caring about the gun, I crawled toward him to pull him off Paul.

"King!"

I set my hands on either side of his neck to pull him up, but then he moved and snapped up.

"Shit!" he said. There was blood on his shirt.

"What happened?" I reached toward him. "You shot him, Paul! You shot him!" I was checking for a hole in King's shirt, but there was none.

And then I realized Paul hadn't said anything—nothing.

"I'm fine," King said, dropping the gun to the floor.

I looked down at Paul. He was squirming, shaking, looking down at blood springing from a hole in his shirt like oil from the earth.

"Paul!"

I pushed King off him.

"Paul! Look at me! Look at me! Paul!" I screamed. "Don't leave me! Please! Stay with me! Paul!"

Chapter 14

I'd been sitting in a chair at Mount Sinai afraid to speak. Move. Do anything. Two detectives I'd known for years were seated across from me with their eyes wide open, inspecting my every muscle movement, awaiting information. I knew not to call or text anyone. Everything I did from the moment I dialed 911 from my apartment could become evidence later on.

I'd already told them everything I could about what happened—how the district attorney came to lie dying on my kitchen floor. The tale went the way Paul had said—he'd shown up at my apartment to check on me after what happened at work, the suspect in a case we'd recently opened showed up at my place with a gun, the suspect shot the DA, I called the police. When they asked for the suspect's name, I replied with what I knew they'd find out anyway: Rig McDonnell.

I'd told that story six times in the six hours it took for Paul to come out of surgery alive. So many times it started to sound like the truth. But, of course, that wasn't how it happened. And, of course, what I'd told them about how King had gotten to my apartment and how he'd left wasn't true either.

I'd said that maybe Rig followed Paul there to retaliate. I'd never seen him before in my life. He pulled the gun. He shot Paul. He ran away. I'd told the false version of events without ever looking to the right, repeating details with not one word out of place.

The detectives seemed to feel sorry for me. There was so much blood on my shirt and hands. Blood everywhere. They vowed to catch the perpetrator. To exact revenge against the person who'd tried to kill my boss, my mentor. Placing his hand on my shoulder for comfort, one detective reminded me, "You know we don't tolerate this against our own. We'll find him. We'll make sure he pays." He nodded and I knew what that meant. I tried to appear excited or encouraged, but inside I was wondering how far away King had gotten.

Before I called for help, I forced him to leave and take the gun. I made him promise to stay away from me. To go as far away as he could for as long as he could. Once it was discovered whose blood was on my hands, everybody would be looking for King. Elliot would shut down the city. There would be a manhunt. If they caught him, King would be lucky to make it to the precinct alive. I told him he'd be no good to me dead, and if he left, at least there was a chance we'd see each other again. He asked me to run with him, but I couldn't. Paul would die for sure if I left him alone on that floor. I couldn't live with that. King grabbed the gun and kissed me. He said he'd send for me once he was someplace safe.

The detectives offered to take me home when doctors came out of the emergency room at 2 a.m. to say Paul would live. But I decided to wait. I didn't know what was waiting for me outside the hospital. Reporters had already started showing up. They'd gotten tips about Paul but probably didn't know I was involved. My walking outside to their cameras and flashing lights would just give them a face to follow, an idea to carry back to their sources, who'd work faster than the detectives. In minutes they'd know enough about King and me to raise the detectives' suspicion, and then there'd be no way out for me. I needed time to think before I made a move. I also wanted to know what Paul was going to say happened at my place. If I needed to run. If I had more time.

When they wheeled him out of surgery and into his room, the nurse told me I couldn't come in because I wasn't immediate family. I'd have to wait until he woke up. She said she'd called Paul's emergency contact, but the woman hung up after saying to call her back if he died.

Sitting across from the two detectives, I noticed a woman I thought I recognized walk into the waiting room. She looked Puerto Rican or Dominican, had huge breasts and a tiny waist. I couldn't remember her name or where I'd seen her. I'd been up for more than twenty-four hours at that point, though, and my eyes were puffy and swollen, so I wasn't sure if I was dreaming or just confused. As she walked toward us, I rubbed my eyes and tried to get a better look without staring.

Once she'd passed and I saw the detectives unashamedly staring at her ass in her blue jeans, I convinced myself I didn't know her and was just delirious. But then she turned and glanced at me, and it came to me instantly: Iesha, the bartender from Damaged Goods.

She caught my eyes and looked toward the bathroom where she was headed, signaling for me to follow.

I waited a second for them to resume their conversation about Strickland and Frantz being found dead.

"Strickland was an asshole though. Wouldn't be surprised if he was working with the dealer. Not one bit," one said.

"Really?" the other one asked.

"Yup. Straight up trash."

"You think both of them were working both sides?" the other one asked.

"I said I wouldn't be surprised."

I picked up my purse and started getting up.

"Where are you going?" one of the detectives asked eagerly.

"Little girls' room." I pointed to the bathroom. "I'll be right back."

Iesha was standing at the sink, looking at herself in the mirror, when I walked into the bathroom.

"Where is he?" I asked.

"Shhhh!" Iesha covered her lips with her index finger and walked toward me. She hugged me tightly and slipped something into my back pocket as she whispered in my ear, "He's safe. Flush it. Okay?" She looked into my eyes and waited for me to agree with a nod. She hugged me again and kissed my check. "Tell him I said good-bye," she said in a low voice. "And thanks for everything— make sure you tell him that." She let me go and walked out of the bathroom.

I went into one of the stalls and pulled out what she'd placed in my pocket. It was a little note folded in half. I opened it and found four lines written in blue ink:

BABOO IS AROUND THE CORNER. HE'LL
DRIVE YOU TO TETERBORO.
    LEAVE YOUR PHONE, YOUR POCKETBOOK,
EVERYTHING.
    TELL NO ONE WHERE YOU'RE GOING.
    YOUR NEW NAME IS QUEEN DONNELLY.

When I walked out of that bathroom at Mount Sinai, I didn't know what I was going to do. What was important. What was right. Even what I wanted anymore. I only knew that I was tired. That I needed somewhere to lay my head and close my eyes and rest. To really rest without interruption. When I saw the detectives sitting across from my empty seat in the waiting area, they almost looked like the rest I needed. I could walk up to them, tell them everything, and hold my wrists out for them to arrest me. To take me away to a cell and close the door behind me. Then I wouldn't have to think about another thing. That would be it. I could lie down and close my eyes and know nothing would ever change again. This was the kind of thinking that led rapists, murderers, thieves, and molesters to confession. If they told the whole truth and faced the consequences, they wouldn't have to lie anymore. Lying was what kept them up at night, trying to hold it all together, cover their footsteps, stay one step ahead. It all became too draining and paralyzing after a while.

I didn't realize it, but my feet were taking me right to the detectives as my brain prepared my confession.

They looked at me and stood anxiously.

"I need to say," I started just as I was about three feet from them, but the nurse who'd been in and out of Paul's room all night came between us and cut me off.

"Kimberly Kind?" she said. "You're Kimberly, right?"

"Yes."

"He's awake. He's asking for you." She grabbed my hands and pulled me into Paul's room. "He's still a little groggy from the surgery," she said, ushering me toward the bed where Paul was lying beneath baby-blue sheets and blankets. "But he's okay to talk for a little while. Just try not to get him too excited. You know?"

"Sure," I said. I looked at the tubes from all of the monitors stuck into Paul's arms. When he was in surgery I'd heard two nurses talking about where the bullet had entered his chest just inches left of his heart. It hadn't exited, and removing it could paralyze him.

"I'll leave you two alone," the nurse said as I sat at Paul's bedside. I felt tears coming to my eyes. "Just give me a shout if you need anything."

When she was gone, I placed my hand on top of Paul's hand on the blue sheet. Only a few months ago we'd been lovers sneaking around Manhattan in the middle of the night. But just hours ago he'd threatened to kill someone in my apartment. How had all of this happened?

"You're here," he said, opening his eyes and smiling weakly at me. "I thought you would leave me."

"No. I wanted to make sure you were all right," I said.

"You've always been a bad liar. We both know why you're here."

"Don't make it sound like I would just leave you for dead." I looked over my shoulder to make sure the detectives weren't waiting in the doorway listening. "Paul, I looked up to you. Before all of this we were friends."

"Before all of this, we were in love," he said.

"No, we weren't. I don't know why you've made it up in your

mind like that. We weren't. We were a cliché—a bored boss and a heartbroken assistant. That's all."

"You never would've said that before you met him."

"But I did. I told you so many times it was over. You never listened to me."

A tear escaped one of Paul's eyes. "I can't let you go."

"You have to."

"I won't." He looked at me hard. "I won't."

"Even if you scream for the detectives right now and they arrest me, I still won't be with you," I said. "Nothing is going to change that."

"You love him?"

"Yes. I do," I admitted.

"Over everything? Over your life? Everything you've built?" Paul looked like he was just coming to understand something.

"I don't think I had a choice."

Paul looked away from me dismissively. Coldly. As another tear slid from his eye, he said, "I'm turning you both in. When you walk out, I'm telling the detectives what happened."

"You going to tell them about Frantz and Strickland too? Or should I tell them that?" I asked.

"You tell them whatever you want. Like you said, you don't have a choice."

"Fine." I started backing away from the bed. I could feel the detectives behind me. See Paul's focus shift from me to them.

"Kimberly, don't leave me!" he shouted, sitting up. But he winced and fell back.

The nurse rushed into the room, pushing past the detectives and me.

"You lie back, Mr. Jackson. You're in no condition to be sitting up and raising your voice at anyone. I heard you all the way up front." She turned to me and the detectives as she rearranged Paul in the bed. "You'll all need to leave the room," she said. "I can't have him upset. He's still weak."

"But we're waiting for his statement about what happened," one of the detectives said.

"It'll have to wait until he gets a little more rest," the nurse said, leaving Paul's bedside and pushing us out of the room before closing the door in our faces.

"Kim!" Paul called out. "Don't leave!"

"So what were you going to say to us?" one of the detectives asked me in the hallway.

"Say?"

"You were about to say something before you went into the room," the other added.

"You said you needed to say something."

"Oh. I was going to say that I was going home to get some rest. I'll come back in the morning to answer any more of your questions. I just need some sleep. Been a long day."

"Do you need a ride home?" one of them asked. "We can escort you."

"No. You stay here with him," I said, walking away from the waiting area.

"Where are you rushing to," one asked, and I almost stopped and fainted, thinking I was caught, "without your pocketbook?" He pointed to my purse waiting in the chair beside my empty seat.

I smiled through my racked nerves and went to get the bag. "Thank you," I said, picking it up. "I don't where my brain is."

When I exited the hospital, it was a little after 3 a.m., so most of the reporters were gone or asleep in their vans double-parked in the street. I walked quickly with my head down and turned two corners, dropping my cell phone into a garbage can on the first corner and my purse into a garbage can on the second corner.

Just before the third corner, I saw a shabby taxicab with a man in a turban sitting in the front seat.

Chapter 15

The fog was so thick when Baboo pulled into the drive in front of Teterboro, there was no way I could believe my flight, or anyone's flight, would be leaving out of the small, private New Jersey airport that June morning. It was just five o'clock, but so hot and muggy outside, the tight air looked like white smoke or milk you could catch in a cup and drink.

I rolled down the back window and reached outside to test the elements. To find a sign, an omen telling me what I should or shouldn't do. I was seeking something to help me make a decision I'd thought I already made when I walked out of Mount Sinai and discarded my belongings into public trash receptacles. My hand in the fog, I reminded myself that it wasn't too late to turn back. To turn myself in.

I tried to hold the fog in my hand. To grasp it and remember the shadows of my life. I was Kimberly Kind. An attorney at law. That was all I was. All I'd achieved. I wanted more. So much more. And I wanted it with King. If I stayed, that would never happen. I realized that when I was talking to Paul in his hospital room. He was never going to give up.

Baboo stopped in front of the terminal.

I pulled my arm in and rolled up the window.

Baboo turned around to me and smiled in his silent way that said so many things. He was wearing his white turban with gold piping around the edges.

"You ready, miss?" he asked so simply.

"I guess so." I sniffled and blinked to hold back contemplative tears.

He got out of the car and left his door open, so the dinging from the car alarm blared a warning signal.

I looked out around the car and tried to see my old world through the fog. There was nothing.

My door opened and Baboo was standing there with a slender white man in a black jacket, who was smiling at me.

"Queen Donnelly?" he asked.

"Yes."

"Welcome to Teterboro Airport. I'm Pope. I'll be escorting you to your jet," he said.

I got out holding an envelope Baboo had handed me when I'd gotten into the car in Manhattan. There was a passport inside. "Queen Donnelly" was beside the actual picture from one of my older driver's licenses.

"No bags, Ms. Donnelly?" Pope posed, looking into the car behind me.

"No. Just me."

"Well, right this way then." He smiled again and turned to lead me through the sliding glass door in front of the terminal.

I started walking, but then I stopped. "Wait a second," I said, turning back to Baboo and running toward him. I embraced him and tried to find in his hold everyone I couldn't say good-bye to. "Thank you," I said to him and all of them. "I'll be back."

I let Baboo go and walked into the airport, promising myself I wouldn't look back again. I didn't realize where I was going until Pope mentioned that I'd be flying on one of Meridian's private jets to Belize. There was another family, the Quinns, who'd be flying with me. If I wasn't okay with that, he could have Ladouceur enlist better accommodations.

"That's fine," I said as we walked right through security and toward a small waiting area that was just steps away. Five chairs were organized before doors that led out to the tarmac where a G6 was being catered to by a crew armed with hoses and brushes.

"Don't worry about the fog. Meridian's pilots are the best money can buy. Everything will be fine," Pope said, looking at me. "Just relax. We do everything from here."

Once the Quinns, a fortyish couple with teen twins in matching Polo outfits, made it to the gate and we boarded the plane, it seemed like the fog dissipated into wind.

I sat in a cushy single recliner toward the back of the plane. There were only three rows though. And one long leather couch the twins had already commandeered. I looked out the window. The sun had just made it over the horizon and burst through the clouds.

I remembered the first flight I'd ever taken. My mother's mother had died and we were taking her body back to Church, Florida, for burial. My parents could only really afford one ticket, but my mother insisted my father find some money so I could go with her. I was just six, but she said she wanted me to see where her people were from. I honestly don't remember anything about the trip. Just the flight. It wasn't a G6, but it was a big deal to be on that airplane. My mother let me sit next to the window. She held my hand and told me not to be afraid. To look right out at the sky and not blink. She said, "There's only rumbling when you're going through the clouds. After that, you'll be the closest to God you can get without dying."

I looked out the circular window from my seat in the back of the G6. We weren't above the clouds yet. The pilot was talking to us over the intercom, something about turbulence ahead and fine weather at our final destination.

After the plane sped up and kicked off from the earth, I looked down at blue flashing lights rolling down the highway toward Teterboro.

"Say good-bye to the big city," the pilot said over the intercom. "Paradise awaits."

Acknowledgements

To Kevin Hunter and Jill Ramsey, my business partners. Thank you for your patience and understanding. To my father, thank you for giving me your love of books. Both reading them and writing them. To Mommy, for giving me my zest for life and a fertile imagination. And finally to my son, Kevin. You're my special gift from God. We begged for you! You're smart, intuitive, and insightful. Thank you for being you. I love you very much!